THE ILLITERATE PRINCE

C.G. LAMBERT

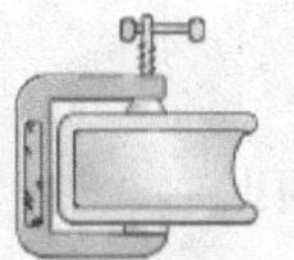

For all those that sling dice

Prologue

Michael had blown off his shift, leaving Eric Prince short-handed for closing. It was the second time that month he had done that, so by all rights, Eric should have given him a formal warning. He resolved to have a little chat with Michael when he came in on the weekend. Plenty of others wanted those hours and now it was he who had to help clean before doing the cashing up and paperwork. It would therefore be a late night, and he had to come in the next morning to open as well. He sighed as he finished wiping down his section. The extra dollar an hour he got for the responsibility of running the restaurant almost wasn't worth it. And it certainly didn't help you make any friends. He'd overheard Sarah and Misty mocking him at the beginning of the shift when they were in the freezer. He'd been tempted to accidentally slam the door shut and let them reconsider their position, while stuck among the meat patties for fifteen minutes. But he'd never do that. He'd have to report the near miss.

It hurt though. They were talking about his acne scars and long hair. He thought he also heard the words "crusty old stoner loser" thrown around. He couldn't do anything about the acne scars, or about his age. The hair and his smoking weed weren't anything to be ashamed of - that was just who he was. But loser? It stung more than it should. Eric's features were a bit coarser than what was considered attractive which made him a little more sensitive to appearance-based put-downs. He scrubbed down the freezer door more aggressively than was warranted.

He'd been at a bit of a loss for what to do after high school. Two of his friends had attended the local community college, but at the time, Eric had been sick of school. One friend had gotten a partial scholarship and headed off to the East Coast to some fancy university. The last of the four friends that Eric used to hang out with managed to get a job in an office, doing something Eric didn't quite get, but by all accounts, making good money without having to be on his feet all day, every day. Eric couldn't figure out what to do, so he increased his hours at the restaurant to full-time for the time being. All that happened close to ten years ago. Since then, his friends that had gone to college had graduated and worked in offices. The friend that had headed to the fancy Ivy League university got a job in New York. On the rare trip back home, he made a point of acting as if nothing had changed, but Eric could feel the faintly detectable air of pity. After Eric moved out of his parents' place, he rented an apartment a fifteen-minute walk from work. He made enough to play his computer games and smoke a bowl, and hang out with his friends. Occasionally he would go to a party or camp in the desert. What more to life was there?

It was close to 1am by the time he pulled the roller doors down over the glass of the windows and headed home. The neighborhood wasn't the best, but at this hour, on a weekday night, there weren't many people around. The street lamps and the bright light coming from the full moon illuminated the sidewalks and it wasn't long before Eric found himself home. He switched on his console and continued his latest game, yet another first-person shooter. Given the time, he decided to only have one joint, pausing the game while assembling papers and leaves. He noticed that his stash was starting to get a little low. He'd have to get in touch with KJ and get some more.

An hour later, he got up and brushed his teeth, headed into his bedroom, where he slipped into his sleep t-shirt and pajama bottoms. He hit play on his stereo. Metallica's Call of Ktulu started to ring out through the speakers at a subdued volume. His stereo was a beast: he'd been persuaded to have a house party the previous summer and the neighborhood had rung with classic rock and metal until the early hours. Now though, it merely purred, the sparse guitar gently relaxing him. He slipped between the sheets on the unmade bed and quickly drifted into an exhausted sleep. Out the window, the moon glimmered silver in the sky, the craters familiar to humanity for centuries.

In a different world, a larger, redder moon stared down at a clearing on a cliff, overlooking the ocean below. A wind whipped off the sea, driving storm clouds deep inland to deposit their moisture. The trees surrounding the clearing bent and swayed wildly under the gusts. Sheltering underneath them was a horse that stood impassively, watching the figure in the middle of the clearing. It was a man, slender and good-looking, slightly taller than average. His jet-black hair was cut short and a closely cropped beard glistened with oil. His cold blue eyes were matched by what seemed like blue tattoos, or maybe stains, on both of his earlobes. He was chanting and gesticulating, the words lost to the wind. The clouds miles away to the North unleashed a lightning bolt that lit up the beaches in that direction. The hairs on the back of the man's neck stood on end as the electric atmosphere near the clearing intensified. A flickering eerie blue-white light grew, attracted to the hands dancing in arcs around the man's body. The path his fingertips traced through the air became outlined in the light, and an intricate electric web built up slowly with each pass. The pulsating threads squirmed and twitched, coalescing into some sort of hemispherical cage, whose highest point was a foot or two above the man's head.

Back in Eric's bedroom, out of nowhere, the dimmest light materialized. A smaller hemisphere centered around his bed got outlined. Eric did not stir, dead to the world. The strengthening light started to compete with the blue LED of the stereo system. The bouncing lights of the graphic equalizer flickered in competition with the alien light. Slowly but steadily, the intensity of the ball of light increased. The hemisphere grew in size until it perfectly encompassed Eric's body.

Back on the clifftop, the chanting man had to squint to protect his eyes from the brightness of the crackling ropes of power which surrounded him. The smell of summer rain on asphalt permeated the air, though the storm had avoided the clifftop. The horse standing under the trees looked on, bored. It didn't react to the sizzling noises, the undulating lights, or to the man chanting in the middle of the dome. And it didn't react when the chanting reached a crescendo, which coincided with the light glowing so bright, it was like the clearing was bathed in noon sunlight. In an instant, the light disappeared, along with the man who had previously stood in the middle of the dome. The darkness of the night illuminated by the paler gleam of the red moon was almost pitch black in comparison with the supernatural light that had been there just an instant before. The powerful glow reappeared almost immediately. This time Eric's prone body took shape in the middle of the dome, lying on the grass in the clearing on the clifftop. The ethereal lights disappeared, leaving him asleep under the watery red moonlight, under the watchful gaze of the horse.

In the meantime, as the final notes of Call of Ktulu faded from the speakers in the finest Dolby 7+1 surround sound, the other man lay naked on Eric's bed. The contrast between the windswept clifftop and the calm of the bedroom was absolute. There wasn't even a gust of air to disturb the curtains or posters on the walls.

In the clearing, a blue slug, that had previously inhabited the brain of the Mage, inched its way toward Eric, who lay on his side still fast asleep. Slowly, it made its way through the grass to the ear which faced downwards. It then eased itself into Eric's ear canal and beyond. Eric didn't stir.

Chapter 1

It wasn't until the wind had exhausted itself blowing the storm clouds far beyond the mountains to the north and the sun had started to peek above the horizon, that Eric started to wake. He groggily looked around before noticing that he was naked. That woke him up. He then saw that he had been lying on some clothing, so he examined it closer. Trousers, boots, a shirt and a jacket. The stitching on the jacket and trousers was almost deliberately wonky as if the machine which had sewed them together had been slightly out of alignment. They seemed to be made well enough though. Absent of any other options, Eric sat down and got dressed. The trousers had a belt with a purse dangling from it, but apart from that, there was no wallet, no phone, and Eric's watch was missing. He was trying to put together some explanation for his situation, but the best he could come up with was that his friends were playing some sort of incredibly elaborate joke on him. Or that he'd been robbed while stoned and dumped in the wilderness Upstate.

"Haha," he yelled as he fastened his belt and stood up. "Very funny, you can come out now." Nothing. None of his friends would knock him out and take him into the wilds. And he was far enough from civilization that he couldn't have sleep-walked. So how the hell had he gotten there? He breathed deeply in an attempt to control the panic that started to well up within him and tried to focus on one thing at a time. The clothes.

He noticed that the clothes weren't the best fit for him. The shirt and jacket were for someone with broader shoulders and the trousers were for someone taller. Eric was half an inch shorter than what was considered average, so the trousers bagged a little at the knees. The boots were soft leather, but even they were two sizes too big. The lack of underwear was also of concern - Eric not being used to going commando.

He shrugged. Whoever these clothes belonged to had left them here in the middle of the field, and Eric needed them. Too bad. If he ever found out who that person was, he could mail the clothes once he got home. Speaking of which, now that he wouldn't be arrested on sight by the police for indecent exposure, he should probably think about how he was going to get home - or more importantly, to the restaurant. It wasn't going to open itself!

He approached the edge of the cliff and stopped a good ten feet from the edge. The view was mesmerizing. He was looking along a beach, golden sands scalloping out bays as far as the eye could see. He must be a hundred feet above the sea here and inland, after the beaches, he could see a patchwork quilt of fields. Hazy in the distance was a range of mountains, barely visible through the remnants of a low mist.

Hmm, thought Eric. Maybe I'm further North than I imagined. Could I be as far as Oregon? Or am I on the Baja Californian peninsula? The scenery was nothing he recognized, both in terms of his own experience and what he had seen in travel brochures or online. *Oh well, best to start walking,* he decided. If there was no way to get in touch with any of his friends now, he'd try and flag down a car and borrow someone's phone from a gas station. Then they could either wire him some money or else, come and pick him up.

Behind, he could see a horse beginning to follow him, slowly meandering while grazing on the grass. Stealing clothes while you were naked was one thing, but stealing a horse was something else. He could definitely get in trouble for that! Eric increased his pace, hoping to sneak away before the horse realized what was happening. The horse shook its head, as if bothered by a fly, and walked after him. Eric couldn't believe it. If there was someone nearby, they would come back and find their horse gone, their clothes gone, and Eric near the horse, wearing the clothes. That could only look dodgy. A faint path left the clearing, heading away from the cliff edge on a slight downward slope. Eric started jogging away from the horse, heading down the track. Behind him, he could hear the jangle of the metal in the tack as the horse broke into the slowest of trots, effortlessly closing the distance between them. Eric steadily increased his speed until he was sprinting as fast as he could down the trail. The horse didn't even break out of the trot. Despite the time he spent on his feet for work, Eric wasn't very fit, so he didn't last long sprinting at top speed. He stopped pretty soon, bent double, wheezing and spluttering, leaning against a tree. The horse casually approached and stood an arm's length away, scouring the ground for a particularly interesting clump of grass.

Eventually, Eric recovered and looked over at the horse, truly examining it for the first time. The leather strapping was plain and unadorned. Unremarkable. But the saddle looked boxy with a high piece in the front. Behind it was a set of saddlebags separated by a bedroll. They were made out of soft leather in two shades, with the flaps in a medium brown and the body in a sandy off white. They looked well-worn but in good condition.

The horse looked up and gave a snuffle, before going back to examining the ground. Eric idly wondered if there was a phone in the bags. Or some food or water. He approached the horse carefully, holding his hands in front of him, and making soothing noises. The horse ignored him, so he reached out and undid the clasp on the saddlebag on the side closest to him. Inside were a leather waterskin and a pair of burger-sized packages, wrapped in strips of what looked like a sort of banana leaf. Hidden underneath the food was a black felt bag, about the size of Eric's fist. It was very light. The wrong shape to hold a phone, but Eric shrugged and paused momentarily to glance around to ensure that he was still alone with the horse. He opened the drawstring and dug his fingers into the bag's innards. It felt like a roleplayer's dice bag. Eric didn't play himself, but he had some friends who did and had seen the plastic shapes about the size of a standard six-sided dice, but coming in various shades and colors and many more faces. He shook out a few into his palm to discover that he wasn't actually correct. While the pieces of plastic were of many shapes, none of the figures were regular and the different faces did not have numbers on them. Rolling these would be pointless. However, they were all a variety of hues and transparentness. So maybe some sort of work in progress. He put them back into the bag, tightened the drawstring, and returned the bag to the saddlebag. Then he walked around to the other side of the horse, passing behind it. To tell the truth, he didn't like the way the horse looked at him, and he worried about getting bitten. When he safely walked around it, he opened the saddle bag on the other side. Again, a quick glance around to make sure nobody saw him rummaging through the stranger's saddlebags. But there was nobody around besides him and the horse.

Inside this saddlebag sat three sacks sitting on top of a majestic large book with a heavy wood and metal cover, with a metal clasp holding it closed. Eric opened each sack in turn. All of them were incredibly heavy and about the length of his forearm in height. They were vaguely cylindrical, with a diameter about the same as both Eric's palms laid out beside each other. They jingled when he moved them. Opening them, he found out why. Each was about two-thirds full of small pieces of metal, something resembling slivers of coins. They kind of looked like coins except that they were way too small. Some had pictures of a person stamped onto one side, but all of them had very small writing in some foreign language. They were all sorts of metal too, some gold, some silver, and at least three or four other shades of brown metal too. Were they some sort of metal-working experiment? Was someone chopping up a lot of foreign coins? Thousands of them actually, if Eric's estimate was any good. He placed the sacks back into the saddlebag and manhandled the book out.

There was no writing on the outside cover, but the craftmanship of it was significant. The corners were metal and the cover was made of a dark stained wood which looked a good finger's breadth in thickness. The edges of the pages were uneven and stained an odd nicotine color. Finally, Eric undid the clasp and opened the book. The interior of the pages was an off-white eggshell and the writing was in jet-black ink. But the text wasn't in English. It was closer to Chinese, with little pictograms arranged in a row, that writhed and changed as he looked at them. Sometimes they would join together with the characters adjacent to them to make a double-sized character. But then their couplet would break up and the character would stay solo for a while, before hooking up with another neighbor. The effect was very much like that time Eric and his friends had done acid in the desert and wandered around staring at cacti as they melted into the sands. Terrified, Eric slammed the book shut, refastening the clasp, and placing it very carefully back into the bottom of the saddlebag. What the actual fuck?

He returned to the other saddlebag and took out one of the banana leaf packages, then unwrapped it to find a pair of corned-beef sandwiches, thick slices of bread with a layer of butter, and a sizable chunk of meat with a glistening layer of fat attached. With a last guilty look around, making sure nobody was coming to accost him for stealing clothes, horses, and now food, he took a bite from the first sandwich. Delicious. He washed it down with long swallows from the water skin, instantly feeling less groggy and much more human. He placed the other banana leaf package with the waterskin into the saddlebag and refastened it. Absentmindedly, he patted the horse on the neck before resuming his way along the trail, this time at a more leisurely pace.

Eric found himself happily whistling as he strolled along the track. He occasionally heard the sound of the horse's tack jangling behind him. It continued to follow close behind. The sun was out - a few clouds every now and then, but as a whole, the day was bright and warm. A gentle breeze blew into his face. He was truly starting to enjoy himself. But the path went on and on. Eric didn't know what time it was when he started, but he had been walking for hours by the time the path popped out from the woods, placing him at a crossroads of sorts. The path joined a semi-paved road that crossed from left to right, each end disappearing into the distance, with nothing to distinguish one from the other.

Opposite the T-intersection, fields of crops stretched like a gray-green sea, interrupted periodically with great clumps of trees. The crops were stubby stalks about waist-high, and Eric had no idea what they were or what they might grow into. He looked to the left, then to the right, and shrugged. One way looked just as promising as the other, so he took the path to the right and started walking. He heard the horse make a whinny. Eric turned to see it shaking its head. Then, without a word of a lie, set off in the other direction, looking over its shoulder to see if Eric would follow. Apparently, he was going in the wrong direction.

14

Eric frowned, deep in thought. What the hell did the horse know about where he wanted to go? Was that the way to the highway? Was this the way to the highway? One way to ensure that he wasn't accused of stealing the horse was to be far away from it when it was found, so continuing on his way made the most sense. But, just on the off chance that the horse knew more than he did, Eric considered that turning in the other direction might be a better option. Besides, the horse had the saddlebags, and the saddlebags had the water, so it might be sensible to go the other way. Mind made up, he turned around and followed the horse.

The road wasn't fully paved, rather there were large slabs of stone that had been sunk into the dirt, a little narrower than the wheel span of a car. Beside the road, separating it from the fields on his right, was a low hedge, about hip high. To the left, the woods butted against the clearing of the path.

Eric wasn't sure how this had happened, but he was now following the horse along the trail. The misfitting boots were starting to rub against his feet, the sweat making an irritant that he suspected would lead to blisters before too long. Another reason to find the freeway sooner rather than later. He paused and looked up. No contrails or any other evidence of airplanes. He listened carefully. No traffic noise at all. Just the birds tweeting and the general background noise of insects. He continued along behind the horse. The sun was dead overhead. He was starting to feel a little overdressed, so he caught up with the horse, took off the jacket, and stashed it in the saddlebag that had held the sandwiches.

The sandwiches. As he moved further down the path, he was thinking about the remaining sandwich. He decided it must be time for lunch and reached over to the horse, who was now walking beside him. As soon as he touched the strap on the saddlebag, the horse stopped. Eric helped himself to the other sandwich and sat in the shade beside the path, eating it slowly while watching the horse lazily twitch its tail in response to the attention of a couple of flies who were bothering it.

Eric placed the banana leaves back in the saddlebag and took a long draught from the water skin. Then he refastened the saddlebag and led the way along the path, confident that the horse would follow. The reassuring jangle of the coins and tack behind him confirmed that this was the case.

Gentle undulations in the terrain indicated that they were leaving the perfect plains of crops and entering a hilly area. The woods to the left were darkening and becoming more overgrown with fallen logs, creeping vines with knee-high bushes becoming more visible. Eric was thankful for the road, where walking was easy. Thrashing through the woods would not be very fruitful.

The fields on his right disappeared eventually, replaced with scrubland, persistent collections of thorny bushes, interspersed with stones and the odd boulder. The hedge separating the road from the fields also disappeared. Eric didn't know how long he had been walking, but the sun was starting to go down and he was getting very hungry. Suddenly, a building came into view, a low-slung single story with a thatched roof and a chimney with a thin wisp of blue smoke, just starting to escape.

When they got closer, a boy of ten or twelve ran out and took the horse's reins. As he led the horse back toward the gate beside the building, he raised his fist to his forehead, as if stabbing himself in the head. Eric was momentarily stunned, first at the sight of another human being, and then at their strange wordless exchange. He still thought of the horse as a peculiar traveling companion rather than as *his* horse, so he didn't move to stop the appropriation. The boy was wearing an off-white shirt and brown trousers with no shoes and had the deep tan of someone who worked outside all day.

Eric made his way to the main door of the building and knocked. It swung open immediately, showing the face of a pretty young woman who beckoned him in while holding her knuckle to her forehead. "Welcome to The Swan, my lord. Please make yourself at ease."

Eric blinked. The woman was twenty, maybe twenty-five, with dark hair, partly plaited along her temple, the rest cascading down her back. She had the most dazzling bright blue eyes and a tiny nose - not the chiseled small nose of plastic surgery but a natural little button. His gaze drifted downward, noticing that she was quite buxom and that the peasant dress she was wearing accentuated this fact most pleasingly before he realized that she was waiting for him to enter or to at least speak.

At last, thought Eric. *Civilization!*

"Ah, I'm not one of the LARPers," he said, "I just really need to use your phone."

She looked thoroughly confused. "I beg your pardon, sir? Lahpers? Phone?" Quizzical looked good on her. Her eyes really were the most brilliant shade of blue. Were they colored contacts?

Eric gave her a winning smile. She really was quite pretty. "I'm not really in the game - I found these clothes out in a field. But all I want to do is ring my friends and take a cab or an Uber or something so I can get back home."

She frowned at this information and scuttled off into the interior of the building. Eric had the strangest sensation that he was watching a martial arts movie, where the shapes the actors' mouths were making was not quite matching the noises that came out. He shook his head and looked around. He was in a large open room with four trestle tables laid out in front of a fireplace, that seemed to be pushing as much smoke into the room as it did up the chimney. The floor underfoot was actually compacted dirt overlaid with reeds or straw. In the fireplace was a blackened metal pot, something that witches would coven around, with a mystery soup bubbling gently within it. Seated on the table closest to the fireplace were three soldiers, wearing random pieces of armor and bright red cloaks. They had their backs to him and were facing the fire. In the corner, the furthest from them, with his back to the wall, sat a brooding stranger, dressed in drab colors and avoiding Eric's gaze by closely examining the plate of broth in front of him. A heel of crusty bread was placed on the table beside him, along with a tall wooden mug.

"Welcome to The Swan, sir! Can I interest you in a room for the night and supper after a hard day's travel? Maybe breakfast in the morning to set you up on your onward journey?"

Eric turned to see a balding man of average height, wearing a grubby white apron over a dark shirt and thick woolen trousers. He looked at Eric earnestly while he waited for his reply. Eric considered asking for a phone again but on second thought, decided to play along. He was very hungry after all.

"Absolutely, that sounds splendid. How much for a room for a night and dinner and breakfast?"

"My beds are soft and the food is delicious. I would only ask for two ribbits - and, and I will feed and water and stable your horse for no extra charge."

Eric was aware that the others in the common room were all listening. Again, he had the weirdest feeling like the innkeeper's mouth was moving much more than was needed to make the words that were coming out. He shrugged and nodded to the innkeeper. "That sounds ok," he told him. His words broke some sort of spell in the lounge. The three soldiers ducked their heads to talk amongst themselves and the man in the corner went back to chasing the broth around his plate. The innkeeper grinned. "The bargain is made! I would ask for payment in advance, my lord. So many distrustful travelers on the roads, you understand…"

Eric felt a moment of panic before remembering he had a purse hanging on the trousers' belt he had… inherited. "Of course, of course," he said while loosening the drawstring and tipping some coins into his hand. Like the others in the saddlebags, the coins were very small and inexpertly made. They were festooned with made-up letters and faded images of kings' heads or animals. Whoever was in charge of the coins for the LARPers was obviously an amateur. "Uh… Which ones are ribbits?" he asked, holding out his hand to the innkeeper. The innkeeper's eyes widened, and he slowly reached out to the offered coins and extricated one particular coin from the pile.

"Oh, this one will do fine, my lord," the innkeeper said slowly without taking his eyes off the coin.

The coin maker for the LARPers may have been terrible, but the innkeeper's acting skills were great, thought Eric. He was doing the whole 'greedy innkeeper taking advantage of the rube' thing really well. Sighing to himself at how he had been implicated in the whole acting scene, he made his way to one of the vacant tables in the lounge area and sat down. His feet reminded him of the many miles he had covered that day. He was certainly not used to such exercise. He would check with the innkeeper or waitress to see if he could get a lift to somewhere closer to civilization after the game had finished. Or in the morning if it was an overnight thing.

The waitress went to the pot on the fireplace and filled a plate with the broth. One of the soldiers made a comment, making the other two laugh raucously. The waitress colored and brought the plate to Eric, placing it on the table in front of him along with a metal spoon and a smallish loaf of bread. "I shall return momentarily with your ale, m'lord."

Eric started on the broth. Chunks of vegetables swam in a milky fluid with an odd nugget of gristly mystery meat. He was so hungry that he could eat anything. It made the dishes they served at his restaurant seem positively healthy in comparison. He made very short work of it, surprising himself with how hungry he was. As he mopped up the remnants with the bread, the waitress returned with a wooden tankard, placing it on the table beside him.

"Would you like a second helping, m'lord? I think with how much you paid; we could certainly fill your plate again." She smiled wryly to herself.

Eric allowed that he could probably fit in a second helping, wondering just how much he had overpaid for the meal and lodging. The soldiers close to the fireplace were starting to get a little loud. As the waitress took Eric's plate to refill it from the pot, one of them grabbed her and swung her around until she sat on his knee. Her face flashed with anger as the men laughed, but whether it was at the joke or at her discomfort, Eric couldn't tell. He could tell that the discomfort was real, though.

"I don't think that she wants to sit on your lap, mate."

Instantly the temperature in the inn dropped, despite the fire behind them. There was a moment of silence where Eric could distinctly hear the crackle of the flames in the fireplace. The soldier with the waitress on his knee stood up, as did his friends, and he guided the waitress behind him, laying a hand on the hilt of his sword. His nose was crooked from many breaks, and his thin lips parted to reveal a snaggle of crooked teeth.

"What," he gruffly asked as he looked Eric up and down, "did you say?"

Behind him, he heard the man in the corner mutter "here we go" under his breath.

"You've gone method, man, dial it back a notch."

The soldier gave him such a look that Eric felt a chill down the back of his neck. "What do we have here, fellas?" The rhetorical question hung in the air as the man's friends started to move forward to either side of Eric's. The man in the center held Eric's gaze.

The voice from the corner filled the silence. "Judging from the stain on his earlobe, I'd say either a mage or someone rich enough to make things difficult for you. Might pay to call it a night."

The soldier held Eric's eye but pitched his voice to carry to the man in the corner. "Dead men don't tend to cause too many problems, now, do they?"

"True, but poor men have no family."

Eric frowned as he puzzled over the response. The soldier didn't share his confusion. Still holding Eric's gaze, he made the smallest of bows. "Be careful on the roads, my lord. There are many dangers lurking in the shadows." He turned toward the man in the corner. "Especially for foreigners." The three soldiers left, calling some garbled obscenity over their shoulders at the waitress as they did so.

The man in the corner looked darkly at his empty plate and muttered under his breath. "Fucking rich people."

Eric shook his head. "Oh, I'm not rich."

The man looked surprised. "You speak Balhish?"

Eric shook his head again. "No, I speak English."

"Eng-lish? Never heard of it."

"Never heard of it? You're speaking it!"

"No, I'm speaking Balhish."

"No, you're speaking English."

"No, my lord. You're speaking Balhish. The Balhish that they speak on the docks, but Balhish nonetheless."

"What, is the waitress speaking Balhish too?"

"Oh, no. She's speaking Driven - the same as the innkeeper. Although, his accent suggests he hasn't left this area, while she's definitely traveled a bit. Your Fredworm is translating for you. If it knows the language spoken to you, it'll translate what you hear and say."

"My what now?"

"Your Fredworm. You didn't know you had one? It's a little worm about the size of your thumb. They're very expensive, how is it possible that you didn't know you had one?"

24

Eric screwed up his face. "Bullshit."

The man in the corner shrugged. "No, it's true. It's why you've got a blue stain on your earlobe."

"Man, you LARPers have some good stories. OK, how expensive are they? $100?"

"Well, each language they learn costs the life of their host, so you could say that they are quite expensive."

"What the actual fuck?"

"You really don't know about them? They get in through the ear and live in your head. They hear what you say and what you hear, and learn the language you speak. Then, to extract them, the host has to be killed. If they don't get a replacement host within a few hours, they die. But they keep collecting languages. Super rare."

Eric sighed. "That's a great story. Or - and hear me out here - everyone is speaking English. What makes more sense? What's simpler? Now, do you guys all go home at night or is this like a weekend thing?"

The man in the corner looked at him for a long time. He was about to say something when he was interrupted by the waitress returning with Eric's second plate of broth. Her eyes were red, and she sniffled a little while serving him. She left without saying anything. Eric watched her leave. In part because he enjoyed the sight, but more because he was on the verge of asking her how she was.

The man in the corner saw Eric's lingering gaze and snorted. "You're wasting your time there, my lord."

Eric looked up, slightly embarrassed. "She is a little young for me," he allowed, not wanting to get into all the other reasons why it might not work between them.

"No, my lord. She is… an admirer… of women." The careful choice of words clearly communicated the situation.

"Really? Oh, ok."

Eric's blasé response raised an eyebrow. "My lord is not scandalized?"

Eric shrugged. "It's not really any of my business," he replied.

The man in the corner shifted in his seat, focused quite intently on Eric now. "My lord speaks quite plainly on such momentous subjects. Is his attitude shared amongst his countrymen?"

Eric nodded, wondering what this had to do with the LARP adventure. "The attitude toward… admirers of both men and women are shared very widely. Certainly not universally, of course. Why, what is the attitude where you are from?"

Instead of answering the question, the man placed a hand on his chest. "I would like to know your name. I am Misan, a merchant of the Jerasi from Heyenne." He inclined his head slightly, before raising his eyes to Eric's with an expectant look.

Smiling back, Eric inclined his head in return and answered. "Hi Misan, I am Eric Prince."

Misan's eyes widened. "Ah, well met, sir. And where are you from?"

Eric thought for a second, wondering whether to mention the country, state, city, or street of his address. He was briefly tempted to state his zip code. Or the area code of his phone number. "Anaheim," he managed.

Misan bowed his head again. "It is a pleasure to meet you, Eric, Prince of Anaheim. I must admit ignorance of your great nation. Tell me, in which direction does Anaheim lie?"

God, this guy was laying it on thick, thought Eric. I'll play along on the off chance that he can give me a lift home. "It is far to the West," he said.

Apparently, this was the wrong thing to say. A look of panic flitted across Misan's face, and he got to his feet in a hurry. "Well, I hope you find this land to your liking. I wish you a safe and speedy onward journey. I must beg my leave of you as I must retire. My journey was very arduous today." Without another word, he hustled past Eric and further into the depths of the inn.

"Goodnight, then," Eric muttered to himself watching the fleeing merchant's back as the gloom swallowed it. He returned his attention to the broth and took his time, trying to figure out why Misan had been so spooked.

The waitress returned a little while later, looking more in control of herself. She seemed lost in thought, but as though on the verge of saying something, but she held her tongue. "Would you like to follow me to your room?"

"Absolutely."

She led him down the corridor that the merchant had also taken when he left. Eric now had a better idea of the layout of the building. A small kitchen area backed onto the lounge, then a corridor leading to the entrance to the stables. Dotted with four doors, each sporting a large iron lock beneath the handle. She opened the one closest to the stable door using a large iron key. "Here it is," she said redundantly.

The floor was matted with straw, beneath which Eric could glimpse bare dirt. The room was bigger than a prison cell, but not by much. The walls were painted with some sort of whitewash. There was a bed, somewhere between a single and double in size. Wooden frame and lumpy blankets. No window. There was a single candle on an alcove in the wall which was stained with a line of soot. The only other feature of the room was a small bucket of water. The waitress smiled encouragingly at him. "Is it to sir's liking?"

Eric attempted to smile, looking around the room, in case she noticed the edges of his mouth were twisted in a rictus of disgust rather than humor. "Lovely," he managed. The LARPers really liked to go all out. Never mind. After breakfast, he'd find someone to tell him the safe word, and then he'd arrange to duck out of this very convincing show.

"There's a chamber pot under the bed. What time do you want to leave in the morning?"

"Uh, nine o'clock?"

A moment's uncertainty flashed across the waitress's face, but she smiled and nodded in understanding before leaving him to his room. The problem with no watch, thought Eric as he tested the bed, was that he had no idea if the time was six, eight, or ten o'clock. The bed was a little lumpy, and the blankets were threadbare - practically transparent in parts. Eric was wearing just his shirt and trousers, the jacket still in the saddlebags from the journey. He decided to head out to the stables to retrieve it. Making sure to take his key, he left the room, heading out the door at the end of the corridor.

The buildings of the inn surrounded a small section of grass, a stone letter O with a well in the middle. Opposite the door to the inn were the stables, obvious in design with the oversized wooden doors and accompanying smells. Eric started across the green, marveling at the moonlight on the grass. It almost looked red. Very red. He stopped and looked up. The moon was red. And about 50% bigger than it should have been. Also, with none of the pockmarks and meteor craters that he was used to. A black shadow was transiting across the face of the moon, so close to the surface that both the object and its shadow were perfectly visible at the same time. Eric stared.

It didn't change. Unlike his trips on acid in the desert, the scene remained absurd but the same. It didn't morph or melt or kaleidoscope into anything else. So he stood, concentrating on his breathing. Waiting for his vision to clear, for the silver of the real moon to reappear. For the moon to snap back to its real size. For the Cindy Crawford mole to stop its movement and disappear. For things to go back to normal. It slowly dawned on him, as he stood breathing in the cool night air, crickets chirping quietly in the woods nearby, that things would never be normal again. That wherever he was, it wasn't Los Angeles, California, the USA, or even Earth.

###

He had not actually made it to the stables after all. At some point, he'd stopped staring at the moon, attempting to snap back to reality, and had walked back to his room like a zombie. Lost in thought.

Wherever he was, there was the same gravity as on Earth. And the same air. Or near enough – he wasn't bouncing around like an astronaut on the moon, and he wasn't gasping his final breaths like a goldfish flopping around on the floor. That was the good news.

The bad news was that he didn't know where he was. And therefore, how to get back home. The only reason he wasn't reacting more was that there was nothing to react *to.* Sure, the moon was too big and too red, but he wasn't going to lay on the ground gibbering and pointing at it. He wasn't in any danger and as far as his experiences in this world had been concerned, he might as well be LARPing or cosplaying a medieval prince. He mentally shrugged and climbed into bed, extinguishing the candle, and eventually, slipped into a dreamless sleep.

When he awoke, he washed his face with water from the bucket. Eric was surprised at how well-rested he was, considering the bombshell that had been dropped the night before.

He put his boots back on, wincing a little at the blisters that had formed where the sweat had rubbed his feet. He unlocked the door and looked around the lounge area. The fire had burnt down to embers but still put out a little heat. The waitress bustled in, still tying her apron.

"Take a seat, my lord, I'll be along with your breakfast shortly."

Eric sat at the same table as the previous night. A couple of seconds later, the waitress brought him a plate loaded with three cakes, a little thicker than pancakes. They were covered in honey and there was a half-melted knob of butter in the center. Eric expected her to leave him to his breakfast, but she sat down opposite him. He smiled uncertainly as he took his first bite.

"You very nearly died last night."

Eric was chewing so merely raised his eyebrows in response.

"And it would have been my job to get rid of the blood. I would have had to replace all the reeds and it would have been impossible to get rid of the smell. You are blessed that the Jeraso spoke for you."

She spoke plainly, but Eric could detect anger behind her eyes. He couldn't figure it out. He was trying to stop those guys from harassing her. Actually, he was trying to stop them from manhandling her, because she hadn't looked like she was enjoying herself. He started to answer but then realized that he didn't know the local rules. He then realized how foolish it had been acting on his sense of right and wrong from his 21st-century American values. Because, wherever he was, he was definitely not in America.

32

"I am indeed blessed. I apologize. I realize that the laws and customs of this land are not that of mine." He hoped that would satisfy her. He took another bite of his breakfast cake. It was light, like an English muffin or a crumpet, and had absorbed the honey and butter so that each bite squeezed the liquids into his mouth in delightful taste explosions. He figured that if he was eating, then he wouldn't say the wrong thing.

"And where is your land? I heard some of your conversation with Misan." She cocked her head. "And I do not believe you are from the West."

Eric slowed his chewing, trying desperately to figure out how much to say. He barely believed it himself, so saying it out loud sounded like a great way to get locked up in the local loony bin. Eventually, he ran out of mouthful and swallowed.

"You are right. I am not from the West. Not the West in this world anyway. I'm from a different world. Where the moon is silver and smaller. I'm sure there are other differences, but I just arrived yesterday, so I'm learning what they all are." He waited, trying to see if what he had said was going to cause an outburst of disbelief, of mockery. Or anger.

She didn't react. "And in your land, people who like people that are the same as them, they are treated well?"

"No, not always. But the law punishes those who don't."

She looked like she didn't believe him. "Everyone in your world treats them well?"

Eric shrugged. "No, not everyone in my world, there are some that don't. Some whole countries. But they are few."

"And when will you return to your world?"

Ah! Now he saw her angle. "I don't know. I need to find my way back to my world. Someone has to open the restaurant."

She either didn't understand his joke or did not care. "Would you take me back to your world?"

Put on the spot like that, Eric really didn't know what to say. "I don't know," he managed. He then decided to take a large bite of the last breakfast cake to buy himself some time.

She watched him closely as he chewed. "I think you need me. I can make sure that nobody takes advantage of you. Like Logan Eze." She looked disgusted. "He told me that you paid for the room and food with a Balhish Geldin. That would have bought the entire inn."

Eric felt his stomach drop. When he thought that the money was just a prop in some sort of medieval live theater show, it really didn't matter. But now he felt the familiar feeling of being taken for a ride. Like when one of his staff called in ill while he could hear the party going on in the background. Thinking quickly, he figured

34

out a way to kill two birds with one stone. But first to find out what it would cost.

"I definitely could do with an advisor. What would a fair wage be for someone to accompany me and give me that sort of advice?"

"I would do it for five ribbits a day."

"And if you were advising me, what would you say about that rate? Am I being taken advantage of?"

She looked a little affronted. "That's a fair wage. It's five times what a fair price is for a night's accommodation and meals. Besides, your wealth won't last long if you are bled dry."

Eric nodded slowly. Now for the twist. "That sounds like a fair wage then. OK, you can have the job, on one condition."

"What's that?"

"You get my money back from the innkeeper. We agreed on two ribbits and apparently, I gave him too much. If you want to have the job, either get the coin back, and I'll give him two ribbits, or he has to give me change."

"I don't think Eze will have that much coin lying around. Give me the two ribbits, and I'll make him give back your coin."

Eric shrugged. "Sure. Now, which ones are ribbits?" Eric pulled out his purse and emptied some of the coins into his hand. She picked through them and found two that looked the same. They were bronze or some other similar brown metal. Eric tried to memorize the markings. A weird squiggle. A man's head in profile. He measured it against his thumbnail. He would have to learn this stuff. He gave the waitress the coins and put the rest away.

"I've got an errand to do before I leave, but I can meet you in the lounge in an hour or so, and you can either give me the change or the two ribbits." She nodded and stood up, a distracted look on her face. Eric got up and headed for the stables too.

Chapter 2

The boy who had taken the horse looked up from where he was sitting, whittling something out of wood with an evil-looking knife.

"Morning, my lord. Your horse is ready," he said.

"Could you please bring the saddlebags to my room? And a pen and a piece of paper."

The youth looked uncomfortable. "My lord, I regret to inform you that your horse would not let me take the saddlebags off him."

Eric wasn't sure he understood. "Wouldn't let you?"

"Aye, my lord. I tried; I did. She let me take off the saddle and bridle, but when it came to the saddlebags and your bedding roll, she wouldn't allow me. And I get the weirdest feeling, it's like she listens to me."

Eric shrugged. Maybe the horse had one of those Fredworm things. "Show me," he said.

The boy approached the horse gingerly. The horse looked at Eric and shuffled its weight from one leg to the other while watching the stable boy carefully. It let him unbuckle the saddlebags, and almost double over under their weight. "My lord, what are in these? Are you carrying stones?"

"The horse looks fine to me," replied Eric. "In the bags? Rocks and stones of the finest quality." It was best that nobody knew how much pure cash he was carrying. Christ, if he was back home, walking through his neighborhood with pockets full of hundreds and someone found out, he wouldn't last long. He would have to keep his secret here too. God knows how good the police were here. But even back home, the police couldn't protect someone from terminal stupidity. "What made you think the horse was listening to you?"

The stableboy looked sheepish. "Just the way she would react when I said certain things. Sometimes she would shake her head or snuffle or move as if she was... Ach, it's silly I know."

Eric shrugged. "Maybe she was." He turned to leave, pausing at the entrance to the stables. "Don't forget the pen and paper." The boy nodded and knuckled his forehead.

Twenty minutes later, Eric finished his count. There were a lot of coins, but really, there were only fifteen types. He'd sorted them into piles on his bed before placing the rest back in the sacks, leaving one of each kind out. The stableboy had brought him a quill and inkpot, along with some sort of soft-bark peel which served as paper. He'd been sure to tell him that he would need to pay the

Innkeeper ten ribbits. Eric thanked him, dug out the required coins from his purse, and thrust them at him before locking the door behind him, leaving the key in the lock, just in case the keyhole grew a nosey eyeball.

Eric noted down the totals of each of the coins that he had. He would have to interrogate the Waitress to find out the relative worth of each, but he was sure that he was incredibly wealthy by the standards of the local people. That was both reassuring as he would not starve or have to sleep under the stars, and he could afford to pay the Waitress many years of wages if need be, but it was also a little distressing. The more that you had, the more people would want to take it from you. Eric didn't know much about different human cultures, but what he did know was that there were thieves and murderers in every single one of them. He would have to be careful.

After he had poured all the coins back into the sacks, pulled the drawstrings closed, and returned them to the saddlebags, he glanced at the book that was still nestled in the dark shadows. He imagined it looking balefully back at him. He wondered if it was banned. Many books were banned, threats to either religious or political power. This might be one. But if it was a clue about how to get back home, then he would need to find a way to interpret it. If the Waitress was on his side (and he still wasn't absolutely certain about that), then maybe she would not expose him even if it was forbidden. It was easy to be paranoid in such a strange world where one had no knowledge of the local customs.

Eric opened the door and saw the Waitress waiting for him by the pot of broth, stoking the fire with a few small logs. She smiled when she saw him and held up his coin. He smiled back, then sat at the table, beckoning her to join him.

"Sit, please. Well done, I will take you with me back to my world. In the meantime, can you look at these coins? Do you know what they are called? What is each one worth?"

She took the handful of coins and told him the names of those she knew and which ones had a set value, frowning as she turned some of the coins over in her hands.

"This one is from Eksland, and these three are from Urbolg. And these are from the old Empire of the Sun but that doesn't exist anymore. The coins are used widely though, especially in the countries which were part of the Empire."

Eric wrote down the names and values of the coins she knew and calculated his net worth. Given two ribbits per night for a meal and accommodation, plus the five per day for the Waitress, he was carrying enough money to last centuries. He looked up to see the Waitress watching him carefully.

She frowned. "What language is that, my lord? The letters are so small and simple."

He looked down at his scratchings, punctuated by splotches where the quill had spilled too much ink. "It's English," he managed. "The language of my land." He didn't want her to deduce the magnitude of his wealth from the tallies on the sheet of supple bark, so he tried to change the subject. "I'm afraid I don't know your name. If I've hired you, I probably should know it, don't you think?"

She looked up and nodded. "I am Imogen of Rodina."

"Nice to meet you," he said. "I am Eric, and I'm trying to get home to Anaheim. I'm not quite sure how I got here, to tell you the truth. The only clue I have is my horse, these clothes, and this book that I found in the saddlebags." He decided to go out on a limb and show her the book. He scanned the room to make sure the innkeeper and stableboy weren't around, before pushing the book over toward her. "Any ideas?" He watched her face carefully, looking for any reaction.

She unclasped the book and opened it. Her face reflected waves of astonishment, wonder, and then disgust. "What book is this? What writing - it's moving!" She slammed the book closed. "I do not like this book at all."

Eric took it back from her. "You don't know what it is? You haven't heard of anything like it?"

She took a second before responding. "No, I haven't. The Mages of the Havelin might know. I assume the writing is magic because it keeps moving. But they live in a city many weeks' ride away from here. It would be a dangerous trip, and there's no guarantee that they would know anything about it. Or about you." She shrugged. "And I don't know anything about anyone traveling from a world with a smaller silver moon. But I guess we could ask on our way to the Mages."

It was Eric's turn to shrug. When you don't have any other clues, the barest suggestion of a direction was as good as any. "When can you be ready?" he asked.

Imogen straightened in her seat. "I will need but a moment to collect my things."

"Could you ask the stableboy to collect my saddlebags and resaddle my horse?"

"Certainly, my lord." She stood waiting.

"Was there something else?"

She looked uncomfortable. "My lord knows… that I like women?"

Eric nodded, uncertain of what she was getting at. "Yes."

"I just wanted to make sure that you knew that was a permanent situation."

Realization dawned on Eric. He nodded, smiling. "Understood."

"It's just that some men see it as a challenge. I would save us any awkwardness and establish at the beginning that we solely have an employer-employee relationship."

Eric gave her what he hoped was a reassuring smile. "I have had many attractive women working for me at the restaurant. I didn't hit on any of them. Once I'm paying, there is no romance." That didn't stop some of his co-managers however.

Imogen nodded slowly, looking at him with a mixture of relief and lingering doubt. "Thank you," was all she said. And with that, she left.

Eric returned to his room and placed the book in the bottom of the saddlebag. He added the ink, quill, and bark, making sure the cork stopper was firmly lodged in the bottle. He looked at how all the items were arranged and wondered if they would be safe on the back of the horse. Shrugging, he decided they would be fine. He wouldn't be galloping anywhere, would he? He'd never ridden a horse before, so if they just walked everywhere, the saddlebags wouldn't get violently shaken.

The stableboy returned and collected the saddlebags. Eric followed him back to the stables and watched him reattach them.

He was surprised that there wasn't a strap to go under the horse, instead, the saddlebags hung down on either side of the animal, just forward of the hind legs, and connected via straps to the back of the saddle. The horse patiently endured the attention, its tail twitching at the odd fly. When the stableboy had finished, he brought the reins over to Eric and paused before handing them over.

"My lord, may I know your destination?"

Surprised at being asked any questions, Eric was momentarily speechless.

"I... I would like to accompany you, if I may?"

While he could certainly afford whatever wages a stableboy would command, the last thing Eric wanted to do was to attract attention with a retinue of followers. "I'm afraid that's not going to be possible," he started. "I don't need a stableboy."

The stableboy started to protest, but Eric thought it best to shut him down. "I'm sorry, but we're going on a very dangerous journey and I don't have any need of your services. I'm sorry, no." Eric used the "my word is final" tone that he used when telling his staff that there were no more shifts for them to work. He took the reins gently. The stableboy looked downcast but nodded, avoiding Eric's eyes, and walked dejectedly back toward the stables.

Just then, Imogen returned with a linen sack over her shoulder. "Is that all you have?" he asked. She nodded. He took it from her and placed it in the saddlebag, the one that didn't hold the book. Then, it was time to leave. "Have you said your goodbyes?" he asked her. She looked at him quizzically and nodded again.

"The Innkeeper was not happy. With the harvest only two months away there will be few people looking for work. He will find it hard to find a replacement."

Eric shrugged. Replacing staff was always a pain, but it wasn't his problem. He led the horse toward the gate, and Imogen opened it for him, closing it after they'd gone through. Eric looked expectantly at her. "Which way?" he asked.

The road beside the inn led away in both directions, woods on both sides, canopying the path with broad green leaves. For some reason, Eric didn't want to go back the way he and the horse had arrived the previous day. It seemed a waste to backtrack on yourself. As if he could or should have known that he would need to turn right instead of left. So it was with some relief that Imogen pointed the other way, leading further into the forest. She watched as Eric led the horse past her and strolled down the path. She hustled to catch up and walked alongside him.

"Aren't we going to ride your horse?" she asked. At the sound of her voice, the horse turned its head as if to say, 'Good question. Well?' At that moment, one of the guards from the previous night came out of the trees ahead of them and tried to grab at the horse's reins. This close, Eric could almost smell the B.O. on him, thankfully hidden the previous night by the smoke from the fire. Even in the outdoors, where a sometimes-gusty breeze was present, he could smell homelessness on him. He was not terribly tall but well-muscled and swarthy looking. His sword was still in its scabbard, his red cloak worn and bare in patches. All this, Eric noticed in the seconds it took the soldier to swing his arm up and grab at the reins.

Time slowed. Behind him, he heard yelling. He half turned to see the other two soldiers at the inn's gate, swords drawn, heading after them. Between them and Eric ran the stableboy, a bag of belongings slung over one shoulder. He was calling out to Eric and Imogen to wait for him. It didn't look like he had seen the soldiers. The horse reared, striking at the soldier that had been grabbing at his reins with his front hooves. One of the hooves connected, caving in the man's skull like an aluminum bowl. The man's eyes rolled into his head. He dropped to the ground in an instant. The horse returned to all fours, and Eric grabbed one of the stirrups and jammed a foot into it. He swung his body onto the horse to discover that he had screwed up and was facing the wrong way. He grabbed Imogen's arm and hauled her up onto the horse. Her dress rode up as she struggled to get on the horse. Behind them, the stableboy had noticed the soldiers and dropped his bag as they approached. The horse bounded forward, away from the inn and the scene developing behind them that only Eric could see. In two seconds, it reached a gallop and sped away down the road, Eric bouncing painfully on the raised part at the front of the saddle, and Imogen, sitting astride the horse just behind the saddle, with her dress bunched around her waist. She looked in pain. The raised part at the rear of the saddle protected her modesty, and she clung to the saddle as if to life itself. Just before they reached a bend in the road that hid the inn from their line of sight, Eric saw a haunting scene unraveling.

The other two soldiers had reached the stableboy from behind, and the man that had confronted Eric the previous night swung his sword overhand in a vicious arc. It hit the stableboy on the collarbone and cut halfway down his chest, coming to a halt with an inch of the blade sticking out the front. A jet of blood erupted from his neck and a frothy bubble of blood from his lips before the horse rounded the corner. The last sight Eric had of the stableboy was the look of disbelief on his face as he stared at the point of the sword, sticking out of his body that was quickly drained of life.

After twenty minutes of bouncing on the saddle and trying to get his other leg over the body of the beast, the horse slowed to a walk and then halted, nosing around on the ground for some particularly lush section of grass. Imogen slid bodily to the ground and lay grimacing in the shadow of the horse.

Eric eased his body off the torture device in the front of the saddle and swung his leg, which was still without a stirrup, over the horse's back, so that he was finally facing forward. He then lowered his weight off the horse and onto the firm ground. Removing the boot from the stirrup, he slumped gratefully onto the ground beside Imogen. Everything hurt. And whenever he closed his eyes, he could see the stableboy. Staring at the point of the blade.

Eric started to shake uncontrollably. It was the first violent death he had experienced in person. One of the homeless drifters who occasionally slept under the trees, out near the bins in the restaurant carpark, had died one night of an overdose and had been discovered by one of the team. Eric had to arrange the calls to the authorities, but that was all. It was death at arm's length. A "civilized" death.

He held his head in his hands and sobbed. The stableboy would not have even been in high school back home. Such a waste. After five minutes, he was beginning to get hold of himself. Then the full magnitude of his predicament finally hit him. He was in a different world, with different rules, different norms, and a different proximity to death. Useless adrenaline still sloshed around in his system, so that even after the sobbing subsided, he still shook. That took a few more minutes to slowly subside. He looked around for Imogen, suddenly embarrassed at his tears. She walked into sight, leading the horse and carrying the waterskin. Her movement was in a weird gait, somewhere between "I've misjudged a fart" and "this is how a duck walks".

Looking across at Imogen, he tried to distract himself from his thoughts. "Who were those guys?"

She handed him the waterskin but didn't answer for a few minutes, sliding to a seated position near him with a grimace of pain on her face. Eric was surprised to see she had hitched up the hem of her dress, exposing an almost indecent amount of thigh. Eric saw why. The headlong dash on horseback with nothing between her legs, and the coarse hair of the horse had rubbed the insides of her thighs raw. He looked away.

"They were the Queen's Guards. They patrol the areas for deserters and bandits. Though, they take advantage of their position and commit petty larceny. And worse." She paused and Eric found himself wondering how the worm in his head worked. It must make choices in a split second on which of the words that Eric knew would match those that were actually said by someone like Imogen in her own language. What would a medieval waitress in an inn know of the word larceny? Eric didn't even realize that he knew the word himself. But he guessed he must have if the worm was interpreting something Imogen had said.

"Falbot is the leader. He comes to the inn periodically and is a complete asshole. The other two are morons, but wouldn't start anything by themselves."

"And if they kill anyone, like me, what would happen to them?"

"If no one saw what happened?"

"Yes. If there were no witnesses."

"They would make up some story about you being a bandit. Or a thief. Or a spy. With the war on, there is a lot of suspicion of strangers."

"Wait, what? What war?"

Imogen nodded, realizing that Eric wouldn't know. "The word among the merchants is that the Dellaran and Ordost are going to war. Well, the rumor is that there have already been skirmishes and armies are gathering. The war will begin for real any day now. But apart from a slight increase in the numbers of patrols and the general unease, there hasn't really been much change from normal."

"Do you think that they will follow us?"

"The guards? I don't know. From what I've picked up listening to their conversations, there is a section of the road that they are to patrol, but most of it is to the south. I don't know how far north they go."

Eric nodded, trying not to think about the stableboy. "OK, so we keep going and try to put some distance between us and them. We'll stay away from soldiers when we can. How far is it to Havelin? You said weeks?" he got to his feet as he spoke, offering his hand to Imogen.

She took his hand, rising gingerly. "There are usually merchant trains leaving from Gerton - that's the next town along the road we are on. I think we should be able to join a train and make it to Havelin in four, maybe six weeks." She thought for a minute. "The war has changed things though. We'll see when we get there."

Eric pursed his lips, watching her moving awkwardly. "Can you ride?"

Imogen looked ruefully at the saddle. She was holding her dress away from her legs. "I don't think so," she managed.

"OK, I guess we're walking then," said Eric, grabbing the horse's reins and leading the way along the path. Imogen followed, grimacing occasionally as the fabric grazed her wounds. They settled into a rhythm, their aches and pains keeping conversation to a minimum, allowing them to focus on where they stepped. Even though the path was well-worn and solid beneath their feet, it only took a misstep on a muddy tree root or a jarring semi-skid to remind them of their bruising and grazes. The path remained under the forest canopy for about an hour before the trees began to thin and the sky could be seen overhead. It was now overcast, but still pleasant walking weather. The forest was less dense here, the underbrush between tree trunks mere isolated creepers and ferns rather than the thick impenetrable bushes they went through earlier.

Eric's butt hurt. He imagined it was a mass of bruising from his less-than-orthodox riding style and the archaic saddle. He also wasn't used to riding a horse, correctly or incorrectly, so his groin was letting him know that it had been stretched in ways that were certainly unfamiliar. So walking was painful. And whenever he closed his eyes, he could see the stableboy. He shook his head to clear his mind of the vision and tried to distract himself.

"Tell me about Havelin. Tell me about the mages. What powers do they have?"

Imogen nodded thoughtfully to herself as she picked her way along the path. "I guess you're asking for specific abilities? Not just what mothers tell their children to get them to go to bed. I know that they keep away from regular folks, but I don't know if that's their decision or if it was forced on them. I know very few courts have had a mage - they're usually forbidden from being involved in human politics."

"Why?"

"If you can't be sure of your thoughts or your emotions around them, then you don't want them around. And while they can wield the power of fire, lightning, and the winds themselves, if you don't know that they're fighting for your cause, then they are a dangerous force on the battlefield."

"What's to stop them from disguising themselves? Pretend to be a diplomat to get into court? And then take over."

"I'm not sure. I've heard of trinkets that detect magic. Presumably, they can detect when a user of magic is near too. Surely if anyone would have such devices it would be the kings and queens?"

"I guess that makes sense. So, could just anybody become a mage? Or do you need to have special blood?"

Imogen frowned as she considered the question. "I do not know - what happens in the Mage's School is not widely known. I have not been around any Mages while they use their magic."

Eric pursed his lips. "Is it possible that all their 'magic' is just tricks? Sleight of hand and misdirection?"

Imogen shook her head slowly. "There are many tales and stories of the power that the Mages have wielded through time. Scars on the earth. Rubble and soot from buildings toppled and burned." She turned to face him more, giving his face a searching look. "Why is it so hard to believe in magic, my lord? Your very presence here, now, is proof that great power exists."

Eric sighed, nodding in agreement. "What you say is true. It's just in my world, magic does not exist. People claim it, but it is all tricks, and smoke, and mirrors."

"My lord would be best served to believe his eyes and forget his own world." She turned to pick her way more carefully along the path. "Or he will find himself run through with a sword or a smoking pile of embers."

Eric didn't reply immediately. How could anyone cast aside everything they knew? All of their frames of reference? Did it extend to his sense of right and wrong? Of when he should intervene and when he should keep to himself? He had the feeling that he would need to be on constant alert whenever he spoke to anyone. The ear thing would allow him to talk to anyone, but he had a sneaking suspicion that this would just make it easier to get himself in trouble. Trusted locals would therefore be invaluable. "You're right, of course. And so, the people in the magical schools. Are they all boys, or can women be Mages also?"

Again, Imogen took her time before answering. "I don't know. All of the Mages I can recall from history in tales are men. And I do not recall if there were female students at the school. But I know very little about the school, so don't take what I say as the absolute truth."

Eric smiled. "I like that when you don't know something, you say that you don't know. You don't make it up."

She looked at him sideways. Eric realized that she was trying to see if he was being flirtatious or genuine. That must get exhausting, he thought to himself. "Tell me more about what the mages do."

She looked at him for a minute before nodding and continuing.

"They study in their towers - first in Havelin, and then when they graduate, they leave the town and build towers in the woods or mountains, usually far away from towns and villages. Sometimes, they set out on expeditions, and you see them surrounded by soldiers and mercenaries, heading off to some ancient crypt or far-off land to retrieve some artifact or to extract some information from a long-forgotten temple. A year later, they will stagger back, half the soldiers missing, and the mage with his arm in a sling."

"You sound like you've seen this first hand."

"Oh yes, the mage Tortle lived very close to my town."

"Well let's go there then - we can talk to this Mage. Is it closer than Havelin?"

"Ah, it's actually on the other side of Havelin, so another month to the north."

"That's disappointing. So how far are we from town?"

She looked at the sky. "We will be at the next inn in a few hours, and then it's most of a day's travel from there. So tomorrow evening we shall have the choice of three inns!"

Chapter 3

Toward evening, they came across the White Swan Inn. It was another single-story building, but this time it had a solid foundation of large stones underneath the white-washed boards and a thickly-thatched roof. Inside, the floor was made of creaky wooden planks, and the large cauldron hanging above the fire held a thick broth with chunky nuggets of meat, nestled beside the slices of vegetables. When they had arrived, Eric had sent Imogen to negotiate with the innkeeper while he sat in the corner of the common room, nursing his beer. She'd come back with the news that she'd managed to get two rooms plus meals for the two of them for six ribbits. He'd just been about to note that this was more than what they'd paid at the previous inn when she held up a finger.

"The broth is better, the beds too, and this is a more well-traveled route. Sometimes I will not be able to get the price you think is fair. Trust me, this is a good price."

He smiled to express his gratitude. "I'm sure it is."

Eric had three helpings and Imogen two after missing lunch during the day. The innkeeper ruefully watched them as he bustled from kitchen to parlor. After they'd eaten, Eric announced he would retire to his room. Imogen looked up, surprised at the early hour. "I can't get in trouble if I'm alone in my room, can I?" he explained.

Imogen nodded. "If we get going at first light, we should get into town in time to see if any merchant trains are heading north."

"Do we really need to be on a train? Surely, if we're alone, we can avoid any troubles. Robbers or such. Certainly, they would leave two poor travelers alone?"

Imogen shook her head. "Robbers and such will still stop poor travelers and might run you through just for fun. And it would be even worse for me. But robbers are not the only hazard for travelers. There are other creatures lurking in the woods who can only be scared off with steel. A lot of steel. You'll be glad of the company. You'll enjoy Gerton. It's huge, almost a city. They even have a library."

"Oh? You can take books out?"

She looked at him, bemused. "You can't take the books away, but you can read them there. If you want to get parts copied out, there are scribes you can hire. And they can copy maps or do research for you if you have a need."

"Oh, we won't need that - I can read just fine. How long will we be there?"

58

"That depends on the merchants. There's a pretty good chance there will be a train leaving from there, but whether we just miss one, or one leaves the day or week after we get there, we won't know until we arrive. If you don't have many clothes, it might pay to buy some more for the trip. The smell of being in the same breeches and shirt for six weeks will keep some of the bandits and creatures away!"

Eric thought of the large wealth in his saddlebags. Sure, a few shirts might be a good idea. And maybe some shoes which fit. He wasn't looking forward to taking his boots off, suspecting that his blisters had burst, and the rubbed raw skin underneath would sting when exposed to the air. "Cool, that sounds great." He heaved himself to his feet and headed toward his room.

The inn hadn't been too busy on their arrival, but as Eric retired, the common room was almost full. The jovial noise and hubbub volume mocked him as he stripped down and lay on his bed.

In the morning, he woke before dawn and blearily pushed the door open. In the darkness, his room felt like a coffin, the air stuffy and a little smoky from the previous night. No window meant no airflow. The door let some watery light in from the common room. He washed his face with the jug of water that was left in the corner. Dressing slowly, he protected the bruising around the inside of his thighs which had gone deep purple against the paleness of his flesh.

He had been right, the misfitting boots had rubbed blisters on blisters. He'd been careful not to burst them, but he wasn't sure that putting on the boots wouldn't rupture them. From personal experience on a micro-LSD dosing trip in the desert, he knew that it was the rubbing of a burst blister that hurt the most. He gingerly put on his boots, doing them up as tight as they would go. There was still a bit of wiggle room, but there was nothing he could do about that. Or was there? He glanced out into the common room. A snoring drunk under one of the tables was the only person visible in the gloom.

Eric undid the boots that had caused him such pain, then grabbed one of the threadbare blankets and found the edge. Tearing a few strips off the end, he used these to bandage his blisters, tucking the ends back into the wrappings. He then got the boots back on. They were a much better fit now. Still not perfect, but there was much less movement. Maybe a pair of boots in the town would be a good idea. The blankets were not shortened by too much either.

He met Imogen as he left his room. She briefly looked up at him and smiled grimly. "I didn't get much sleep last night."

"They were quite noisy, huh?" he smiled back.

"Sure. That's probably it."

The smell of wine on her breath gave her away. She picked her way through the benches to the cauldron on the fire, the embers barely glowing now. Taking two metal plates and two coarse wooden spoons, she ladled broth onto his plate and handed it over with a grimace. She was frowning at the window as there were no curtains, and even though the glass let in only about half the light from outside, it was still too much for her hangover. Eric sat at the nearest bench and turned his attention to the broth. She sat next to him, tentatively prodding at the meat. Wafting the steam toward her nose, she took a test sniff,.

She took a spoonful after seeing his quizzical gaze. "Sometimes if I drink a lot, my nose gets too sensitive, and just the smell of certain foods makes me throw up. I think I'm ok though."

"How're the legs?"

"Terrible. The wine helped. For a couple of hours last night, I couldn't feel them at all. Now my head is throbbing too much, but once that wears off, I might be in a little bit of pain."

"Do you want to leave slightly later? Go back to bed?"

She shook her head, wincing as it proved a little too vigorous. "No, if we want to make sure we get there in time to see the merchant trains, we will have to leave straight away. And I'm in no shape to ride, so we're going to have to walk. So, we should get our gear together and head out."

They finished their broth and headed out to the stables where the horse was waiting, saddled up, the bags firmly secured, and a water skin sitting in the space between them, behind the saddle.

The sky was awash with a low gray cloud - not threatening rain, but promising a more temperate day ahead. There was a chill in the air this early in the morning and Eric was glad for his jacket. Imogen was wearing a wrap over her shoulders. They headed out in companionable silence. Eric was not even thinking about mounting the horse with the bruising around his thighs. The road was beginning to appear more permanent, the grass worn to dirt where cartwheels had run, and the odd hollow or hole filled with stones or rocks and packed down with more dirt on top. They had gone for about two hours when Eric noticed other travelers quite some way behind them.

"Hey, look - travelers. Shall we wait for them? You know - for safety."

Imogen paused to take a swallow from the water bottle. "They're a long way behind us. Besides, we have nothing to worry about here. It's the roads to Havelin which are dangerous. There will be more travelers too as we get closer to Gerton."

True to her word, as the last remnants of the woods melted away and the fields of crops spread out in all directions, they spotted more people on the roads, going in both directions. Eric and Imogen were occasionally passed by lone riders, galloping down the road, a satchel slung over their shoulders, and a sword bouncing at their hips. A large emblem was usually embossed on the satchel.

Imogen noticed Eric frowning after seeing one such rider. The emblem had been a winged horse.

"That is Gerton's crest. The town where we're going," she told him.

"We call that animal a Pegasus. The winged horse."

"Pegasus? Hmmm… Here it is a *Lopharer*. They don't really exist, but there is a myth about them. If I remember correctly, one of the old gods made them drag the sun and moons across the sky. There's a smaller winged horse for the smaller moon and a red one for the red moon."

Eric tried to remember any mythical backstory of Pegasus but came up blank. He could vaguely recollect something about wings melting due to being too close to the sun, but that didn't involve a horse at all.

A few hours later, they stopped for lunch. For some time, the road had been open, with fields on either side. There were no more low stone walls or even flimsy wooden fences, with the lateral strips of wood interlacing with the upright poles. They found a widening of the road, where they could be sure not to get run over by a galloping messenger, and sat beside the path. Imogen pulled out two pies from the saddlebags. They were a little different from what Eric was accustomed to. They were more like mini towers of pastry, a hand span in height, and a fist in diameter. He accepted it thankfully and observed how Imogen ate it. She nibbled the end cap of the pastry until she had cleared it away. Then, she squeezed the filling to the surface and ate it with dainty mouthfuls. Eric did the same. The dish was effectively pastry filled with a broth, very similar to the one they had had the previous night. The pastry was quite thick but had been half soaked in the gravy, dissolving so you could not quite be sure where the pastry stopped and the broth started. Delicious though.

They washed it down with most of the water and hit the road again. The horse, who Eric would have to name at some point, had been grazing calmly on the grass near the path, not wandering into the fields at all. Imogen noted this.

"Your horse is very well trained."

"She is. Though, like these clothes, I found her. She is not really mine."

She nodded. "Well, we will be at Gerton in maybe three, four hours. And after we ask about the train, maybe we can get you some more clothes."

"Some boots that fit might be a good idea too," agreed Eric.

Another rider flew past.

"I didn't see the emblem on the rider's satchel. What was it that time?"

"That was the lion's head of Toblemore."

"Oh, not another Lo… Lorarer? What did you call the winged horse?"

"Lopharer. The town we're going to is big enough that it could be called a free city in other realms, but the leader of this county, Earl Blackhammer, does not want to give up that much power to the Mayor. So, you sometimes see messengers delivering for the Earl, and some for the Mayor. And occasionally the Duke."

"The Duke? The Earl? The Mayor? Why do they all have messengers?"

Imogen looked at him. "So… The town has a mayor. If the town gets big enough, it tries to be a Free City. The County belongs to the Earl and the Earl has to give fealty to the Duke. The Duke owns many counties, some of which he governs directly and some through his Earls. The Dukes all owe fealty to the Queen. So Gerton has a Mayor, an Earl, a Duke, and a Queen."

Eric was worried that she'd start rattling off their names and expect him to remember them all, so he pretended that what she said was obvious. "What I meant was that if each of those layers had their own messenger service, then there would be four different sets of messengers. It strikes me that it might be a little inefficient."

Imogen considered this. "Yes, but wouldn't it make it easier for people to intercept the messages and read what they shouldn't? Better to have people you trust who only work for you, no?"

Eric inclined his head in agreement. "True. I think my people have solved that problem, so it makes sense to have a shared infrastructure."

As Imogen frowned, Eric wondered what his Fredworm had translated infrastructure into. Never mind.

"If you could guarantee that nobody could look at the messages, then that would gut the messenger services. There would be fewer riders, fewer horses, fewer stables."

"Fewer inns?"

"No, the messengers ride hard and continue through the night. It's dangerous work."

"What about messenger birds?"

Imogen looked at him blankly. "Messenger birds?"

"Yeah, some birds always return to their home no matter how far away that is. So, you take them in a cage and put them at the edge of your kingdom. When you need to send a message home, you tie it to the bird's leg, and they fly home as soon as you let them go."

Imogen was watching him with a wry grin on her face.

"How do you fix the message to the leg? Surely the bird would have to be huge to fly with so much parchment tied to the leg?"

"No, you make the writing small, the paper small, curl it up like a scroll, and tuck it into a metal tube that you stick to the bird's leg."

Imogen's gaze fixed on the ground in front of them as she considered this. "And your people do this?"

"Well, we used to. Never mind, forget it. Tell me more about your life before you came to be at The Swan Inn."

They walked in silence for a few minutes before Imogen responded. "Think of the happiest you've been. Now think what it would be like if you knew that was going to be the best you would ever feel. And that it is all in the past. So, all you have left are memories. An aching hollowness. But obviously, you cannot just stop. You keep looking for happiness." She looked at him for a long time. "That's why I want to go to your world. Everything here is set up to get in the way of finding that happiness. My happiness is sin here."

Eric nodded slowly. "I understand. I'll do everything I can to bring you with me. But don't think it will be simple or easy. One of the first challenges would be that you don't speak the language there. You also won't have any cultural knowledge. I don't know what people like you talk about on dates, but you won't have the background that everyone else who grew up in my world does. Maybe we need to get you an earworm thing like the one I have. How expensive could they be anyway?"

"I could learn. Just take away that one barrier to my happiness. I will do the rest." They walked in silence for a bit longer before she turned and shot Eric a grin. "You are very easy to talk with, my lord. You must have people telling you their secrets all the time?"

Eric gave her a wry smile in return. "That's not a good thing."

"Oh?"

"People confide in you, and you prove yourself to be someone who can keep your mouth shut, so they share more. Eventually, they realize that they've shared too much. And so, they panic. I don't know if they suddenly comprehend the embarrassment that could be caused by any slip-up, or maybe it is the full realization of just how much you know about them. But if they then decide that they need to distance themselves from you, they make up some story to justify the change in the relationship. And so, you overhear some story that they've told other people - total rubbish of course - and you understand what has happened. There's nothing you can do about it, but you wonder how to prevent it in the future. What do you do? Limit how much you know about people? It's a little frustrating."

"I imagine that in your position, you would also have to pick what is flattery and what is genuine."

"At the restaurant? Yeah, sure, but everyone learns pretty quickly that I don't play favorites with the roster. Some of the other managers are less resistant to the flirting. I actually prefer it that way. The last thing I need is the smiling and simpering to try and gain favors or change my mind."

Imogen looked confused.

"The weight of leadership, I guess."

She smiled in understanding, but Eric wasn't sure that extended to her eyes.

Their road was joined by another and it widened a little, adding more space on either side of the compacted earth. There were more people on the road as well: they could make out three other groups in wagons pulled by oxen at various distances ahead of them. Not long after the other road joined theirs, there was a jangling of tack, and a group of four horsemen, riding in pairs passed them at a trot. The men were all wearing different types of armor, all were carrying swords, and two also carrying bows. They examined Eric and Imogen with great curiosity as they passed. Obviously, something interested them, as there were some discussions between them as they rode further away, frequently turning to take another look, before eventually losing interest and focusing on the ride.

Eric frowned at the scrutiny and shot Imogen a questioning look.

"You don't have a sword, my lord. It's very unusual for any traveler not to have a sword. If we were farmers on the way to a market, that would be different. A merchant would have guards. A tinker or musician would have the tools of their trade. But you don't fit any of those categories. It obviously provokes suspicion."

Eric didn't get it. "I don't get it, what could I be?"

"If you had priest's robes, then you could be a priest. If you had grubbier clothes, you might be a pilgrim. Though there are precious few pilgrim's paths near here. No, I think they were most concerned that you might be a mage. It might be best if you gained a sword when we get to Gerton. Just to make it less conspicuous."

"That makes sense, I guess. What the hell is that?"

They had come caught up to one of the wagons ahead of them. It was simple, wooden, with one large wheel on either side. What had almost stopped Eric in his boots though was the creature that was pulling the wagon. Instead of two oxen standing four or five feet high at the shoulder, there was one ox that was somewhere between six and a half to seven feet high at the shoulder. Its horns were prodigious, but it was the musculature that was so unusual, its shoulders and neck being incredibly well developed, and the body and hind legs being a little less so. It reminded Eric a little of a furless buffalo that had gone to the gym excessively. And maybe missed leg day.

As if knowing that it was being stared at, the creature snorted. Eric could see that it had a ring through the nose which was held by the waggoneer, who had a long switch in their other hand. The bed of the wagon was covered in a high stack of hessian bags, laid first in one direction and then the other, and covered in a rope net and cinched tight.

"That? That's an auroch. Like a super ox. Very strong." She noticed Eric staring in disbelief. "You don't have cattle in your world?" Eric barely noticed that the earworm hadn't found a matching English word for auroch.

"Our cows are a little… smaller. And our bulls are not as large. We do have buffalos, though. They are a similar shape but smaller and with furry bits around the shoulders."

Imogen gestured toward the auroch. "They are common in the areas near the ocean but less so in the highlands. And not at all in the mountains. Some people say that's because they can't see too well and trip and fall from the passes. Some say that they don't have any fur, so they freeze."

"Can you ride them? Imagine that running toward you!"

"They're too wide across the shoulders and the angle of the back means that where you would have room to sit would be wobbling around far too much. And they're not of the right temperament to put up with someone on their back. Not for long, anyway."

The driver of the cart was sitting on the far right of the bench of the wagon, craning his head to see past the beast pulling it. He noticed them looking at the auroch and smiled, revealing missing teeth. He knuckled his forehead, and Eric spotted he was missing a couple of fingers too. But the action reminded him of the stable boy, so he turned away, frowning. Imogen noticed this.

"Risk of the trade."

"Huh?"

"The missing fingers. The windmill has a large millstone that grinds the grain to make flour. When they need to mill more grain, they winch up the upper stone, place the grain on the lower stone, and lower the upper one back on the grain. Occasionally, the ropes or the winch slips or something breaks, and this huge round stone drops down, crushing anything below it. He's lucky it was only a finger or two."

"I'm sure he doesn't think so. How does he count to ten now?"

She smiled wryly at the dark joke as they slowly pulled away from the beast, the wagon, and the man with the missing fingers.

Chapter 4

A few hours later, the long straight road with fields on either side disappeared to the right over the brow of a hill, opening up a view of the city below it. As Eric and Imogen stood to one side of the road, she showed him a few points of interest. Gerton was nestled at the intersection of two rivers. It was surrounded by a wooden wall, about twenty feet high, and studded with towers. Eric couldn't tell how large the city was as there were various hillocks and tall buildings hiding the other side of the city wall. It was big though, probably the size of three or four city blocks from back home, populated by crooked three and four-storied houses, white-walled behind thick wooden beams, and stained a deep yellow-brown from fire smoke, soot, and age. They seemed to have glass windows and tiled roofs rather than the thatch that the inns on the road had sported.

"Well, don't stand there gaping, my lord, we have made good time, but if we just miss the train leaving, we may be looking at a week before the next one goes."

Eric shuffled after her, thankful to be making progress toward the mages and potentially, toward finding a way home. The non-stop wooded roads and inns they had passed had made him think that was all this world had to offer, so he was glad for the trappings of civilization, as primitive as that civilization may have been.

It turned out they were another thirty minutes away from the town proper. The road followed one of the rivers toward Gerton, then crossed it in a long low bridge, nestled on wooden supports over the wide river. The bed of the river was covered in large gray stones, and the water level was very low: it covered only about a quarter of the river bed. Imogen noticed his gaze.

"The river takes the snow melt in the spring and fills the bank entirely. Sometimes, if we get heavy spring rains, we get flooding. Too much water coming from two different rivers, you understand. When that happens, the bridge floats away and has to be replaced. It's happened twice in my time."

They joined various wagons and livestock heading into and out of the city over the bridge, at times having to wait until some blockage or another was worked through. The gates were on the other side of the river. There were no railings along the side of the

74

bridge, so Eric made sure that they were a good foot or so from the sharp drop to the stones below. When they reached the other side, he could see that the wooden palisade sat upon a low wall, formed by the stones from the river bed, packed together in some gray mortar or mud. The gatehouse was manned by two bored-looking soldiers, chatting to each other and ignoring the traffic heading in and out of the city. They didn't even look up when Eric, Imogen, and the horse headed through the gates to make their way inside. On the other side, there was a cobbled square with three wide roads, leading away into the interior. The crowds coming into the city fanned out along the different paths, competing with those wanting to leave. Even though the air was filled with yells, oaths, and discussions, the general vibe of the place was relaxed, with only short spikes of ill humor.

Imogen led the way through the crowds. They were just leaving the square when Eric caught a violent motion out of the corner of his eye. Glancing toward it, he just managed to see a man land thirty feet away, disappearing into the crowd. The path he'd inscribed in the air between them and the landing point was obvious from the looks of the people along it. A gap appeared around Eric's horse, those closest finding a way of imposing on the personal space of their neighbors. The horse, for her part, looked nonchalant. Eric frowned, trying to figure out what had happened, but soon got distracted by the city, looking in wonder as they made their way down the wide central street.

While the main street was wide and well-lit, the side alleys were much darker. The houses on them were crazily built, each floor at a different angle, so the higher they got, the closer they were to their neighbors, some almost touching the houses on the other side of the street. The view reminded Eric of some forest parts of the path, as the sky was at risk of etching a single line through the coverage where the canopy didn't quite meet. It took Eric a few minutes before he noticed the biggest difference between Gerton and the cities he was used to back home - there were no words anywhere. No signage, no billboards, nothing. Oh, there were placards outside various buildings, showing what was inside - a beer tankard for a pub, a spool of thread for a tailor, a cleaver for a butcher. But there were no street signs, and obviously, no neon lights. The lack of advertising hoardings or even ads on park benches threw him. Almost like the city was too new and hadn't been lived in properly yet.

The crowds had died out entirely by this point, making walking an easy activity, and Eric found himself enjoying the exercise. The pain from the saddle had diminished pretty much entirely, and he was sure the deep purples of the bruising must have faded to yellow. As the only person who would have been able to confirm that was Imogen, he had kept his suspicions to himself. He breathed deeply, trying to place the strange smells, which mixed and merged in the afternoon air. It wasn't long before Imogen stopped outside an inn, turned to him, and asked him to wait for her. He shrugged and turned to the horse. Without anything else to do, he found himself trying to make small talk with it.

"So, did you have a good trip?" he gave the horse a reassuring pat on the neck. If he didn't know better, he would have sworn that the horse looked surprised. He was about to continue the one-sided conversation when Imogen came back.

"This way," she said, leading them through double doors into a courtyard adjacent to the inn. "I got us a good deal for tonight by promising to wait here if we have a week's wait for the trains to leave. And there's time for me to check them out before nightfall. What do you want to do while I get that done? You need clothes and a sword, but I should be with you for that."

"You mentioned a library," Eric responded. "I could have a look in the books, try and find more information about the mages."

She nodded. "That's a good idea. And then I'll swing by and bring you back here."

The plan settled, they dropped the horse off at the stables, leaving her in the capable care of a bored stableboy about fifteen years of age. They took the saddlebags up to their rooms, Eric happy to see a heavy door and a solid lock. He pocketed the key, then followed Imogen down the stairs, and back out the door to the street. As they passed a street vendor, Imogen bought a pair of fist-sized paper bags, handing one to Eric as they walked. He opened it to see what looked like nuts, the warmth of which was still coming through the bottom of the bag. He picked one out and was just about to eat it when their aroma hit him. A warm earthy scent greeted his nostrils. He crunched it to discover a truly amazing flavor. They had been roasted in something sweet, though he couldn't pick out whether it was honey or something else. Delicious. He grunted his appreciation at Imogen as he helped himself to another one. She smiled back.

It took about half an hour to reach the library, the road making its way up and down the gentle undulations and occasional hills. The uneven surface spoiled the uniform layout of the cobblestones, and frequently there were large gaps in between the stones, filled with hard earth, probably in an attempt to even out the surface. The library itself was a large building on top of a hill with a nondescript doorway. Unlike the other houses and buildings, it was stone and gray mud on the ground floor and wooden on top. Imogen reached over and gave him a coin.

"They will charge you a threffening to browse. If you need anything copied, there will be a scribe who will do it for you, but it might be worth getting an idea of how many pages you need copied. Then, I will negotiate a good rate for them. I should be back in an hour, maybe two. Fingers crossed I return with positive news."

He felt like a child being given a coin for sweets at the local store. He climbed the steps and pushed the door excessively. His eyes took a second to get used to the dim interior. During that time a youth, fifteen at the most, came shuffling over. He knuckled his forehead and smiled. He was about the same height as Eric, with dark brown hair forming a wild mane down to his shoulders. His eyes were a little too close together and darkened, like he was wearing eye shadow.

"Hello, I'm Anton. How can I help? Do you need a map? Research? A book copied?"

Eric smiled back. He wanted to keep his cards close to his chest but didn't know how to phrase a question to get the information without tipping at least some of his secrets. "Um… I'm heading to Havelin and wanted to know more about the mages there. Do you have any books that discuss the sort of abilities they have?"

The boy pursed his lips and stared into the space to the left of Eric's head. "There's a history of the journeys of a discoverer from three hundred years ago. I think he swung past Havelin. And there's a memoir of a mayor of Havelin from seventy years ago that might mention something like that. But it sounds like you would want an in-depth book about the mages themselves. We don't have something like that, but there might be one in the library at Eles."

"Ah, Eles. Where is that exactly?"

"Oh, it's on the way to Havelin. Come this way." He led Eric over to the other side of the building. Eric could now see the layout more clearly. A mezzanine floor around the walls held bookshelves. There were bookshelves all around the walls of the ground floor and reading desks in the vacant middle area. Frosted glass windows, high on the walls, let in a milky-colored light that didn't do too much to expose the interior. Which may explain the dark circles around the eyes of his new friend. Or maybe it was just a lack of sleep.

Anton had led him to a large map on the wall. For the first time, Eric appreciated the full context of the lands he found himself in. He followed Anton's finger, pointing to where they were. He was astonished that the writing on the map was some weird language, consisting of scratches and boxes in various combinations. Instead, Eric focused on how he had gotten to Gerton, proceeding to follow the roads along which he had traveled until he found the little promontory where he had originally found himself. Anton cleared his throat, drawing Eric's attention to where he was now, pointing to a city high up on the wall.

"Havelin," Anton explained. Nestled in one of the colossal forests between Gerton and Havelin was another city, marked with a square and two diagonal lines scratching its upper line. "Eles."

"What language is that?" asked Eric, pointing to the writing on the map.

Anton frowned. "Balhish" he replied. "The language we're speaking."

Eric sighed. He kept thinking that every language he spoke was English. And he knew how to read and write in English. So, he naturally thought he could read any language that he could speak. It was becoming immediately apparent that he was going to have to make some adjustments to his understanding of his abilities. If he was staying longer, he might have to learn how to read and write all over again. But seeing as in two or three months he would be back at home, there was no point.

Eric would not allow himself to entertain the idea that he might not be able to get back home. Or that he wouldn't find what he needed from a book in the library. If he allowed himself to think about the possibility that the answer might not be in the book, or the mages might not be able to send him home, he would totally fall apart. The plan was his rock, his anchor. It would work. It had to. He would get home. And take Imogen with him. She would need to learn how to read English, but that would probably be best to do after they had made it back. He had lots of money though, so maybe he could fill the short-term requirement with another hire.

"Can you show me the memoir of the mayor of Havelin?" he asked Anton.

Anton shrugged and led him up to the mezzanine floor, then along to one of the corner shelves. A very short examination of the bottom shelf ended with the triumphant presentation of a soft leather-bound book. It was about the same size as an encyclopedia volume, but instead of thin pages, these were thicker and with rougher edges.

Eric took the book and opened it at a random page. Rather than letters, there were more of the square boxes and their nefarious cross-hatching.

"I can't read," he told Anton, crestfallen.

Anton shrugged. "That's fine, my lord. Would you like me to read the book and make you a summary, or would you like an exact copy? Or is there a particular page you would like me to copy?"

"No… Thank you. Oh, how long would it take to make a copy of the map? Maybe just focusing on the area between here and Havelin?"

"If you wanted something just for navigation, I could have that by tomorrow lunchtime. If you want something for your wall, we're looking at months."

Eric was still stuck on not being able to read.

"My lord?"

"Uhhh… How many people know how to read? Like on average?"

"My lord?"

"Say, in this town. How many would know how to read?"

Anton nodded. "Serfs and peasants don't know, obviously. In Gerton, the soldiers won't either. The merchants probably would. The trades people may or may not. The clergy do, obviously. All the lords and ladies do too. And people like me, members of the Scribes Guild, by definition do. So, I don't know, maybe one in ten?"

Eric looked around the library with fresh eyes. "All these books, the knowledge…"

Anton smiled. "Little nuggets of knowledge. Shelves of them. And this is just a small library."

Eric looked around. Sure, the library was small in comparison to the grand civic buildings back on Earth, but it was one of the larger structures in the city.

Anton saw Eric's disbelief. "Comparatively. Some of the libraries in the capitals would dwarf this one. Thousands and thousands of books, and scrolls, and tablets." Anton smiled widely at the thought of all those books.

Eric gazed around at the knowledge that was denied him, not able to see the bars locking it away, while Anton reveled in the access. He bitterly wondered if Anton would still be smiling that broadly if that ability was taken away from him.

"Ah, yes. My friend is returning in an hour, is there anywhere I could wait for her?" He couldn't even wait with a book to kill the time.

"This way, sir."

Anton led him to a side room. A bench with an inkwell and quill pen sat in front of a sturdy seat. A skylight far above flooded the room with a milky light.

"I'll come and get you when she arrives, sir," Anton said before leaving Eric alone with his thoughts.

As soon as the door closed, Eric cupped his head in his hands. He'd never thought about being able to read before. It had always been a given. Throughout his schooling, everyone had known how to read, even the athletes. By adulthood, all but the absurdly rare exceptions had learned to read and here he was. No, he was being unfair to himself. He was a stranger in a foreign land. You wouldn't put an American in the middle of China and expect them to be able to read the local newspaper, right? And he would be back in the United States as soon as he got to the mages and paid them to send him back. So it would be, what, two, three months? Also, it wasn't like he was missing anything: the books they did have here were only vaguely pertinent.

He was getting a little miffed if he had to be honest with himself. He had a good thing going back home. Well, maybe not good. But comfortable. The restaurant didn't pay well, but it was enough for how he wanted to live his life. There wasn't a huge opportunity to meet women – sure, he could have hit on the customers, but he'd rather keep work and romance separate. He had his games and his bong, and his friends. He didn't have any great goals such as writing a screenplay or learning an instrument, but he was happy.

And then there was this place, where he really didn't belong. A kid had gotten killed because of him. Death seemed to be a way of life here. Common. None of the things one would imagine in a magical world were present where he was now, and he'd played enough games based in such worlds to know what to expect. *Oh, you want to go to Havelin. Fine, pay this much, jump on this flying creature, and speed-travel there.* Done. He was also getting sick of everything he did being wrong. His thinking seemed totally at odds with how the world operated. But with Imogen being his advisor, maybe he would be able to learn the lay of the land. Instead of acting straight away, maybe he should check with her to see if what he wanted to do would get him in trouble. Maybe a secret little hand gesture or something. That might save his neck. And, hey, maybe the mages in Havelin would be able to teach him some magic. That would be awesome. He'd wait until KJ and Finn came over next, and after they'd had a few tokes, he'd turn a rock into a frog or something. That would freak them the fuck out. But he was done being a passenger in this world. He was going to push the envelope more. What was the point of having all this money without being able to get ahead because of it? Why shouldn't he just hire his own army and walk straight to Havelin immediately? Or buy a bunch of horses and gallop there, leaving the bandits, the monsters, and creatures behind him? He smiled to himself. *Goodbye Eric, Shift Manager. Hello Eric, Shit Starter.* Besides, nobody knew him here. And no one knew all the jokes from late-night television. Maybe he could regurgitate those jokes and become a troubadour? If they shared the same sense of humor that was. Jokes about the TSA at airports might not land too well here. Their moon wasn't even the right color.

Just as he was just coming to a conclusion, there was a knock on the door. Expecting Imogen, he turned, only to be surprised by seeing Anton. His face was lit up with a huge grin.

"My lord, I think I've found exactly what you were looking for!" He placed a very thick book on the desktop, the thud it made shocking Eric. "I found this in the few texts we have that were written in the Softo language, which is why I wasn't aware of it when you first asked. These are the memoirs of one of Havelin's great mages, Marion the Wise. They were imprisoned in Suffloti last century and, subsequently, found themselves with a lot of time on their hands. It's large, but I'm sure that I should be able to find what you wanted to know about the mages. It might take a while though, you can see how big the book is."

"How long are we talking here? I may have to leave Gerton soon."

"Maybe a month?"

That was too long to wait in Gerton. It would be good to have the information before getting to Havelin, but it didn't seem a good idea to delay the travel. After all, he'd find out as soon as he arrived anyway. "Could I borrow the book?"

"My lord?"

"Can I take the book with me?"

"But this is our book. It belongs to the library - to the guild…" Anton's immediate response faltered as he saw that Eric was serious. Eventually, he continued. "I don't think that's possible, my lord. I would be happy to make a copy, or read it and make notes to answer any questions you had. I could send you a summary?"

Eric rubbed his chin and stared into space. "OK, so I can't take it with me. And even if I could borrow it or buy it, that's no good to me, because I can't read it. If you summarize it, the summary would make its way to me when I can no longer use it, and on top of that, I would not be able to read it."

Anton nodded.

"Anton, do you want to take a trip to Havelin?"

Anton blinked. Made an attempt to speak but nothing came out. Tried again. "I have always wanted to go to Havelin. The mages have a magnificent library there, a pair of libraries, in fact. But it's very dangerous. And I have my duties here. More importantly, I doubt that the Chief Librarian would allow the book to leave the library."

Eric nodded, rubbing his chin. "Just out of curiosity, how much would it be to replace that book?"

Anton shook his head. "No, my lord. It's not just the value of the book. It's the income that the book could generate over the years. And the time it would take to make a copy."

"Ballpark." He was watching for any confusion at the term, but the earworm must have found a local equivalent.

"Let's say 100 orams for the copy and 400 orams over the next century - maybe 500 orams in total."

"So, what if I told the Chief Librarian or whatever you call him that I would give him 500 orams, and when he gets the book back, he gives me back 400 orams?"

"And how would you persuade him to release me for the time there and back? And, more importantly, how would you keep me safe?"

"It'll take three months to get there, so six months there and back, right? What would pay your wages for six months? Double it. What's that?"

Anton didn't answer straight away. "Ten Orams." And then he frowned. "But the Guildmaster won't let me go just like that. You can't just reduce everything to money. There is my learning and my work here. My life is here."

Eric smiled at him. "Do you want to go? The libraries. The people that you'll meet. It will make for some great stories that the other men in the inn won't have. Look, if that doesn't appeal, just say the word. But if it is something you want, let me know. I'll speak with your boss."

Eric could see Anton weighing up the offer. He didn't know whether the prospect of the adventure finally won or whether Anton just couldn't see his bosses going for it. Either way, he eventually nodded, smiling. "If you can get me the leave to go, I would be glad to accompany you."

Eric grinned. "My friend will be here shortly to collect me. We'll return tomorrow to talk to your boss. Will he be here?"

Anton nodded. "He has other guild work to attend to in the mornings, but by noon he is usually in his office here. Do you want me to ask him about it or would you like to broach the subject yourself?"

Eric couldn't see any benefit either way before deciding that the more time they had to come to terms with the possibility, the better chance they would come to the correct conclusion. "Yes, you can tell him." Anton smiled and left him to his thoughts.

Imogen returned not long afterward and briefed him on the way back to the inn.

"The last train left five days ago."

"Shit. But doesn't that mean that the next one will be soon?"

"Normally, maybe. But with the war and everything, there are fewer merchants traveling between cities, so fewer people are waiting here for the next train."

"But surely with more soldiers around the roads, it will be safer?"

She looked at him for a second. "If men want to avoid being levied and becoming soldiers, they leave their village to camp out in the woods and badlands. When they do that, there are limited opportunities to get food. Or money. So, they rob travelers. And then those farmers who cannot avoid the levy, sometimes decide not to remain soldiers and desert. If they get back to their farms, they might be tracked down and made to return or executed for desertion. So, they—"

"—turn to being robbers as well." They skirted around a wagon that had broken a wheel on a gap in the paving stones. The horses were still hitched and the sacks of grain were strewn around the scene. Thankfully, it looked like none of them had split open. The team of wagoneers was in a yelling match, much to the amusement of the surrounding crowd.

"So how long do we have to wait? Would it be worth it to leave tomorrow and try to catch up with the train that left five days ago? Surely, we could make better time?"

Imogen nodded thoughtfully. "There are merchants waiting here already to warrant a train, but they will wait another five days to make sure they have a big enough group. The Train Captain wants a large train. If you wanted to catch up with the other train, you could buy me a horse and set off, but we'd catch them up in five days, maybe six. Once we hit the Underhills, we would be in danger from the Moolean. They don't attack groups, but two people on horseback? They would love that. They love horse flesh. And that's assuming that some bandits have not strung up a line between trees that we gallop into." She shook her head. "Our best bet is to wait."

Eric grinned wryly. "And that would be an additional two horses. I am going to hire a scribe. He can figure out what the mages can do - he's got a book, a diary, which will tell us all we need to know."

Imogen looked surprised. "And he was allowed to come? The Scribes Guild is known for their love of books. I'd be surprised if they let one of their scribes, and more importantly one of their precious books out of their sight."

"I'm going to meet the boss tomorrow at noon to negotiate."

"Good luck."

Chapter 5

The next day, they ventured out in the early morning air. The streets were already starting to thicken with the constant traffic of the beating heart of the city. Eric tried to figure it out. He could see what were obviously farmers, entering the town, wagons pulled by oxen or by one of those enormous aurochs, and occasionally, by a stunted pony. The wagons tended to be a flatbed between two large wheels, very occasionally between four wheels. Typically, they were piled high with sacks, filled with flour if the white streaks against the grey-brown sack fabric were any indication. Sometimes the wagons carried logs, planks of wood, or blocks of stone. They weren't always a single type of cargo though, a third of the wagons carried wicker baskets holding fruit, vegetables, and fish or other meat. The aromas suggested those weren't always fresh. But there were also smells of spices and other scents that Eric couldn't place. There weren't any wagons clearly carting large piles of spices, so Eric assumed those were in some of the mystery sacks. The outbound traffic was more limited, with emptier wagons, and the occasional drunk in the flatbed sleeping off whatever debauchery had occurred the night before. Most of those were steered by a less drunk farmer. On one occasion, Eric saw a wagon with the sole occupant asleep on the back and the two oxen meandering down the street. He was almost tempted to stop so he could see what happened, but like a woman possessed, Imogen was wasting no time getting to Tailors' Row.

Eric expected it to look like Rodeo Drive in Los Angeles. Plate glass windows and haute couture. Instead, the windows were solely to illuminate the interiors - a forearm length of glass positioned high on the walls, with no displays of dresses at all. The placards outside each of the shops showed what kind of clothing was sold. They passed three shops with variations of a dress on the placard - one with the red dress encircled with gold rope or thread, one with the green dress in front of the rising sun, and the last with a blue dress with a silver flower. But Imogen led them past the shops, down an alley off the main road, where the buildings threatened to touch three stories above them. The sliver of morning sky did nothing to illuminate the gloom, and wouldn't, Eric realized, until the noon sun could penetrate to the ground below.

Imogen stepped down to a door, which was set a foot below the ground level. The placard out the front showed a pair of men's breeches. It was faded and had been repainted so many times, that it looked almost like the breeches had three legs. Imogen opened the door without knocking, ducking so she could go under the low doorway. Eric followed closely behind. His eyes took a minute or two to adjust to the darkness inside. A row of candles along one wall was the only attempt to illuminate the room. An elderly woman, knitting with her eyes half closed, sat behind a desk. A fireplace with a low bed of embers still glowing kept her warm. She looked up when they entered and smiled upon seeing Imogen.

Imogen embraced her warmly and whispered something in her ear. The older woman nodded and cocked an eyebrow at Eric. Imogen nodded and the older woman returned to her knitting. Imogen took Eric's hand and led him to one of the walls. She slid it across, revealing a passageway. She pulled Eric into it and returned the wall to its place, plunging them into darkness. As Eric's eyes again started to adjust to the lack of light, he noticed the outline of a doorway just in front of them. Imogen was already opening the door, leading him further into the bowels of the building. They were now in a well-lit room, with a long table in the center of it. Along the far side was a line of mannequins, wearing shirts in various shades and designs, and in different stages of completeness. The tailor working on them had already stood up and was coming to greet Imogen.

He reminded Eric of a leprechaun. Sure, he was only just shorter than Eric, but he was dressed in a fetching green-based palette, he had a buckle hat on, and his white beard was topped with eyes that glinted mischievously. "A pleasure as always, Imogen," he said, as both he and Imogen touched the tips of the fingers of their right hands and wiggled them gently.

They turned to Eric. Imogen presented him with a sweeping arm gesture. "May I present Eric, Prince of Anaheim in America. My lord, this is Mo. The best tailor in the realm."

This was the first time Eric had been introduced to anyone. The stable boys had placed a fist to their forehead when they had greeted him, so in absence of any other gesture, he did this also while saying "Very nice to meet you, Mo."

Mo looked surprised by his gesture, and inclined his head toward Eric. "Likewise, my lord." Turning toward Imogen, his smile broadened. "My dear, it is good to see you again. What can I do for you? For you both?"

Imogen returned his smile and nodded toward Eric. "We need some clothes for Eric. Something which fits. Something nice. For traveling, not court."

Eric piped up. "But nothing that will attract attention, or scream 'rob me!'"

Mo was nodding while stroking his beard and looking at Eric. "How long?" he asked.

"We leave in five days."

Mo winced. And then nodded. "Are you snow-bound? No? OK, I can get you four shirts - Caretan cotton, not the local hessian - two pairs of trousers, and a jacket. And I'll send you to Timmy Twofingers to get some better-fitting boots."

Imogen smiled. "Thanks, Mo. I knew you were the one for the job."

Eric looked from one to the other, waiting for the cost to be brought up. Seeing that the two of them considered the transaction completed, he cleared his throat. "My thanks, Mo. Just out of curiosity, how much will all that cost me?"

Mo glanced briefly at Imogen before answering. "Of course, my lord. Of course." He frowned. "Forgive my impertinence, and apologies Imogen, I do not wish to embarrass your friend, but I'm curious. Eric is a Prince, yet you address him as 'my lord', not 'your majesty' or 'your highness'. While his manners are definitely not of our lands, he tugs his forelock to a tailor and has none of the... arrogance one expects of the ruling class. I'll give you a price, Eric Prince of Anaheim, but should it be a price for royalty, or one for a runaway farm boy pretending?" Mo's tone was jovial, respectful, but his gaze was piercing, watching for a reaction.

Eric smiled, a little confused. "I'm not a farm boy," he said evenly. A farm boy wouldn't manage a shift or have to open in the mornings.

Mo inclined his head in a mini-bow. "Well, in that case, my lord, I think due to the short time frame, the sum of four drahms would be appropriate."

Eric glanced at Imogen. She kept her eyes on Mo, but gave the slightest shake of her head. "I think that would be an acceptable price should I be traveling with piles of gold, Mo. As it is, funds are shorter than that. Shall we say two drahms?"

A shadow of a smile flicked across Mo's face. "My lord wishes to rob me! Two drahms would just cover the costs of the fabrics - I did say Caretan cotton, did I not? And with the tight time frame, I will not be able to accommodate any of my other clients—"

Imogen interrupted him. "We have other merchants to see this day, Mo. Shall we skip to the part where we agree on three drahms without a half hour of hysterics?"

Mo shut his mouth, which was still open, mid argument. He looked between Imogen and Eric, half bemused, half hurt. "As you say, my lady, as you say. Three would be a fair price." He looked at Eric for agreement.

Eric nodded, relieved not to have to go through - a half hour, of further negotiations. Really?

Mo recovered quickly. "Everything should be ready before you leave."

Imogen led Eric back to the thoroughfare which opened out into the main market square. There was a steady throng of people coming and going, or just milling around talking. Eric stopped dead in his tracks, staring around him. He finally put his finger on what had been bothering him since they had arrived in the city. Everyone was white. There was a little variation in skin tones, but none of the broad spectrum of color that he was so used to from Los Angeles. No Koreans. No Chinese. Certainly, no African Americans, no Puerto Ricans, or Mexicans. As he scanned the crowd in the market square, he mentally tried to find the most extreme skin colors - the pastiest white and the most swarthy. He couldn't see any red-headed folk. There were some blondes and the odd auburn, but nothing red like an Irishman. And at the other end of the scale, there were none of the dark-skinned Europeans, like Italians or Greeks. Imogen had stopped and was watching him closely. Eric caught her eye and shook his head as he let her lead him further into the marketplace. He would have to ask about it when they had a moment alone. How would you frame such a conversation? Probably it would be safest to just ask about skin and hair colors. Should he mention the environments which led to the colorations? He knew that it was hotter where people with the darkest skins come from, but what made Asian people look the way they did? How would he describe them? Without being racist?

Imogen was waiting for him by a stall in the corner. A well-muscled man of average height, jet black hair, tumbling down to his shoulders, greeted them both as Eric approached. There was a rack of swords, flanking bellows beside an anvil. The swordsmith was less muscular than the gym bunnies that Eric knew from back in the US, but the muscle looked sinewy, more earned from activity with purpose. He had a twinkle in his eye as he saw Eric noticing his physique.

"What can I do for you both?" The swordsmith asked. Eric expected him to have tattoos, but he couldn't see any.

"My lord needs a sword," offered Imogen, nodding toward Eric.

The swordsmith sized Eric up and down. He gently took Eric's right hand in both of his. The difference in the hand size was almost ridiculous. Eric's slim limbs were dwarfed by the swordsmith's. They were like catcher's mitts, smooth leather save for a ridge of callus through the palm. Whatever analysis was being performed was over, and his hand was released gently. The smith stared into space for a few seconds, stroking his chin in thought.

Eventually, he shrugged. "I have two that might be agreeable." He turned to the sword rack, and when he returned in sight, he was holding a sword with the blade resting on one enormous forearm. For Eric, brought up on Conan, computer role-playing games, and movies, the sword was ludicrously underwhelming. The width of blade was less than one of Eric's hand's widths across and its length was shorter than his forearm. Eric didn't even bother to look at the hilt or cross guard.

"Where's the rest of it?" he asked. It looked like something for a child.

The swordsmith nodded as if expecting the reaction. "My lord has not the physique for a sword for butchery, this one will be a better match for a man of... intellect. The handle is honest sharkskin. It balances–"

"What else do you have?" asked Eric, trying to hide his hurt. Imogen was watching him closely.

The swordsmith returned the sword to the rack and was engaged in finding the other sword for a good minute, Eric growing more impatient as the seconds ticked by.

"Here is the other one," the swordsmith said as he turned. He held it out along his forearm, his hands dwarfing the hilt again. Eric could not tell the difference between this and the first sword, except for this one had writing inlaid into the middle of the blade. Five busy characters each a thumb's width square.

A choice of two, and one with writing on it. Not exactly a hard decision, right? He reached for the hilt, and the swordsmith swiveled so that the handle was pointing toward him. He carefully took the weight. The sword felt alien, like an awkward appendage. It was surprisingly heavy, like when he'd picked up a friend's electric guitar. There was a density to it which made it difficult to translate the desired motion into reality. Eric very quickly realized he had no idea how to use it: if it was going to be used in anger, he would definitely need some sort of lessons.

Imogen and the swordsmith were both watching him. Anything he did with it would give away his ineptness, so instead he carefully handed the sword back to the swordsmith and nodded to Imogen. "I think we'll need a scabbard and a sharpening thing."

"A whetstone."

"Yeah, one of those." He wandered away, waving to Imogen, ostensibly to idly flick through the racks of swords while Imogen ran through the familiar pattern of the negotiations. That was one thing he would not miss about this world. Give him a standard ticket price and let him get on with life. He would have to get Imogen to arrange some sort of sword training. Would the swordsmith be able to train him? If you made the sword, would that mean you would know how to use it? And had he actually made it? Or was the swordsmith like a used-car salesman? Buying and selling second-hand swords. He giggled to himself as he remembered the typical lies car salespeople would tell, stories such as a car being in very good condition, because it was previously

102

owned by a little old lady, who drove it to and from church, one day a week. What would the equivalent of that story be over here? Oh yes, the sword was previously owned by a little old lady, who only used it to slaughter on Sundays on the way to church.

The swords he was looking at now were more like what he had in mind - big, thick blades, wide. Grooves down the middle of them. A couple with wavy edges. Long ones. One with a whole novel written in the middle of it. A pity he couldn't read it. Speaking of which, he would need to get someone to read the writing on the blade of the sword he'd just bought. It would be typical if it said something derogatory. Like a poorly chosen bumper sticker. Or a tattoo in Chinese script that said something like "stupid dumb white person."

Imogen caught up with him, holding the sword in a scabbard in. She carried it in one hand, not bothered by its weight. She smiled and held it out to him. "A good price, my lord. I caught the start of tears in his eyes."

Eric smiled back. Imogen definitely seemed to like her work. "Uh… Who would be a good person to teach me how to use it, do you think? Could the swordsmith do it?"

Imogen gave him a look. "Definitely not him. He seemed on the edge of crying, and that's the last person you want swinging a sword at you! No, I think we should be able to find you someone who can show you the basics. Oh, sorry, I'm sure you're already a very good swordsman." She seemed concerned that she might have offended him.

Eric gave a small smile. Self-deprecatory. "It couldn't hurt for a refresher. Where to next?"

"Boots and then back to the library. This way, my lord."

As they left the swordsmith's stall, their path took them directly past the swordsmith. Imogen led the way, and as Eric made to follow, the swordsmith caught his eye. When he passed him, the man leaned forward, and spoke very softly, "My lord, if you find yourself in combat, I suggest that you run."

By the time Eric registered what the words meant, he was already past the swordsmith. With a confused look over his shoulder, he forged back through the gathering crowds to ensure he stayed close to Imogen.

The bootmaker was on the other side of the square, and Imogen was not dawdling. Eric hustled to catch up to her and took a second to watch her. There was a bounce to her step and a ready smile on her face. Evidently, being paid to shop agreed with her.

The bootmaker had a shop that opened onto the square. Stepping inside, they found themselves in a cozy open area with benches along the walls. Imogen had evidently been there before as the shopkeeper instantly started walking towards them when he saw her, greeting her with the wiggling fingertips and gushing exclamations. After a minute, Imogen introduced Eric to the bootmaker, reducing his title to his first name. "Eric of Anaheim." The bootmaker bowed from the waist, her blonde braid slipping over her shoulder, only to be returned without thought as she looked him up and down. "Emerald the Bootmaker of Gruden," Imogen announced.

"Emerald?" Eric asked, puzzled. He looked over to Imogen. "Not Timmy Twofingers?"

"Mr. Twofingers is fiction. Emerald is the best bootmaker in Gruden. You will have to meet her sisters Ruby and Pearl," laughed Imogen.

"My parents were venerators of the Earth goddess, our names honor the gifts of the Earth," said Emerald with a bemused forbearance. "But my lord did not come all this way to hear about naming ceremonies now, did he? How high do you like the cut of the boot, my lord? I have some which will cover your calf to the knee, but the fashion for the court appears to favor boots cut to the ankle only. Would my lord favor style or substance?" Both Imogen and Emerald seemed to be watching him for his response, a little too interested. He got the feeling this was one of those loaded questions that single girls read in magazines and woe betide you if you don't select the correct response. Eric didn't have much time for those sorts of games.

"Knee-high will do just fine. Thank you, Emerald. Actually, I'm more interested in the fit across the foot. I have been wearing these ill-fitting ones for so long, I dare say that the blisters are the only things keeping them on."

Emerald grinned broadly. "Of course, my lord. Let's slip one off. I'll take it out the back and see if I have anything close to it." She put words to action and disappeared through a door behind them. Imogen sat down beside Eric.

"You look like you are having fun."

"I must admit this job is the absolute best I have ever had, my lord. Nobody is trying to sleep with me, I am getting good prices for the things you want to buy, and I am being paid well for my time. Also, I am getting to see friends of mine that I have not seen for a year or two. Plus, the promise of a new world to explore. A good day indeed when you stepped into The Swan."

Eric smiled back and nodded. While they were waiting, he thought about the names of the bootmaker and her sisters. And how confusing it was for people of this world to refer to it as Earth when it was very much not the Earth. Not Eric's Earth anyway.

###

The sun was well and truly overhead when they made their way toward the library. "Does my lord wish to have his lunch before or after we visit the scribes?" asked Imogen as they pushed their way through the more crowded areas of the marketplace.

"Let's get the talk with the scribes over with, in case I need to make alternate arrangements" Eric responded.

The light was gamely trying to illuminate the interior of the library as they went through the door. But the darkest corners still remained covered in gloom, and the strong beams of light managed to pick out the motes of dust which lazily swirled through the still air. A hacking cough filtered from one of the rooms in the back. Anton recognized Eric immediately and hurried over to greet him.

"My lord, so good to see you again! I must admit to suspecting that it was not going to happen. But the more I think about your offer, the more I like it. I only hope the Librarian assents. Let me fetch him."

Imogen gazed around the interior of the main room, running her hand into the grooves, carved into the back of the thick wooden chairs, and occasionally caressing one or other of the shelves. Eric, for his part, stood patiently, making his face take a neutral or hopefully amiable stance. Back in his home world, he had only had mixed success with negotiations. The odd wins (championing one of his team in a performance review, and getting the schedule he wanted over the last holiday period) nestled amongst a rather larger collection of failures (every other request for a bonus or a raise, every attempt at asking someone out). But hey, new world, new Eric, right?

The Librarian waddled over behind Anton. He was balding, with tendrils of combover silver where there wasn't gray. He was short and quite rotund, with a beaked nose and bad teeth, and reminded Eric of a grotesquely exaggerated version of Danny DeVito's Penguin.

"Librarian Troy, this is the man I was telling you about. Eric Prince of Anaheim. My lord, Librarian Troy of the Scribes Guild."

The Librarian inclined his head slightly toward Eric and fixed him with a beady eye, reminding Eric even more of a bird. He smiled, which looked more like a grimace, at Eric.

Eric decided that after his experiences meeting people earlier in the day, he'd match the manners he was greeted with. He returned the bow, a little deeper than the one he'd received. "Librarian Troy, a pleasure! Has Anton told you about my offer?"

Troy paused while blinking and licking his lips, his tongue darting out of his mouth just far enough to moisten before retreating back. At last, he nodded and grimaced again. "My lord, yes, Anton has communicated the main points of the offer. I must admit that it would be quite impossible. He has many tasks, and as

108

for leaving with the book, that would be out of the question. The Guild has very strong rules about that sort of thing."

Eric smiled broadly. "Librarian Troy - I'm sorry, is that the correct way to address you?"

Anton spoke up. "It is more correct to address him as 'My Bookish Master' while we are in the Library."

"If we are following the most correct forms, of course, my lord," confirmed Troy, a treacly smile spreading over his face.

"Of course, My Bookish Master. It seems to me that there are two concerns that I need to address. The first is that of Anton's proposed absence. I can see why that would be unacceptable - there is work that needs to be done, and if there is nobody to do it, then… Well, that reflects badly on the Guild, does it not? Income not earned; maintenance not been done. That does make sense."

"My lord is very wise."

"And if you had to put a monetary value on that labor, how much would that be, do you think?"

Eric noticed two things at the same time. The first was the change in the posture of the Librarian. He was now more attentive, more interested in what was being said. Eric guessed that was the Librarian switching to negotiation mode. The other thing he observed was that Imogen had circled around and was now within earshot, standing behind the Librarian. Good. He would be able to be guided by her knowledge. That would help with getting a good price.

"Two doons."

Imogen's eyes widened in shock. She frowned behind the Librarian and shook her head. Eric made a show of considering the offer. "That's… interesting," he said after a while. A pause. "And the other concern that I must address is that of the valuable book that I need to have interpreted."

The Chief Librarian's eyes narrowed. The tip of his tongue reappeared - flicking between his lips weirdly - almost as if tasting the air like a snake. "It is, as I am sure you are aware, a very valuable book, my lord." The honorific was tacked on as an afterthought. "We would be bereft to be without it for any length of time. And the journey you are proposing sounds very dangerous. We would be bereft, positively bereft, if anything happened to it while in transit." Eric wondered if that sense of loss would be reflected if anything happened to Anton. "And the regulations are quite clear. We cannot allow any books to leave the library. So, I'm afraid while I can let you have Anton, I cannot let you have the book. Regulations, you understand." He smiled, again more of a grimace than anything else.

Eric returned his smile, wider and more genuine. He was on familiar ground here. Dealing with the head office at the restaurant was a constant negotiation of impossible regulations. Even the glee with which his original request was turned down was straight from all his interactions with HR, Legal, and Operations. You only get somewhere by changing the angle of attack. And ignoring their reveling in their power by laying on friendliness.

"The book is, as you say, very valuable." He smiled at Anton to try and include him in the description of its value. "And so, I would be happy to leave a deposit to make you whole, should I not return with it." The Librarian's eyes lit up at this thought. Behind, he noticed Imogen about to say something before he silenced her with the smallest shake of his head. "As for the regulations," he said, pausing to rub his chin and contemplate the ceiling, "Surely they don't apply to books being transferred to other libraries? I hear there are two libraries in Havelin?"

He could see the Librarian weighing up the prospect of not one but two obscene payments versus the regulations. And now there was a barely plausible reason to support allowing it, he could almost feel the weight of the coin in his purse.

"But we have received no such request from the libraries. And while they are in a different country, and in a self-governing city no less, our guild still governs them."

"But, My Bookish Master, how do they know that you hold this particular book?" The librarian looked confused. "Wouldn't it be prudent to show it to them? To see if they wanted to borrow it?" Behind the librarian, he could see Imogen trying to stifle a smirk at the frailty of the argument. Anton also looked surprised that the concept was being considered. The Librarian on the other hand seemed to be weighing it up carefully. After a while, he nodded.

"Yes, and Anton would have to go then to present the book to the librarians of each of the libraries to ask if they would like to have the copy. Yes, that would work."

The look of startled surprise on Anton and Imogen's faces was a joy to behold.

"Which brings us to the amount of the deposit. Which we would return of course, on the safe return of the book."

"And Anton," smiled Eric.

"Of course, and Anton."

The librarian looked uncertain for a second, his eyes darting from side to side, matching the tip of his tongue. "That particular book is in great demand, so we would have to say ten dooms as a deposit."

Imogen's eyes were wide in shock, and Anton looked like he had stopped breathing entirely. Before Imogen could signal him, Eric nodded. "Two dooms that you keep and ten that you hold for safe return of the book and Anton."

"My lord–" Imogen started.

"We will pay the amount when we leave in two days. Anton, will you be ready? Good! Shall we be on our way, Imogen?" He led the way out of the library, Anton making a show of showing them to the door, leaving the Chief Librarian stunned and frowning.

He rather thought that Imogen would explode, her lips pursed with barely contained indignation. She was obviously waiting for Anton to leave them before unleashing on Eric, so he made a point of pausing at the door and leaned closer to Anton.

"Are you sure you want to come? I cannot promise safety," he blinked away the memory of the stableboy, "But I can promise it will be nothing of the life you know in the library. The Chief Librarian can compel you, but I want to know, what is your decision?"

Anton smiled broadly. "My lord, I have thought of nothing else since you mentioned the journey yesterday. An adventure like this does not come very often. It'll be a tale worthy of the page. I am ready." His eyes started to tear. "Thank you, my lord. Thank you!" He turned and returned to the darkness of the library, wiping at his eyes with the sleeve of his robe.

Eric smiled to himself and turned into the baleful glare of Imogen.

"My Lord, how can I help you if you insist on negotiating for yourself? You quite got taken advantage of there. Do you know what you could have bought with that sum?"

Eric held up a hand to forestall the barrage. "You are right, Imogen, I apologize."

"My job sir, is to–"

"Look, it's like this: back home, I can read. Here, I can't. And the answers that I'm looking for are in that book, I can feel it. Clues to the way back are in that book. Normally, I would just read it. Can you imagine what it's like to have that ability just taken away from you?" She shook her head. Eric continued. "The words are just there. On the page. I don't have much, but at least I had that, right… And…" he blinked back tears. "And so, I might have paid too much. But I'm not just paying for Anton's ability and time. I'm paying for the certainty of finding out what is in that book. And that's worth paying for."

"Aren't you afraid that he will try and renegotiate the amount when we leave?"

"Not really. If it is as high an amount as you say, we are practically buying Anton and the book. If he does push for more, then we leave. There is zero chance that he won't chase us down the street, agreeing to the original amount once he figures out that we're serious."

They headed back into the streets. "Tell me, Imogen, is the train the best option? Is there not a different way of traveling? Some mystical creature? Or can I not hire guards directly?"

"I am not a mage, and know not of any in town, so could not begin to think how magic could get us there any faster. All the mercenaries are in the employ of one or other of the local lords to fight in the war."

"And mystical creatures?"

"I have never thought that such could carry people and be so common as to be talked about as if they were horse or cattle. You will have to tell me of such creatures from your world, my lord, if I am to be prepared for them when we arrive."

Eric nodded. "The journey sounds like it will be long, so we will have plenty of time to talk about it. But lastly, why should we not buy you a horse and ride hard until we get to the city of the mages?"

Imogen looked at him wryly. "The Bendies usually show the bones of those who travel without them on the first or second day. It's their way of justifying the fee."

"Bendies?"

"You will see, my lord. And seeing is believing. The things which are between here and Havelin are faster than horses."

Chapter 6

Eric was sweaty, sore and pissed off. He made his way to where he'd arranged to meet Imogen and reflected on what he had learned. Imogen had arranged for him to get a lesson from the local swordmaster and it had not gone well. It had started well enough, with a short conversation where he admitted to not having any idea of what he was doing, and the master looking at his physique and nodding. The actual lesson was the swordmaster showing him some patterns to practice. And that was it. They went through them a few times, enough for Eric to start feeling fatigued from moving the heavy sword in ways unfamiliar to his body. He needed to stop and rest a few times, and the swordmaster grew impatient, indicating that in a battle it was a little unlikely his opponent would allow a "two-minute break for some water." Eric was annoyed at the superficiality of the lesson and, unfortunately, it showed. Looking back on it he wondered if he'd expected to learn the secret moves which would always win every battle, similar to when he discovered a special combo in one of the computer games he played. Left arrow, left arrow, up, right, right, attack, attack didn't really translate to real-world motions.

The swordmaster had asked if he would like to finish with some sparring and, well, let's say there were no broken bones but more than a little bruised ego. At least he knew how to draw his sword, wear it, and show it to other people. So that was something, right?

The previous day he'd sent Imogen off to arrange the purchase of the wagon and their supplies. As he approached the square where they had arranged to meet, he noticed that she was waiting by a flatbed wagon and a pair of oxen yoked to it.

The marketplace was awash with wagons and men, armed with spears, who were wearing various different pieces of leather armor. The wagon train was assembling in the predawn light - there were twenty wagons of various types.

Imogen had changed from her dress into tight trousers and a well-structured jacket with tails. The seams of the jacket were lined with geometric shapes, picked out in a bold yellow, which offset the darkness of the green. She had also found a hat.

"Wow," said Eric. "You look… different."

Imogen struck a pose, before a more serious look came over her face. "It's more for practical purposes, my lord," she said, "if we are to be in danger and need to move quickly, I thought it best not to be tripping over skirts. And the trousers keep the bandages in place."

"Well, they're certainly... snug," he said, trying not to look too closely.

She smiled and gestured for him to follow her. She led him to the middle of the trail, giving Eric an opportunity to inspect the other members of the train.

The recurring theme was definitely thick wagons with large wheels, carrying heavy chests. Sometimes the chests were surreptitiously hidden behind sacks of grain or under bolts of cloth, but it was something Eric pretty quickly picked out as they passed each wagon in turn. The carts themselves were more robust than the ones Eric had seen on the road to town. The wheels were up to his shoulder and made from solid wood with studded thick iron bands around the rims. The animals pulling them were more often than not the auroch that he had seen before, placidly waiting. Occasionally, one would drag one of its foot-long horns along the cobbled street, grinding the end down, and leaving scratches and a slight groove in the surface of the stone.

Imogen turned and saw him watching the auroch. "They have to keep the ends short, otherwise the horns grow in a curve and actually impale their own skull. If they get longer than two feet, they're not able to stunt the growth, and a month later, you have a dead auroch. A traveler at The Swan once told me he had seen one such auroch run head-first into a cliff. The impact broke the horns off near the skull. The auroch apparently picked himself up, shook his head, and then wandered off. I didn't believe him at first, but then a different traveler told me of a cliff in that same general area that looked as if miners had been chipping away at its face, and whose base was littered with shattered auroch horns. They're strange beasts."

At this moment, the auroch they were passing turned and watched them go by with an inscrutable stare, stolidly chewing a mouthful of cud.

"This is us," Imogen said at last. Ahead, Eric could see their wagon, his horse saddled and tied to the back, and two plain oxen harnessed to the front.

"Not the auroch?"

Imogen grinned. "They are impressive, aren't they? No, they attract attention. The only people who can afford them are the rich folk, the ones that are good to rob, the ones that we want to make sure that we don't look anything like."

The bed of the wagon was a riot of sacks, barrels, and what seemed to be a spare wheel that peeked out from the bottom of the pile. Imogen watched him as he stared at the supplies. "All totally needed. We're going for three months, and a lot of that is through lands where war has been brewing. We might not be able to barter or buy supplies between here and Havelin."

"Wow, there's quite a lot there. Was there any change?"

Imogen looked embarrassed. "There's a lot less money remaining than I thought there would be, my lord. I also got some spare parts for the wagon, and since there are three of us, a lot of food. I tried to save money by getting grain and a hand mill instead of flour, but there wasn't much left." She handed the coin pouch that he had given her, almost completely spent, with only a few coins clinking together in the bottom. Eric had populated the purse with a small handful of coins from one of the sacks, so it hadn't actually reduced his total wealth by any noticeable amount. He was just aware that if he started taking the wealth for granted, pretty soon, it would all be gone.

Eric opened the purse and looked at the coins, then at Imogen, and back again. "Well, tell me that you got us good deals, at least," he said with a smile, pulling the drawstring to a close and placing it in his jacket pocket.

Imogen grinned back and clambered up onto the waggoner's seat, awkward but enthusiastic, and twitched the reins. The oxen lumbered forward. "The best! I was even able to get waxed cloth for a lean-to when we camp, as well as sleeping stones."

Eric clambered up beside her, frowning upon hearing 'sleeping stones'. "What are—"

Imogen's grin broadened as she interrupted. "They're stones that you keep in the campfire. Then, when you go to sleep, you slip them under your blankets, and they keep you warm all night."

Eric wryly looked at the sky. While there was the softest puff of a cool breeze, the lack of clouds promised a fine and hot day. "Will we need the heat at night in the summer?"

Imogen joined their cart to the growing line underway. "It can still get quite chilly at night, and when we're in the Gash, the light of the sun doesn't penetrate the canopy of the trees, so it can be very dark even in the middle of the day. That means it gets quite cold."

They rattled along the streets toward the gate, Eric interested in the views of the city from his different perspective atop the wagon. He found that he could frequently peer into the ground-floor windows if they were open, so he tried to piece together insights into the lives of the inhabitants from the snippets of activity visible within. The gentle sway of the wagon and the odd snort from one or other of the beasts of burden were all that spoiled the quiet air. As they drew closer to the gate, Eric could see Anton and Troy waiting. Anton had a small bundle over one shoulder and the larger rectangular block of the book wrapped in a blanket. Troy was muttering under his breath while Anton was gazing at each wagon as it went past, clearly not listening to him.

Imogen pulled the wagon to halt, out of the convoy, just in front of the two men. Eric made his descent and headed toward them. He had already populated a coin purse with the required coins, so all he had to do was hand Troy the money and get Anton on board. And the book.

"My lord, I'm glad that you have not changed your mind."

"Not at all, Troy. I have your money here." Eric placed the pouch with the coins into the pudgy librarian's hand. But he did not immediately let go. Smiling, he continued, "Remember our deal. I will want the deposit back when I return the book." He then released his hold on the pouch, turning as Troy tipped the coins into his palm to count them. "C'mon, Anton, let's get you into the wagon. You've got a book to read!" Eric helped him up and then returned beside Imogen. Anton started to move a few of the bags around to try and clear a spot to sit. Imogen twitched the reins, and Anton stumbled to his knees as the oxen lurched forward, putting them back into the line of wagons.

As the wagon train exited through the gate, Imogen frowned and half turned to Eric. "My lord, are you planning on returning to Gerton?"

Eric smiled back. "The plan is still as we discussed, I'm going to return to my world, and I will do everything I can do to take you with me."

Relieved, Imogen nodded. "But–"

Eric held up a hand to stop the question. "Why make a point of telling him I was going to come back for the money? It's a backup plan. If we can't get back to my world, I might need a pot of gold to live off until I can work out plan B. And I don't like our friend the librarian. Having money he can't spend, and the worry of when I might return, will hopefully make for some sleepless nights."

Imogen watched him carefully. "You're… not all that you seem, my lord."

Eric wondered if that was a good or a bad thing. To change the subject, he referred to the train which was moving slowly along the packed dirt path that was leading them out of the city. "I thought that we would have guards? What were we waiting for, if not the guards?"

Imogen returned her attention to the oxen. "The Bendies will be meeting us at the ford across the river. It's about an hour away. Technically, we're under the protection of Earl Blackhammer, so if any bandits tried anything, they wouldn't last long. He's a cruel taskmaster, our Earl. He keeps those on the wrong side of the law on their toes, anyways."

"Bendies?"

"You'll see." Imogen studiously focused on the oxen, and Eric took the hint, lapsing into silence. The early morning birds were the only source of noise, their twittering punctuated by the occasional snort of the oxen and aurochs, the constant creak of the timber wagons, and the rattle of the metal in the harnesses. The pace of the train was similar to a slow walk, and the plains separating the woods from the city allowed Eric to marvel at the volume of commerce, represented by the wagons. Most of them had four wheels and low sides, some even flat beds, their sacks, boxes, and chests strapped down with ropes and chains. Only one had a fabric covering like those on the mid-west Oregon Trail back on Earth.

Eric noticed that Anton had made himself a nest of sorts amongst the sacks and was studiously examining the book, the blanket over his knees and his lips slightly moving as his eyes followed a long bony finger across the page.

The road left the city, crossed a plain of fields, and ran along the side of a forest for most of the first hour. It then descended a gentle bank to the side of a river. From what Eric could see, the water only filled a quarter of the space between the sides, the bottom covered in fist-sized blue-gray rocks. The water flowed lazily, a distinct lack of white-water making Eric believe it was safe. The road on the far side of the river was dotted with about twenty men, all wearing

124

dark leather armor and carrying spears. Eric turned to Imogen, who nodded. "Bendies."

The train forded the river and then stopped on the other side, some of the last wagons having to pull alongside the earlier ones to find room out of the water. All the waggoners and passengers dismounted and walked to the head of the train in ones and twos. Imogen and Eric joined them. A red-headed man with a prodigious beard stood at the center of the semi-circle, waiting for them all to arrive. Beside him was one of the leather-clad men Eric had spotted from a distance.

He stared.

The man was the first person of color that Eric had seen since coming to this world. And he couldn't place him, the color of his skin was just... different to anything Eric had ever seen. And since Eric had lived in a major city, he had seen quite a few shades of skin. The color was darker than the many Hispanics that Eric had worked and studied with. It wasn't as dark as the darkest brothers from the street, but it was a different... shade? There was a purple undertone to it. The man noticed Eric was staring and returned his gaze. Embarrassed, Eric switched attention to the red-haired Train Master.

"Greetings, travelers! I will be brief. This man and his group will keep you safe. Mark their words. If anything happens to you, we're not going to send your belongings to your next of kin, we can't delay."

The leader of the Guardsmen made eye contact with one or two of the drivers and nodded to each of them before turning on his heel and going back to his men. Eric stared again. While he had been distracted by the coloration of the guardsmen's leader, he'd not noticed that the leader had extremely bowed legs that made walking seem more like a waddling motion. Imogen nudged him. "See, Bendies."

Eric shook his head in disbelief, noting that while the guardsmen all shared the same skin color, the leader was the only one who had the extreme leg shape. "It's like he's carrying a storm drain between his knees," he said, almost to himself.

He and Imogen turned and headed back to their wagon. "Tell me about the Bendies."

"They live up in the mountains. Well, they used to. The leaders still do - they're the ones with the crazy legs. Some of them live in the valleys leading up to the mountains. These ones were originally a mercenary band, but as I hear it, there was some disagreement about payment, so they refuse to serve any of the local lords or ladies anymore. Fortunately, they've settled into guarding this route through the Gash and they know the territory and the dangers. We should be fine." She looked devious, and pitched her voice so that Anton could hear. "They rarely lose more than one in three wagons of the caravan."

On cue, Anton's face appeared above the sideboards of the wagon, a panicked look on his face. "One in three?! But that means that one of us won't make it!"

Suppressing a smirk, Eric boarded the wagon, carefully holding his sword out of the way. Imogen boarded also, ignoring the increasingly shrill demands for more details from Anton, before Eric decided to take pity on the youth. "I suspect that Imogen may have been a little provocative, Anton. We'll be fine." As Anton settled back into his nest, Eric shook his head softly at Imogen. He cautioned her under his breath. "It's going to be a long trip. It might be a good idea not to panic Anton into an early grave."

Imogen rolled her eyes at him. "Fine. He's too easy anyways."

They had made their way to the knot of leather-clad guardsmen that had been steadily decreasing as pairs of the warriors had peeled off and attached themselves to one wagon or another, in a pattern that Eric could not discern. Two of the men, each carrying a long spear over their shoulder, left their group, and started walking alongside Eric's wagon, and only briefly looked up toward them before beginning to talk softly to each other.

"He's not going to be much use in a fight, and unless the dweeb in the back is a mage, the only one of any value is her."

His colleague snorted. "Her nose is too small. And she's too skinny. But, any port in a storm, right?"

Eric leaned over. He could ignore the gibe at his expense, but he didn't want the guards making Imogen feel uncomfortable. "I don't think she's your type, buddy."

The man discussing Imogen's shortcomings fell over, his spear falling harmlessly onto the grass alongside the path. The other's eyes widened. After a minute or two, he composed himself as his colleague got to his feet, brushing himself off, and finding his spear. "Ah, you speak Kisho. Where did you learn that?"

Eric smiled despite himself. "A long story."

The man smiled back. "Fortunately, we have a long journey ahead of us. I am Vollo of the Kishan and this is Giran."

Eric placed a hand on his chest and bowed slightly. "I am Eric Prince of Anaheim. My companions; Imogen and Anton." He indicated them each with a nod.

At the mention of his name Vollo's eyes had momentarily flashed with alarm. He was a half a head taller than his companion, with a slightly fuller beard. Both had waves of long straight black hair that fell around their shoulders, and beneath the stiff pieces of armor, Eric could see the ripples of muscles. Still the weird purple sheen though. Now that he was close enough to make out their facial features, he could see that their noses were a little larger than

128

what would be considered normal back on Earth. Not wide at the bottom as if the nostrils were permanently flared though. They appeared larger because of a twisted bump higher on the bridge of the nose. But Eric couldn't tell whether that was natural or due to their noses being broken in some fight. Vollo noticed the scrutiny.

"I meant no disrespect, your... highness?" he said, unsure of the correct honorific.

"Call me Eric," said Eric.

"Understood, my lord," responded Vollo. Giran nodded his agreement. Imogen was watching them, the look of incomprehension indicating that the earworm was doing its job. Anton seemed engrossed in his book.

"So, what should we know about the route? What can you tell me that will keep us alive?"

The two guardsmen looked at each other.

Vollo eventually broke the silence. "Chances are pretty good that we will make it through the Gash without incidents. It's always a gamble though. On the other side, we have a long journey and the dangers are more... human in nature. No less dangerous though."

Giran grinned. "Our pay would be a lot lower if people thought the journey safe though, so keep it to yourself, if you would be so kind?"

Eric thought about the days wasted, waiting for the Train to form up. And about the chunk of coin it had cost to buy and outfit the wagon. He frowned. "So, there's no danger?"

Vollo switched his spear from one shoulder to the other. "Oh, I wouldn't go that far, my lord. Maybe one in five trips gets through totally unmolested. And maybe one in three make it through the Gash without an incident. But those are good odds."

Eric tried to get his head around the numbers. They didn't add up for him though. He shrugged. The guardsmen were on the ground and had been on the route themselves multiple times, so he had to defer to their knowledge. They seemed to think it not worth worrying about, so he resolved not to lose sleep either.

Twenty minutes later, they passed the skulls. The meadows with wildflowers on the side of the path had slowly been narrowing until the forest on both sides pressed against the path. The sky above was still visible though, and the underbrush lining the floor of the forest under the canopy was light, so that you could see the occasional patch of ground through the tree trunks and bushes. A gap in the trees on the left was causing each wagon ahead of them in the train to pause for a few seconds before progressing. When they came alongside, Eric could see why.

The gap in the tree line bordering the path exposed half a clearing in the forest. In the center of the clearing was an impressive pile of skulls, stacked one on top of the other, all facing outwards. Eric gave up counting them after hitting thirty, primarily because one of the sides of the pile had collapsed, rather spoiling the symmetrical layout. The skulls there had spilled over that side of the clearing, some upside down, some face to face with the dirt. Anton had poked his head up and was looking at the skulls wide-eyed. Imogen twitched the reins and the oxen lazily plodded forward.

"What happened there?" asked Imogen.

Eric turned to the guardsmen. "Which forest predator stacks the skulls of their food so neatly?" he asked with a smile. The guardsmen concentrated on scanning the tree line ahead, avoiding the question.

The wagons rattled on through the morning, the path slowly climbing in altitude, the forest on both sides obscuring any sort of view so that their world shrunk to just the path, the trees, the guardsmen, and the rear of the wagon that was immediately in front, about twenty feet away. The sunlight that was warming the day, now found them unprotected by canopy, and it was becoming uncomfortably hot. Eric turned to Imogen.

"Do you think we'll be stopping for lunch at all?"

"I don't think so, my lord. We'll stop for nightfall - there's a clearing that we'll have to make. That's why we had to leave so early. It's a fixed number of hours from Havelin - a long first day. There are set camping sites along the road. It means we have to get started early in the morning and can't wait for too long if someone has broken wheels or lame animals."

"There isn't any room to maneuver or to change directions. If some bandits put a road block, we wouldn't be able to go around them, would we?"

She smiled. "There will be no bandits on the road to the Gash. Or beyond it. No bandits until we get to civilization. The forest won't let us get robbed."

Eric looked at her sideways. She didn't seem to think she'd said anything untoward. Eric frowned. Was it just a turn of phrase or did she think that the forest was alive? Like "sentient" alive, not just "alive" alive. "Did you pack anything to eat during the day? Or would it just be breakfast and dinner?"

"Would my lord like to take the reins? I will see if I can rustle something up to take the edge off until we stop." Eric focused on taking control of the oxen as she disappeared into the back of the wagon. But, in truth, the oxen seemed to be so docile and slow that he imagined that if the driver fell asleep on the waggoneer's seat, the oxen would make their own way to the clearing. He heard Imogen rustling through sacks and muttering to Anton to get him to move.

Ten minutes later. "My lord?" He half turned and she passed him a thick cut sandwich, a slab of meat and leafy green peeking out the side.

"Many thanks, Imogen." She looked like she was about to say something about having her lunch while he drove the oxen. He waved her concerns away. Eric noted that the guardsmen had briefly glanced up at the sandwiches that he, Imogen, and Anton were now enjoying.

The afternoon plodded along as slow as the oxen. Eric and Imogen took turns with the reins, and the guardsmen seemed to be always just out of voice-shot. Eric wondered if he had inadvertently annoyed them. He was glad that Imogen wasn't filling the silence with chatter. The quiet was peaceful, and given what the guardsmen had said about their relative safety, he was starting to enjoy the pleasantness of the day. He was not used to being so relaxed – normally, he was either at work, on the way to work, or asleep. The hours that were not allocated were certainly not spent outdoors, staring at a pair of oxen's asses while they lumbered through a peaceful forest. The sun had passed overhead, and the path was now in light shade, though the heat of the day was just building.

"Do we have any water?" he asked Imogen, half turning so he could look into the back of the wagon.

"Certainly, my lord. We've got three waterskins and a barrel. Let me fetch one."

While he was half turned, Eric noticed that his horse was wandering behind the wagon, occasionally staring off to the left or right before plodding along. When he looked closer, the reins that he thought were attaching the horse to the back of the wagon were dragging along the ground. The horse would periodically pause to nibble a little of the grass that grew between the wagon wheel ruts in the path. Eric shrugged to himself as he settled into the waggoner's seat and focused on the path ahead of them. If the horse wanted to wander off, it had already had plenty of opportunities.

Hours later, the sun, hidden behind the trees, was starting to dip behind the horizon. The eerie gloaming half-light of dusk was pierced by some sort of bonfire ahead that turned out to be in a clearing in the forest. The train of wagons formed a circle around the fire, with about the same distance between the edge of the forest and the fire in the middle. There was usually about a wagon-length gap between each one. As soon as they all came to a halt, there was a bustle of activity - the oxen and auroch were taken out of the harnesses, fed, and watered.

Vollo disappeared into the forest nearby as Imogen saw to the livestock. Giran stood alert, scanning the perimeter, but Eric couldn't detect any concern radiating from him, so he figured that they were relatively safe.

Imogen bustled around the wagon, preparing the camp. Within minutes, she had set up the lean-to and was setting up a cooking pot. Eric had trouble seeing in the dark, with the campfire constantly frazzling his eyesight. He wondered how Imogen coped. He also noticed that Vollo had rejoined his colleague, and they were being visited by another guardsman. He noticed that the newcomer handed the other two a square of some sort of food, to which they grimaced but thanked him. Could it be that military rations were devoid of taste in all worlds?

He caught Imogen's eye as she dished up the evening's meal – some sort of stew, apparently. "Would we have enough for our new friends?" he asked, pointing toward the two guardsmen. She shrugged and then nodded. "Give me a minute," he said, walking over to them.

They stood with their backs to the fire and wagons, about twenty feet between them and the edge of the forest. "Hi," he said as he approached, not meaning to startle them.

They looked around and smiled. "Good evening, Eric."

"I was wondering if I could trade your dinner for a plate of mine?"

They frowned, and Giran snorted. "You want a slice of hotopty? I'll take that trade in a second!" Vollo looked puzzled but nodded also.

"I'll send Imogen over with your plates," he said, heading back to the lean-to. When he got there, he saw that Anton was already starting his meal and that Imogen had also filled four other plates. He nodded back to the guardsmen. "If you could take them theirs, that would be awesome. Thanks, Imogen."

She nodded and headed off, returning moments later with the two square packages that Eric had seen the guardsmen being given. "My lord, why not just give them the stew? We have plenty? And why would you trade for slices of hotopty? It's like eating rocks, sandy rocks. The flour they are made with is so coarse!"

Eric took his plate and began to eat. The stew was much less watery than those he'd had on the journey to Havelin and the cuts of meat had almost no gristle. The broth was thick and hearty. "I'm just currying favor. So that if they have to choose one wagon to save, they will save ours. Should anything happen, of course. And by setting it up as a trade, we're not making it a weird social thing, where we feel obligated to feed them at every stop. Imagine that we have enough food for the three of us, with a little bit of a safety margin, right? But not enough for two extra mouths?"

Imogen nodded as she thoughtfully speared a buck of meat. "My lord is right. I haven't heard of anyone sharing their food with the guardsmen. I know that they travel lightly, so I guess they only have traveling food. The smells from the cooking fires must be a special kind of torture."

"Let me taste the hotopty. It would be good to know just how bad it is."

"Here, take both, I don't want it. If we're ever in a position where that is the only thing to eat, we're practically dead anyway."

He nibbled the corner of one of the squares. It looked like a roofing tile. Square, dense, and with a feeling that water would not be able to penetrate the surface. To say it tasted like dust would not do it justice. There was a texture, like a vein of honey had been added to try to bind the thing together and maybe add some sweetness, but the dryness of the - was it a cake or a bread? – sucked all the moisture and sweetness out of the vein, so it was a thread of slightly more dense dust in the center. Imogen was right. A dire day indeed if this was all they had. He pocketed both packages and took his plate back to where the guardsmen were standing.

They both looked up at his approach, smiling broadly. "I hope you're not going to back out of the deal, Eric," said Vollo. "A deal is a deal!"

"I think you both got the better of the deal. I'm not sure I'm a fan of your Bendie bread."

Their smiles dropped. The fork paused mid bite. Giran's eyebrows raised in surprise. They didn't say anything. The light of the fire behind Eric played across their silent faces. Eric felt a slight chill. He tried to figure out what he'd said that was so offensive. "Um, did I say something wrong?"

Vollo was the first to recover, slowly resuming chewing while never taking his eyes off Eric's. "You use that slur in our own language. To our faces. That is new."

Giran just stared. The cords in his neck and shoulders were tense. The vein in his neck pulsated.

"Oh, I am so sorry, I did not know. I meant no offense. I didn't realize that was a slur!"

There was a long minute of silence.

Vollo was the first to break it. "Giran, what happened the last time someone called you a Bendie?"

Giran kept his eyes on Eric. "I don't know. And nobody else knows either. They never found the body."

Vollo continued. "And when was the last time someone called you a Bendie to your face?"

Giran finally broke his gaze, turning to his colleague. "It was that Grealish fellow with the tics. And he was 'Bendie this, grkkk, Bendie that, grkkk.'"

"And before that?"

"Nothing I can remember since I was a child."

"I guess we can add another group to that list. The insane, the children... And the ignorant. If you value your life, Eric, I'd suggest you don't use that word again."

Eric nodded vigorously, the pulsing vein in the neck of Giran burned into his memory. When both guardsmen had returned to their plates, he frowned, weighing up whether to ask a question. These were the first people of color he'd seen in this world, and he needed to know more. "So why is your leader the only one with legs... like that?" he managed, wondering if he was pushing things too far.

"He wants to know how we can be Bendies if we don't have bendy legs, Vollo."

Vollo nodded as he chewed. "Our people, the Kishan, came from the mountains around Turnesque. Well, originally. As we grew in numbers, we spilled down into the surrounding valleys. Our leaders still come from the mountain villages, and they speak Kisho like you. And they have the bowed legs. The men, the women, and the children. The further down the valleys we live, the fewer of our people have bowed legs. You would think that the mountain villages would empty out and everyone would live in the valleys instead, right? No, the elders say that it's a sign of their breeding. Of their right to rule. And therefore, they stay up there in the everclouds, only seeing the sun a day or two each year, while those in the valley enjoy years of four seasons like the rest of the world. The more able elders lead bands, who guide travelers through the Gash or across the desert. They ignore the wars of the ruling classes and focus on keeping people safe. It's honest work."

"So, why is your bread so bad?"

Both guardsmen erupted into laughter. The explosion of honest emotion evaporated the tension of Eric's faux pas. Vollo opened his mouth to say something but was cut off by a rasping roar that came from the forest. Judging from the way both guardsmen froze and looked at each other, Eric could tell the situation was serious.

Chapter 7

"Back to the wagon, Eric!"

Eric followed the command. The fear in his eyes must have shown as both Anton and Imogen leaped to their feet, their plates and stew flying into the air. Behind him, the two guardsmen were backing into the circle of the wagons, warily watching the forest. Eric had no idea what to do. All around, the other travelers seemed similarly confused, some watching food in hand, while others gathering up their belongings that had only just been laid out in camp.

Thirty seconds later, there was a thrashing in the underbrush near the wagon and a mob of creatures came swarming out of the darkness. Eric stared at them as they sprinted past the wagon, some crashing directly into the campfire in the center of the clearing, spraying embers into the night sky, and others circling the interior of the wagon circle. They were about waist-high, vaguely birdlike, with two scrawny legs, a rotund belly, and a long neck, which balanced a surprisingly large head that seemed to be almost entirely taken up by two large dark eyes. The ones that had burst through the campfire were making an eerie high-pitched 'screee' noise, and the others continuously looked around the clearing, as if they were not really taking in the details of what they were seeing. The scene reminded Eric of the baby emus he'd seen on a desert farm - the chaotic running style and inquisitive head movements were as hilarious then as they were now.

"Ha, how cute!" he exclaimed. "What's the problem? Why are you so on edge?"

Vollo was still facing outward, toward the forest. He turned over his shoulder and yelled, "Get on the wagons! Quickly!"

Shrugging, he collected Anton and Imogen, helping them up onto the back of the wagon. As soon as they were up, what seemed to Eric like a komodo dragon came bursting through the underbrush and into the light. It would have been about knee high, solidly built, and all teeth and claws, three or four feet long down on all four legs. No tail. Vivid orange and brown diagonal zigzags.

Yelping to each other, the emu-like creatures fled through the wagons on the other side of the clearing. The dragon creature made to scurry after them, but then noticed the two guardsmen. It paused and let out that same rasping roar they had heard earlier. Eric blinked at how loud the creature was. It then attacked the men.

It charged straight at Vollo's legs. The spear points were quick enough, but it was a near run thing. One took it in the shoulder, and the other glanced off the creature's face, leaving a nasty wound but not arresting the assault. The creature impaled itself on the spear that had stuck its shoulder, driving it further into its body. Eric could now see the reason for the cross spikes, set a little way down the spear from the point. He had thought it to be some sort of religious thing: 'make your weapon look like a cross' sort of thing. But he realized it was there to stop any creature who would not let being impaled get in the way of trying to kill their impaler. The creature wasn't wasting any time with the biting attempts either, snapping aggressively every couple of seconds as it got closer and closer to Vollo. Giran recovered his stance and rejoined the attack, striking the creature through the belly. The spears were now at such an angle that the only way it could get closer to the men would be to rip itself apart across the two spears. No sound came from it now, except a gentle wheeze as it expired.

Eric was surprised that it wasn't noisier around them. Surely everyone was fighting the monsters? He looked from his vantage point on the wagon. Some of the waggoners were watching him quizzically, but there was a calm that told him everything he needed to know - there were no other komodo dragon-like creatures around. The emu critters had all disappeared as well, so Eric, Anton, and Imogen looked like they had all spontaneously decided to clamber aboard the wagon. A curiosity.

Vollo and Giran extracted their spears from the corpse of the creature and wiped the gore from the points. Then, unexpectedly, they both headed away, toward the trainmaster's wagon. Eric was just about to call after them when he noticed Imogen looking at him from the back of the wagon. "What happened? Why are we up here? What were those things?" He realized she had not seen the smaller predator.

Time froze as another giant roar echoed from the other side of the campsite. The same emu creatures came charging back through the wagon circle, some bursting again through the fire, sending another shower of sparks into the sky. They were followed by the screams and yells of the guardsmen on that side of the clearing. Numerous low-slung four-legged creatures came bursting through the ring of wagons, roaring. Anton and Imogen screamed, Anton burying his head under a blanket. From nowhere, Imogen held out a knife, backing further from the edge of the wagon. Eric struggled with his sword, before finally clearing it from its scabbard. It felt cumbersome in his hand, nothing like a baseball bat, which was the only weapon he had wielded prior to purchasing the sword. It was denser and, once swung, had a mind of its own. He attempted to hold it with both hands, trying to remember the lessons of the swordmaster. Of course, that had all been about confronting a human opponent!

One of the predators charged up to the wagon, this one not bellowing but making a husky "yup" noise. It had fixed its gaze on Eric who watched it come closer, trying to figure out when to swing. He could see it readying itself to strike, so he decided this was the moment for his attack. He would have timed it perfectly if the creature had any sort of vertical leaping ability. But, for whatever reason, the creature did not manage to get anywhere near the bed of the wagon, so Eric struck air, and toppled over as he followed through. The sword embedded itself in the top of the side of the wagon bed. Eric hastily rose back to his feet and put a foot on the side to pry the sword out of the wood. Panting at the effort, he frantically looked around to see where the nearest threat was coming from.

They were safe for the second - a pair of the emu creatures came sprinting past them, distracting the predator. As it sprinted off after the emus, Eric backed closer to where Anton and Imogen were sitting, just behind the waggoner's seat, as far as they could get from the back of the wagon.

"Are you ok? Anton, you?" They both nodded. The noise of the battle randomly spiked in volume as one or other of predator, prey, human, or oxen bellowed, yelled, screamed, or made some inhuman sound.

"Another one!" yelled Imogen, pointing. Sure enough there was another creature. Or the same one as earlier? Charging toward them. Again, he swung, again, the creature's leap was insufficient, and again, a chunk was taken out of the top of the wagon's sideboard. Eric didn't know if they were dodging his sword or if he was just inept but didn't really have time to think about it. He recovered and stood again far enough from the edge to feel safe-ish. His sword unbloodied but zero injuries. A nil-all draw so far.

The wagon lurched as something hit it, and Imogen momentarily grabbed his leg to steady herself from her seated position. Eric patted her shoulder as he moved a little closer to see what was going on. At the same time, as he noticed that one of the predator creatures was camping underneath their wagon, one clawed leg holding down an emu creature while it casually chewed on the carcass.

Eric moved closer, readying his sword. He calculated its length versus the length of his arm, and the distance to the creature from the back of the cart. He would have to be lying down on the bed of the wagon in order to reach the critter or leap down onto the ground beside it so he could hit it. He slowed as he neared the wagon edge. He could leap with the sword pointing down like a spear. Or... Or he could just leave it. It looked like none of the komodo dragon creatures had sufficient power in their back legs to jump high enough to be a threat to anyone. The one nearby seemed content to chew on the emu critter.

Eric looked at the other wagons and the clearing. The flames of the bonfire in the center both illuminated the scene and ruined his ability to see in the nearer shadows. Most of the other travelers were standing on their wagons too, mainly just moving silhouettes, but a few dark shadows on the ground appeared too large to be the emu creatures. Eric didn't look too closely at those.

The komodo dragon below him suddenly stopped chewing and looked across the clearing, making a gurgling sound. Eric tried to spot what it was looking at and saw the guardsmen coming across the clearing, an amorphous blog of leather, hair, and spears in the night. Eric expected the creatures to flee before them, but the komodo dragon look-alikes all turned and attacked. Not all at once, which would have made them difficult to deal with, but one by one. When they attacked, they were met with at least two spear points, pinning them to the ground. Eric watched the guardsmen circle the campfire, efficiently dealing with the remaining predators. They didn't have to hunt them at all - the creatures attacked the men without hesitation.

The battle finished with a whimper. One of the guardsmen, who Eric hadn't met, came over.

"Anyone hurt?"

"No. I don't think so. Imogen, Anton, are you ok?" They gave worried nods.

"They look unharmed, good. We should be ok tonight, but if you want to feel safer, sleep on your wagon bed. Are your oxen injured?"

"Shit, my horse!" thought Eric, looking over to where Imogen had tied it up. The two oxen stood impassively, staring at him, and chewing. His horse was gone, though.

"My horse is missing!" Eric told the guardsmen.

"OK, missing one horse, oxen are ok. Good." The guardsmen made to move onto the next wagon.

"Wait, what about my horse?"

The guardsmen didn't seem to care. "Uh... It'll turn up tomorrow. Or it won't. I'm just checking if each wagon will be able to move out tomorrow. Or if anyone got hurt."

"Wait, what were those things?"

"Those? They were rinca, hunting ratites. They don't usually hunt at this phase of the moon. I guess we got lucky. Or unlucky. I have to go." The guardsman noticed the chunks taken out of the side of the wagon bed and the sword that was still in Eric's hand. He didn't say anything, but Eric detected the start of a smirk on the guardsman's face.

Man, swords were hard. Eric concentrated on putting the weapon in its scabbard, wondering why his hand was shaking so much.

"Here, my lord, have a drink of this." Imogen handed him a small earthenware bottle. He took a swig and gasped. Whatever it was, it was strong – it burned like brandy.

"Thanks," he coarse whispered, handing it back. He slunk to a sitting position, adjusting the sword as he descended. "I think I'll just have a little rest here."

"You were very brave, my lord. None of the creatures got to us."

Anton was still hugging the book to his chest, looking like he might cry. "Is this what it's going to be like every day, my lord? I don't think I can do this–"

"You heard what the guardsman said," interrupted Imogen. "The rinca don't normally hunt at this time. We were just unlucky. Here, help me find the cooking equipment."

"... I don't really want to... Are there any of those things left?"

"The guardsmen got them all, come on, I'll help you down."

Eric wrapped a blanket around his shoulders and waited for the shaking to stop. This was not what he was used to. Unruly customers, homeless people sleeping near the dumpster out the back, these were the things he knew and could deal with. Late shipments, occupational health and safety briefings he knew how to handle. Humans and unearthly creatures trying to kill him were not in the same category. He knew the shaking was just the adrenaline from the fight, but the smirk on the guardsman's face haunted him. Also, not being able to hit anything with his sword really pissed him off.

They relocated everything onto the back of the wagon and tried to settle in amongst the barrels and the sacks of grain. It was anything but comfortable. Eventually, Eric drifted off to sleep.

He awoke with the dawn sun peeking just above the tree line and surveyed the ring of wagons. The sunlight revealed that they had not been the only ones who had decided that the ground was not safe. The camp was breaking, with most of the other travelers having a hasty bite to eat as they harnessed their livestock and prepared for a full day's trek. He nudged Anton and Imogen. "We'd better get ready, we don't want to be left behind."

The others, bleary-eyed and still half asleep, looked around in a daze. Eric climbed down the back of the wagon and realized he had no idea how to harness the oxen. But the least he could do was pat his horse. His horse! There it was, looking at him as if to say "...and?" He went over and patted it on the neck. He looked at its legs, looking for bites, or blood, or any sign of any wounds. Nothing. He let out a breath he didn't know he had been holding.

All he knew about horses was that if they broke a leg, you had to shoot them, which, thinking about it, was weird.

Eric let the stress and frustration of the night wash away as he held his head against the horse's. It was comforting. It didn't judge him. In fact, the only thing it did was follow him and stay out of the way. And it looked after itself. The perfect companion.

"What's it saying?" Imogen called out to him.

"Hmmm?" he asked, turning to face her.

She had the oxen harnessed and was preparing the back of the wagon. "The horse. It looked like it was whispering in your ear," said Imogen, smiling at the absurdity of the possibility.

He smiled back. "It was just telling me how it slept in the trees to keep away from the monsters."

A flicker of doubt crossed Imogen's face before the smile reappeared. "Well, we're two minutes away from leaving, my lord." Ahead of them, the first wagons were already heading out of the clearing and back onto the path.

"Right, let's go." He got up on the seat beside Imogen and turned back to the horse. "Are you coming?" Who snorted and wandered behind them as they set off.

Eric alternated between loving the pace of the train and missing the modern conveniences back on Earth. Even a bicycle would be faster than this! Let alone a car or a plane. A car would make short work of those predators. There was a man walking along by himself, part of the train, keeping up with the pace. He was obviously without enough money for a wagon of his own or even for a seat on someone else's.

He was definitely not one of the guardsmen. Speaking of which, upon leaving the clearing, Vollo and Giran joined them, raising eyebrows in silent greeting. They also noticed the solo traveler and rolled their eyes, altering their course to stay on the other side of the path from him. The solo traveler pulled off the path and waited for their wagon to pass. As they did, he began to walk alongside them, giving Eric a chance to get a good look at him.

He was about Eric's age, but a better build, and with a little more height on him too. He had pleasing features and a somewhat scraggly beard. Blue eyes, black hair, and a beard, with a large mouth filled with pearly white teeth. He didn't appear to be armed, but carried a stick over his shoulder, with a bag attached to the end of it. He smiled at them as he walked alongside. Eric was puzzled when Imogen ignored the newcomer entirely, furiously concentrating on the oxen. Mentally shrugging, Eric made eye contact and raised a hand in greeting.

"Well met, fellow traveler," the stranger began. "I'm glad you made it through the night unscathed. My name is Bary."

"Well met," answered Eric. "I am Eric, this is Imogen, and that's Anton." Imogen didn't respond, and Anton seemed to be totally consumed by the book.

Bary didn't seem offended but focused an intense gaze on Eric. "Quite the commotion last night! Did you manage to kill any of the creatures?"

Eric shook his head. "We were lucky."

Bary nodded. "I think we were all very lucky. I'm heading to my new position, leading the congregation in Rea. Where are you heading?"

"I'm heading to Havelin to… do some research in magic."

A shadow came over Bary's general countenance. "Ah, magic. I would wish you luck in finding what you are looking for, but the use of magic is unnatural and an affront to the gods." He looked vaguely disgusted. "And its use always extracts a dire cost from the practitioner."

"Really?" asked Eric. Even if Bary was totally against the use of magic, he might still provide some insights into how and who used it, and what they could do. "I must admit the land I am from does not have anyone who uses magic." Bary's eyes lit up. "Why is it so bad?"

"Its use changes men." Eric felt Imogen tense. "Having the power over the natural world, or one's fellow man is unnatural and mocks the gods' powers. Only the gods should have the power over the elements, or the power to change a man's mind."

"Can women not use magic?"

A dismissive wave. "Oh, some lesser magic, some healing, trivialities. But the great mages have all been men. And they have paid the price."

Eric frowned. "What price?"

Bary blinked. "All users of magic pay a price. Those that prey on the minds of men are shunned by right-thinking people. You can't trust your own thoughts if you encounter one. How do you know if you are really their friend or whether you are getting a good deal if they control your thoughts? There is no place for them in a good society."

"Oh! I thought you meant that the use of magic costs some portion of your soul or something. Some deal with a demon or some such."

Bary looked at him closely. "There is always a price. What do you know about healing?"

Eric shrugged. "Nothing. As I say, there is no magic in my land."

Bary continued. "Even you must know about healing. When your bone is broken, it must be mended. That's just moving the two parts of the bone back to where they were, the fragments go back to where they should be or are removed so they don't damage anything else. Simple. In fact, that's all healing is, right? Making the body back to what it was like before. But what about death? What is there that's different about a body before and after it dies?"

Eric smiled. "The ax wound in the head?"

Bary's smile didn't quite reach his eyes. "Let's say the death was from old age. What is the difference? That's the spark of life, right? Returning that spark back to the body will bring them back."

Eric shrugged. "Sure, I guess."

"And what do you know of heaven and hell?"

"If you were good during your life, you go to heaven and are surrounded by your friends and family. If you were bad, you go to hell to be tortured by the devil."

Bary frowned. "That sounds like a Grealish fable. But anyway. Sure, that's one take. Do you know why? Do you know what actually happens when you die?"

Eric smiled back. "Unfortunately, in my land, the only ones who truly know, can't tell us."

Bary raised his eyebrows. "Really? Here we know. They do tell us. There's a white light that they travel towards. When they reach it, their life repeats itself over and over again. Snippets and scenes. And when you've been good and the scenes from your life are fulfilling, then you feel nice. But when you have done something wrong, you feel ashamed. And these scenes repeat. So I guess there is some truth to your claim that you are tortured, but it isn't the devil. It's yourself. And there is no heaven - just those same stories about your life. More than not, with your friends and family involved, so I guess you are surrounded by them. And you'd most likely have pleasant memories about them, so I guess that would be heaven."

Eric nodded. "I guess that's a great theory."

Bary looked at him askance. "Theory? It's the truth. Those practicing their magic to bring people back have unlocked that secret. But at what cost?"

"Well, I guess the healers would be in demand, like doctors in my world."

"That's certainly true. But healers can only bring so many people back. And when they do, the results are not always the same."

Eric leaned forward. "What do you mean?"

"If it's been too long, or there has been too much damage that cannot be healed, then bringing the spark back does not bring that person back. Their body lives, but the person is no longer there. Or they are only partially there. Some memory, some elements of their personality but not all. I don't know which is worse - having a blank drooling husk, or someone who is close enough to the person they were but doesn't recognize you. And after paying for the spell, to have your loved one so close and yet so far, would be infuriating."

"Cost? Who could possibly charge to bring back a loved one?"

Bary smiled. "You are being naïve, Eric. Everybody gets paid for their labor. Why else would they do it? I go to my new posting and my congregation will provide me a house and meals. I will bring them closer to the gods with my sage counsel and wise words about how they should lead their lives. And if everyone knew the words, and therefore no one needed a healer to bring their loved ones back, then no one would die."

Eric frowned. "And would that be such a bad thing? Eternal life doesn't sound too bad to me."

"Very naïve again, Eric. The body wears out. If a man lives to eighty and then dies. And you bring him back. How long will he last for? Another year? A month? A day? And the healer?"

"The healer?"

"How many times can you bring people back? If it's just about saying some words, surely they can teach that and anyone would be able to do it, right? And if not, then why shouldn't some ruler kidnap you and make you bring them and their family members back to life whenever they die? Some kings have done just that."

"But that's not an argument against the use of magic, that's an argument against slavery."

"Slavery? Oh! So as long as they are getting paid for their labor, that should make it all ok? Who decides who gets brought back from the dead?"

"Ah, I think I understand what you're saying. If it's Capitalism, then only the richest people get brought back, if it's Communism, then in theory, the most beneficial people get brought back. But in reality, it's the country's rulers, and if it's Medieval times, then the King gets to decide."

Bary looked confused. "I don't understand half of what you just said, Eric. But I think that you are beginning to see the issue."

Eric shook his head. "I don't think I am. What's wrong with magic?"

Bary looked exasperated. "It's unnatural. It takes powers that only the gods should have."

Eric nodded. "You said that before, but I'm not sure I understand. What is natural?"

"What would exist without human intervention?"

"So, humans make tools. Are those tools natural?"

"No, by definition, they're man-made and, therefore, unnatural."

"But what about other animals that use tools? Like monkeys?"

Bary looked confused. "I don't think we have those animals here, Eric. What does a monkey look like?"

"Sure you do, we share an ancestor. They look like us but shorter, more hair. Long arms, live in the jungle."

Bary laughed. "So, is it your father or your grandfather who is this monkey, Eric?"

Eric sighed. "So, if all tools are unnatural, what should we do in a drought? Should we just die? And what about your house that your congregation is going to give you? Isn't that just a tool? Isn't that unnatural?"

Bary shook his head, looking like he was starting to get angry. "I am only referring to the unnatural tools, Eric. Using magic to stop the drought would be wrong. Keeping water in barrels would not be wrong."

"And that is regardless of the method of stopping the drought? If I threw magic powder into the air, then that would be just as wrong as if I took a magic rope and dragged the clouds to where the drought was?"

"Yes, magic rope and magic powder are both wrong. It's the magic."

"But let's say that I found a regular rock that when you threw it into a fire, it created a cloud, and caused rain. Would that be wrong? Assuming there was no magic at all?"

Bary thought about that for a second or two. "No magic at all? That would still be wrong."

"Why?"

"Because the control of the clouds, and rain, and wind, and snow is the sole job of the gods, not of men."

"I think I'm beginning to understand now. Tell me, can anyone talk to the gods?"

"Anyone can pray, but sometimes you need a priest to interpret what the gods tell us."

"And if someone used magic to control the wind, and clouds, and rain, then they wouldn't need you to interpret what the weather gods tell us, would they?"

Bary looked at him with thunder in his eyes. "That's not the case at all. Magic is wrong. You will find that out when you do your research, Eric. There are some others that I need to talk with on this journey. Fare thee well." And with that, he doubled his pace, leaving them in his wake, heading further up the train.

Imogen was trying to conceal a smirk. "The followers of Tamki tend to annoy people by constantly telling them how to live their lives. I haven't heard of anyone making them storm off though. My lord truly excels in rhetoric."

160

Chapter 8

Eric watched Bary head toward the front of the train, a little puzzled by the reaction to their conversation. He now recognized the gaze of the preacher to be the same as the intense look the homeless and drugged had when they managed to scrape enough for a meal and came into the restaurant. While they were waiting for their food, they would latch their gaze onto the nearest person and spill all sorts of conspiracy theories and garbled streams of consciousness. And, God forbid, you encountered them while taking trash out to the garbage bins out the back. You just didn't know what they would do, and without the counter between you and them, there was always the possibility of physical harm. You learned to recognize the look. The only reason Eric hadn't realized that Bary had the same look was the coherent conversation coming out of his mouth.

The rest of the day limped along, Eric and the others falling into a routine. It wasn't a varied one and mainly consisted of concentrating on keeping the wagon in their place in the train and moving. If it wasn't for a the slight variations in the terrain and surroundings, Eric was sure he'd fall into a coma of boredom. He was tempted to break it up with some exercise, but the previous night's attack made him reluctant. Maybe the next day.

The path was steadily rising, and while the view remained resolutely consistent, the density of the underbrush was thinning and the tree trunks were getting slimmer. More stones appeared in the dirt of the path and the sky was more visible through the canopy of the trees nearest the edge of the trail. The sun was hidden behind a thick layer of white clouds, low against the layer of trees.

By the time the train entered the clearing for the night, about an hour before sunset, the temperature had also dropped, making Eric thankful for his jacket. Again, a fire in the middle of the clearing promised a modicum of warmth, but Imogen turned to him as they pulled into place in the curve of wagons. "My lord, do you want me to set up the lean-to?"

Decisions! "I think we should be safe enough back on the ground - the guardsmen said so. And they will be on guard at night, so we should be ok. And besides," he said, theatrically straightening his back, "whatever is on that wagonbed is too lumpy to sleep on two nights in a row."

Imogen smiled and proceeded to set up camp.

"Anton, could you give Imogen a hand, please? Also, after dinner I'd love to know what you've found out from the book, if that suits you?"

"Of course, my lord."

The evening's meal was the same, or near enough the same, as the stew they'd had the night before. So either Imogen had scavenged the remnants after the attack or else that was the standard meal for him to expect. They'd had the whole day to get over the previous night's attack, and the time had brought some perspective to Eric's thinking. He'd been promised a dangerous trip and the pantomime of the skull pyramid had added to that frame of mind. But when it happened, there had not been any tree roots attacking them or some dragon breathing fire from the skies. No, they had been unlucky enough to be at the wrong place at the wrong time as a pack of rinca had hunted a flock of ratites. And nobody had been killed. The creatures could not even leap onto the wagon bed. They had been unfortunate enough to be hunting when they should not have been, so even though so far the ratio of attacks per night was a solid one to one, Eric was confident that there would be no attack that night.

When they started eating their meal, Eric turned to Anton. "So… the book?"

Anton swallowed the mouthful he'd just taken and nodded. "As we discussed, my lord, it's very promising. The mage has included a lot of details. Which means that when we get to the good bits, we should get insight into the things you want to find out, but until then, that same detail is going to take a while to get through."

"So what can you tell me so far?"

"It's actually a lot of the personal back story about where they had come from and how they came to be in the prison. This Marion was from Frahm - that's in the foothills of the Bisonnette mountains, and was a full mage, graduating from the university in Salet. There are a few pages on that part of his life, but they mention that the universities are all run a little differently, so I'll skip that unless they mention Havelin. Then they discuss how they were caught, and go into a lengthy diatribe on how it was unlawful. I'm not sure whether that was due to the spells that the university used to track them down or the magic they used to capture them. The details aren't clear, but the tone is very pure."

After they'd eaten and stowed the plates and cutlery away, they settled down to try and sleep. The bonfire in the middle of the clearing had died down to a dull glow of embers, and the shadows of the guardsmen on their rounds flickered against the backdrop of the trees. The first test of Eric's leadership decision-making in this world was coming - would they survive the night?! Eric had not

164

chosen the sleeping arrangements but had ended up in the middle. Imogen had laid out the bedding and indicated that the middle berth was his, and he found himself a little ashamed when he caught himself feeling relieved that any attack would get to him last. His dark sense of humor had phrased it: *I'll get the chance to escape while the creatures are halfway through Anton.*

The predawn light was a sort of vague lightening of the overcast sky - the figures of the travelers breaking camp and the guardsmen finishing their rounds in the near silence, indication that not only had they survived the night but had also slept all the way through and were well rested. Eric rubbed his eyes as he surveyed the clearing. Imogen and Anton repacked the wagon. As he walked past, he nodded to Vollo, who in turn slowed.

"You're in for a treat. We'll be on the slopes of Mount Erevin this afternoon, and you'll be able to see the length of the valley. It's a great view." He spat into the trees. "Worth the trip alone," he said with a smile.

Eric looked forward to the view all day. The path was boring, the oxen were boring, and his colleagues were boring. He was probably boring too. Normally, when he felt this way, he would smoke a bowl and get out of his head for a while. Maybe he had to talk to Imogen about getting some of the local equivalent. But that could be dangerous if they had something similar to Prohibition or the War on Drugs in effect. The last thing he wanted was to be the poster child for some Zero Tolerance politician. Maybe best to save himself until his return to Earth. By the time they had had lunch, he was wondering how he would survive the weeks ahead. He realized that the slowness of life in this world would require a sizable adjustment to his expectations and to his ability to amuse himself. With no books available as he was functionally illiterate here, and no phone or other gadgets due to the technology situation, he was going to have to figure something else out. He thought he could try and gain information by talking to his fellow travelers, but judging from their reaction to Bary, it might be an impossible task to break through their understandable reluctance to engage. And he couldn't interrupt Anton from his reading. The information in the book seemed like the key to figuring out what magic there was here and who would be able to help him and Imogen get back to Earth.

The first sign that they were close to the view were the wagons ahead, which started to stop and start like freeway traffic when there was a breakdown ahead. They had been climbing in altitude, with the woods on either side of the path thinning more and more until Eric could see at least twenty feet into the forest. The underbrush limited to ferns and occasional bushes and the canopy above allowed ample views of the undersides of the clouds. They first paused at a bend in the path and, while Eric could see the outlines of the wagons ahead of them, he couldn't even begin to figure out why they'd come to a standstill. The whole train did not usually stop after setting of at dawn until they pulled into the campsite a little after sundown, so to have a mid-trip pause made Eric think there was some accident up ahead. Maybe a wagon had thrown a wheel or toppled off the path down a bank somewhere. Speed, he thought wryly, would obviously not be a factor in such an accident. After a couple of minutes, they resumed their movement. So Eric thought that whatever had occurred (a deer in the path? Something falling off one of the wagons ahead?) was over and dealt with. But then there was another pause for a couple of minutes. And another. And another. Infuriating. It was half an hour of this stop - start progress before they could see far enough ahead to where the pausing was happening. A clearing, or more of a thinning of the forest, alongside the path as it reached the brow of a hill before it disappeared back down its the other side. Each wagon would stop and all the occupants would crane their necks as they looked at something to the left. After a little while, one of the two guardsmen stationed at that point would bang their spears on the wagon and the wagon would resume its languid pace, the occupants still craning their necks as they continued down the hill and disappeared from sight. So the pauses were being caused by whatever view was available through the clearing.

Eventually, it was their turn. From this height they could see all the way up the valley. Red-brown earth exposed as cliffs faced each other. The cliffs' faces were about a mile or two from each other, the valley between a verdant forest, thick, and twisted. The trees were not the constant height of a man-made forest. Sporadically taller trees poked out to the canopy, bestowed with vines and creepers, all competing for the attention of the sun. The valley narrowed as it moved further away from their vantage point, gradually the walls of the canyon meeting as if the forest had never existed and the farm lands on the upper level continued looking unblemished as far as the eye could see. It didn't take a superior intellect to realize that something large and round had traveled at some speed and gouged out the valley before coming to a rest at the point where the valley ended. Eric tried to figure out how big it would have been to survive hitting the ground at such an angle and to have traveled so far, shaving off its surface, before finally coming to a rest. Judging from the stark difference between the farmlands on top and the dense forest below, whatever had landed, had encouraged the tree growth as well.

The guardsman rapped his spear on the side of the wagon. It was time to move on. "Do you know anything about that valley?"

Eric asked Imogen as they rattled over the brow of the hill and along the path, down the other side. She shook her head. "Anton?" He in turn shook his. Fascinating. After the look-out, they descended into the valley itself. This far up, the red earthen cliffs were maybe five miles apart - an hour and a half, maybe two hours walk if it had been a straight line over paved roads or as track. Without the path through the trees, you would have to walk through the underbrush, which would have surely made the trip closer to a week, Eric thought to himself.

The camp at nightfall was in the shadow of the cliff face, on the far side. In fact, one side of the clearing was just the cliff face, looming almost a hundred feet above them. Eric left Anton and Imogen making camp and sought out Vollo. He found him watching a family of waggoners making camp, close to the path, where they had entered the clearing. He looked up as Eric approached and broke into a huge grin.

"Eric! Are you interested in swapping food again?"

Eric smiled back. "Are you kidding? Have you tasted hotopty? No way! I'm actually after some information, if you know?"

Vollo visibly swallowed his disappointment but nodded.

"What can you tell me about this valley?"

"Ah, it is magnificent, is it not? What would you like to know?"

"How did it get made? Who made it? How long has it been here?"

He nodded through the litany of questions. "It is a wonder, isn't it? The trees are old enough to grow fifty feet high in some places, and yet the valley has only been around since my father was young. He told me of the time when it was created. From the mountains, they saw a flash at night, and then there was a huge bang. All glass was broken, anything that had been repaired fell apart. The goats and sheep were spooked, and the cows stopped giving milk. It was summer, but the snow at the top of the mountain was shaken off and slid down halfway to the villages. And for a year after that, the sunsets and sunrises were an eerie green glow. When the next traveler came to the villages, there was talk of the new valley and how it blocked the normal routes, leading to an enormous detour. Over the next ten years, the path was cut through the forest at great cost to human life. The first Kishan work groups had been hired to help cut the road through the forest, and what they learned in protecting themselves was incredibly valuable. So they stayed on to guide and guard the travelers through the forest. The route kept growing, and the teams would go out for longer each time, making more money than farming rocky barren land in the mountains, eating hotopty, and milking bad-tempered goats. Occasionally, there would be an attack on the train to remind the travelers that it's wild country"

"Like we had?"

"Oh, no, that wasn't really an attack." Vollo turned his eyes heavenward as he tried to find the words. "That was a scuffle between creatures that we happened to witness. No, you would know when you had been in a real fight. Anyway, sometimes we get through totally unscathed. Then, inevitably, the question is raised 'why did we need to pay you so much? What purpose did you serve?'"

Eric nodded. "And those that have seen battle don't begrudge the cost."

"Those that make it, of course."

Eric gestured toward the wagons. "And are we safe here tonight? Will we witness any more… scuffles?"

Vollo smiled. "We time our trips through the Gash with great care. It's never foolproof, of course, but we minimize the chances of an attack. We got unlucky, that's all."

Eric nodded. "That's great to hear, it truly is. Thank you for telling me about the valley too. Sleep well tonight." He turned and made his way back to the wagon, accepting a plate from Imogen with a nod and a smile, then settling down to eat and think.

Back on Earth, he'd worked his way up the hierarchy in the fast-food restaurant, and one thing he'd learned: when a visiting member of head office said 'Trust me' you could not do anything but trust them. The only people that ever said, 'Trust me,' were those that you could not trust. The platitudes of 'we'll be ok,' and 'there is little danger' were obviously designed to placate the travelers. Eric wondered how much of a disadvantage they would be in if there was another attack that night. The predator creatures they had seen didn't seem to have done any damage to the humans in the camp, so maybe if they set up some sort of warning system, then that would give them enough time to clamber up onto the wagon.

He looked up to see that Imogen and Anton were both watching him as he stared into space.

"My lord?"

"Sorry, were you saying something?"

"No, but you hadn't moved for some time. We were getting worried."

"Just thinking, that is all. Imogen, do we have anything we could rig up around the lean to, about ankle-height, which might stop those predators we encountered that first night?"

She thought for a second, the flickering of the flames across her face mimicking thoughts flitting through the ether. At last, she said,

"Actually, my lord, there is. I have some yards of fabric that we could wind between the poles of the lean-to and the wagon, starting at the ground level and going up to about knee high. And if we hang the pots and pans from the top, then anything trying to get over or through it will make a noise that should wake us up."

"Excellent thinking! Awesome, let's put that up before we go to sleep."

Anton frowned. "Why don't we just sleep in the back of the wagon?" Both Imogen and Eric tried to answer him, but he continued as he realized the reason. "Because it's so uncomfortable, of course. Sorry."

They worked quickly. Eric paused momentarily, looking at the bolt of fabric and then back to Imogen. She looked a little guilty. "It's a gamble, my lord. I've been told that this type of fabric is almost impossible to find where we are going, so I have used a portion of my salary to buy the bolt of it. If I'm right, I will be able to double or triple my money."

"And if you're wrong?"

"I have many friends who are tailors and would be happy to take it off my hands. Truth be told though, my lord, it was a little more expensive, so I should have just paid it off by the time we arrive at our destination. Fortunately, there aren't many shops between here and there to spend my salary."

"Well, it's lucky for us that you did. Thanks for letting us use it as a warning system!"

She smiled wryly. "I have a vested interest in keeping us safe, my lord."

Eric nodded as they all bedded down under the lean-to. "As do we all, Imogen, as do we all. Good night."

The next morning, they awoke, looking at each other and smiling. As they packed down the camp, Eric examined their early warning system. Nothing. No indication of any animal activity, no bite marks, no scratches, or any other sign that something had come there at night. The problem, he thought as he joined in packing the wagon, with precautions was that you never knew if you were lucky and the measures taken were unneeded or whether they worked and had kept you safe. He shrugged. At the restaurant, they had manuals and processes that addressed all the risks the company had thought about over the years they had been operating. Health codes, employment law, all codified, and strategies put in place to minimize the chances of the risk happening, or to minimize the impact if bad events did occur. Eric was trying to mentally put something like that in place for his life on this planet, however short that hopefully would be. Just until he got back home. He smiled as he looked around at the clearing of wagons, breaking down their respective camps. He didn't have to be the most intelligent person alive - relying on the decades of operational excellence that he'd learned as a manager would give him a huge leg up. What was that saying? In the land of the blind, the one-eyed man was king.

He was smiling to himself as their wagon left the clearing, passing the guardsmen on the way. Ahead of them, the other wagons seemed to be going even slower than normal. It soon became evident why that was the case as they began the uphill trek toward the top of the hill that overlooked the valley, the switchbacks zigzagging up the sheer cliff. While the cliff they climbed had looked like brown earth from the other side of the valley, this close, it was a dark brown sandstone, flecked with streaks of silver metal, about the length of a finger. The oxen barely paused at the bottom of the hill before snorting and leaning into their harnesses. The angle was such that the odd ceramic jar or bag that had not been secured properly in one of the preceding wagons could be seen lying on the side of the path, but they had stowed their own gear well enough, and it all stayed in place.

Imogen was obviously a little concerned with the switchbacks. By the time they reached the top, she let out a long breath that Eric hadn't realized she'd been holding and deflated slightly, the tension visibly leaving her body.

Eric leaned over so that Anton couldn't hear them. "Hey, you did well."

Imogen smiled back. "Thank you, my lord. I must admit that I haven't done this much droving before."

"Well, I could not have guessed that."

They drove along the path for a few minutes in companionable silence. The day had dawned overcast but was burning off as they plodded along. By the afternoon, the guess was that they would have a fine day again. The terrain on the other side of the Gash was farmland, golden fields of grain, approaching harvestable size, spreading out in both directions on either side of the path. The path itself, now that it had left the Gash, was heading across this plain toward a wood. It was miles away at present, but the line for the trees stretched out for as far as the eye could see to the left and right.

Imogen looked up. "I guess we should enjoy the sight of the sky while we can. When we get into the forest, we will be under cover for quite a few days."

"Have you been this way before?"

"No, but even in the limited travels I have done, you hear things. Merchants in inns, market places, tinkers - all great sources of travel information."

"And what did they say about this place?"

"Not much. The only person I can remember talking about this area said that the land between the Gash and the Greenwood Sea was empty farmland. It looks like that might have been during sowing time, because it's certainly a different sight now."

Eric stood up on his seat and craned his eyes in every direction. And then sat down quickly in case the wagon rocked too much.

"Anything?"

"No, I was thinking there might be a farmer's house or something. But no, nothing but the grain in every direction. It only stops at the forest and at the cliffs that we've just come up."

Imogen frowned at that. "There should be a road which runs along close to the edge of the forest. It eventually leads to Sladdy, the capital of Ordost."

"Where is Ordost?"

She looked at him for a split second. "My lord is definitely not from here. Ordost is our country. We've been in it the whole time. And will be for the majority of our trip. We cross over into Western Pittoos toward the end, and Havelin is in Maclesh, but most of the time we'll be in the land of Queen Rennia."

Eric shrugged. Would there be any point in learning any of this if he was just going to be returning home?

"My lord… My lord, what is your life like in your world?"

"As I said, Imogen, while there are people, who think as they do here about people like yourself, there are laws to protect you. And good people act on those laws."

"Yes, my lord. You mentioned that. But what is your life like? Day to day? What would you typically do on a daily basis?"

Eric was quiet for a while, the typical day playing out in his mind. Waking up, breakfast on some sugary cereal. Brushing his teeth and showering. Heading to work. Either an opening or closing shift, consisting of checking that other people had done what you've told them to do a hundred times. Begging teenagers to come in when their coworkers call in sick because they're hungover or at high school detention or both. A stint at the drive through window. Customer complaints. Karens. The homeless guy, who throws up on himself or, worse, in the corner booth. Head office drones coming through to throw their weight around. Performance reviews. Then that blissful time when the shift was over. Back home to smoke up large while blowing away some enemies of the state in a computer game. A dinner at one or other of the local fast-food restaurants. A weekend spent out in the desert. Or at the beach. Or just hanging out at the skatepark. Rinse and repeat.

Imogen waited. What to tell her? A little white lie? A small stretch of the truth? He didn't want to lose face, but… What was wrong with telling her about his life? Was there something wrong with it?

He smiled wryly at her. "Day to day? I wake up – "

The wagon in front of them suddenly jerked and lifted, all of the supplies and equipment sliding out the back, sprinkling with a cascade of crashes across the path. The oxen tethered to the harness bellowed in alarm as their haunches rose unceremoniously into the air. Imogen and Eric's eyes widened simultaneously as they saw something moving under the wagon, the waggoner and his passenger tumbling from their seats to land heavily on the ground.

The wagon was flung into the grain on the side of the path, the oxen breaking free of their harnesses as they landed among the wreckage, their calls rising to painful screeches. The thing was now exposed. It stalked forward toward the waggoner and passenger. They still lay dazed on the ground, staring back in disbelief as it approached. It was like someone had shaved a lion and then injected it with steroids. A lot of steroids. It moved with an arrogant swagger, padding forward almost silently toward the people on the ground. Eric focused on the only color on its face – the pink lining of its nostrils. Until it opened its mouth, making Eric and Imogen scream. Double rows of sharp fangs were briefly visible, until it snapped its mouth shut around the head and shoulders of the waggoner, and then leapt into the sea of grain to the left of the path.

It had taken mere seconds. The stunned quiet that followed was broken by the ragged breathing of the passenger, lying on the ground, staring in disbelief at the headless remains beside them, and the sobbing oxen, hidden off to the right of the path.

One of the guardsmen came running toward them, his spear at the ready. Eric tried to find the words to shout a warning. But then stopped himself, knowing that the guardsman would look up at the sound, which could potentially stop him from seeing another attack. Another guardsman followed, and another. They appeared to be looking behind Eric's wagon. Eric was suddenly filled with a sense of dread. Anton screamed from the wagon bed behind. Eric turned to Imogen, shouting, "Drive!"

The wagon lurched forward as she smacked the ass end of the oxen with the twitch and yelled "Move, you slovenly sluts!"

Eric looked over his shoulder to see the grain swaying on both sides of the path behind them and the eyes of the wagon driver behind as big as saucers. Anton was slowly and ineffectively moving his legs to back further away from the edge of the wagon, not realizing his back was against the rear of the driver's seat - there was nowhere for him to go. His horse was calmly moving her head around, snorting occasionally, and stomping her feet as she scanned the grain on either side of the road.

The passenger on the ground in front of them must have heard them coming and rolled away, disappearing from view. Ahead and behind, the silence was split by the guardsmen yelling to each other and trying to coordinate their movements. Attempting to figure out where this thing was. More pandemonium greeted them from far in advance of the column. Eric couldn't understand it. How could the thing move so quickly? It had been behind them, and now, was attacking the front of the column. What was that, a half mile away? In seconds?

As they jostled their way along the path, Eric tried to figure out the best course of action. They now had two guardsmen running alongside the wagon toward the front of the train, and they were passing three or four heading the other way. Behind them, Eric could see the rest of the wagons in the train driving their oxen as fast as they could. They were quickly approaching the next wagon ahead of them, a family of four, pulled by an auroch. The animal was attempting some sort of a gallop but was hampered by the chains of its harness. As they got closer to the back of the wagon, they saw the grain to the left of the path sway apart, and the creature emerge and stand in the middle of the path, sniffing the air, oblivious to the approaching wagons. The auroch saw it and finally figured out how to gallop, breaking part of the harness in the process, and heading into the sea of grain to the right at ever increasing speed. The bellows of the driver and the screams of the family were swallowed by the grain as they bumped their way off the path.

This left Eric's wagon charging headlong toward the creature. It now faced them. Eric stared straight into its eyes, expecting to see hate or some other familiar human emotion. But there was nothing there. Nothing he could read anyway. The two guardsmen sprinted toward the creature, and beyond it, Eric could make out more spear points on their way. The creature leapt over the guardsmen, disappearing into the grain with barely a rustle marking the landing. The thing was quick. And it was silent.

The guardsmen faced the grain, where the creature had leapt and formed a line. One of them waved Eric past. The oxen were moving as fast as they could and the horse was trotting alongside, periodically pulling alongside the back wheel on one side of the wagon and then dropping back to pull alongside the other back wheel. He reminded Eric, in the weirdest way, of a Secret Service man protecting a President in a limousine by running alongside, one hand on the fender closest to him.

They very shortly came across the remnants of the commotion they had heard earlier. A wagon was on its side, its contents spilled along the path. Both oxen lay on the ground in front, still harnessed, and the wooden spars that ran alongside them snapped off, unable to take the dead weight. As they sped past, they could see that both oxen were missing their heads, jagged ripped flesh exposed to a swarm of black flies. There was no sign of any people, living or dead.

"What can you see behind us, Anton?" called Eric. No response. Eric turned to see Anton's back shuddering. He whacked him, not hard, over his shoulders. "Anton! What can you see?"

"Uh… I can see three… no, four, wagons behind us. There are a bunch of Bendies coming after them. No sign of anything else, my lord."

"Good. Let me know if you see anything else, OK?"

"Yes, my lord."

"You're doing OK, Imogen, keep them moving, and we'll be safe enough soon."

She didn't say anything, just gripped the reins harder. Her face was a study of serious concentration.

A few minutes later, they came up behind the wagon in front. There were about six people in the back, staring wide-eyed all around them. A middle-aged woman was comforting two pre-teen children. The auroch was shaking its head from side to side, looking on the verge of breaking the harness and escaping alone. Spilled sacks of grain and broken barrels spoke of the violence of their escape.

Imogen slowed the oxen slightly to match the speed of the wagon in front, Eric silently urging them to go faster. There was no room on the side of the path to overtake without driving through the grain, and the last thing Eric wanted to do was to lose any more visibility. He didn't think that anything would save them from the creature, but he would like to at least see it coming before it… well, he preferred to be able to see all around them.

"What can you see now, Anton?"

"Six wagons, the Bendies have moved to the back of the last one I can see. I think that's all the wagons. How many can you see in the front?"

"I can't see the front of the train. When we camp tonight, I guess we'll find out how many are left."

Imogen finally spoke. "Are we safe then? Have the creatures left us?"

Eric frowned. "Creatures? Wasn't there only one?"

She shook her head, still focusing on the path and the oxen. "No, my lord. There were definitely two. They had different markings. And one had blood down its front. The second one didn't have that."

Well, that explained how they had attacked different parts of the train so quickly. "I don't know. The train seems to be slowing, so I figure we must be out of danger. We're not far from the forest edge."

The wagon in front actually stopped entirely, and Eric craned his head. More wagons in front of them had also stopped. One of the guardsmen walked past, coming from the back of the train. Eric called after him.

"Is it safe? Stopping here? Shouldn't we keep moving?!"

The man ignored him, fingering his spear, and keeping an eye on the grain on one side of the path or the other. He wasn't running but he certainly wasn't dawdling either. Eric turned to see if anyone else was happy with staying still when they should be concentrating on putting more miles between them and whatever the two creatures were. The driver of the wagon behind was nervously watching the grain on either side, the men in the wagon behind him were standing on the driver's seat, peering out over the grain, which rippled when the wind raced along it. Nobody was shouting or complaining, so while there was a definite tension in the air, there was no panic or loud arguing. Eric didn't like it at all. He contemplated getting down and walking forward to see why they weren't moving. The obvious danger of moving around was outweighed by his desire to get the hell away from whatever those things were.

"I'm going to find out why there is a holdup. Don't wait for me, move up when the wagon in front does. I'll come back and find you."

Imogen looked at Eric like he was insane, so he gave her a jaunty smile, expressing a confidence that he definitely did not feel, and patted his sword. "I'll be fine." Her eyes only widened, and as she was about to say something, he concentrated on making his way down to ground level. He made it there without tripping himself up but definitely felt unsteady on his feet. Adrenaline was making his legs wobbly, he thought, taking a breath to calm himself before keeping a hand on the hilt of his sword to remind himself it was there, and headed forward along the path.

It took Eric a few minutes to get past all the wagons ahead of them, a few of the passengers calling out to him to find out what was going on, why they were stopping and what those things had been. The fear in their voices wasn't quite terror, but nobody was happy with stopping. Ahead of him, he finally saw the lead wagons and the guardsman chief talking to one of his men. As he approached, the guardsman took his leave, and the leader nodded to Eric.

"You are Eric?" the man said, taking in the sword and his clothes.

186

"I am," said Eric. He was about to ask his questions, but the leader continued.

"What do you do for a living, Eric?"

How to describe what he did? "I am a manager," he said after a second.

"Ah, another leader of men," the leader responded. Eric looked at him sharply. He didn't know what his earworm had translated 'manager' into, but he suspected it didn't represent someone, who made barely more than the minimum-wage staff that he oversaw. "You're aware of the burden of leadership, then." He looked impassively around them.

In the pause which followed, Eric leapt in with his questions. "How many of them were there?"

"The tunco? Just two."

Imogen was right.

"And three guardsmen killed, seven waggoners, four wagons destroyed, three aurochs missing in the fields, two oxen dead, and one missing."

"Did we even kill one of the tunco?"

The leader barely suppressed a smirk. "I would be surprised if any of my men even touched one of them with their spear. The tunco are a force of nature. We are truly blessed that they breed so slowly, otherwise, they would overrun the world. We've had worse. The good news is now they've hunted, they'll lay low for a while, and they keep the other predators away, so we will have three or four nights of peace. By the time they decide to hunt again, we should be well and truly deep in the woods. They don't like the woods for some reason." He turned to face Eric directly. "So, how do you know our language? And here's the curious part: you know our language but call us 'Bendies' to our face? How does that work?" The leader's gaze held no malice.

"I have an earworm," Eric said, tapping his earlobe.

The man nodded slowly, thinking. After a second he continued. "I have not introduced myself. I am Tas of the Kishan."

"Eric Prince of Anaheim," Eric responded before he could stop himself.

"Ah," said Tas.

Desperate to change the subject, Eric continued. "So will we go back and get the wagons or bury the dead?"

Tas shook his head. "No, we keep going. Everyone knows the terms of our train. We continue."

"We just continue?"

"Always. We go on. There is only forward. You can never go back. They were my people. I will have to tell their families how they died. My prince, that is the burden of our role as leaders. We

188

are accountable to our people. Go back to your wagon, we will be leaving immediately."

Chapter 9

Eric did as he was bid and hurried back to his wagon, ignoring questioning looks and exasperated inquiries from the other travelers. As he approached their wagon, he could see Anton and Imogen having some sort of conversation which petered out as he approached. He clambered up to his normal seat, and let them know what was happening. "We're heading out. Apparently, this is a safe spot because the tunco will be feeding on their kills for the next few days and won't follow us into the woods."

"Why have we stopped? Are we still in danger?" Anton scanned their surroundings intently.

"We needed to regroup; we have to keep together for safety."

"Good news, my lord. The sooner we leave this place, the better."

It only took five minutes before they were underway again, the relief on their faces very evident. Every minute they were moving was another notch of stress leaving their bodies. Every minute the hurried scanning of the grain stems closest to them slowed slightly, and the time between standing on the seat to have a look across the top of the grain stalks lengthened. They'd been on the move for maybe half an hour when the train came to a halt again. Instantly, Eric stood up onto the seat and tried to figure out what was going on. The edge of the forest was very close now indeed, and he figured that if the lead wagons had not entered the forest itself, then they must be incredibly close. He could make out a bit of a gap running along the edge of the forest and realized that there must be a road between the fields and the forest.

"What is it, my lord?"

"I can't see anything," he said. He scanned the other travelers ahead of them. There was no panic, no exaggerated movements, or attempts to flee. If it was the creatures, then they hadn't attacked… yet. A minute or two later, the train resumed its progress. They could see the forest looming in front of them, and beyond the wagons, the path entered the woods, looking to all the world like a dark tunnel in a cliff of trees. Just before the road disappeared into the forest, though, there was a crossroads, with the path Eric had surmised running a foot away from the edge of the forest in both directions. Slightly off the side of the main road, a group of ten soldiers on horseback were waiting with the leader of the train, and the leader of the guardsmen. As they approached the crossroads, the train leader nodded and moved out to the middle of the crossroads, gesturing for them to pull out of formation. Imogen glanced over to Eric, who pursed his lips.

"I don't like our chances of outrunning them," he murmured. "Better do what they say."

Imogen pulled the wagon over to the side road and brought the oxen to a halt.

Eric nodded to the guardsmen leader and raised a quizzical eyebrow. The man looked away and strode in the direction of the forest. *Oh, this does not look good,* thought Eric. The leader of the soldiers was dressed in chainmail with a large breastplate sitting on top. His helmet slung down his back between his shoulders. A mane of long blonde hair ended just above where his collar would have been. He walked his horse over to the side of the wagon.

"Queen Rennia of Ordost requests the company of Eric, Prince of Anaheim and his companions at their earliest convenience."

"You have caught us at a most inconvenient time. We are on our way to Havelin, and this train is the only way for us to get there. Please, pass on my regrets that we cannot meet with her. As much as we would normally wish to, of course."

A look of surprise flitted over the train master's face, but the soldier merely blinked. "Unfortunately, we will have to insist. She would not hear of missing the opportunity of meeting with you.

And I'm sure the wagon master will take most good care of your wagon and belongings, won't you?"

The train master looked uncomfortable. "My lord, one of my men can drive their wagon and feed and unlimber their oxen each night. But we cannot be held responsible for anything that is missing from their wagon upon their return."

The soldier looked bored. "Why else do they pay you then if not to look after them? And their wagon?"

The train master shrugged. "We promise nothing. The forest is dangerous. The Gash is dangerous. The whole trip is dangerous."

Eric kicked himself. He would have to go with the soldiers, otherwise they would just take them anyway. And then they would make him leave all his belongings behind. At least, he would be able to take his money if he could get his horse saddled up.

"Put Vollo and Giran on it. I know them."

The train master sadly nodded. "I will put Vollo on your wagon. Giran was taken by the tunco."

Eric closed his eyes for a moment. Another one gone. He sighed. "Will you give me a minute to saddle my horse?"

"I cannot see your horse, your majesty. Is it invisible?"

Eric looked around. His horse was nowhere to be seen. He'd definitely seen it after the attack. She hadn't even been breathing hard. And now where was she?

The soldier gestured to the troop. "We will ride two to a horse."

There seemed to be no benefit to delaying any further, so he descended to the ground, helped Imogen down, and then accepted the book while Anton descended. Back on the wagon's bed, the saddlebags, their cash, and the mystical book all nestled among the grain, flour, water, and other supplies Imogen had provisioned. He prayed it was still there when he returned. If he returned.

The soldier barked orders, and soon, the book was in a saddlebag, Anton and Imogen were on the backs of two of the horses, and one of the other soldiers was reaching down to help Eric up onto the back of his horse. He remembered the last time he'd tried to get on a horse. He took a second and worked out which way his legs needed to go. He gripped the back of the saddle with both hands and threw his leg over the back of the horse. The soldier grunted and grabbed his arm, hoisting him up. Somehow, he managed to find a position that prevented him from sliding off the horse. He prayed they would not have to gallop anywhere. The bruising on the inside of his thighs was still a painful memory.

The soldiers set off at a trot, Eric on the second row of horses after the leader. Despite the danger of falling off, he half turned to make sure Anton and Imogen were following. Both seemed to be riding better than he was. For the next hour, he clung to the saddle or to the soldier riding the horse, muttering curses under his breath the whole way. They paused after that hour, the golden fields of grain finishing in a straight line, while the woods continued to their right. In the distance, across the grassland, lay the foothills leading up to the mountain range he'd seen from the Gash. Sitting on top of the foothills was a castle, about two hundred feet across, a bold set of walls about thirty feet tall, with a square tower poking above them. It took another hour and a bit to get there, and Eric was thankful when they rode up the path, leading to the gatehouse. He'd had time to note the pennants and flags fluttering above the keep, and the many helmeted heads of soldiers patrolling the battlements. They clopped over the wooden drawbridge into a stone courtyard, which looked like a Renaissance Faire on steroids. Tents and soldiers were everywhere. The very occasional woman hustled along delivering some supplies, not dawdling, and usually followed by raucous jokes and laughter from the soldiers.

They passed through another gatehouse into the base of the large central building, a stout round tower that was the focal point of the castle. Eric slid off the horse inelegantly, landing awkwardly but without a tumble on the cobbled ground. They were led into the interior of the castle, up narrow stairs and along too many corridors to memorize. Eric was thankful they didn't have to plan an escape, so he didn't need to know the way back by memory. There was no way he would be able to find his way back under his own power. Eventually, they reached a wider corridor with guards against each of the doors. They were led to a smaller door at the end of the corridor and found themselves in a compact room, with wooden benches arrayed in rows in front of an altar. Stained glass windows allowed a many-colored light to filter into the room. Eric was startled, thinking they were in a chapel, and started to look around for any Christian imagery. There was nothing he recognized - certainly no crosses or beams of light from the heavens. More depictions of fields of grain and mountains with mines or caves. No sign of humans tending the fields or heading into the mines.

An elderly man in long robes entered the room and bowed. "Your highness, welcome to Castle Timker. My name is Rehm, and I am the Chief Counsel to her majesty, Queen Rennia. I will shortly take you through to your audience with the Queen, but can I trouble you to please disarm yourselves? Your weapons will be most safe in the Chapel for the duration of your stay."

Eric shrugged, then slid his sword from its sheath, and placed it on one of the benches. He noticed a momentary look of panic on Rehm's face, but it quickly went away. Imogen apparently had a dagger, which she placed, still in its sheath, beside Eric's sword. Rehm looked expectantly at Anton, who stared back blankly before figuring out what was being silently asked.

"Oh, no. I do not have any weapons. Only my mind," he continued, tapping his temple with a finger.

Eric suppressed a smile.

"Well, if there are no further weapons, I will just advise you against the use of any and all magics in her majesty's presence. The wards protecting her are quite vicious, and we wouldn't want another Baron Greele incident now, would we?" An almost evil smile flitted across Rehm's face at the memory of the incident. "Please, follow me," he said as he led them out of the room.

Anton followed first, and Eric leaned close to Imogen. "What happened to Baron Greele?" he asked.

"He attempted to cast a spell in the Queen's presence," she answered as they left the chapel and crossed the hall. "Some say it was a harmless spell to show deference to her, some say it was an assassination attempt. Either way, whatever wards were in effect caused him to die in a quite spectacular way. They were washing his remains off the walls for days afterwards. Some say that they're still finding bits of him in that room weeks later. Here we are."

They had entered a large open room with vaulted ceilings, held up on many pillars throughout the room. On one side of the room sat the Queen, slightly raised on a dais with a high-backed throne, topped with a wooden box that had her coat of arms emblazoned on the front. The queen was in her mid-twenties, so of a very similar age to Eric and Imogen. She was sitting, but didn't seem overly tall. She was quite slim, bordering on malnourished. Prominent collarbones and cheekbones. Pretty by both the local customs as well as Eric's. Dark straight hair. Eric was too far away to see what color her eyes were.

A pair of guards, armed with impressive long axes stood either side of her. There were more guards at each of the doors leading into and out of the room. On the far side of the room were the ladies of the court, and opposite the throne were soldiers in armor and older men in tunics and trousers. Rehm stepped to one side and bellowed unnecessarily loudly.

"My Queen! May I present Eric, Prince of Anaheim, and his companions, Anton, Apprentice Librarian of Gerton, and Imogen. Prince Eric, the Queen of Ordost, rightful ruler of South Redes, North Redes, and the Salmon Isles, Protector of the Lands of Gold, and most worthy of her family."

Eric noticed a flicker of annoyance flash across Imogen's face at her apparent unimportance in the court. He also wondered what her preferred job description would be. He would have to figure that out before he had to introduce her to others.

His introduction had caused a little bit of a stir amongst the ladies of the court. He also noticed an air of confusion amongst the soldiers and menfolk. All were looking at him expectantly. He stepped forward and nodded in the direction of the queen. "Nice to meet you," was all he managed. A titter spread from the ladies and a shocked silence replaced the confusion from the other gallery.

The queen's smile froze in place, but she was all cordial politeness. "Prince Eric, welcome, I must admit I was surprised to hear of a member of a royal family, albeit of a country I had not heard of before, traveling through my realm without the courtesy of sending their regards. Especially one traveling with a pair of my citizens." Here she looked over to Imogen. Not Anton and Imogen, just Imogen. Eric noticed that about half of the ladies of the court were equally taken with Imogen and her tight leggings. There was a significant difference between Imogen's choice of clothes and the attire worn by the ladies. Eric had mentally characterized their clothing as "generic medieval." It consisted of a full skirt, with a fitted bodice, and some kind of cotton shirt or blouse underneath. Imogen's display of legs had obviously attracted a lot of attention.

"If my counselor has told me the truth, you seem to be heading to Havelin. That would entail taking my two citizens away from their country. Rehm, have I given permission for these two to leave the borders of our fair nation?"

"No, my queen, you have not."

Eric looked in confusion at Imogen. She nodded and leaned closer to him. "Technically, the queen has the power to forbid any of her subjects from leaving the country. It's almost never enforced, so nobody pays it any mind."

The queen was waiting, looking expectantly at Eric. Eric took a deep breath. He actually had some experience in this sort of situation. Dealing with senior management from head office gave you some idea of the buttons that needed to be pushed.

"Apologies, Queen. I must admit I find myself in your fair nation through no plan of my own. I am seeking knowledge in Havelin that might facilitate my return home. Imogen here is acting as my most trusted advisor. My counselor, if you will, while I am here. A task, which she has performed extremely expertly, I would be at a loss without her. She gives me the background knowledge of your land and customs."

The queen blinked when he claimed that Imogen was his counselor. Eric guessed that a woman in such a high position in a royal court might be a bit of a shock.

"And Imogen, what say you? Does the Prince speak the truth?"

Imogen cleared her throat. "Yes, my queen. I am given great trust and allowed to get on with my responsibilities without interruption or impediment."

"And these responsibilities? How much does he have you doing?"

Imogen smiled. "Everything, my queen. I organize the provisions for the trip, I drive the oxen, remove the harnesses, and look after the animals at the end of the day. I make camp. I negotiate for supplies and with the train master."

Rehm frowned. "Prince, could you not have found a man to do all these things? What does this Anton do?"

Eric had been watching the queen. There were certainly power issues there! "Anton has his own skills that are valued highly. He concentrates on those because he is the only one who has them. I would no more ask him to perform the responsibilities that Imogen performs than I would ask him to pick up a sword. Imogen has performed her duties admirably, and I am blessed with her service."

The queen watched him carefully, nodding slightly. He had the impression he was being measured. "I must admit I do not know where Anaheim is, your highness. Is your country bountiful? Its people are plentiful?"

"Oh, yes, I think at last count there were three hundred and twenty-something million people in America."

There was silence in the room, with a single guffaw from someone amongst the men.

Rehm gave him a condescending look. "Maybe your highness is not aware of how much a million is? Maybe in Anaheim there is a different counting system?"

Eric looked blankly around. "One thousand thousands. One million."

The queen continued quietly. "And how many soldiers could you put into the field?"

"So, we share our military with the whole of America, not just Anaheim, but I think it's something like a million men and women. Maybe half of those in the field."

The room was silent, surprised blinking all around.

"Your nation sounds mighty indeed; I would like to visit it one day to… strengthen the relationship between our peoples. Where did you say it was located?"

"I am led to believe it may be far to the west. One of the reasons I am traveling to Havelin is to find out exactly how to get home."

"Ah, I understand. Your country is so far away that you don't know how to get home. That makes sense." The counselor seemed to be playing semaphores to the Queen using his eyebrows. "Oh, yes. Actually, I have a sensitive matter to discuss. Would you be able to help me out with a matter of some import? We need to address the problem of some ogres in the land. And while you are gone, I'll keep my two citizens safe until you return, I will even give them safe passage and letters of introduction for when you cross the borders."

Imogen tugged at his sleeve, and he bent his head close. "She wants your army. But seeing as its too far away, she seeks to gain some benefit from having you here. But beware, your safety is not her concern. Many a visitor of royal blood has ended their life as a result of some quest."

Great! Smiling ingratiatingly, he attempted one last time to escape intact.

"Your highness is most kind, but I really need to get to Havelin."

"I'm afraid in this case it would have to be alone, as without the letters of introduction I'm afraid I cannot let my citizens travel freely - there is a war on after all. I'm sure you understand."

Eric had been blackmailed enough to recognize it. And to know when he didn't have any options. "Your highness is most generous, I would love the opportunity to help in any way that I can. If I can aid in neutralizing the threat of these ogres, will you promise to release Anton and Imogen from any and all travel restrictions?"

The queen looked every inch the cat who had got the cream. "I so promise. Bring them in, Rehm."

Four strangers entered the room, none of them had weapons, but two were in full plate armor, helms held under their arms, and one was in chain mail, over which he wore a surcoat of white with a red circle in the middle of it. The fourth stranger was in brown robes, a rope belt tied around his waist with a pouch on it. Imogen leaned closer to Eric as they walked forward.

"My lord! These are the four adventurers whose escapades have been widely reported by bards in inns across the lands! Hergsa there (she gestured to the taller of the two in full plate), is a knight of the highest honor. He single-handedly saved the orphans from burning in the city of Salet. The healer, Lioko, there in the surcoat, holds the health and life of men in his hands, and saved the Queen's father from a hunting accident two years ago. The King died the next week of an assassin's blade, but everyone agreed it was good of him to heal him after being gored by the boar. The mage, Firsl, wields power beyond the knowing of mortal man, and some say that he has deals in place with four demons, promising his soul to each of them in exchange for the powers he has. He then tells each demon, who comes to collect, that he has given his soul to one of the others and so manages to keep them hunting each other instead of him."

"And the fourth? The other one in plate armor?"

"Yeah, that's Jhara."

On cue, Jhara broke the silence of their entry. "Could we get on with this? I've got a potion on the boil back in the castle."

The Queen directed a frosty stare at him before continuing. "Thank you, noble sirs, for coming so quickly. My messenger assures me that he delivered my summons a week ago."

The Knight replied, giving Jhara a warning look. "There were… issues with our traveling here."

Jhara, Lioko, and Firsl all muttered to themselves. Eric couldn't quite make out what they were saying, but it seemed that some disagreement was bubbling below the surface.

"As I said in my letter," the Queen continued a little bit of steel edging into her voice. "A tribe of ogres is stealing cattle in the farmlands near Nocco, and they are hiding out in a cave system in the hills nearby. Two squads of my soldiers that I sent have failed to return and are feared dead. I need the ogres dealt with, so that the farmers will harvest the grain, and I can feed my soldiers in the war that is underway. And since you will not join my war…"

More mutterings about vows, being forbidden to dally in local conflicts and bad timing.

"… I would ask that you do this little task for me instead."

The four of them shared looks before Hergsa finally bowed. "As you wish, my queen."

"Good. You will take the Prince of Anaheim with you. He will be most helpful."

They barely looked at him. "Really? Ok, whatever. Let's go."

The counselor took Eric, Anton, and Imogen back into the chapel to collect their weapons. Then he led Anton and Imogen away, while Jhara poked his head in the door.

"Coming?" he said as Eric was trying to catch Anton or Imogen's eye to say goodbye or to give them words of comfort. To no avail. Eric turned back to Jhara, who smiled, and then led him out of the castle, again their route instantly forgotten.

Chapter 10

The four adventurers cast lots to see who would take Eric. He thought the three winners laughed a little too hard when Jhara lost. Eric clambered behind Jhara on his horse, and they set off. The pace was more of a walk than a trot and rather than dwell on their reluctance to get to where they were going quickly, Eric thought he would try and gather some intelligence.

"Your armor seems very light. I thought it would slow your movements."

"It's light enough. It's a bit cumbersome, but it's really the padding and the chainmail that make it heavy. You're not from around here, are you?"

Eric was glad he was behind Jhara so he would not be able to see the panic in his eyes. "What gave it away?" he asked, kicking himself for whatever it was.

"Little things. Not knowing how heavy armor is. Not being particularly practiced with your sword. The way you speak to commoners. I dare say, you're not the first peasant pretending to be royalty, and you won't be the last. So, are you adventuring for fame and fortune?"

"No, I'm trying to get home. I have to get to Havelin."

"The ogres aren't really on the way to Havelin. Why are you here with us?"

Eric paused, wondering how honest to be. "The queen is blackmailing me. She's holding my friends effectively hostage until I do this thing."

"Ah yes, the lovely queen. She is good at blackmail and coercion. And getting what she wants."

"But surely when you heard she was in need, you came running to her aid?"

Jhara snorted. "We're not your usual heroes. We're the ones you call when you need things done, and you're too desperate to care exactly how they get done. Do you see Hergsa there? He has been killed so many times that he's just a little maladjusted. He's obsessed with honor which, of course, makes him easy to manipulate. Lioko there? Our healer? We all have a little healing magic ourselves, so he's always trying hard to justify his position. And Firsl, our mage? He ducked out of the university in Doris Bay in Frekenhardt just before graduation, so unless we find a spell in some treasure somewhere, he'll never learn any new ones. And so

208

many of us know a little magic, but anything remotely related to magic has to be his area of expertise. It's a matter of pride for him."

Eric had played enough games to know that in any party you needed to cover all the skills available, and after a tank (someone to take damage), a DPS (damage per second – a mage), and a healer, you usually had someone who could disarm traps, pick locks, pick pockets, and sell the stolen loot.

"What, no thief?"

"We only trust each other a little as it is, how much do you think we'd trust someone who advertises themselves as a thief? If you're unconscious, I know my sword, or my rings, or my gems aren't going to mysteriously disappear. Which helps me go into battle with all my skills, rather than hanging out near the entrance so I can make a quick getaway." Jhara paused, frowning. "Is there no magic in your world?"

"No, not really."

He heard the man snort. "I don't believe you. So, if you were a thousand miles from your family and you heard your father had a day to live, what would you do?"

"A thousand miles? I would take a plane to get there."

"And what is a plane?"

"It's like a wagon. But it goes very fast. In the sky."

"And can anyone drive it?"

"No, you need a pilot."

"OK, so you need a mage - a pie-lot - you called it?"

"Yeah."

"And here's a question for you: could you learn how to be a pilot? If you had enough time and money?"

"I could, yes."

"OK, nothing you've said sounds anything different than a mage. Or a sorcerer, or a wizard, or a witch, or whatever you call it." Jhara spat into the grass on the side of the path. "And how about making a person you don't like dead? If they're within an arm's length, then you hit them with your fist. A pace back, you hit them with a sword. A hundred yards, you have a bow. Further away, you might have a siege weapon."

"Ah, ok, you'd shoot them."

"Like with a bow and arrow? Or a crossbow?"

Eric wondered how to describe a gun. Or a machine gun. "Like a crossbow. Or a thousand crossbows all in one. And it can reach out to a mile. A tool to project death out to a mile."

"Ah, like a siege weapon, good against buildings but not against someone on the move - in a cart or on a horse?"

Eric nodded, though wondered if Jhara noticed the gesture. "No. It could still hit a moving target at that distance, not all the time, but with a skilled user, it is deadly accurate. Our army also has other weapons that are like a thousand archers, all in one tool. And other weapons that project deadly force over the horizon."

"Beyond the ability to see?"

"Beyond what the naked eye can see, yes. But we have other tools that allow you to see very far indeed. And even kill beyond the seas. We even have weapons that can destroy whole cities."

Eric expected Jhara not to believe him. Surely what he was saying would be beyond a medieval adventurer's ability to comprehend? But Jhara just nodded. "And that's not magic?"

"No, because you can see how it happens."

"Could you do it now? Could you kill Firsl?"

Ahead of them, Firsl half turned in his saddle, puzzled. Was he in danger?

"No, I don't have a gun, and I can't make one because I don't have the tools."

"Could you make the tools?"

"No, I don't have the tools to make the tools."

"If I brought engineers and tool makers to you, could you explain how to make the tools that make the tools?"

"No, I know some of the concepts, but I don't know the details. I don't need to; I just buy the tools. Or, I just buy a gun."

"Sounds like magic to me."

Eric wasn't happy that the distinction seemed so hard for Jhara to understand. Maybe time for a new subject. "Could you explain to me how to cast a spell?"

He half turned in surprise, and Eric concentrated on not falling off the horse. "You are a strange one." There was a pause as Jhara searched for the right words. "There are certain words, magic words, that can redirect energy. Sometimes that's just the energy that is everywhere. The small spells use it. But sometimes, when you want to do larger magic, you need a source of energy. The greatest mages harness storms or fires or other natural phenomena. Historically, that is also where the most damage has come from. Mages fighting each other tend to destroy the surrounding areas."

"But can anyone say the words? There's no special bloodline that enables only particular people to do magic?"

"It's a bit more involved than that, but yes. If you learn a spell, you can cast it."

"And can you cast it many times? As many as you want?"

"No, there is only so much energy in any place. Once it's gone, it takes time for it to come back. Some places have no energy at all. That's where magic can't work."

"And tell me, how do you learn to cast the spells?" Eric continued.

"Well, it takes a long time to learn the skills you need to be able to read the spell, and then you have to be guided to learn how to channel the energy required to actually cast it. We have whole universities that teach magic. You have to swear loyalty to advance further than the easiest spells. And some people never quite learn enough to be useful. So, the world is full of people like us. Those with just a few spells - enough to make a living as a troublemaker. But some know more spells than others."

"And who are the great mages?"

"Historically? They were the men who could wield enormous power and make great changes to the world."

"Men? No women?"

Jhara looked at Eric skeptically. "Women? They typically don't get too far in the study of magic."

"Why is that?"

"I don't know - too busy having babies, I guess. Or maybe they don't want to be magicians."

Eric frowned. "How many do you let into the universities?"

"Me? I don't run the universities. But it is harder for them to enter. When I attended, there were maybe three out of a class of a hundred."

Eric looked rueful. "Maybe there would be more women magicians if you let more into the universities."

"Sure, that's true. But some women don't even go to universities, and they do magic."

Eric shook his head. "You just finished telling me that you do spells by knowing the words to use and saying them. And you learn those words by reading them. But now you say that women don't need to do that?"

"There are more women healers than men, and no university teaches the advanced healing magic that women know."

"Have you seen anyone cast that advanced healing magic?"

"Sure, you get beaten down by enough monsters, and eventually you need all manner of healing cast on you."

"And was there any difference between the spells that they cast on you compared with the spells that you cast?"

Jhara considered how to answer. "The more powerful spells take longer to cast. You need to accumulate the power and release it in the way that is required for the particular spell. The healing spells we've had cast on us were more advanced than anything we could cast at the time. But no, they weren't any different. The healer called forth the power, then spoke the words, and healed us."

"And you can't remember the words?"

"Oh no, many people have tried to remember the words of a spell. Getting it wrong can be quite catastrophic. Especially in a battle. If you miscast even one of the spells we use, all sorts of fun things can happen. You'd think that the words of a spell would be similar or the same as the other spells. And I guess they are. For some of my spells, the words are the same. So I suppose it's the rhythm that you say them with or the gestures or something that make them different somehow. I don't watch other spellcasters to see how they do it: I'm concentrating on my own thing."

They rode along while Eric tried to digest all the information he'd just been given. There was always the chance he was being fed lies, but Jhara didn't seem to give a shit about anything and was incredibly candid. Not in the "I'll hide my lies under a smattering of truth" way, but more in the "here's all the truth, if you can't handle it, it's your problem" way. Eric had had one or two of those types of people in the restaurant. They didn't last long, but you always knew where you stood with them. And they responded to the unvarnished truth.

Presumably, then, the magic that had transferred him here would have had to be very powerful. And therefore, there would be few mages who could cast such a spell. Which would mean that there might even be one fewer if the caster had ended up on Earth. Otherwise, where was the caster when Eric had passed through?

"We're getting close," the mage said.

Hergsa broke away and scanned the horizon. In the hours they'd been riding, the forest had been left far behind them. The terrain continued to be rolling hills, with rocks peeking out of the dirt, and scrubs and clumps of barbed bracken. Further away from the barely detectable path, the hills became more jagged, leading to some dramatic slabs of rock, haphazardly arranged at weird angles, like some giants had played jenga with slabs of the mountainside. Judging from what had happened thus far in this world, Eric carefully looked around to ensure that was not in fact the case.

They dismounted near some scraggly-looking trees, tying the horses to the branches. Shields were retrieved from backs and backpacks appeared from saddlebags. Eric looked around. There was no sign of a tower or farms. "Hey, is this the right place? There's no farm or tower."

Lioko rolled his eyes. Jhara smirked and turned away.

Hergsa shook his head. "If you saw a pile of bodies in front of a door, what would you think was going to happen if you knocked on it?"

Eric shrugged. "I'd expect to join the bodies, I guess."

Hergsa turned to face him. "So why would you go through an entrance where you've already been told that people have not returned from? Seems a little silly, right?"

"OK, so where are we going instead?"

"We know that the cave complex that comes out at the tower and the farm has a few other entrances. One of them collapsed in what looks like a landslide. Another is home to a family of brethrets, and there's no way we're fighting those. Even one of them means certain death as our friends have already proven… which leaves this one."

"And this one is safe?"

All of them smirked. "There is no such thing as 'safe'. This is the best of the bunch. Some very distasteful people live here, Eric." Hergsa paused. "Touch nothing. You go at the back and carry the lantern. If you hear anything behind us, you click your tongue twice. This is important. Touch nothing. If there is a lever, do not pull it. If there is a chest, do not open it. If there is a statue, you can guarantee that it will come to life and attack us. If you trigger some sort of trap, then we might be attacked by more than we can handle. So do nothing that could unleash something. These are the rules."

Eric nodded. "Sure, I understand." Secretly, he was happy that there was no expectation of any sort of competence with his sword. "I guess I can fight one-handed."

Jhara smiled nastily. "You're more likely to cut your own leg off. Keep the light shining, you're carrying all the oil, so don't smash the lantern, or there's a chance you'll go up like a bonfire."

"What are we expecting to face?" Eric asked, finally realizing that he was voluntarily going into danger.

Jhara nodded. "I told you he'd be a chatty one. Some alchemists have set up shop in this branch of the caves. They have rented those out from the ogres. So, the theory is that the connection between their caves and the ogres should be lightly guarded. And with any luck, we'll find their water source, then use a little poison and we have no ogre problem anymore."

Eric was shocked. "You're going to poison them?"

"Well, did you expect us to kill them all? There are supposed to be over a hundred of them. They already killed twenty soldiers, so we can assume that probably half of them are trained and armed. If they formed a nice orderly queue, we could probably go through a hundred soldiers, but the awkward thing about trained men is that they don't take turns attacking you one after another. And that's considering there are no bowmen. Or anyone who can use magic."

"Won't the alchemists know magic?"

"Hopefully not, people that use chemicals tend to try and exercise their power using those rather than magic. The groups don't tend to overlap."

Hergsa the Knight turned to them with a scowl. "So, are we going to talk all day and hope the ogres die of old age?"

With that, they headed up the hill to where the gray slabs of stone were sitting in the afternoon shadow. As they approached the cliff face, Eric saw that the ground was strewn with stones, ranging in size, the largest being of the size of a man's head. At the base of the cliff was an opening, maybe ten feet tall, shaped like a rhombus. Or a trapezoid. Eric had never been good at geometry.

Hergsa showed him how to change the oil in the lantern, how to hide the light by closing the hatch on it, and how to light it, using the flint striker, which was tethered to the lantern by a stretch of light chain. Eric watched Hergsa closely, trying to figure out if there was any resentment in having to show what must have been pretty basic skills to someone, but there was no eye rolling or muttered insults. Eric already had a satchel with six flasks of oil slung over one shoulder. The bulbous flasks were made of soft leather and created a comforting pressure in the small of his back. He waited until the others had entered the cave, then took a deep breath, and stepped in behind them.

The cave mouth opened onto a corridor that seemed more like a void, formed when great slabs of stone had shifted. This meant that the ceiling would be the flat underside of some seam of rock, cocked at a jaunty angle for twenty feet, then there would be an odd-shaped gap, and then some other form of ceiling continuing afterward. A chaotic collection of mismatched walls and ceilings only brought to Eric the fact that they were at the mercy of whatever cave-ins might or might not happen. And there was a lot of stone suspended above them.

The light was steady in the lantern, though the crazy rock cast weird shadows, and the silhouettes of the other men frequently obscured the proportions and the direction of the corridor. The only sounds were the clink of the armor and the scuffing of leather against the stone walls. Eventually, the corridor seemed to stop, until Eric got closer and could see that the end point of the corridor was in fact a wall with foot holds carved into it. About twenty feet above them, the corridor continued. Far above that, Eric could just make out the afternoon sky, a brief gray-blue rectangle amongst the darkness of the tunnels.

Lioko went first, holding his sword in his mouth as he climbed, his shield on his back, and the footholds sufficiently deep enough to support his weight and provide good grip for his gloved hands. He made good time with his climb. After a brief pause upon reaching the top, he made a point of stealthily slithering over the lip and then signaled for the others to come up.

Hergsa took the lantern up with him. When Eric gave him a questioning glance, he whispered that if they were attacked at the top of the corridor, they would need to see, and therefore, couldn't be left in the dark the whole time until Eric gets to the top. Eric could see the logic but hated waiting for his turn in the deepening shadows at the bottom of the cliff. He wasted no time after he was given the signal to climb up. And reclaimed the lantern.

The new corridor was not natural. It had been hacked out of the stone with tools, which had left marks along the walls, ceilings, and floor. Whoever had carved the corridor, must have been the same height as humans or been given instructions to make the corridor that size, because there was plenty of room for them to stand up, and almost enough room for two of them to stand beside each other. This also meant plenty of space to swing a sword.

The mage pulled out a scroll and started making marks on it. Eric got closer and was disappointed that it was not magical. He was marking out a map of sorts - or more of a sketch of one. A tiny corridor, ending in the footholds, was obviously indicating their entrance point. They headed forward along the path, the mage counting the paces and marking every hundred on the map. The corridor was gradually leading downwards. They continued in this manner for maybe thirty minutes before the terrain changed.

Eric didn't see it immediately; he first noticed the change in the body language of the others. They were more alert now, more careful with their footing, scanning their surroundings with more vigor. They spread out when they arrived at the clearing, and Eric held the lantern higher than normal so that the light would illuminate the inside of the room.

The room was large - probably about the same size as his restaurant back home if you included both front and back, and laid out in the same rectangular shape. They'd entered along one of the shorter walls. The area around the entrance was a jumble of crates and barrels, possibly at one stage nicely lined up but deteriorated into a mismatch of shapes and sizes since then. The containers filled about half the space, the shadows receding once Eric got to the middle of the room. On its far side, a single door faced them. It was closed. Around its edges, Eric could make out a soft orange glow - maybe a fireplace in a room on the other side?

Eric waited until the others made their way to the other side of the room, each one taking their time and looking around. He was surprised that none of them opened any barrels or crates, but then maybe storage rooms weren't where treasure was kept. Apparently, the mage had finished the map because at some point they gathered at the door and gestured for him to join them.

He stood directly in front of the door while the knight began to open it, achingly slowly. The mage and healer stood to either side of the door. Jhara stood beside him, his sword in hand and jaw flexing. He still wasn't wearing his helmet; Eric would have to ask him about that when they got someplace that they could talk.

The door opened into a corridor, and Eric was beckoned forward after the mage and healer, who had followed the knight out into the corridor, each of them moving slowly. The mage briefly trailed one hand along the wall, looking at his fingers puzzled before returning

222

to marking the number of steps on the map. The orange glow that Eric had seen turned out to be a half dozen torches held to the wall by metal sconces. A scar of soot on the stone wall indicated that the torches or their predecessors had been burning here for a long time. The corridor itself seemed much more finished than the last one they'd seen. It had two branches, one heading left and one right from the storeroom. The others had turned right, so that's the way Eric went. He made sure to peer down the left side before he followed everyone, not wanting to be stabbed in the back. Jhara pulled the door closed gently and followed closely behind, slowly walking backward more often than not.

Ahead, the corridor branched off again, the spur running for about twenty feet before ending with two doors facing each other. One of them was open, but no light spilled out from the room beyond. The mage looked at the knight, who nodded before returning to face the corridor ahead. The mage hurried after him, glancing briefly into the room before returning to his place in the party. He murmured the word "bedroom" as they progressed forward.

Eric was worried. There was the corridor to the left of the storeroom, there were one, maybe two bedrooms from the side corridor. Was he the only one concerned about having so much unknown real estate behind them? If they were discovered, they would be in danger of having more opponents approaching from two other sources behind. The party seemed to know what they were doing, so he kept his opinions to himself. But did they know what they were doing? They seemed powerful enough to back-talk the queen, but did that prove any success in terms of dungeon raiding? Had they been lucky with the dungeons they'd been in? He bumped into the mage who turned and glared at him. He sheepishly held up the non-lantern-carrying hand in apology and looked around. The corridor came to a stop at a large wooden door. Eric was used to rectangular, tall, thin doors, with a door jamb around the edge, which tended to block most of the light beyond. And there was always a door handle, usually a knob or lever for opening. So far, in inns and castles, he had seen arched doorways, almost as wide as they were tall, and the doors blocking them had ranged from thin strips of wood with finger-width gaps between the boards at the flimsiest end of the scale, all the way up to the one in front of them. The door facing them had been bound by three strips of a dark metal running side to side, and some sort of black sealant or glue had been used between the boards. The wood itself was incredibly dark and, judging by the shiny reflections the lantern light was picking up, seemed to have been stained or varnished at some point. If he had to guess, Eric would have picked the thickness of the wood as being probably half a foot deep. *Would that sealant make it airproof or waterproof?* The party assembled before the door, and the knight made to push it open.

Eric had seen enough police shows on TV to know that when trained teams burst into a room, they were supposed to look in all directions to make sure that the attacking force wasn't ambushed by anyone hiding behind the door. So he was a bit surprised when the door was pushed open, with some effort by the looks of things, and then the party hustled haphazardly into the room.

The room was about the same size as the storeroom that they had entered through, but it was split into two levels. They were on the upper one and were protected from a ten-foot drop by a five-foot balcony of stone, carved out in intricate shapes. In the middle of the balcony, a staircase connected the levels, a single set of stairs heading down to the one below. A door on the far side of the lower level was the only other obvious way of getting in and out, and at first glance, there was nothing else alive in the room, no danger apparent.

The upper level had more barrels and a workbench with glassware and chemistry-type equipment. The lower level was bare, save for a large checkerboard, which was laid out to cover the entire space in front of the door. So even if you jumped the fifteen feet from the balcony to the lower floor, you would still have to deal with that obvious trap.

The knight headed toward the workbench, followed by the others, but Eric caught the glint of something on the ground in front of them. "Wait!" he said. But it was too late.

Chapter 11

The knight stumbled on the trip wire and tumbled to the ground. Behind him came a slam as the door swung shut, Eric turning in time to see Jhara move toward the giant metal ring in the center of the door. The knight got up almost immediately, retrieving his sword, and walked in a much more relaxed fashion toward the workbench.

"Always the tripwire," said the healer at normal volume.

The knight turned his head and laughed. "It's this fucking helmet, I can never see near my feet."

Eric looked from person to person, confused why they were being so noisy. The mage saw him and smiled. "With that noise, anything nearby would have heard us, and we've lost the element of surprise. Until we leave this room of course. But the thing about dungeons is that you usually can't pass off that sort of noise as just being the wind. Or a dog in the night."

"Bring the light over, Prince," called out the knight. He was by the workbench and had levered the top off a barrel. Eric came over, holding the lantern up to allow more light to fall on the surface of the liquid. "What do you think it is?" he asked. Eric's eyes watered being this close to the liquid. It wasn't anything flammable, but he'd been around cleaning products and industrial fluids enough to know that whatever it was, it was strong.

"Probably water," answered the healer before Eric could say anything. "Hey, remember the time when all our equipment got stolen, and we ended up in that sorcerer's den? You found that barrel of water - smaller than this one, and you were going to try and use that as armor?"

The knight laughed, pausing above the barrel. "That's right, and the tap of the barrel was at groin height, and you were going to–"

The door on the lower level burst open and two robed figures walked in, standing just in front of the checkerboard. They bellowed something, the tone, volume, and indignation translating 'What are you doing here?' even if Eric could not understand the words. He was just realizing that the earworm wasn't translating these two newcomers when the two figures ran across the checkerboard, tracing out a pattern of steps on the squares that Eric was too slow to understand he should note. They walked toward the stairs as the others of the party made their way to the top of the stairs and waited.

The stairs were wide enough for both the knight and healer to be side by side, the mage and Jhara standing a little further back and slightly off to the side, which allowed them to see the newcomers going up the steps over the top of the balcony. Eric stood awkwardly, holding the lantern high, and wondering if he should draw his sword.

The knight bellowed. "Hold the top of the stairs, we have the high ground!"

The two robed figures climbed the stairs slowly, gesticulating and chanting more words in the unknown language. Then Eric saw his first magic. The mage pointed at the robed figure on the right and spoke a few words. From the air around his hand, a glow of light intensified until it reached a point that was painful to look at. At that point, it formed a finger-length line, like a dart or a short arrow, and zoomed straight at the robed figure, prompting a yelp and a brief cessation of the gestures and chanting. The other one completed whatever it was - a dance? a ritual? And hurled a jar of something at the knight. It was a small pottery jar, maybe the size of both fists held together and flew true like a baseball. It burst on the shield of the knight and small shards of the pottery went flying everywhere. That didn't seem to be the point of the missile, though, so the sticky black liquid that had been held within stuck to the shield. It was even more viscous than oil - more like very dark maple syrup or molasses, but shot through with sparks of the white-blue light that the mage had hit the newcomers with. The knight grunted through his helmet and threw his shield down the stairs at the approaching alchemists. It was a bad throw, resulting in the shield clattering into the shadows on the floor below. When Eric returned his attention to the knight, he was standing holding his sword in both hands.

The healer was waiting for the alchemists to get to the top of the stairs, concentrating on holding his position beside the knight, readying the oversized hammer, and loosening his shoulder muscles. Jhara was apparently casting some sort of spell, the occasional word barely discernible over the clatter of metal and clank against the stone.

At last, the two alchemists made it to the top of the stairs. Eric blinked in disbelief. Their hands were on fire. At least that's what it looked like. An eerie green fire flickered over their leather gloves; metal studs were visible through the flames. Eric looked for any sign of a liquid dripping off the gloves and falling on the floor, but couldn't see anything. Maybe it was a trick? A liquid that burnt prettily to scare people?

That idea went out the window when the healer struck at the closest alchemist. He missed as the alchemist swayed out of reach. On the follow-through, the alchemist punched him square in the side of the head. A shower of sparks erupted from the impact point, and the healer screeched. Eric could see from his vantage point that there was a large scorch mark on the side of his face and he could smell singed hair.

The knight was having a better time, his sword point tracing lazy figure eights in the air while he waited for an opening. The alchemist in front of him was also looking for an opening. Any forward and backward movement was made a lot harder by the stairs. Eventually, he stepped forward and aimed a punch at the knight. The sword was slower than the punch, but Eric saw the knight shrug and deflect the force of the blow off his shoulder while allowing the alchemist to get closer. The knight pivoted, bringing his sword across the body of the alchemist, the robes ripping open in a spray of blood. The alchemist's body toppled off the side of the stairs, landing with a sickening crunch on the floor below.

Eric glanced over to Jhara who was still gesticulating, brow furrowed in concentration, beads of sweat on his forehead. Flickering lights drew beams from the shadows, their intensity increasing as they spun around his head. Eric wasn't sure what spell it was, but judging by the length of time it was taking, he figured it might be a big one.

The healer thudded to the ground, sparks dissipating from where the now last-standing alchemist had struck him. The mage called out to the knight and grabbed the healer's body, dragging it away from the top of the stairs, beside the balcony. The knight swung his sword wildly, more to distract the alchemist than to try to hit him, and it worked - the alchemist had to concentrate on where he was putting his feet to avoid toppling off the stairs. The battle had seemed a foregone conclusion until Eric realized there was someone else who had crossed the checkerboard and was now removing a sword from his scabbard.

The newcomer was dressed in a dusty red leather armor, all straps and studs. He was well-built, tall, and broad across the shoulders, with a square face, showing a well-groomed goatee, lined with jet-black hair, cut short. Eric half expected the man's sword to be on fire or to attract sparks, or lightning, or something, but it was nothing special. Eric placed the lantern on the floor and ran over to the healer's body. "What can I do?" he asked the mage. The mage looked over to the knight who was backing away from the top of the stairs while the last alchemist followed, his glowing fists even brighter than they had originally been. The mage looked like he was going to say something but instead stood up and started yelling guttural words. Shit.

Eric realized he would be useless in a sword fight. Observing the way that the man in red was holding his sword, it was clear this wasn't his first rodeo. Eric looked around, desperate to find a way to contribute to the fight. Maybe the barrel was holding something dangerous enough to work as an area-effect weapon. Then, it might get both the alchemist and the man in red. He ran over to the workbench. Behind him, he heard curses, clangs, and crashes. There was even a thwip! as something whizzed past his ear, a small explosion momentarily illuminating the workbench in blue and green. He pulled the lid back on the barrel. Years of obeying health and safety regulations inflicted a momentary shock of guilt - this certainly didn't count as moving bulk liquids in a safe and controlled manner. He glanced over his shoulder. Things had changed - the mage and the knight were both down! There was no sign of the alchemist, but the man in red was looking right at him as he wiped his sword on the mage's robes.

By this time, Jhara had finished whatever he'd been doing and was now swinging his sword in an intricate pattern, standing beside the balcony. A soft blue glow surrounded him, making shadows dance as he maneuvered toward the man in red. He dismissed Eric with a sneer and turned toward Jhara. As the man in red closed the distance to Jhara, Jhara hopped up onto the balcony, and then, in the same motion, leaped off it, flipping backward to the floor below. Eric could not see him down there, but the man in red wasted no time following him, doing a slightly less elegant jump from the balcony.

Seizing the opportunity, Eric rocked the barrel on its bottom rim. He was not confident that the lid would seal the barrel, so could not drop the barrel onto its side and roll it. Instead, he got the weight of it onto the rim and rotated it, trying to mostly keep it upright. He spun it along this rim until he got closer to the stairs. He figured he could wait until Jhara got away and then try and roll the barrel down the stairs, aiming at the man in red. It was something, anyway. He banished the thoughts that it was only water or some other innocuous liquid. He made it to the bodies of the mage, the healer, and the knight, avoiding looking too closely at them. Being that near to the stairs, he could see the man in red and Jhara below, fighting.

Jhara danced like a gymnast, leaping over the red man's sword gracefully, before launching attacks of his own, darting forward, feinting, and parrying in a sensuous single movement that never really seemed to end. There were a few dents in his armor though, and a jagged gash in his chain mail. The man in red was his equal. While Jhara was all bodily elegance, the man in red was less physically showy and all swordplay. The blade always seemed to be ready for Jhara, parrying and counter-attacking with an ever-increasing speed. The man in red was trying to back Jhara toward the wall between levels, but Jhara was too dexterous to allow that to happen, pivoting and spinning until the stairs were to his back. The man in red found himself beside the two bodies of the alchemists. Without taking his eyes off Jhara, he crouched slightly, touching the body of the closest alchemist, and speaking a few words. Jhara attacked again, but was parried and countered. He then had to step back to ensure he wasn't hit. The man in red was taking advantage of the reaction, stepping over to the other alchemist's body, and repeating the crouch and touch.

Blinking uncertainly, both alchemists got up off the floor. Eric was sure that the one he'd seen fall must have had broken bones, if only from the fall, let alone the wounds from the knight. He could see no evidence of their wounds at all. Jhara noted that the balance had definitely moved against him and started up the stairs. The man in red pointed after him and bellowed something. Both alchemists hurried after him, closely followed by the man in red.

Eric levered the lid off the barrel and heaved against it, trying to topple it. It resisted him. Over the barrel, he could see the head and shoulders of Jhara as he reached the top of the stairs. He redoubled his efforts, turning so his back was to the barrel and squatting, so that he could use his legs to get more leverage. Success! He felt it moving as he looked up at Jhara who had jumped over both the barrel and Eric. Eric concentrated on rolling free as he toppled after the barrel. It tipped all its contents down the stairs, the stone sizzling and smoking as, whatever the liquid was, it interacted with it. Jeez, if that's what it did to the stone, what would it do to people?

Eric got to his feet and looked over the balcony. Both alchemists were screaming, their legs below the knees missing. Splashes of the liquid were burning wherever they touched. Behind them, the man in red was looking at his own legs in disbelief. The armor was in tatters and he was missing huge chunks of flesh. Steam or smoke was still rising from the stone of the stairs. Jhara walked past Eric, down the stairs, stepping very carefully on the edges of each step to avoid what was left of the liquid, until he came to the two alchemists. With two swings of his sword, their severed heads rolled down the remaining steps. They didn't seem to notice. The act felt like a mercy.

The man in red looked up as Jhara approached and snarled something at him, but Jhara didn't pause and hacked him down with his sword. The man in red tried to block the swing, but lying on the ground with very little maneuverability or leverage made the gesture only partially successful. Jhara made short work of him, the savage butchery in stark contrast to the elegant sword dancing he had previously performed.

Eric let out a breath he hadn't known he'd been holding and looked around. The door on the upper floor was still closed and the lantern still burnt, illuminating the workbench and the bodies of the party. Apart from the sizzling of the stone and his own breath in his ears, it was completely silent.

Jhara climbed back up the stairs and knelt beside the healer. Raising a hand to the ceiling, he said some words. The summoned power gathered light, which competed with the lantern light, casting the healer's head in a cold blue light. "Go down and loot the bodies. Let me know if anything else comes through that door. Take the lantern."

Eric nodded and grabbed the lantern. He tiptoed down the stairs, keeping to the edges like he had seen Jhara do, trying to avoid any remnants of the liquid. To be fair, there wasn't much left anyway. But it had left scars on the steps, splashes and drops, burning holes and gouges into the surface. There were maybe two small puddles of it that he very tentatively stepped over on the way down.

And then he got to the bodies. The very first thing he did when he reached them was vomit. Everything in his stomach came out loudly and messily, eventually Eric aimed over the edge of the stairs. Feeling drained, he looked back up to see Jhara watching him. His head disappeared and was replaced by flickering blue light, so Eric figured the healing was continuing. Or was he raising the dead? He hadn't heard any breathing or seen any pulses from the other members of the party. He hadn't had the opportunity to check either, so he didn't know if they had just been unconscious or if they had died. Would they have enough to continue or would they turn back? Their first fight had almost ended catastrophically. Maybe this quest was too difficult for them.

He returned to the task at hand. The recently beheaded body was still seeping blood from the neck, and the rest of it that he could see was a gray-blue color. He gingerly patted down the body, glad that there was no face staring back at him. He eased the gloves off. They were more rigid than he thought they would be, stiff leather with a fist-sized bulge of metal sewn into the back of them. He put them in his satchel. A coin purse also made its way into the bag, as well as a gold chain. How had he come to this? He was robbing the dead and killing people. This was not the path he had chosen for himself.

The second body also revealed gauntlets, a coin purse, and this time - two gold rings. All went into the satchel. He looked around. There was no sign that Jhara would be ready any time soon. Also, he still had yet to inspect the man in red's body. He made his way further down the stairs.

The red armor had certainly seen better days. There were big gaps where a splash of liquid had burned its way through or was damaged by a sword blow. Checking this one turned out to be easier as there were no pouches or purses. There was nothing of value on the body either, just a knotted piece of string around the man's neck. It resembled a necklace without adornment and was made of a few strands of rope, plaited together. The sword lay nearby, a little longer than Eric's and a lot thicker, too heavy for him to comfortably wield, though lifting it two-handed was certainly easy enough. The flickering on the upper level continued, the occasional low murmur of voices accompanying it.

Eric shone the lantern further around the floor of the lower level, getting closer to the door and the checkerboard in front of it. This is where the alchemists had come from, so he was on alert for any sign of additional foes. He was ready to scamper back up the stairs at the merest suggestion of an untoward sound. As he got closer to the checkerboard, he could see that the liquid had certainly had an effect on its surface. Whereas there were gouges and signs of impact on the stone stairs, there was very little left of the checkerboard. Either it was made of thinner or softer stone or it was susceptible to whatever the liquid had been. Below the checkerboard, he could see a pit. Five of the squares of the board had been supported by pillars rising up from the floor. The rest of the floor of the pit was covered with spikes. It appeared that if you did not stand on the squares supported by one of the pillars, you would naturally fall through the wooden square into the pit below, and presumably be pierced by one or more of the spikes. If you were lucky, you would fall straight down and "only" get pierced through the feet. If you lost balance and pitched forward, there was a good chance you would land lengthwise on the spikes and enjoy an acupuncture session all the way along your front.

He wasn't even keen on trying to jump from square to square, knowing where the pillars were. He would wait until the rest of the party were ready to rejoin him. The leap between pillars was not far, barely an exaggerated hop, but he was sure if there was anything slippery underfoot, it would surely lead to spiky time. There was nothing else of interest in the lower level, so he headed up the stairs to check out the alchemist's workstation.

He passed the others from the party, all lying on the floor at the top. They looked about done in. Glancing at his passing, they barely managed weak smiles. He continued past them, trying to give them time to regain their composure. There was a soft glow from Jhara's sword which illuminated the group. They obviously didn't need the lantern. So, instead, Eric went over to the workbench. Now that he was getting an idea of how the alchemists operated and the way that the gauntlets had worked, he could see how the workbench might support that.

There was metal working gear - not anvils and blacksmith-type tools, more the finer tools like those jewelers used. There were also leather working awls and needles, such as some he recalled from shop class in high school. The chemicals were many and varied, some jars on the workbench and others in bulk, like the barrel he had used in combat. There were labels on some of them, but in such hieroglyphs, they were useless. It's not as if they were in some vaguely familiar Earth language so he could read them, allowing him the small chance of trying to figure out what they might contain.

Jhara came over. "You did well. We'll need a couple of more minutes before we continue, but then we'll be good to go."

Eric looked over his shoulder to the recuperating party members. "I wanted to ask them what it was like to die, or were they just unconscious? If there was a tunnel of light or Saint Peter at the gates."

Jhara's eyes widened, and he moved closer. His voice was an insistent hiss. "Oh, no. You don't ask them anything like that. That's not something you ask a man. That's between him and his god. Or his conscience."

"But they would be able to clear up so many questions. What happens after we die, that sort of thing."

Jhara shook his head. "No. Just, no. I sometimes wonder if we lose a part of ourselves each time we come back from the brink. Some people never come back. Small wounds, very healable. But they just don't come back. The worst ones are when they come back but they're… changed."

Eric wanted to know more, but something about Jhara's demeanor dissuaded him. Instead, they waited for maybe another five minutes before they were ready to continue. They took their time hopping from pillar to pillar in front of the door, leading away from the lower level. The door on the other side opened easily, and they returned to the previous marching order, Eric glad for his position toward the rear. The corridor continued straight on. Then there came a slight stirring in the air. Fresh air was coming from ahead of them. They came to a tee section with indistinguishable corridors, leading both to the left and the right. The fresh air was coming from their right.

Jhara came up behind Eric as they paused. "If we were on a normal mission, we would head to the right, secure our exit, search for treasure, and then come back here and continue on to go deeper. Because we're working for she-who-must-be-obeyed, we're going to turn left and go deeper."

"Oh, so you do know that you are exposing your rear to the other parts of the alchemist's area, plus whatever is between us and the outside world?"

Jhara cocked an eyebrow. "Oh yes, we are definitely aware of that, your majesty."

Chapter 12

They walked along long passageways, more often than not on a downward angle. Eric wasn't looking forward to the return trip: all the uphill ramps would be murder on his quads. They had been moving for maybe half an hour, Eric watching the mage make the measurements and markings on the map all the way, before they could see the flickering of lights ahead. Jhara whispered in Eric's ear. "Close the window on the lantern."

Eric did as he was bid, closing the little door on the front of the lantern, which almost doused all the light coming from it. As he did so, the others were still, all of them as one, listening to the rock and stone around them. Ahead, they could hear the movements of many people. Not the martial sounds of armor and weapons, more the low murmuring of regular folk going about their business. The occasional guffaw of a joke. Mothers calling out to their kids and the corresponding shrieks thereof.

They crept forward, occasional scuffling of leather or creaking of the armor were the only noises. And even then, it was quiet enough that the noises coming from up the corridor well and truly drowned it out. The corridor ahead entered a cavernous space and passed over it to the other side like a catwalk above a factory floor. The corridor continued to be made of stone. Eric was not sure how it was suspended as there were no ropes or other cabling attaching it to the ceiling, which was only about ten feet above them, but about fifty feet above the floor of the cavern. This was covered by a sprawling city, or so it seemed.

The unit of habitation was an open-air tent, with four posts covered in fabric or furs attached on three sides. The beds were made of multiple layers of furs that were the only things within. They weren't laid out in uniform rows and columns, but more haphazardly filling the space, with the only planning rule appearing to be that the vacant fourth wall of each dwelling should never face the vacant fourth wall of any other dwelling. It didn't take Eric too long to figure out why. They didn't need a roof if there was no rain, they were underground after all. And apparently, there were no leaking ceilings from overhead water sources. So, for privacy's sake, you wouldn't want to see into your neighbor's home.

The creatures moving around had to be the ogres he had been told about. They were not too much different from humans but were taller and leaner. Eric didn't know how that worked with subterranean people. Surely, they should be short like dwarfs?

Otherwise, they would be forever bumping into the ceilings of low corridors. While they were definitely slimmer and probably about seven feet tall on average, they also had a rather prominent pot belly. Even the children and women. They were similar in coloration to Eric himself, with a splattering of lighter or darker splotches, randomly applied. Facially they looked like some of the edgier baristas Eric had encountered in coffee houses, except their piercings and aloof attitudes were matched by a protruding tooth and slightly pained expression. It was weird. This was Eric's first encounter with a non-human race. He was fascinated. They were so different from humans, and yet so very similar. Not like bad science fiction on TV where they just added some glue on prosthetics and gave them all character names with Xs and apostrophes.

There were numerous exits from the cavern below, and there didn't seem to be any restriction of movement. Periodically, one or two of the ogres would leave the area or return, sometimes holding a large mushroom over their shoulder like a bale of hay. Eric could have spent hours watching them from his vantage point, trying to figure out how many there were and how they constructed their society, pecking order, that sort of thing, but he was gently nudged from behind. He looked up to see that the rest of his group had reached the other side of the catwalk and were waiting for him and Jhara to join them.

He crouched-walked across to them. "How many of them are there?" he whispered.

The mage glanced past him. "Maybe a few thousand. In that cavern at least. We don't know their fighting strength - is it one in ten? Or one in fifty? It makes a big difference."

Eric nodded. No wonder the Queen was interested in neutralizing them. Such a lovely euphemism. There might be a thousand soldiers on her back doorstep. That's a dangerous position to be in if you were at war. But the ogres weren't what he was expecting. They looked more like *people* and less like monsters. Were they really going to poison them all?

The knight turned from his position at the head of the party. "We have to find their water supply. It's the only way to get them all."

"Are we really going to poison them all? There are women and children down there."

The knight looked taken aback. Then he frowned and looked expectantly at Jhara before turning to continue along the corridor. Jhara came up to Eric.

"Having second thoughts, Eric? Poisoning a little less of a noble act than you are used to?"

Eric wasn't sure what to say. So, he said nothing.

246

"We owe a vow of fealty to the queen. She has given us land and a busted-up castle in exchange for aiding her when she needs it. We have begged off any involvement in wars which pisses her off majorly. So, she asks us to do the things that she can't do herself. Things that she can't ask her noble knights to do either. True, some of those things are distasteful. But we can't just not do them. And we certainly don't need someone without that level of obligation making us feel like shit when we are doing what we have to do."

"So, you're just following orders?"

"Something like that. Ask yourself what will happen if we don't do this thing." Eric thought of Imogen and Anton. "Could you live with yourself? That's the equation."

"And living with the consequences?" he asked.

"That's life," Jhara said bitterly as he followed the others down the corridor.

Eric followed behind sullenly.

The corridor continued along and then turned a corner. They waited until they were all together. There was something about this corridor that seemed different from the other one they had been traveling along, even though the walls were the same stone. Eric looked around. The corridor was long and straight and that by itself was unusual. They were not used to looking a hundred feet down a corridor. Great visibility. They could see anyone coming the other way. The ceiling also confused Eric. It started forty feet above them and came down at a forty-five-degree angle to meet the ten-foot ceiling level for the rest of the corridor about halfway along. He just could not see what purpose that served. Almost like someone had decided they wanted a forty-foot-tall corridor and then changed their mind while it was being built.

They crept along it, cautious about where they put their feet, and looking at the walls and floors for any signs of traps or clues as to why they were all on edge. They had reached the halfway point, where the ceiling was now only ten feet high but consistent for the rest of the corridor.

"I don't like this," Eric said quietly.

The mage turned to him, one hand on his map, the other holding the nub of charcoal he was using to write with. "Look, nobody wants to kill all these ogres either–"

"I mean the corridor. Something feels wrong," interrupted Eric.

"I feel it too," said Jhara. "No hatches in the ceiling for boiling oil. Now that we're away from the larger ceiling, there are places for hidden archers, and if any come from the end of the corridor, we can hide behind the knight's shield."

They continued, getting closer and closer to the other end. The knight felt it first, taking a step and managing a grunt, looking at his feet. Jhara, behind Eric, managed to get out a "What the–?" and then they all started sliding forwards. The corridor floor tipped beneath them. Eric half turned as he slid to see past Jhara. Behind them, the whole corridor floor had pivoted and was pointing up to the angled ceiling. The floor was all one piece and so their end had dropped down like a seesaw, sliding them into a room that had been hidden underneath. They landed in a tangle of limbs, and it took them a few minutes to extricate themselves. Eric, thinking quickly, had cushioned the lantern from the collision at the bottom of the ramp with his body, hoping that it would stop it from spilling lit oil over all of them.

Thanking his lucky stars, Eric shone the lantern around their new position. They were in a stone room, about ten feet cubed with a wooden hatch in the ceiling. With a creak, the slide that had deposited them in the room swung back to the vertical. Eric shone the lantern up to see what had happened. There was a forty-foot ramp leading back the way they had come, the ceiling in fact being the underside of the corridor floor that up until very recently they had been walking on. Effectively, they had been striding along a thin layer of stone that pivoted in the middle. The start of the corridor had been supported by the stone below, but the second half had a ramp under it. Their combined weight had dropped that down, the corridor they had been walking along tipping into the air, sliding them down into the ten-foot room. When the slide had no more weight on it, it tipped back up to a horizontal position.

Now they were trapped. "Looks like there are only two ways out," Eric said. "Either someone else comes along and gets caught by the trap, we jump over them as they slide, and pin the slide down with our weight…"

"Or we get out through that hatch in the ceiling," Jhara finished.

"Or we get out through that hatch in the ceiling," Eric repeated.

The healer and knight started to work out the logistics of how they might manage to lift each other to reach the underside of the hatch while Eric looked around the room. It was small so it didn't take him too much time to study it. The only thing that looked out of place was a black gemstone with dust on it, placed on the floor, in the corner. It was about the size of Eric's fist and seemed to be half embedded in the stone. Either that or it was only a half-fist-sized stone stuck onto the flat floor. The only way to tell seemed to be to try and pry it out. Jhara came over to check it out too while Eric was examining it. Nothing happened when Eric gingerly pushed it. So, it wasn't a button. He glanced up at Jhara who looked exasperated.

"We were in a pit trap a little like this about a year ago. Tulli, you don't know him - he was the mage before Firsl joined us - found a button like that one there. We didn't have a hatch in the ceiling and the pit was deeper. Much deeper. Before we could stop him, he had pushed the button and water started coming into the top of the pit. There's a reason I said not to touch anything."

Eric gulped. "Sorry. So, what happened to the mage?"

Jhara sighed. "He thought he was fine as he was in his robes. He got them off so they wouldn't drag him down and floated to the top of the pit as the water rose. He thought he was very clever. 'Sorry about that!' he called down to us."

"Why were you at the bottom of the pit? Didn't you swim up to the top as well?"

Jhara tapped his breastplate. "Plate mail armor. Good against swords, spears, and clubs. Not known for its buoyancy. The three of us were stuck on the bottom until our breath would run out. This usually means death because it takes so long to get off. Fortunately, the button also opened a secret door which allowed us to walk out and climb the ladder out of the water next door."

"What happened to the mage? Did he catch up with you?"

"Unfortunately, there was a slime clinging to the ceiling above the pit. The mage floated up and was dissolved. He didn't figure it out until he was encased by the slime. There was nothing left of him but our memories and his final words. 'Sorry about that!' How do you plan on getting the stone out?"

Eric tried hard not to think about being in a flooding hole and then being enveloped in a lime green jelly. He focused on the gemstone instead. He cast around for something he could use to leverage the gemstone out of the encasing stone. He unsheathed his sword, thinking he could pry it out. Jhara stopped him. "No self-respecting swordsman would use his blade in such a way. You'll notch it and since it is so thin, it might even snap if you put too much stress on it."

Eric nodded and put his sword away. The sword of the man in red was still slung across his back. He was very thankful that he had kept the sheath as well. Falling down the slide would have been more dangerous with a naked blade flapping around. He unlimbered it from his back and unsheathed it.

"That's better," said Jhara. "Hang on, let me have a look at it." He bent over and looked at the stone, spitting on his finger and rubbing it. "It's black but covered in dust. Not the shiny black of obsidian, mind, but a dull black. If you had enough of it, you could carve a figurine or use it to craft game pieces. Or even dishes. That would be the envy of your neighbors because they would look different from anything that they would have. But it's not a valuable stone. You're probably wasting your time."

"Could it be magical?"

Jhara stepped back so that the mage could get closer. Firsl barely paused. "Definitely not. I'm not detecting anything magical about it at all."

"Ah well, I'll still try. You never know."

"Sure, your funeral."

Eric got the point of the sword into the groove around the edge of the stone. Levering it back and forth did very little, except grate a little of the surrounding rock into a fine dust. Funny, that didn't seem to be the type of dust that had been on the stone when they arrived. Behind him, the healer and knight were having a heated discussion about who would be better on top and who would be best to support the other. Jhara went over to help, only to increase the raised voices in the discussion to three. Eric ignored them and redoubled his efforts with the stone. One more voice would just add to the din, so he might as well focus on something else. If it wasn't a button, then what was it doing there? It didn't look like it naturally occurred in this place, so what was it for? Who had put it there? He gouged a good line in the rock with the sword. That was some sort of progress anyway. Behind him, the discussion now included the mage who was making the very reasonable suggestion that he be at the top of the pile of bodies, and that maybe they should form a pyramid with the knight and Jhara on the bottom and the healer in the middle.

"Tonight, drama at the National High School Cheerleader Championships!" Eric muttered to himself. The gouge was able to be enlarged a little with judicious use of force with the sword. He could see what Jhara meant. Nicks were appearing along the edge. It was fine though; he couldn't use the sword as it was too big. Also, the others had assured him it wasn't magical, so it was just treasure to be sold once they were out of the dungeon. In terms of value per weight, it was actually more beneficial to find a sack of coins with the same weight. So, it was disposable as far as Eric was concerned. Which meant that he was quite enthusiastic when it came to trying to get that stone out of the rock around it. He started making good progress. The noises behind him changed from vocal disagreements to grunts of effort and scuffling. "It moved! It's almost out!" he said, half-turning.

The mage had indeed managed to scale the others and was balancing precariously on the hunched back of the healer. One of the mage's feet was on the healer's thigh, the other was firmly planted in the middle of his back. The healer wasn't having much fun as the mage tried to find a supportive position. The mage was probably a couple of feet away from the hatch, making it a little more than ten feet high. Eric returned to his effort and jammed the point of the sword into the significant gash that he'd managed to get into the rock. Using brute force, he pushed his entire weight and strength at the hilt of the sword. With a pop, the stone came out and rolled to a halt in the corner of the room.

"Ha! I got it!" He bent and looked at it closely. It didn't seem worse for wear, all the damage done by the sword had been inflicted on the wall. Feeling very chuffed, he placed it in the satchel and turned to see how far the others had gotten to the hatch.

The mage was standing with both feet on the back of the healer. His hands were just about scraping the underside of the hatch when it flew open, and a small object fell amongst them, smashing on the ground. Once again, the hatch shut with a thud. It was unexpected enough to topple the mage. The shift in weight on his back toppled the healer too. The four of them collapsed into a pile of bodies and curses. The object which had been dropped into their room started sizzling and hissing, making Eric feel faint. Whatever it was, it was fast acting. As Eric slunk to the floor, he distinctly heard someone above saying, "I'm glad there are no large ones - they're always so heavy!" before he passed out.

Chapter 13

Eric awoke in a cell. His arms felt like they were manacled behind his back, and his mouth was gagged with something unclean that stank of sheep or some other animal. He tried hard not to gag, breathing through his nose. His head hurt and his lungs felt like he had run a marathon or smoked a shipping container of cigarettes. He looked around. He was in a prison, that much was clear. Each cell was large, but there were no benches around the edges or any other form of comfort, just a thin layer of straw on the floor and conflicting smells, none of them pleasant. The other members of the party were there, similarly trussed up. They were all still wearing their armor, but no weapons were in sight. Eric's satchel was missing, as were both of his swords. None of the party seemed to be awake.

They looked like they were in one of maybe ten cells, all about twenty square feet. A corridor ran between them and there were five cells a side if Eric was seeing straight. The repetition of the metal bars made it hard to see if there were four, five, or six on each side. None of the others seemed to have any occupants. Footsteps approached, making Eric panic. Should he pretend to still be unconscious? Too late - three ogres walked over, talking amongst themselves.

"Which one had the hotopty?"

"The one in green over there - the one that's awake."

"Right, take him to Gonnagonna, kill the others."

"Wait," he croaked through the gag. The ogres came closer, still peering through the bars. Now that he was near them, he could see each of them had one tooth that jutted out of their mouths from the bottom jaw. Two of them had it on the left side, one had it on the right.

"It sounds like that one is trying to speak!"

"Careful, might be a mage. Can't trust those."

"His hands are bound. He won't be able to cast anything. Besides, it sounds like he's speaking Farovian. Bring him here. Take the gag out."

They unlocked the door with a comically oversized key, attached to a ring along with many others. One of the ogres entered the room and grabbed him by the manacles, hoisting him to his feet. His gag was removed, and he was brought to the door of the cell.

"What was that, human?" said the one with the tusk coming out on the right side.

"I said 'wait'," said Eric. There was general astonishment from the ogres.

"Haha, he speaks funny."

"Funny or not, it's still Farovian!"

"And why should we wait, human? We have our orders."

Eric coughed and spat. He desperately needed water. "Don't kill them," he managed. "I have to talk to your leader."

The ogres shared a look. There was a brief discussion, that ensued in hushed tones and more than one suspicious look directed at Eric. Then the debate concluded and a decision was made. "We will take you to Gonnagonna. You can tell him how you got hotopty. And then you and your friends will die."

No pressure.

His hands were still manacled as they led him through tunnels and up staircases with a few rough pushes and cuffs. Again, Eric's ability to memorize the path failed well before they reached their destination. If he had to make his way back to his friends, he would need help. The room he found himself thrust into was a mirror of the room where he had met the Queen. Broadly. Certainly, there was the throne, where the ruler sat, and a selection of advisors. Although, the throne seemed to be made of human bones. The armrests appeared to be a line of skulls missing their jawbones, their vacant eye sockets staring at him. The advisors were not split by gender and were fewer in number. They shared the clothing styles that he had witnessed from the catwalk above the giant campsite earlier: an off-the-shoulder number in what appeared to be goatskin for the women and some variation of a loincloth for the men. There were five or six of them, arrayed on smaller seats, but still looming over him from their seated positions. The ceiling was a little higher here than in the corridors feeding into the caverns, and Eric was very conscious of his diminutive status when being surrounded by the giant ogres. It didn't help that all of the ogres were armed with clubs of one type or another, usually, a stone head attached to a curved stick or bone, tucked into a belt or held loosely.

"More humans? They are like cave locusts, too plentiful! Kill him and his friends and put the bodies with the others."

"Gonnagonna, this one had hotopty on him! And he speaks Farovian!"

For the first time, their leader looked at Eric. Eric stared back. He hadn't seen many ogres up close so was fascinated by the features that could tell one from the other. The different pigmentation made that easy, with each ogre having two or three shades of skin tone laid out in different patterns across their bodies. The fang in this case rose from far to the left of the mouth and made him look like he was chewing a cigar. This ogre had very bushy eyebrows, errant hairs poking out at all angles. They didn't seem to have any other facial hair. He hadn't seen any of them with mustaches or beards. So not at all like the dwarves that he expected to see in mines and caverns.

"Is this true, human, do you speak our language?"

"I do, King," Eric replied, looking carefully for subtle signs of a reaction to his words.

"So how do you come by bread from the Kisho? They do not sell it because none will buy it. They do not give it away because they know how terrible it is. Did you steal it?"

Eric shook his head. "I traded for it," he said with a laugh. In truth, he had forgotten it was in his trouser pocket, having been there since very early in the trip.

That seemed to be the most hilarious thing the ogres had ever heard. Eric thought it would be like if you had traded for nuclear waste. Or had given your cow for magic beans.

Gonnagonna shook his head as the laughter subsided. "And what does the human have to say before I kill him and his friends?"

Eric looked around. "I come from Queen Rennia. She sent me to see what happened to the soldiers she sent here looking for some thieves."

"Thieves? We are not thieves. We are peaceful people. We just want to farm our hihigi, raise our moga goats, and be left alone."

One of the advisors piped up. "Except Gaddaboo and his men who don't want to farm and want to raid the human farms for cattle. They are larger than moga goats and easier to take."

The ruler looked miffed at having been so directly contradicted. "Yes, except Gaddaboo. But Gaddaboo does what Gaddaboo does."

"Ah, no offense, but the human people don't know the difference between Gaddaboo and his followers and those that follow you. They are one and the same to the Queen."

"That does not seem fair," the King responded.

"It is not," said Eric. "And she must help her farmers. She must stop the thieving. And so, she will send more and more men to stop them."

Again, one of the advisors had something to say. "Why do we speak with this one? Let him wallow in the same pit as the others, and then do the same for his friends."

The King silenced them with one raised hand. "Humans breed very fast so there are many of them. They run amok above ground. They will keep coming and, eventually, the traps will not stop them anymore. It will be like the Caverns of Despair all over again." Both king and advisors were silent for a moment, recalling some collective racial event.

"Do you honestly want peace? For you, and your children, and your children's children?"

The King looked up. "Keep talking."

"The humans fight a war amongst themselves. They seek an end to the thievery. But they cannot have a fighting force of this size behind them when they leave for battle. So, they will seek to come here in their thousands."

"They have so many?" asked one of the advisors.

"Less than a day's ride from here in the castle."

A different advisor nodded. "This is unfortunate. With such a large army, they may get through our defenses and traps. But we will kill many of them, and our people will escape back into the deeper tunnels."

The King looked somber. "We must stop running. This is our home! We will live here. We will farm here and, if needed, we will die here. We have collapsed the bridge at the Caverns of Despair. The lichen-eaters cannot follow. And we will pay in blood for the humans to leave us."

Eric spoke softly into the silence that followed. "What if you didn't need to fight a war with the human queen?" That got their attention. "If you showed that you had captured the thieves and punished them, and in exchange for living here in peace, you offered to fight for her in her war?"

One of the advisors had an issue with that. "You are forgetting we killed her men. What kind of queen would forgive such a slight?"

Eric thought about that for a second. "True, but you could blame that on the thieves. Rogue operators who you punished as soon as you found out. You believe in the rule of law."

The King considered what Eric had proposed. "And those that came with you? We will not release you all. That would be a weakness."

Eric could sense success. "I tell you what, send an emissary - one of your people - with me to the queen. We'll propose you join her and see what she says. If the emissary does not return in two days, you kill the others and prepare for war. If she sends him back, then you will still need to prepare for war, but at the end of it, you come back and enjoy a life of peace."

The King was sold but had to do his due diligence. "Your queen, is she trustworthy?"

"She's not my queen. I don't know how trustworthy she is, I know that she is trying to defend her kingdom. That always forces people to make hard decisions. But it also may mean she's open to ideas that might otherwise not make sense."

"You have given us a lot to think about. Return to your friends, we will call you in an hour with our decision."

One of the advisors had to have the last word. "Or to kill all of you."

Eric bowed. "As you wish."

The others were conscious when he returned to the jail cell. The jailors didn't gag him this time which he was thankful for. But after he told his tale to his party members, they all looked furious at him. Obviously, they did not approve of his deal. There was a lot of grunting and muffled angry noises. He pleaded his case. "It was the only way I could think so they would not kill us all out of hand. You've seen how big they are. It would be smash, smash, game over." He didn't know which part of the plan they had issues with, but there was a lot of eye rolling. "I don't know what you're complaining about - I haven't sold you out. If this doesn't work, I will die too, you know!"

An hour later, the jailors took him back to the throne room, and, in what Eric chose to interpret as a positive sign, they brought his equipment. Of course, that might just have been to dispose of it in the same place as his body. He didn't like the thought of that. At all.

264

Chapter 14

The throne room was a little different upon Eric's return. The advisors had left as did the jailors after dumping Eric's gear on the floor behind him. There were only two ogres there now. The family resemblance was striking. The tufty eyebrows had not gotten out of hand just yet, but the King's son was the spitting image of his father, with the same patterns of skin tones, and more notably, the same tusk positioning.

"We have decided to send you an emissary to talk to the Queen. He is just a soldier but will report back to me how he is treated. If we do not see him within two days, we will prepare for war with the Queen, and we will kill your friends."

Eric wondered who the King thought he was fooling with the cover story of his son being a regular soldier. But he couldn't think of any advantage to telling him that he saw through the bluff. He didn't even see if he should tell the queen. The more success he had as a diplomat, the more he knew it wasn't really something he was any good at. The biggest uncertainty was going to be how the

Queen responded. The fate of the other four members of the party was literally hanging on whether he could persuade her.

"Most kind, King. I will do everything I can to broker a lasting peace, but it might take a meeting between the queen or her representatives and your people before peace is assured."

"That is true. Soldier, do your duty."

The soldier nodded, and Eric retrieved his equipment. The only item missing from his stuff was the lantern. Eric was so relieved to be free and on his way to safety though that he didn't inquire about it. The soldier led the way out of the room, and so began the long trip out of the warrens. As they walked, Eric found himself crossing numerous catwalks over the settlements far below. The second catwalk he crossed made him suspect they were doubling back on themselves and seeing the same settlement again. So he picked out the tents in the top left of the settlement, and whenever he looked at subsequent settlements, he compared them to the mental picture of the original. They did not repeat. There was always a variation. The ogre population was a lot larger than anyone had anticipated. He had thought that maybe they would have a few hundred individuals and maybe an armed force of fifty to a hundred at most. He was adjusting his estimation higher and higher as they ascended. The prince of the ogres introduced himself as Gallo, and as they swapped names, Eric asked him what emissaries carried to indicate that they came in peace. He was hoping it was something universal like the white flag back on Earth. Gallo didn't know, and Eric wasn't sure whether that meant that he didn't know that was just the human emblem for peace or if there was nothing universal in this world. He hoped he had the chance to speak before any military patrols found them. The last thing he wanted was to be haunted by the ghost of Jhara because Eric had let Gallo be killed on sight by trigger-happy soldiers.

When they arrived at the entrance to the caves, there were two horses saddled and waiting for them. Eric noticed they were saddled in the Queen's livery. He winced. He wasn't sure whether that would make things easier or harder. He turned to Gallo.

"Do you have any of the spears that would have the queen's emblem on them?"

Gallo turned to one of the ogre guards who were milling around the entrance and spoke softly to them. He went away and returned momentarily with a long spear, embellished with the queen's pennant. Eric took a couple of goes to mount his horse. It seemed a little nervous around the ogre. Gallo's mount was even more skittish, but he got into the saddle with the ease of a practiced horseman. Then they were off. Sort of.

"Do you know the way?" Eric asked Gallo. Getting lost for a day would certainly put the rest of the party at risk. More risk. Gallo looked over at him, grinned, and nodded. Eric took a little while getting the butt of the spear into the stirrup, but then they were underway for real.

Eric was happy to ride along in silence, not wanting to tip his hand that he knew that Gallo was Gonnagonna's son. While he did, he thought about the poison in his satchel. It kind of felt like having a nuclear bomb. Would you be able to do anything with it? The threat of it had value but having it meant you either got mugged or arrested for it. Only a psychopath would actually use it. This meant that not only did he not want it but that getting rid of it would have to be hidden from Gallo. He couldn't tip it out because it might cause an ecological disaster. And he couldn't sell it as only another psychopath would want to buy it. Because they would want to use it. He looked over. Gallo was doing a great job riding. He smiled when he noticed Eric watching him ride.

"Farovians ride moga goats underground. They're smaller than these horses, but the principles are the same. Mogas goats have more legs though." The ogre made the full-sized horse look almost like a Shetland pony. They rode in companionable silence for an hour. With being unconscious and underground for so long, Eric had totally lost track of time. Judging from the position of the sun, it was early in the morning, with the clear skies promising a fine autumnal day.

They were discovered about another hour later, the thundering of hooves alerting them to the presence of the patrol. The pennant gave them the opportunity for Eric to explain that Gallo was an emissary from the ogres and that they sought an audience with the queen. One of the soldiers rode off for the castle while the rest of them formed a guard of honor around Gallo and Eric. They had been perplexed that Gallo was not armed and that Eric had two swords, one comically too big for him. But it had helped persuading them the mission was genuine and not a trick. So, at a slow trot, the group made their way to the castle. This time they were greeted by crossbowmen at the gatehouse to the keep, and the chief counselor guided them up through the back, to the throne room.

Again, the return trip to a throne room was different, with fewer advisors in attendance. It was educational as to which of the queen's court were the most important. Eric was surprised to see only one soldier, whereas the female section of the court was half populated. The Queen however did not seem pleased to see him.

"Prince Eric, I sent you to kill all the ogres, instead you brought me one living one. And where are the others from your party?" The subtext was obvious. How did you survive when it looks like you couldn't fight your way out of a wet paper bag, and the others were the heroes from legend?

He smiled. This was going to be tricky. "Your majesty, you sent me to make sure the ogres are not a threat. If you will listen to me, you will learn how I propose to do that and to give you an additional 500 soldiers for your upcoming campaign."

Her reaction was nowhere near the enthusiastic acceptance he was hoping for. "I can't feed the soldiers I have at the moment. In a month, the grain will rot in the field because of the tunco."

Eric looked thoughtful. "Your majesty sees two problems; I see one opportunity. Agree to take on the ogres. Give them the caves they already occupy in exchange for their loyalty. No different than any other lord swearing fealty. And you can't afford the men to root them out. I have seen their numbers - they are many. But give them the chance to prove themselves. Say that they have to kill the tunco. Then, they will either kill the monsters and get you the grain you need for your campaign or they die and you are no worse off."

There was a shocked silence.

"We would then be cavorting with monsters. What about my men? What about the thievery?"

"They speak an intelligent language. They have caught those responsible for your patrols being killed and justice has been done. They have sent an emissary to begin communication between your people and theirs. As a gesture of their goodwill." He paused. "When we spoke, you said that if I solved the issue of the ogres, you would allow my friends to accompany me on my travels. I have solved the issue with the ogres. I don't know if rulers in your land keep their word. The old rulers in my land were notorious for not doing so. But I was hoping this land would be different."

The Queen drew herself up straight. "This Queen always keeps her word."

"Good, I will send the emissary back to the caves. The ogres should take a day or two to prepare themselves. Then, you shall have a troop of battle-hardened troops to add to your army, striking more fear into the hearts of your enemies."

There was a beat, and then the chief counselor spoke. "The war has not begun, Prince Eric, how have they been battle hardened?"

Eric turned to the emissary. "Gallo, who have you been fighting in the caverns?"

"The lichen-eaters."

He turned back to the Queen. "The ogres have been fighting the lichen-eaters, your majesty."

The Queen blinked in surprise. Evidently, she knew of the lichen-eaters. Eric didn't know whether that was a human group or another race. But they sounded mean.

"Five hundred soldiers who have just been bloodying the noses of the lichen-eaters sounds like a great addition to your army, no?"

The Queen was silent for a while, considering. Eventually, she raised her head. "Your plan is beginning to sound acceptable," she intoned.

Now is the time to strike, thought Eric. They were on the hook. "Oh, there is more, I suggest you send your best linguist back with the emissary. You will need someone who can communicate with the ogres. And as we have established, I must return to my quest. So would you be so kind as to release my colleagues? We must catch up to the train before they get too far ahead."

He thought that she would keep him dangling but the response was immediate. "You speak wisdom, Eric, Prince of Anaheim. Make it so. Rehm, who is your best linguist? Send him back with the emissary. Castellan, prepare for an additional five hundred men. Bring out the Prince's colleagues and an escort. You may wait at the stables for your escort to be prepared, Eric. It should not take too long."

He smiled his thanks and nodded.

They were escorted to the gatehouse beside the stables on the ground floor. Gallo turned to him. "How did it go?"

"Send my regards to your father, and tell him that the Queen has agreed to the deal. She seems to be impressed with the reputation of your men already."

"Success then! But you don't seem pleased."

"In my world, our leaders have a history of promising citizenship for fighting in wars, but when peace comes, citizenship is sometimes less forthcoming. Tell your father to be on his guard. Remind him that I do not vouch for the Queen."

"My fa- Gonnagonna is a suspicious man, Prince. The leadership of the ogre tribes is not a position where sleep is deep."

"Well, go with my best wishes, and tell him to release the others. He will keep to our agreement, won't he?"

"My… leader is honorable. He will release them."

The chief counselor brought a young man out to them, and he took the horse Eric had ridden on the way here. Gallo stepped astride his horse, and they headed out of the castle, the route lined with staring human soldiers.

Not long after, Anton and Imogen were led out of the keep.

"Anton! Imogen! Did they treat you well?"

"It's good to see you again, my lord!"

Imogen looked as if she wanted to say something but held her tongue.

The patrol of horsemen who was to return them to the train emerged from the stables. The leader pulled up next to Eric. "Are you ready to go, Prince Eric?"

He was about to say that he was, and then try and negotiate the rump of the horse, when one of the Queen's courtiers appeared, lifting her skirts as she hustled over to them.

"A word before you go, your highness." Imogen's eyes widened as she recognized the courtier. The courtier was slim with a cascade of straight blonde hair, which framed a very handsome face. The blouse under her dress was only very loosely laced, exposing a glimpse of cleavage.

"I have a note for your eyes only, your highness."

Eric blinked in surprise. This could be awkward. "One moment," he said to the leader of the patrol. He walked with the courtier a little away from the others. The note was sealed. He couldn't beckon over his designated reader because the issue was obviously private. He didn't take the note from her hands. And he couldn't read her look. "A sealed note. Do you know what it says?"

His response seemed to throw her. "Uh... maybe."

He smiled winningly. "Why don't you tell me?"

A puzzled frown flitted across her face. "My queen is looking for a fruitful relationship with the rulers of other nations. While we don't know where your nation is, the size of the military makes it sounds like it might be a good match for my queen. Your skill in diplomacy also leads her to believe that."

Eric started to say something. A flustered polite refutation, but she continued.

"My queen also asked me to state that the creation of the heir is the most important part of a royal marriage, but that as long as that occurs, there's no end of... *possibilities* in making the relationship as exciting as it can be." The twinkle in her eye drove straight to Eric's crotch. "While the crib in the royal bedchamber fits one, the *bed* is a lot larger."

"Ah... can you pass on my extreme thanks for, er, such a kind offer. If my return home wasn't as pressing as it is, I would be happy to explore the... er... possibilities you've raised."

She looked at the note. "Will you not take the note, your highness?"

Eric smiled sadly and shook his head. "I cannot. For reasons of state, I am not allowed to enter into official correspondence while I am out of my country. A distinct disadvantage to be sure, but the rules are the rules." He hoped that his bullshit sounded believable.

The lady in waiting nodded slowly before bowing, a distinctly mischievous smile barely suppressed. "Well, if you ever change your mind, I'm sure a favorable offer could be negotiated. I think we'd both enjoy that. Travel safely!" She headed back toward the castle.

Eric returned to the others who had been watching him and the lady in waiting.

Imogen was the first to speak. "What was that about, my lord? You have turned quite red!"

Chapter 15

The ride back to the woods to catch up with the train gave Eric time to reflect on the events of the last two days. He had been used to making hard decisions at work, but walking the tightrope between the demands of head office, the demands of the staff, and his own morals was a lot less important consequences-wise than the parties involved with his recent negotiations. Fundamentally, he had done the right thing since he, Anton, and Imogen found themselves on the way back to the train in one piece. Who knows, maybe his horse and treasure would all still be there too? But there was enough going on to make him pause. Would Gonnagonna allow the adventurers to leave? Would the queen actually follow through on the agreement that Eric had made on her behalf? Would the ogres be able to kill the tunco or would the queen turn on them and kill them before, after, or during the hunt? Would she be able to? Would the ogres be more powerful than the queen's army? Would the king of the ogres be able to control his people? So many questions. Was he reading the offer correctly? Was he being offered unlimited sexual freedoms while in a marriage as well as the power of being king? Or would he merely be the consort, who had no power? Of course, the queen would expect him to bring an army to the table. But he had - the ogres. He shook his head. Man, Earth was looking simpler.

His memory of the tunco's attack brought him more and more alert as they approached the fields of grain. He noticed the men in the patrol were not exactly on edge as they trotted to the beginning of the fields.

"Aren't you worried about the tunco?" he asked over the jangle of the harnesses.

"There's typically a patrol along the edges of the grain fields - along the road covering the perimeter. The tunco tend to stay in the grain fields, so if they do attack, you only have to head a little way into the forest, and they won't follow."

"What about the plains around the grain fields? Do they follow you there?"

"They tend to stay in the grain but it's not always the case. We lost two men who thought they were safe once they were out of the grain. They only kill to eat, so we have a few days of peace after they've killed. And they know there are aurochs wandering around in the grain, so even then, they should be quiet for a little while."

"Ah good to know, thanks."

"No problem."

278

Before too long, they were at the crossroads where they'd been picked up from, the sun waning in the sky and the shadows lengthening. If Eric was right that the train would travel two or three miles an hour for about a day, they were about twenty-five miles away. A marathon, more or less. Eric considered what the current worst-case scenario was. It would be for them to be dropped off at the entrance to the forest when night fell, then to have to walk for, say, six hours to catch up with the train, which would happen at about midnight, and to find the horse gone, the treasure gone, and the train under attack from the forest equivalent of the grain-fields tunco. And! And, in the battle, for the book to get damaged - maybe dropped in the fire. In that case, all possible leads on how to get home would be gone! And all possible ways of finding more information – gone too. And Eric would be left with minimal opportunities to make money, except maybe as a translator of the spoken word. Maybe that would keep him in roast chicken and flagons of wine? Constantly thinking of worst-case scenarios was starting to get wearisome. His imagination was too good!

He blinked. While he'd been musing, they had entered the forest. The sudden change in the light had broken him out of his reverie. They were riding slowly, moving from a trot to something faster than a walk. The path was very well-marked and seemed to be clear of roots and branches. The clouds were visible through the canopy and the gloom was enough to see by, but Eric was still concerned by the possibility of something tracking them in the woods. He didn't think they could overshoot the train, not if the passengers camped as they had at the other stops along the way. The big bonfire in the middle of a clearing, surrounded by the train of wagons would be hard to miss!

The woods here were quite noisy, with one bird or another making whooping noises, crashing through the bushes on the side of the path, or settling on branches high above. It took Eric the better part of an hour to realize that these were not harbingers of an attack like the ratite. He recognized that he had been exposed to the most dangerous parts of nature, and it would take him a little while to readjust to what was a more normal appreciation of what danger was. Unless he was now acclimatized to the natural danger level of this world, and only now forgetting what it was like on Earth.

He looked over to the other riders, especially the ones carrying Anton and Imogen. Imogen was riding well, looking comfortable behind her soldier, her trousers being a much better-suited piece of clothing than the dress she'd been wearing when Eric had first encountered her. Anton, on the other hand, seemed like he was always coming down whenever the horse was going up, and rather than the smooth synchronized movements of Imogen and her rider,

Anton's head bobbed along at twice the rate that his rider did. It wasn't long before Eric had trouble seeing the other riders in the dark and his butt was starting to get very numb. Not long after that, they could make out the sure signs of a bonfire ahead through the trees. A few minutes later, they had entered the clearing and were circling it, looking for their wagon. The riders ahead of Eric dropped off Anton and Imogen, both of them awkward on the dismounting, and Eric realized why when he came to slide down off his ride. His muscles being stiff and sore made the novel actions cumbersome, and he very nearly stumbled and fell as he landed on the ground. He stretched his back and staggered over to the wagon. His horse had been tied to the same tree as the oxen and turned to give him an angry look as he approached. Vollo sat up from the bed of the wagon and blinked at them before realizing who they were.

"Eric! Welcome back. I almost didn't think that I would see you again! I'm sorry I didn't set up camp - I didn't know that you'd be back tonight."

"That's all right, thank you for taking care of everything while we were away. Were there any issues?" Eric deposited his satchel and the man-in-red's sword on the bed of the wagon as he spoke, especially glad to be relieved of the extra weight of the sword.

"No, nothing, plain sailing."

"Ah, grand. Imogen, did you and Anton want to have a look at setting up camp? I'll walk Vollo back to the train master."

"Of course, my lord," answered Imogen.

As they walked the short distance, Eric turned to him. "Vollo, what do you know about ogres?"

He blinked in surprise. "Me personally? Nothing. But my father used to tell me stories about them. The caverns under the mountain linked to the caves they used to live in. Our people used to trade with them, and sometimes travelers would come through in either direction. Why is that?"

"I bumped into some of them, not too far from here. They mentioned that they had fled the caverns they'd been living in. Do you speak their language?"

"No, only some of the elders do. Not many of them anyway. Why is that?"

"They could probably do with some human friends - they're about to become the next addition to Queen Rennia's Kingdom."

Vollo's eye widened. "Our people have had a long relationship with the ogres, but I'm surprised that they have agreed to such an arrangement. On my return home, I will talk with my father and the leaders in the mountains. It would be good to rekindle the friendship." They had reached the train master's wagon. "All your belongings are intact, Eric. Your horse turned up not long after you left and stayed with us the whole time. It didn't like being tied up, that's for sure."

Eric smiled. "It's like that. Thanks again for looking after everything. Good night."

He walked back in the dark, the bonfire being a clue that it was in the early hours of the morning - the flames were far from their peak but the fire was larger than the mound of embers they usually woke to at dawn. The only movement was the other guardsmen doing their rounds, their spears casting crazy shadows along the tree trunks on the periphery of the clearing. The noises of the night had died down, but there was still the occasional fluttering of wings or the bizarre bird calls from the forest.

He headed back to the wagon and settled carefully into his spot between Anton and Imogen, who were both already asleep. He drifted off too not long after his head hit the rolled-up blanket that served as a pillow. Instantly, he awoke to the dawn light. The bonfire indicated he had been asleep for four or five hours, roughly the whole time between their arrival and dawn. This surprised Eric because he felt like no time had passed. He was still tired, and he had to nudge Anton and Imogen awake, getting dark mutterings and grumbles as a response.

They moved like zombies, preparing the oxen and wagon for the day's travel. Eric wanted to check the contents of his saddlebags but didn't want to do it where Anton could see, so knew he would have to get some time alone. It seemed a little churlish to send him on some errand so early in the morning when nobody was particularly awake or in a good mood, so he knew it would have to be later in the day. In the meantime, all there was to do was suffer through the day and maybe steal a nap at some point.

His eyes weren't really taking in the surroundings, he was just rocking along in the "existing" state of affairs, known only to the hungover and sleep deprived. It took him a few minutes to realize that Anton was actually speaking to him.

"My lord, I found out some things yesterday from the book."

"Uh… ok."

"I had a lot of time in a room with good light, and without the constant motion of the oxen and cart, I was able to make good progress."

"That's great."

"Marion the Wise is a very interesting person. They were imprisoned in Red Sede last century and subsequently found that they had a lot of time on their hands. Marion went to Red Sede specifically to learn about a particular type of magic - controlling people's minds."

"Wow – that's impressive." Eric wasn't sure how that would work. Would it be like the stage hypnotists he'd seen on tv?

284

"Yes, that was the reason they ended up in prison. The council of archmages has very strict rules on what kind of magic is allowed to be learned or practiced. I'm not quite sure of the distinction because they seem to contradict themselves a few times there."

"So nothing about traveling to other worlds then?"

Anton paused to think about that before continuing. "No, nothing there. But how they got into prison is quite fascinating."

Eric wondered how fascinating it could actually be, but then he remembered that as it was, he had nothing else to do, so he may as well hear the whole story. "So how did he come to be in prison?"

"We don't know if Marion was a man or a woman, my lord."

"Does that really matter?"

"Actually, it does. You see, two hundred and some years ago, there wasn't a restriction on what types of magic you could or could not learn or practice. It was a bit of a chaotic time. Progression at the schools of magic tended to be based on the power of the mage, but it turned out there were some spells that changed the way people thought about the caster. In some cases, they could be compelled to do things, and in some cases, they were totally in the control of the caster. Again, the writing is not clear and that might be the same spell doing all three or just an indication of the power of the caster or how weak-willed the victim was."

"OK."

"So people who somehow learned that spell or spells could become incredibly powerful. We don't know how long the spells lasted, whether the victim was forever in the control of the caster, or just for a certain length of time. This opened up a huge interest in counter spells and magic that could protect them from that kind of mind-control spells."

"That makes sense. There's always been a battle between attack and defense. Armor improvements lead to weapon improvements."

"Well, it also led to some very interesting social changes."

"What do you mean?"

"So, the mages worked hard to protect themselves from each other, but nobody protected the non-mage population."

"Huh?"

"Not all the people in the universities and colleges of magic are mages or students. They couldn't possibly do their own laundry or cook their own meals. When powerful men decide that they want… certain things… and have the means to not only have them but make other people think that it was their idea, no matter how out of character those things are… well, you can see how that gets very debauched very quickly. Eventually, enough of the students and non-mage staff figured out what was happening and most of them left - none of them could afford the kind of protections required to keep their minds their own. So the mind-controlling mages started to go out to the villages, first of all for cooks and laundry maids, but later… Anyway, the local villagers either moved or started to attack mages on sight. Village magic sprang up, usually superstitions nonsense involving trinkets and home-made solutions that supposedly protected the wearer. Slowly, the lands near the schools emptied, the schools ground to a halt, and the mages who were still there turned evil. Not all schools were totally taken over - those that held out tended to become male only and went to great lengths to exclude gay people. Do you know why?"

"I don't know - was it related to the general anti-gay attitudes?"

"Oh no, mages now are actually quite liberal."

"So liberal schools stopped taking on women and gay men?"

"Yes. Well, actually women stopped going to the schools if they suspected there was a chance of the mind control magic being taught or practiced."

"Nobody likes being made to do something they didn't want to do," Imogen interjected.

"Yes, Imogen, nobody likes to be forced to do things that aren't in their mind. But why did they ban gay men?"

There was a pause while they all considered this. Eric got it first, answering his own question. "In case they learned how to do it.

And then the straight mages found themselves doing things that they didn't want to do."

"Yes, my lord."

"But that doesn't make sense - the adventurers I went with to the caves had a mage, and nobody attacked him on sight or worried about him taking over their mind."

"That's right. There was a war. The evil in the schools was rooted out by right-thinking mages, both men and women, and the whole branch of mind-control magic was forbidden to be taught, learned, or practiced. Eventually, people slowly came back to the schools to learn, cook, or do the laundry. And the villages closer to the schools filled up again, so things went back to normal. Then maybe eighty, ninety years later our friend Marion came into the picture. They start their memoir in prison and give the circumstances of their capture and incarceration. Then over the pages, they explain more of the back story of what they tried to do and how they got caught. But the best part is that it looks like he, or she, explains how the school is structured and how power is distributed within the university. It should be most enlightening."

"Wow, you have done well. Thank you for that, is there any way of identifying a mind-control mage? Or of noticing whether some sort of mind control spell is being cast? I'd hate to miss a clue."

"Marion calls spells such as these 'glamors'. But they haven't mentioned any way of detecting them or what the counter-magic spells or items look like."

"OK, well, keep an eye out for that sort of thing, we might need to be on our guard."

"Of course, my lord."

"Actually, Anton, would you mind doing me a favor? I need to know the distance between the front of the train and the rear. Would you be able to pace that out for me? Best to do it twice, just to make sure it's accurate."

Anton frowned. "Surely that distance would change depending on corners, hills, and many things like that?"

Eric nodded at the very legitimate concerns. "Yes, but I do need the distance as it is now. It'll give you a chance to stretch your legs."

Anton looked uncertain.

"The guardsmen are all along the train, you will be safer closer to them than you are here with us! Off you go."

Anton nodded and smiled. "See you soon," he said as he slid off the bed of the wagon.

As soon as he was twenty feet away, Eric slipped over to the back of the wagon, ignoring the questioning look from Imogen, and started going through the saddlebags. The horse watched him from behind, free to wander but obediently staying behind the wagon.

Eric had been keeping track of expenditures and how much he'd been giving Imogen, but with all the upheavals, attacks, and fleeing on horses, he was convinced there would be some shrinkage, a gap between the amount of cash he had and the amount he should have. Back home, the dangerous part of cashing up at the restaurant each night was blaming the cashier for any shortfall. He didn't want to blame the guardsmen, Anton, or anyone else on the train for coins that might have been misplaced or lost during the tunco attack. But, fortunately, they were all there. The amount matched to a dime. Or a penny. Or one of those little brown coins with the picture of the man with three heads. Imogen cleared her throat, and he glanced up to see Anton approaching. Eric put down the sacks of coins and covered them with the blanket that was used to wrap the book. To explain his presence in the back, he picked it up, and made a show of looking at all the weird and wonderful letters.

As Anton passed, looking up and quizzical, Eric patted the book and nodded. "Still can't read it."

Anton didn't pause but continued on toward the back of the train, looking over his shoulder at one point, and shaking his head as if trying to figure something out.

Eric rearranged the saddlebags and tightened the clasps. Then he sighed in relief. If the spells to get back were expensive, judging by the weight of the coin, they still had a chance of being able to afford them. And if there was only enough for him, at least Imogen would know how much she would need to raise herself. Maybe he would be able to help her out. Maybe he could start up a fast-food restaurant here. Being able to get the same food from any outlet must surely be a service that the local people would be willing to pay for? Or would he be able to earn enough as a translator?

A glimpse of an idea flitted across his mind. If he didn't have enough money, maybe they could borrow some from the Queen. Of course, that would be dishonest, and he didn't really like contemplating it. His mind wandered, probing the thought like a tongue, worrying about a bit of food stuck between the teeth. If he couldn't borrow the money from the Queen, maybe he would have to marry her to provide some sort of value in exchange for the money. Although she seemed much more interested in an army. And if he ran off with the money and Imogen without providing an army, that would be universally frowned upon. Not the honorable actions of a prince! From the Queen's point of view, it would make quite the country and western song: I lost my money and my husband when he ran off back to his world with a lesbian serving girl, leaving me with a bunch of ogres.

Eric finished wrapping up the memoir in its blanket and got back into his seat just as Anton walked past on his way back to the front of the train. "Anton? We probably only need one measurement. How far is it?" Anton told him a number of paces. "Great, thanks for that, hop back up now if you like?"

"Do you not trust Anton, my lord?" Imogen asked as Anton got himself settled.

For a few seconds, Eric considered how to answer. "I trust Anton, but he is young and might inadvertently let something that endangers us slip. Even if it is an innocent comment. If he does not know any details, then this cannot happen."

Imogen cocked her head. "And me, my lord? Will I let anything slip?"

Eric suppressed a grin. "I trust your street smarts, Imogen. Also, you are used to keeping secrets."

Imogen nodded. "Was it all there, my lord?"

Eric let his relief show, smiling broadly. "Yes, we won't be begging for our supper in Havelin when we get there. The Kishan took good care of our possessions."

Imogen half turned to look at the horse, placidly plodding along behind them. "I don't think that it was just them."

Chapter 16

Eric tried to do the math. For the three days and nights he'd been on the train, they'd suffered two attacks. He was counting the first one even though they had not really been in any danger. There had been more than enough danger on the second attack. At that rate, in a three-month trip, he would find himself in battle sixty times. If you counted the night he missed while serving at the pleasure of the Queen, it still worked out as something like forty-five battles. His chances of surviving to the end didn't seem that great to him if that was the rate at which violence would be experienced on the road. It was boredom, piled upon boredom, interspersed with the chance for instant death. Kind of like being a pilot. Or in the army, or police. Except in those professions, you could learn the skills that would presumably help keep you alive for longer. Sure, he could try practicing what he had been taught by the swordmaster, but the warnings and admonishments to stay out of battle were even more top of mind. Maybe he could do something with the alchemist's gauntlets?

He rustled in the satchel that he'd been given together with the oil for the lantern. The gauntlets were there, nestled amongst the little leather flasks of oil. He got one out, put it on, and made a few gestures, trying to remember what the alchemists had said and done when they were wielding them. Nothing happened.

He looked closer at the gauntlets. They were made of stiff leather and fitted reasonably well on Eric's smaller hand, maybe a little looser than he would like but comfortable enough. The stitching was about what he'd come to expect in this world - not the uniform and tiny stitches of the sewing machines on Earth, but longer and more irregular. The product of real people, real craft. The stone looked like it had come from the bed of a river. Blue-gray and uniform in shape, it didn't seem to have been ground down or chipped, almost like it had been naturally formed. It peeked out from the leather that was holding it to the glove. The stitching there looked like it was wire or some other sort of metal. It could also just be a thick cotton thread in a color that made it look like metal.

Not having immediate success in activating the gauntlet, Eric turned his attention to its back. No clues there either: though the wire threads splayed out in a wide-reaching pattern, kind of matching the bones of the hand within. Weird. The threads looked almost like the branches or roots of a tree, depending on which way was up. And while the threads on the palm of the glove seemed to

294

be holding it together along the seams, or maybe holding the stone firmly attached to the glove, the threads on the back seemed decorative. Eric weighed the gauntlet in his hand, considering his options. It struck him that the glove could maybe be activated by a spell. But the alchemists had not seemed to be spell casters. Sure, they wore robes, but what was it the Knight had said - they used magic through objects, rather than… what? Instead of spells? But they had been gesturing and yelling things when using the gloves. Didn't that mean they were casting spells? So, let's say those weren't spells, would he have to know the moves to make the things work? Like a cheat code from a game. Or like a kung fu move or something? From a video game? Sonic boom! Well, if it was a set of gestures, it would be very unlikely for him to guess it, right? But if it wasn't a move or a spell, then was it maybe a switch, or a button, or a shock that made it work? He looked closer. There was nothing he could recognize as a switch or button. He had, of course, pressed the stone, but nothing happened. No audible click or a tactile response indicating that anything had changed.

Eric made a fist. Nothing. He twisted in his seat and hit the edge of the wagon. Ow; but nothing. The other two were watching him, Anton, directly, Imogen out of the corner of her eye. He took off the glove and handed it to Anton. "Any idea what this does?" he said.

Anton looked at it carefully, turning it around to look from all sides before shrugging and handing it back. "No idea at all, my lord. It's a glove, obviously, but I have not seen one like it before."

"Have you read anything about something like this? In any of your books?"

"No, my lord, nothing."

"Ah, ok. Imogen?" Eric handed the glove over. Imogen switched the reins to her left hand and flipped the glove over, examining it closely.

"No, but I know a tailor in Havelin who might be able to help. Or maybe not, but at least it's someone we can ask. It's a glove, so that might mean he can help, but it's got a great big stone in it which would mean it would be useless for anything you would normally wear a glove for, so… that kind of rules him out. But we can try."

"Ah, cool. Thanks."

"Uh… my lord, is it permissible to ask where you got the glove from?"

Eric smiled. "Of course. When I was on my mission for the queen, we encountered some alchemists. They were wearing these gloves, and I'm trying to understand how they work."

"They're magical gloves?"

"Yeah, I guess so. Green flames came out of them."

Anton was looking at him wide-eyed. "Really? Wow, that's awesome."

Eric nodded sadly. "It would be if I could figure out how to make them work. Maybe Imogen's tailor friend in Havelin might be able to help. We'll have to wait and see, I guess."

The rest of the day drifted along monotonously, the views of the sky few and far between under the canopy of the trees. For lunch, Imogen broke open some fruit that looked like a brown watermelon but turned out to have a flesh that was not too dissimilar to coconut in both texture and flavor. It was a welcome change from the incessant cycles of stew.

Eric was on edge all afternoon, expecting some sort of dangerous creature to attack them, but by the time the evening closed in, he was almost disappointed that none had. The guardsmen didn't seem to ever relax, but their attentiveness was professional. Eric watched them carefully to see if their demeanor ever changed. If they were worried, then he needed to be worried too, but he couldn't ever tell if they were being professional, relaxed, or something else.

As always, they made it to the campsite after dusk. Imogen asked about the bolt of cloth, and Eric shook his head. The tunco had shown the futility of that protection. Dinner was more stew, less meat, and more vegetables. Sleep was interrupted periodically by some great bird thrashing through the brush, but nothing attacked them. Bleary-eyed breaking of the camp, more slow-moving oxen. The occasional update from Anton on what he had found out. Rinse and repeat. A week under the canopy of the forest. A wagon in the train, toppled into the river after breaking an axle, and being washed down the river, drowning the waggoner and his oxen, the oxen harnessed to the dead weight of the wagon, the waggoner not able to leap clear and being wrapped in the fabric cover on the back of his wagon.

As they popped out the other side of the forest the skies above were bright. Fields stretched in both directions, but the road continued toward another forest on the horizon. There was the occasional solitary town around the path too. The town was surrounded by a wooden wall that nothing more than whole trees felled from the forests and dragged to a waiting hole to be re-erected and bound to their neighbors. The houses within were single-story stone affairs with reed roofs. The discrepancy between the height of the walls and the height of the houses struck Eric as humorous, until he started wondering if there was something roaming outside the town for which such tall walls were needed. That froze the smile on his face.

Imogen restocked their larder with what was left from the market. There were slim pickings after the first wagons had been through, but she wheedled and wangled, managing to get enough fresh food for the next leg of the journey for a good price. Beyond food items and the odd farming implements, there were few trade goods or luxury items in evidence. The people wore plain clothes, showing signs of many repairs, but by and large clean. Most of them wore some sort of weapon, usually a large knife at their waist. Eric weighed up whether to get a night in the nearby inn and catch up with the train in the morning, convinced it would be easy to do on horseback. A nice bed would give him a good night's sleep. And he had the money. But that wouldn't be cool.

They left right away, the straight road a novelty for the trip. Eric enjoyed the new view of the train - an uninterrupted stream of wagons, with the guardsmen dotted around them. There were now twelve wagons altogether, a couple of new ones joining them at the town. Eric realized that he hadn't even bothered to learn the name of the town.

The walls and the knives reawakened Eric's paranoia, and he spent the remainder of the day keeping an eye on the fields on either side of the road. The farms here were not growing the same grain as the previous fields. Rather, the square fields were covered in rows of what looked like waist-high fronds. They were densely packed into the fields, which themselves were surrounded by stone walls, about knee-high, and were then topped by irregular wooden planks in a kind of fence that matched the height of the fronds. The effect was that for the surrounding areas, there was a checkerboard of the fields as far as he could see. Being able to see that far, offset Eric's paranoia a little.

They made camp in one of the fields, which was empty when the bonfire and wagons arrived. The walls reflected the warmth of the fire and stopped the increasingly strong wind. They were treated to a baked meat dish: the flesh was placed in a pottery bowl, that was then thrust into the innards of the bonfire and extracted fifteen minutes later, using one of the planks in the fencing on top of the walls. Eric thought the meat might have been chicken, but there were way too many legs. It simmered in a vegetable sauce, not unlike a tomato paste in consistency, but a deep purple color, which he found very off-putting. There were plenty of leftovers that sat in the pottery bowl on the wagon bed while Imogen, Eric, and Anton slept, satisfied, and with full and warm bellies.

The next day, they entered the next forest. After that, the days started to blur. The only activity that broke the monotony was the progress that Anton was making with the book. Also, bad things happened. Not attacks, though Eric's paranoia came and went, and he was constantly trying to gauge how concerned the guardsmen were by looking at their body language. No, these were smaller things. Well, smaller for their crew anyway. Another wagon broke an axle. A man was bitten by a snake while relieving himself in the woods. Someone found some liquor, drank too much, and fell into the bonfire. He wasn't burnt too badly but was in great pain for a long while afterward, whimpering in the night. There were also days under forest canopies and across plains of grain when they saw the start of the harvest, teams of men swinging scythes through the stalks of grain, and stacking them in sheaths on the back of flatbed wagons. Other times, the plains were barren, grassland or meadows studded with stones, rocks, and what looked like gorse to Eric. Big thorny bushes with different colored flowers anyway.

The weather stayed pleasant by and large. When they were exposed to the rain, Imogen ran around the wagon, attaching the lean-to to the bed of the wagon, giving their belongings some shelter. At those times, Eric wished he had spent some time thinking about the design of the wagon: if he had attached ribs, similar to those on the wild west wagons, then they all might have had some protection from the elements. As it was, the back was protected, but they got wet. The wagon that had been washed away crossing the river had been similar enough to the wild west wagons. If it hadn't been disabled by breaking an axle, Eric might have been able to negotiate with the owner to grab the ribs and attach them to his wagon. All the gatehouses and bridges in the places they had been had sufficient headroom to accommodate something like that.

The food went through cycles too. Way too much stew for Eric's liking. They could tell when they were approaching a town because the meat would start running out. But the best days were those when there was something interesting to eat. And they tended to be regional. The watermelon that was more like a coconut. A large pumpkin-sized vegetable, striped with green and purple, that when cut open revealed five fist-size seeds, which were something like a pitless peach. They were very sweet. The fronds they passed turned out to be starchy green vegetables. When Imogen baked them in the pottery bowl, their edges caramelized the sugars within, almost like a roast potato.

Spending so much time with each other, with nothing to do but keep the oxen from wandering off the track, meant that they got to know each other's back story quite well.

Anton was the third son of a less-than-successful merchant and had two older sisters, in addition to two older brothers. His father started off reselling wool and other fabrics, before moving on to sourcing stone and masonry for the cathedral and castle construction in the south of Ordost. The difference between what he could buy the stone for and what he needed to pay to get it shipped to the sites tended to edge closer and closer to the amount that the people building the structures could pay, so the money got harder to get. Anton's mother had been from a mercantile family too. She had also known how to read. She taught all the children the skill and as the money dried up, they all moved out to make their own way in the world. Anton loved reading, so a job doing exactly that was perfect for him. His career path seemed set - ten years as an apprentice, followed by five as a journeyman, and then either applying for a grand librarian position, if one was available, or alternately, moving into the guild house to perfect the administration functions. Solid work. An honest trade. A life of respectful toil. He didn't particularly enjoy the dangerous aspect of the travel, admitting to being "just a little scared" during the battles that they had already been involved in. Eric had chortled at the masterful understatement. Being on their journey had already made Anton the most well-traveled of both his family and the entire guild in the town. He thought that he might find a nice girl back in Gerton, settle down, and have a family when he returned.

As the story built up, Eric nodded to himself. He got it. It seemed that few skills in this world were recognized as transferable, so getting into a trade and staying in it was the only way of securing stable employment.

Imogen, on the other hand, was a very different person. She was the younger of two girls born into a tailor's home, in far-off North

Redes. Her mother had died in the first of three waves of plague that had ripped through the country, and her father had retreated into the comfort of his work. Her older sister had found a love match that hadn't sat well with their father, who had eventually worked out a match of his own through his guild. When the older sister had eloped, preferring the relative poverty of her love match with a traveling tinker to the loving embrace of a man three times her age and four times her weight, her father had redoubled his efforts to get Imogen married off instead.

Imogen had always been the most interested in the tailoring her father did and had called on his fellow tailors, supposedly to pass on his regards. She had used other manufactured reasons too, but in reality, she did it because she felt a connection with certain of his fellow guildmates. Not the amorphous mass of a man that he had tried to marry off to her sister, but there were three or four of the others that seemed… different. More like her, somehow. On their side, they seemed to recognize something within her too. It was certainly nothing romantic, but as time went by, she realized that they saw her as the person she was, whereas most of the other people she came about only had a glimpse of a single facet of her identity. It was either as someone who could do something for them, someone who they could fuck, or someone who they might be able to gain benefit by knowing.

She only realized just how different she was when she spent time with one of her favorite tailors, Pred. Pred was a wizened hunched-over balding man, with a halo of white hair and spectacles which he would always peer over at her. His niece was visiting from the neighboring city, and Imogen was fascinated. The woman was a few years older than her. During the visit, Pred told her no fewer than three times that she would catch flies. She didn't realize what that meant until he told her that whenever Messa was in the room, Imogen's mouth would gape open as she watched her going about her business. She was enthralled. She very quickly learned to hide her interest, lest she be ostracized by the rest of society. Her tailor friends never made her feel bad about the feelings she was starting to develop. In fact, she suspected that they held, or had held, similar feelings of their own for members of their own sex.

Her relationship with her father deteriorated as the matchmaking efforts increased. As she blossomed into a woman, it became harder to reconcile her self-image of a fine upstanding member of society with the thoughts and desires she had in her heart. With the help of her friends, she learned to recognize the signs and little giveaways that someone was of her own kind. That was, assumed the people themselves knew, of course. There were a few times that someone Imogen would have sworn was gay turned out to have not come to that conclusion themselves. Or maybe had decided not to allow themselves to believe it. Eric had wondered how open Imogen would be around Anton about her sexuality. They seemed to have a trusting relationship. He supposed that if you were planning on leaving this world and going to a better one, you would have a certain abandon.

Imogen's first romantic relationship with a woman had ended abruptly when her father had noticed the change in her demeanor and had put one and one together. He came to a slightly incorrect conclusion however, expecting another elopement for a love match, and was perplexed when he discovered the cause for Imogen's distraction was female. If Imogen was expecting to be treated differently because of the loss her father experienced after her older sister left, she was sorely mistaken. She was cast out, bouncing between her tailor friends until she could find gainful employment. Her romantic relationship had died before it really got started, her girlfriend terrified of being outed and losing her position as a governess. Imogen gathered what savings she had, along with some gifts from her friends, and worked her way across the countryside, not quite sure where she was heading, but knowing it had to be a better place, somewhere she could be herself in peace.

This was why she had jumped at the chance to follow Eric. He was wary of sharing too much about his own life back on Earth. Worried that if it became known that he was not actually royalty, someone would look at all his wealth and decide he had come about it through dishonest means. This could prevent him from returning home – he could get locked -up or have his belongings confiscated. If spells were expensive, or if just getting someone to cast them was impossible, he would be stuck here. With no toilet paper, toothpaste, refrigeration, television, or ganja. He'd been hanging out for a smoke since he'd gotten here, especially after the attacks and his experience in the tunnels. It was exactly what he had needed to get over the shock of actual physical violence and having someone trying to kill him. But no, there were no Jamaican flags or Bob Marley posters, or five-leafed emblems on people's clothing. He had no idea how he might get hold of some. Or even if they had anything like that here. It would be just his luck if he was asking for something with a mellow, all-over body high, and ended up strung out in a psychedelic rage after ingesting enough of the local equivalent of PCP to embalm a rhino.

Eric had thought that, from the outside at least, his own story sounded a little bit like the doomsday cultists he'd read about online back on Earth. The ones that were usually found dead alongside their flock in some bizarre mass suicide that happened after promising to take them to a better world, where all perceived failings in this world would not follow them. Eric knew that wasn't the case here. But maybe those charismatic leaders thought the same.

So onward they traveled, the insights from the book giving him some idea of how the college of magics was constructed. Unfortunately, it was what he would have guessed about the structure of any school. There was an administrative office and academic staff that taught theories about magic. The actual teaching of spells seemed to be an afterthought, and judging by the way Marion wrote about it, there were only a very few spells that were learned by the beginning students. As people progressed through the ranks, the spells they learned tended to be in their specialization. But in the first five years, there were very few mages who had a unique spell book. Eric didn't know whether that was a good or a bad thing. On one hand, he hoped it would mean there were a whole group of mages who would be able to cast the spell to take him and Imogen back to his world. On the other hand, if the spell was too advanced, there was a very good chance that the number of mages who were able to cast it would be tiny. He was hoping that the spell needed would be common so that the price he would have to pay would be lower. There was too much uncertainty.

Of bigger concern was the advancement system within the hallowed halls of the university. It was not too different from the guild system he had learned about from Anton and Imogen. It was some sort of apprenticeship, where the basics were learned from a master, followed by a period during which the journeyman was able to contribute more fully to their master's work, concluding in an opportunity for the student to become a master themselves. And depending on their standing within the guild, there was an opportunity to gain additional rank as a grand master or equivalent.

Within the magic school, there seemed to be allusions to ceremonies and rituals in addition to the graduations. He couldn't tell if graduations were like his high school back on Earth, where you just had to perform to a certain level, attend for a certain number of years to graduate, and then be released into the world. Or whether it was more of a mastery situation, where you had to prepare a piece of work of a sufficient standard to prove that you could. Or a combination of both - a master suite after having spent five years as a journeyman tailor, for example. From what Anton could tell, there seemed to be at least two other rituals or ceremonies that somehow connected and committed the mage to the advancement of the school. Some proof of loyalty. It kind of made sense when Eric thought about it. What would stop anyone from doing what needed to be done for ten or fifteen years, and then, after learning the advanced and most powerful spells, heading out into the world to do terrible deeds for personal gain? That had not gone well before those controls were put in place apparently. What Eric couldn't figure out was whether that sort of magic constituted mind-control magic or not. That would be strange: using the forbidden magic to guarantee that nobody could use the forbidden magic! He wondered idly how well an ancient and powerful school would react to having that sort of hypocrisy pointed out to them.

Chapter 17

They sat on the wagon, looking across the river at the city. They didn't say anything for a while, just sitting, staring. The rest of the wagons of the train continued their way through the large gatehouse. The guardsmen were congregating just outside the gatehouse, an unceremonious farewell to a two-month journey. But Anton, Imogen, and Eric were staring at the city beyond it. The destination they'd been traveling toward for the past seventy days.

Havelin sat on an island in the middle of the river, the road somewhere on the far side exiting the city through a similar gatehouse, hidden by the impressive stone walls that ringed the edge of the island. On the other side of the city, the road carried on straight as an arrow across the vacant plains. They had seen the city as if through a haze for the last two or three hours, and it was the fact that they could finally catch a clear glimpse of it that made them pause. Eric figured that there was some kind of magical spell keeping them from seeing it clearly from afar, but he couldn't figure out the purpose of such a spell. It wouldn't be to protect the city from artillery or siege weapons as it was the details that they couldn't make out from a distance. You'd still be able to hit the walls, gatehouse, or whatever else you were aiming at. It wasn't as if the whole city could move while under attack. Was it?

Imogen twitched the reins, they pulled in behind the last wagon, and crossed the bridge. Eric waved at Vollo as they went past. The guardsmen smiled and nodded in return. The guardsmen's leader watched him warily until they were through the gatehouse and out of sight. And just like that their journey was over.

On the other side of the gatehouse was a large courtyard, with evenly spaced cobblestones that were almost uniform in size and shape, the edging of the road merely being where the oblong blocks changed from laying side-to-side to end-on-end. The roads were wide and there was space on each side in front of the buildings for pedestrians to walk along, free to stop and look in shop windows or converse without having to worry about being run over by a horse or a wagon. The other wagons in front of Imogen, Eric, and Anton were making their way deeper into the city, so they retained their place at the end of the train. They discovered the endpoint of the journey when the wagons entered a giant central courtyard in front of enormous black wrought iron gates, beyond which they could see the University. The courtyard was bordered on two of the three remaining sides by the interior of the strong walls that

312

encircled the islands. The side facing the university buildings consisted of large merchant houses, three or four stories high, with crisscrossing timbers and white walls with steep gabled roofs. But the best views were to be had toward the university.

It wasn't the height of the towers that made them impressive, rather how many of them there were. When Eric thought of castles, he pictured those at Disneyland, a single tall tower with a number of middling buildings behind the imposing wall. What he could see now was the same imposing wall, but with a much more elaborate series of towers behind it. In fact, there was nothing *but* towers, jammed into the available space within the boundary wall of the University. They tended to be the same color stone, vaguely the same construction, and more or less the same width. What really stood out for Eric were the walkways strung between the towers. They hung from beams protruding from the towers, some midway up the height, some nearer the top, and all made from wood and rope, and swaying slightly in the breeze. Occasionally, Eric could see a robed figure scurrying along one or other of the walkways, walking with a swaying gait that he guessed would be so they could actually make forward progress while walking on the uneven and moving wooden boards.

Below on the courtyard, the wagons were splitting up, some heading through the gates into the university. The majority of them though were heading to the right of the gates, between the walls of the university and the exterior walls toward the remainder of the island, where the city which supported the university was situated. There was little to be gained from gawping at the spires, so they followed behind, knowing that the sun would set in a few hours and very aware they had no accommodation planned.

It took them ten minutes to reach the city proper, popping out of the narrow alley between the defensive walls into a city which looked like it had evolved more than had been planned. Even Gerton with its slightly skewed taller buildings that touched high above the alleys seemed more well thought out.

Eric took a look at the width of the streets of the city. They were large enough to take the oxen and the wagon, but there wasn't much room. If they had to turn around then there would be an issue as the oxen were notorious for not liking to walk backward while in their harnesses, and they usually had to be delimbered and turned manually.

"How about you go ahead and negotiate some accommodation, Imogen? Stabling for the oxen and the horse, and beds for the three of us. It would be good to sleep in a bed that isn't on the ground for once, wouldn't it? Oh, and food. I'm sure you're sick of cooking, right?"

314

She smiled her thanks, and he gave her a sizable number of coins from the purse. It was noticeably lighter than when they had started the journey but was still at least half full. The other sack had not been touched yet either. "How long will we need the room for, my lord?"

Eric thought about that for a moment, rubbing the wispy beard that now covered most of his chin. He was sure it would start filling out soon. Maybe. He'd never tried growing a beard as work preferred him freshly shaved, so leaving it to grow, he was discovering that he didn't really have the genes for facial hair. "Let's start with a week. I have no idea how long it will take us to find what we need. And tomorrow you can try to sell the oxen, the wagon, and what's left of our supplies."

Imogen dimpled and curtseyed. "I will return momentarily, my lord," she said before heading into the city.

Eric watched her go. It was weird, the contrast between the order of the university and the chaotic collection of buildings on the other side of the walls. Anton shifted in the bed of the wagon, leaning over the lip separating the waggoner's seat from the rear. "I guess we're here now, my lord."

Eric turned, puzzled. "I guess we are, Anton. What are your plans now?"

Anton seemed reluctant to answer. "Well, my lord, I think by rights, I should head back to Gerton on the next available train."

Eric nodded slowly, seeing Anton's predicament. "That is what we agreed with the most learned librarian if I recall correctly."

Anton continued. "But if my lord needed me, then I could see if there is a library I could continue to research on your behalf. And we could check when the next train is leaving to make sure that I get to Gerton in good time."

Eric tried to keep the smile off his face. "We would certainly have to get you back as soon as possible, but we might have a few things to check, so it would be very advantageous for you to stay for a little while. Just until we have all the information that we need, of course."

Anton looked relieved. "Of course, my lord. Once you have everything you need, I will leave you and Imogen, and head back home. With Marion's memoir, of course."

Eric nodded emphatically. "I think that we have extracted all we can out of Marion's memoir, haven't we?"

Anton had finished the memoir and had started back through it a second time. He wasn't able to quote verbatim from memory, but he certainly knew the contents by heart.

"So, how about tomorrow, you head out and find out what you can about the university, and how we get access to their library. But keep your wits around you - we're not on the train anymore - there aren't any guardsmen to come to our aid here. And it might be that the people are more deadly than the creatures we encountered out on the trail."

"I'll be careful, my lord. I did survive on my own in Gerton."

Eric inclined his head in an apology. "Of course, apologies, Anton."

They waited for half an hour. While the sun hadn't gone down quite yet, the air was cooler and the moons were visible by the time Imogen returned. She looked troubled.

"Problems?"

"No. Yes. I'm not sure, my lord. I have found us lodging for a week, but it took me four inns before finding one that didn't charge an arm and a leg"

"Awesome, well done. No problems with the stabling?"

"No, my lord."

"Well, what is the problem?"

"I got some strange looks, I guess they're not used to women wearing trousers here."

"Ah, ok. Well, let's go. It will be dark soon."

They headed deeper into the city, Imogen navigating them through some pretty tight streets with ease. Eventually, they made it to the inn. Imogen and Anton saw to the oxen and horse, and Eric went inside to freshen up. Not long afterward, they regrouped in the dining room for supper. There was a large fireplace there with a spit on it, a small dog walking on a wheel that rotated the spit, and a large animal carcass rotating on it. Periodically, the serving girl would pour a sticky liquid onto the flesh, drizzling it from a small bowl. Occasionally, some of it would drip off the meat into the fire with a hiss, releasing a sweet smell into the room. For dinner, they got slices of the meat carved off in front of them, with some roasted vegetables that turned out to have been cooked in the spill tray of the spit, so were naturally smothered in the sauce as well. It was delicious. They all ate more than they should have, ending up slumped on the benches in a meat-induced stupor. After waddling up the stairs to their rooms, they slept more comfortably than they had in a very long time.

In the morning, Imogen headed out to sell the oxen, wagon, and assorted supplies. Eric made sure to give her the man-in-red's sword. Her eyes widened when he handed it over to her. The notches in the blade would obviously lower the price she was able to get for it, but not having it around would definitely lighten their load. And, as he had been told, it wasn't magical, so it seemed to be safe to get rid of it. Imogen looked bemused and headed out.

Anton too was heading out. His was the most pertinent activity which would further their mission. Which left Eric. He had been focusing on the immediate task for so long, whether that was getting onto the train, detecting any danger while on the train, or dealing with the Queen and the ogres. Now that they were at Havelin, he was very much at a loose end.

He was tempted to stay at the inn and just veg out but decided it was much more important to try and find his feet in the city. So he went out and got thoroughly lost. His theory that the island, basically a boat-shaped piece of land in the river, with the university at one end and the rest of the city at the other, would mean it would be impossible to get lost. Surely, if you ever found yourself unsure, the walls along one side or the other would allow you to orient yourself, and you could therefore navigate to where you wanted to go. The conceit of this became apparent somewhere around the second hour of wandering, and it wasn't until later in the afternoon that he realized the island wasn't shaped like a thin boat such as a canoe or kayak, but more of an aircraft carrier. It had a narrow bit at one end that was widening considerably before abruptly finishing at the end.

Until then his wanderings allowed him to see the different construction styles and categorizing the buildings on the island. He was starting to recognize patterns. The oldest buildings tended to be closer to the wide end of the island and were made of the darkest wood. They were the most ramshackle. The next layer were the white-walled buildings, with wooden cross beams on the outside for support. These were usually newer but sometimes sat on top of the older foundations. Finally, you had the newest buildings. Those tended to be made of stone - but not the large blocks that he'd seen in other settlements, these the small stones that were found in the river banks. They were embedded in some sort of cement and must have been lighter than they looked because not only the foundations were made of the stone, but the whole walls, all the way up to the roof of the three- or four-story constructions. Eric must have looked pretty suspicious, examining the pebbled walls, stroking his chin and figuring out whether he would be able to climb them. He eventually decided that it wouldn't really be possible: the stones were too small and did not allow enough purchase. But that was only if the buildings were uniformly spaced out and perpendicular to each other. And that was the issue. The buildings were so tightly packed that it would be trivial to get onto the roofs by finding where two buildings were adjacent to each other at less than a ninety-degree angle. That made climbing up the walls pretty easy. You wouldn't have to be a parkour expert to do that.

Eric eventually found his way to one of the markets in a square, toward the east side of the city. It was the same as all the other markets he had seen: small stalls, usually a wagon with the oxen lazily waiting behind it, a farmer offering a selection of vegetables, chickens, or ducks in cages, maybe a sack or two of grain or flour. Occasionally, there would be a pen with a bunch of sheep. Or the odd cow. Eric wished he could figure out the relative prosperity of a town just by examining the market. Surely a more robust market would be a sign of wealth? Although, wouldn't that really mean the farmers were doing well? Having so many stalls might indeed imply that the farmers were doing well, but if nothing sold, then that would mean the city folk was not doing well. Eric ran a hand through his hair. Man, maybe he should have paid more attention in class.

He got back about the same time as everybody else. They reassembled in the dining room over an evening meal. This time it was some sort of ham salad. Big thick cuts of ham, served with flatbread and various vegetables. Fewer greens than Eric was used to, and more orange and purple. But they all tasted fine. They could have used a little mustard though. Maybe they didn't have mustard here?

Anyway, Imogen had done well disposing of the oxen and spare parts and had even gotten a good price for the sword, which she was happy about. She was even happier with the price she had been able to secure for her bolt of cloth. She smiled and jingled her purse.

She had also managed to find out more information from her tailor contacts. Her smile faded when she repeated what she had learned.

"No luck with the gauntlet, but my friend said that it would be incredibly unlikely that anyone would cast a spell for us. They didn't think that was how the mages operated, and in fact, they probably had not even thought of that as an option."

"What do you mean?"

"Well, and I'm just repeating what they said here, apparently mages are incredibly selfish and self-serving. They really are only learning their spells and their magic so that they can cast spells on themselves and seek glory and immortality. As I said, that might just be my tailor's prejudices coming through there."

Eric smiled. That did seem very prejudicial. But concerning all the same.

Anton, on the other hand, had had less success. He had found the main gatehouse to the university but had been stopped by the guard at the gate. Evidently, his robes were noticeably different from the mages' robes, and so he was not going to be able to enter without a sponsor – someone inside, who could vouch for him. And of course, without being able to go inside, he wasn't able to meet anyone who might want to vouch for him.

"Did you try to bribe the guard?" Imogen asked.

"What do you mean?" asked Anton.

"Sometimes when you want to go somewhere you are not allowed to, you can offer some money. Just don't say something like 'how much would it take for me to bribe you?' That's not an elegant way of doing it."

"Oh. How would you say it?"

Imogen looked uncomfortable. "I might say something like 'How much would a temporary pass be, so I can get in touch with my sponsor and get you what you need?' But you really have to watch how you ask for that. If they want to be awkward about it, you could lose your money and not get inside. You have to read the guard."

"Ah, ok, maybe I'll try that tomorrow." He looked over to Eric who hurriedly nodded. There weren't many avenues that he would not try to find that spell… and someone to cast it.

They retired for the night, ready to try again the following morning. Anton would attempt to bribe the guard, and Eric and Imogen would see whether they could broaden their search by heading around the inns, hoping they could at least talk to a mage. They thought that everybody had to blow off steam at some stage, and therefore, there should be someplace where mages could drink. Eric didn't want to consider the possibility that mages only went to bars on campus. That would really put a fly in the ointment!

The morning was a little overcast, and breakfast was some sort of oatmeal with crunchy raisins. Those turned out to be a fruit with a natural crisp skin that gave it a pleasing snap when you bit into it. Eric was just glad that it wasn't an insect as when he first saw the dish he thought that they were small cockroaches.

Imogen led the way to the first inn and was recognized by the innkeeper as soon as she walked in. He was a larger man, weirdly pear-shaped, with most of his bulk below the waistline. His face didn't really show his weight and could have appeared on a much thinner man. He was a little shorter than average, probably approaching middle age.

"You again! Where did you end up staying if you don't mind me asking?"

"We're over at the Brass Knuckle."

"Ah, that Jaxon will be the death of me, undercutting me at every turn. When he runs out of that pork, you come and see me. I'll give you a good deal."

"We will indeed! While we're here, we were just wondering if mages come here to drink?"

The innkeeper was on edge immediately. "Sure…" he drawled slowly while looking from Imogen to Eric and back again. "Why?"

"We're looking for a mage who can cast a spell on us."

As the man stared back, it finally dawned on Eric just how ridiculous that sounded.

"It's a particular spell," he explained. The explanation didn't really help much though.

"I'm sure," said the innkeeper. "You'd have to be some kind of idiot to allow a mage to cast just any spell on you. But, out of curiosity, how are you going to dictate which spell they cast?"

"Well, I'm going to pay them, surely they are honorable men and will cast the spell that I paid for? Won't they?" The look on the innkeeper's face was a mix of incredulity and amusement.

"Uh... The mages are not tradesmen who will put up a wall to your dimensions. They are beholden to themselves; they do not answer to us. They have a university, not a guild. There's no checking of their work or method for claiming that they short-changed you. There's no maker's mark."

Eric's face fell. "Ah, yes, that makes sense."

"But yes, to answer your question, sometimes a mage will come in and have a drink. They're human too, right?"

"I guess so."

They went from inn to inn getting very similar responses. It was approaching lunchtime by the time they arrived back at the Knuckle. Anton was waiting for them. He hadn't had much luck either.

"I didn't have any luck at all with the guard. It was like he didn't want the bribe or something."

"That's always the possibility. And if you push too hard, they might report you."

"So how do we get Anton into the library? He's not a student, he's not staff, and we don't know how to bribe the guard, so how do we get him inside?"

"In the laundry hamper?" suggested Anton.

"Through the sewer?" suggested Imogen.

"I think I might have better luck with the hamper, my lord."

"Well, if we can't go over the walls, then I guess maybe we can go under the walls. Won't the sewers be dangerous though?"

"Again, maybe just being brought through the gate in a laundry hamper would be enough - they come and go quite regularly."

"Are all the outlets of the sewers above or below the waterline? And, more importantly, what would be crawling around down there? In another city, they had all manner of problems with groffrey. Do you know what they are? Little pond animals that grow into dog-sized pests. They eat mice and insects and are really cute when they're young, but then, after three months, they change shape and grow extra legs. They become get quite hideous, so the owners then put them in the sewers."

"I don't think that–"

"Oh, that's right, Gerton doesn't have sewers, right? Everything gets flushed down the street. Anyways, if the mess the groffrey caused is a benchmark, who knows what a bunch of mages would be flushing down the sewers?"

"My lord, I really cannot go through the sewers." Anton's voice had gotten quite high-pitched by this stage.

Eric sighed. "Ok, fine. We can try the laundry. Imogen, can you please ask around and try to gather information on how the whole laundry system works? Anton, do you know what you would do if you could get into the university? Do you know where the library is or how it operates? Do you need a library card?"

The others looked at him in confusion.

"Oh, sorry. Library card: an indicator of belonging to a library. Is there anything that would indicate you belong there?"

Anton shrugged. "I guess I will have to find that out when I'm inside, my lord."

Eric shook his head. This was not a plan with much meat on it. "Imogen, could you take Anton with you and try to find out what you can about the laundry system, and what credentials you would need for the library?"

"Of course, my lord. What will you be doing this afternoon?"

"I'm going to see a man about a dog."

Their looks of confusion brought Eric a perverse pleasure.

Eric headed back to one of the inns they had visited in the morning. The innkeeper greeted him warmly, and Eric ordered and paid for a drink while surveying the bar. A few dodgy-looking folks in the shadows, making nefarious plans, no doubt. A merchant regaling a table of ladies with his latest mercantile exploits. And in the corner, nursing a very tall beer, was a mage. Jackpot! He looked to be a little older than Eric, but Eric didn't know if that would make him a student, a graduate, or even staff. There was so much they didn't know about the school despite having read Marion's memoir.

Eric headed over and pulled up the chair opposite the mage. Who looked up, extremely surprised. "Hi," said Eric, smiling warmly. "Can I buy you a drink?"

"Nah, I don't think so, I've got one. Besides," said the mage, "I want to be alone."

"Are you sure? I'd like to–"

"I'm sure. Off you fuck."

Eric was about to try again when the innkeeper's hand came down on his shoulder, a little heavier than a friendly pat, and the innkeeper smiled down at him. "Best drink your drink somewhere else in the bar, kind sir," he said. He watched as Eric moved away toward an empty seat that was closer to the entrance, and then followed him. "It might just be a good idea not to bother the

328

patrons, good sir. They could be a little prickly, and when they've had a few drinks, some of them are downright dangerous. Nobody wants to be bothered when they just want a few drinks, right?"

Eric agreed with him and finished his drink. He headed to the next inn; the failure still fresh in his mind. He thought about his approach as he walked. He needed to align his interests with the innkeepers, he decided. Again, the innkeeper recognized him, and again, he ordered a weak beer, drinking it at the bar.

"Innkeeper, you strike me as someone who would be keen to earn an extra coin for very little work."

The innkeeper was all ears at this. "I'll allow that you have me intrigued," he said.

"I wish to ask a mage a question, and I know that sometimes they frequent your inn. What I would like to do is to give you a coin every time you tell me that there is a mage in your bar."

"What do you want a mage for?"

"As I say, there's a question I need to ask him."

"I can't have you interrupting my customers. I'll get a reputation, and they won't come back!"

"Well, the mage won't know that you told me that he would be there. I walk in, ask the question. You walk over and say 'Are you bothering this man, you'd better leave'. At that stage, if the mage is interested in my proposal, he'll say that everything is fine, and I will sit with him. If he's not ok with it, then you will look good for keeping-riff raff away from your customers. What do you think?"

The innkeeper considered it. "Ah, but how am I going to tell you that he's here?"

"You send a boy. I'm staying at the Brass Knuckle. So you send a boy to tell me there's a mage here, I pay the boy a coin for the message. Then I come here, and if there is a mage, then I will pay you a larger coin."

"What kind of coin?"

Now Eric was stuck! Maybe he should have gotten Imogen to do the negotiation!

"What do you care what kind of coin? It's literally money for nothing!"

The innkeeper paused for a second, considering the offer before grinning and pulling out a twig from behind his apron. He snapped it in half, saying "The bargain is made!"

It didn't take long to finish off the rounds of the inns, making the same bargain with each of the innkeepers. He didn't want to try and persuade the first innkeeper, thinking that it might attract too much attention to himself. As he headed back to the Knuckle, Eric congratulated himself on coming up with such a plan. Now he just had to wait.

When Eric got back to his room, Anton and Imogen were already there, looking depressed. They'd both been less than successful with their intelligence gathering. First, the ladies who did the laundry for the mages had been incredibly suspicious of the amount of curiosity shown about the process of how soiled linens became clean. There were very few satisfying answers to the challenge 'why do you want to know?'

Second, they still hadn't been able to get past the guards at the gate. And suggesting that maybe there could be some sort of payment to allow them through temporarily didn't get any traction.

After debriefing them, Eric got Imogen to show him the least valuable coins that he had. Even those were still quite valuable though, so he got her to swap those with the innkeeper for the denominations low enough to warrant being paid to someone who told them of a mage in an inn. He very soon had a pocketful of appropriate coins, and all there was to do was wait.

They supped on pork ribs, served with a barbecue sauce that was more spiced than sweet, but really brought out the flavors of the meat. It contained something resembling paprika but more earthy. The meat itself fell off the bones, it was so tender. If anything like that got to Earth, it would cause a stampede. Eric could imagine it on a bun at a baseball game or served at a candlelit dinner in an upmarket restaurant. Delicious. They had nothing to do but eat and nurse drinks while hoping someone would come through the door with good news.

It was actually starting to get quite late when a boy of about eight came through the door. He paused when he got inside and scanned the interior, before fixing his gaze on Eric and walking up to him. "Throm of the White Swan sends his regards, my lord," he said, holding out his hand. Eric smiled and thanked him, before handing him one of the coins. The child scampered out into the night and Eric turned to the others.

"Showtime!"

Chapter 18

The White Swan was one of the closer pubs to the rear gatehouse that was used to access the university. It wasn't very full when they arrived. Anton and Imogen took up seats near the door. Eric walked over to the innkeeper, who indicated a man in the corner, drinking alone. The man was definitely wearing mage's robes, so Eric deposited a coin in the innkeeper's hand and approached him, uncertain how to begin the conversation.

The mage looked up as Eric got closer, a little surprised to be accosted. Eric had not rehearsed his opening line, and it showed. "I would like you to cast me a spell," he said, kicking himself immediately after, realizing how cumbersome it sounded.

The mage was older than Eric, maybe thirty or so, with the beginnings of a goatee that would look quite fetching when it started to fill out. "Go away," he spat, returning his attention to his beer.

"But I'll pay!" Eric called over his shoulder as the innkeeper led him away. He collected Anton and Imogen, and they headed back toward the Knuckle.

"Shouldn't we stay there and try again?" asked Anton.

"I don't think starting a bar fight will endear us to either the innkeepers or the mages of Havelin," Eric replied. "Besides," he said, "we have to be back at the Knuckle in case a boy comes in from one of the other inns."

Eric turned to Imogen. "Why are so many inns called 'The Swan'?"

In the semi-darkness under the street lights, he saw her smile. "There was a legend about a Berberber, an enormous supernatural being, twice a normal man's height, with purple skin. Anyway, this Berberber captured a wandering king. The king bargained that he be allowed to leave the prison and wander along the river bank as far as a swan could travel in a day. The Berberber agreed. The next day, the two of them rode to see how far the swan had traveled. While they were looking for it from the river bank, the king found it nestled in the reeds beside the river. The Berberber was very easily distracted, so the king threw a stone into the middle of the river, and while the Berberber's back was turned, he killed the swan and hid its body. The two of them continued onwards. Each time the king found a swan, he would distract the Berberber, kill the swan, and hide the body."

"That's terrible!"

"True, but in this manner they made their way back to the king's kingdom, the Berberber getting more and more upset as they got closer. Without finding a swan, there was no way of restricting the king's permitted exercise area. Until they stepped over the border to the king's lands. Then, he had the Berberber arrested and killed. And as a sign of his gratitude, he made the swan the symbol of safe travel and created a law against mistreating them. That's why inns are very commonly called 'The Swan', or sometimes, 'The White Swan'. As if there are any other colors of swans!" They finished the story just as they arrived at the Knuckle.

They didn't have to wait too long. A different child entered, again scanned the room, before recognizing that something about Eric matched the physical description that they have been given, and came over holding his hand out.

Eric looked down at the hand. "And where have you come from, my little friend?"

The street urchin looked a little rougher than the previous one but answered the question. "The Ogre's Delight - where's my money?"

Eric smiled at his brusqueness and paid him his coin.

Again, they headed over to the inn in question. By that point in the day, the lanterns had been turned down, and the shadows in the inn's common room lengthened considerably. At this late hour, there was only one patron, moodily looking into the bottom of an empty wine glass, as if hoping to find another, undiscovered mouthful somewhere in there. Eric was tempted to not pay the innkeeper as it was so obvious who he was looking for, but he was too honest for that, so passed by the bar and handed over a coin.

Eric sat in the chair opposite the mage and waited until he noticed that Eric was there. This one was more inebriated than the previous one and was actually quite a bit older than any of the other mages he had seen. A thick salt and pepper beard hid most of his face. His eyes were blue and piercing, if currently unfocussed. Maybe a staff member?

"What do you want?"

"I'd like for you to cast me a spell. A particular spell. To send me back to my home. On a different planet."

The mage stared at Eric for a few seconds, and Eric wasn't sure if he had actually heard him. "And what do I get?" he asked eventually.

Wow, we're negotiating! thought Eric. This was going well!

"Money," he said. But that didn't have the effect he was hoping for. The man looked unimpressed. "A lot of money," Eric added.

"I have money. I don't need more. What else have you got?" The mage looked like he was enjoying Eric's discomfort.

"What do you want?"

"Twenty virgins and the Spellbook of the Arch-mage," the man grinned, showing perfect teeth.

Eric still couldn't figure out whether the mage was negotiating or wasting his time. "I can do ten virgins, but the spell book might be a bit of a stretch. How about five virgins, and I throw in one of the stray dogs I have seen around the city?" If he could get him laughing, maybe Eric could talk sense with the man.

The mage stood, a little unsteady on his feet. He leaned closer to Eric. "You have nothing I need; you can get nothing I want. Talking with you is a waste of my time. Enjoy the rest of your evening."

Eric recoiled, as much from the alcohol on the man's breath as the meaning of the words. This was not going well.

The mage navigated his way to the door and, with a bellowed farewell to the innkeeper, left the inn, slamming the door behind him.

Eric sat at the table for a second, recovering from the disappointment. The innkeeper came over and collected the mage's wine glass. And then surprised Eric by sitting in the mage's newly vacated chair, fixing him with a quizzical look.

"I can keep taking your coin, as can Throm at the White Swan, Jorm at the King's Head, all of Havelin's innkeepers, but I have the feeling that at the end of the week, you are going to be short a purseful of coin and you're not going to have the answer you're looking for. Why don't you tell me what you are actually looking for? Who knows, maybe I can help?"

Eric sighed and rubbed his face. "We're seeking one who can perform magic. I have… questions."

"And nobody wants to answer your questions, hmmm?"

"No."

"Well, to be fair, what would the staff and students need from the likes of you and me? They're learning how to move mountains and make smarter animals, and we're here trying to earn a crust. To them, we're ants, asking for answers. They don't have the time for things that are unimportant. And we are unimportant. Listen, it's not all bad. They pay well, and they don't start fights. But if you start pissing them off, you're going to learn some answers to questions like 'what does it feel like to be shocked to death?' and 'how far can my feet be pulled away from my head before my neck or ankles give way, and which would give way first?'"

"Are they all like that?"

The innkeeper leaned back in his chair, arms behind his head. "No, not all of them. Most of them, yes, but not all. Every now and again you'll get one, always a student, always before graduation. They'll come in all furtive, acting like they're looking for the answer to their own questions in the bottom of their glass. Always with the look like they are haunted, or maybe hunted. They jump at their own shadow and appear as if they're sleeping rough. Sometimes, they hang around for a couple of months, and sometimes for longer. It's a pattern I've noticed. We've got one currently, a larger lad. Likes his lager. And his food. Bit of a scent on him if you know what I mean. A bit grizzled."

"Why is he grizzled?"

The innkeeper leaned forward now. "Where I come from, we have a saying for someone who finds out more than they should. We say that they saw the whole of the moon. Like too much truth for one person. This young mage, he looks like he saw the whole of the moon."

"How do I get hold of this guy?"

The innkeeper looked thoughtful. "I've been seeing him off and on maybe once every couple of days? Tell you what, if I see him, I'll tell my boy to tell you that the moon is rising. That should be worth a bit more than just a copper coin, hmm?"

"Two? Or ten?"

"Make it twenty," the innkeeper said, his eyes twinkling in what lantern light was left.

Eric led the way back, the others curious as to what the innkeeper and he had spoken about. "I was just following up on a lead. My initial approach doesn't seem to be working, so I'm pivoting." At their confused looks, he explained. "Just tweaking the plan. Instead of trying to talk to every mage who comes into an inn, I'm looking for just one."

Anton frowned in the darkness, briefly illuminated by one of the street lanterns along the main road. "But won't that make it harder to find them?"

"Harder, yes, but much more likely to have luck talking with them."

They left word with the innkeeper at the Brass Knuckle that they were to be woken should any child come bearing a message. After that, they went to bed.

The next day was spent waiting and waiting and waiting. They had the breakfast cakes when they woke up, some sort of ham sandwich for lunch, and the ribs again for dinner. There was no sign of any child couriers all day. The innkeeper got a little terse after they asked him for the third time whether there had been any messages for them. Eric went to bed that night feeling they had wasted a day. But with no other leads, they were in a holding pattern.

The next morning was kicked off by a knock on Eric's door. He answered it bleary-eyed to see the innkeeper standing at the doorstep, smiling, and a ten-year-old boy next to him, with his hand out. "The moon is rising, mister. But that's bullshit because it's daytime, and it's already in the sky. Give me my coin." Eric paid him and flicked the innkeeper a coin for extra measure. Then he got dressed. He was more sleepy than excited, and the constant failures were dampening his expectations. In spite of that, he collected the others, and they made their way back to the Ogre's Delight.

It was empty of patrons, save for one, sitting in the corner with his back to the wall and a view of the door. He was in mage's robes and was carrying a lot of extra weight, his face supporting heavy jowls. His eyes were dark and puffy from lack of sleep, and his lank hair looked greasy and unkempt. In short, he looked like he needed to lose fifty pounds, and have a shower and a haircut. He looked up as Eric and the others walked in and watched them warily as Eric walked toward him, alone.

The mage was eating breakfast, some sort of porridge or polenta, with chunks of fruit cut into it. As Eric approached, he called out to the innkeeper. "Another breakfast for me and my friends if you please." He sat at the table beside the mage, figuring that one of the reasons he hadn't gotten anywhere with the other mages was because he had been too familiar with them.

"How is it?" he asked the mage as he sat on the wooden stool.

The mage obviously didn't know how to respond. He flicked his eyes toward the door and then back to Eric. "Good," was all he could manage. The innkeeper had been right, there was a scent on him. Actually, the innkeeper had been polite. Eric had been near enough to homeless people to recognize the ingrained body odor of someone who was sleeping on the street.

"Great, great," continued Eric, trying to figure out how to coax the mage out of his shell. The innkeeper came over with his bowl of polenta, and Eric handed over a large coin. The mage gave a secret smile as the innkeeper left them.

"You should have negotiated better. The breakfast should have been a lot cheaper than that. Even for the three of you."

Eric couldn't quite pick how old he was. Probably the same age as he was, maybe a little younger. "Yeah, you're right. Thanks for the pointer. My name is Eric, what's yours?"

The mage was instantly circumspect, constantly measuring the distance between him and the door. "My name is for my friends," he said sullenly.

"Ah, a cautious man, an advisable trait indeed. You never know who wishes you ill. Trust me, I do not wish you any harm. I only want to know the answers to a few questions, if you can spare the time?"

"Are you from the university?"

"No, but I do want to talk about magic. You can leave anytime you want though." The mage looked up at the door, then at Anton and Imogen who were sitting right next to it. "Imogen, could you and Anton please sit further away from the door, please?" They moved their plates and went further into the innards of the inn. Eric shrugged as the mage looked at him, and then turned his attention to the meal in front of him. "Or," he said, not making eye contact, "we can eat our meals in silence, and we can go our separate ways. But I think that you have a tale to tell. A story that you need to share with someone. What do you think?" He glanced up to see if the soft sell was working.

The mage looked conflicted. In fact, he almost got up to leave, before thinking better of it and settling back into his chair with a sigh. "Fine. You pay for lunch, and I'll tell you my story."

"Lunch? But we've just had breakfast?"

"It's a long story."

"Then, let's start at the beginning. As I said, I'm Eric, that's Anton, and that's Imogen. And you are?"

"Oram. I am Oram of Fendel in Eroo."

"Well met, Oram."

"Thank you. I am… or was, a student at the university. Up until recently anyway. Things happened."

"Oh? What kind of things?"

"There are a number of ceremonies to pledge your loyalty to the university. These are serious pledges, promises made in blood and with dire consequences for breaking them. Our year had more students than normal, so we ended up having two of these ceremonies: one in the morning, and another in the afternoon. I was beside myself with curiosity - nobody would tell me what the ceremony consisted of. And there was no way I was going to wait until it began to see what was involved. I had figured out that you could climb the outside of the ceremony hall and peer in the window while standing on the little annex shed. Anyway, I was watching as they led the class through the incantation. The light was coming through at such an angle that they had to blink in the sunlight because they were facing the windows. I was watching closely, so as my friend cast his spell, I saw a speck of light - a sunbeam - fly up his nose. It was so brief you would not have even noticed it unless you were looking for it. Then the next person cast their spell and the same thing happened. I shouldn't be telling you this, but I have no one else to talk to. If I speak to anyone attached to the university, I will be cast out."

"Can't they find you? Aren't you worried that they'll track you down here?"

"Not if I don't use magic. They are supposed to be able to track you once you have attended the ceremony. Although, mages go missing and aren't found, which makes me wonder if that is just hearsay. It's difficult to split out what is actual ability versus what things might have been in the ancient past, and what never-was.

They can ask around if they like and find me, but I really don't think that they care."

"A mage on the loose? Surely you are too powerful?"

"No, they lose so many before the ceremony that they really only treat you like a member of the university once you've gone through the ceremony. I think they probably think I have fled the city like everyone else who decides to retire from student life."

"And why haven't you?"

"I don't know," he said. There was a long pause. "I was all ready to commit to the university, to further my knowledge of magic, and play my part in casting spells of great power. But seeing that thing invading my friend's body made me reconsider. The only reason to put something into someone's body would surely be to control them? I know that the purpose of those ceremonies is to commit to the university, but that seems like–"

"Like you would be their thing?"

Oram frowned, considering what Eric had said. "Yes, but when you see the graduates, it doesn't feel like they are empty: they are still the same people. And if that's the case, why do they need the… whatever it is?"

"Don't take this the wrong way, but could it be possible that you imagined it? Or… that it was indeed a sunbeam? Or a bit of dust?

Picking out the light? And because of the angle you were watching from, it looked like it was entering their body?"

"Anything is possible. I have thought about this for so long, hoping and praying that was the case. But in my heart of hearts, I know what I saw. And it scared me."

"What are you going to do?"

Oram blinked. "I never thought of that. I know I can't go back, but that has been my home for so long, and every plan I had made for my life featured the university at some stage and in some form. But now… I don't know. I can't go back and don't know where to go forward. I'm lost."

"Would you like to help us?"

Oram sat looking into his beer for a long while, weighing up the offer. He looked up at Eric, then at Anton and Imogen, then back to the beer. He sat staring at it for so long that Eric glanced into it to make sure there was nothing floating in it. After a long pause, Oram turned to him.

"Sure."

Chapter 19

"Do you want to tell us more about the ceremony? I was told that mages are forbidden from using mind-control spells," began Eric.

Oram looked surprised that he knew that. "That's true, for many years now. Periodically, someone talks about someone they know, hearing about someone who thought it would be ok to cast a mind-control spell. And how their head explodes, or their face melts, or some other catastrophic occurrence."

"So, it can't be the university doing mind-control magic, can it? That would be hypocritical."

"I don't know. But even seeing the sunbeam going into the body connected the dots for me. A lot of the things I had learned that never quite made sense, all of a sudden clicked."

"Like what?"

Oram leaned back in his chair. "So, if magic actually involved tiny sunbeams, then where do they come from?"

"That's a pretty good question. What did you learn at school?"

"We learned that magic is all around us."

"Like 'in every living thing' all around us? Like the Force?"

Oram frowned. "I don't know what the Force is, but no, not like that. More that, literally, there are sunbeams all around us, too small to see."

"Unless the sunlight hits them just right."

"Yeah. But in addition to 'magic is all around you', we also learned that there are dead zones with no magic. So, presumably, none of these little sunbeams exist there. And there are zones where even more magic is present."

"You don't have to be Einstein to figure out that there's going to be more magic at a mage university," said Eric.

"Whatever an Ein-stein is, right. But there are these zones away from universities where the magic is concentrated. Where animals are… different. Smarter, more social, faster, with more muscles. Where trees grow faster, have more fruit, you know, everything is just better."

"Are there a lot of these zones?"

"There are a bunch, but when you ask more questions, you find they all look similar. Some lush valley, maybe centuries old, maybe recently-formed. But it is always a valley that comes to a point and is surrounded by very similar legends of its making. We're talking about different cultures, on different continents, but the story is always the same. You only piece these stories together over time. They might tell you something when they teach you about the students in one of the other universities, in another country. And to get there, you have to travel past this or that crater. Or this or that valley. Like the Gash in Ordost."

"We went through there."

"Weird place, right?"

Eric nodded.

"So, at each of these places, eventually the concentration of magic lessens and presumably it drifts away."

"OK, weird, but OK."

Oram leaned forward, all intensity. "Eric, where do these things come from? These balls of magic from the sky? My father was a sheep herder. He'd spend long days out in the pastures with the sheep, and when the game was harder to find as winter approached, he'd have to fight off the wolves that came down from the hills. Living rough out in the world, he would tell me the stories that his father had told him about the gods throwing lightning and thunder at each other, thus creating the storms. They would manufacture some sort of reason for that. So we have our warring gods, and each storm is a battle. But if these balls of magic are just like that, then fine, there are gods rolling balls of magic to the ground in between throwing lightning and thunder at each other. But if what I saw means that magic is not a gift, wrested from the grasp of the gods, and it's in fact something mechanical, then who is sending these balls of magic to us? I would actually prefer to believe that it all comes from the gods because that is less scary. Lightning? Oh yeah, this god fighting with that god. Magic? Yeah, abilities stolen from the gods. But the alternative? Magic just being some sunbeam shoved up your nose? Balls of magic sent from the sky from someone? So, let's just say, I've been trying to figure things out, and I'm not getting anywhere."

Eric frowned back at Oram. It sounded like the mage would prefer a supernatural explanation for magic, rather than seeing evidence for it with his eyes. And what his mind was telling him. "Might there be clues in these scars? These valleys?"

"Funny you should say that. Periodically, some of the university staff will head out to one of these scars on a research expedition. We joked that it was a chance for them to get away from their families, drink too much, and sleep with their research assistants. But now I'm not sure. What do you think they would be looking for?"

"I don't know, but I'm not keen on going back to the Gash. It's too dangerous."

"Yeah, fair enough. So this spell, what do you know about it?"

"Literally nothing: just that I was in my bed at home and woke up here."

"Are you sure it was a different world? Could you have just been moved a long distance?"

"Well, apart from the moon being the wrong color and the wrong size, you might be right."

Oram smirked. "Fair enough. OK, so I don't know all of the sorts of spells that the library has."

"If we can find it, could you cast it?"

"Probably not." He saw Eric's face drop. "Look, it's like this. The magic that you learn before you become a mage proper are all localized magic. 'Shock that person'. 'Heal me'. 'Heal them'. 'Make me stronger'. 'Make me more agile'. That sort of thing. But once you commit… Well, I'm only operating on what I've heard. But they are more expansive spells. Affecting the weather. Changing animals. Bringing people back from the dead. Traveling miles with a step. And maybe even traveling between worlds. But all those take exponentially more power."

"Ah."

"Yeah, it gets weirder. The day before the ceremony, I met a man who had something similar to what you've got: that blue spot on your earlobe. But he had a blue smudge on his eye. He told me he could read anything in any language. So I thought I would show him a page from my spell book. Bear in mind, I had spent a year just learning the alphabet of the language that spells are written in. And the mother fucker could read it!"

"What happened? Did he cast the spell?"

"No. Oh, he said the words alright. I damn near fell off my chair when he spoke them. But he did not have the rhythm correct or any of the gestures."

"So the hand motions, are they required?"

He frowned. "Everything is required. The gestures - I mean, do you think it takes so long to learn magic because we're learning little dances and patterns of hand motions just for fun? The alphabet, how each letter is pronounced and how other letters change and modify the pronunciation. If you get that wrong, the spell splutters and fails. The fun part is when you don't get the timing right when it comes to both the words and the gestures. Then the spell either fails, gets misdirected, gets underpowered, or…"

"Or?"

"One of the reasons the ceremony of commitment waits so long is to make sure we're only getting the good mages, those that can pronounce all the words the right way, the ones that can pause at the right places, and make the right gestures. Because the more powerful magic can go really awry in a big way, and if you don't pump enough power into the spell, then the magic will take it from you. Leaving you an empty husk. But that's not the most interesting part."

"Hmmm?"

"The man could read the words as well as any mage. He could see the letters and knew the pronunciation. That was impressive."

"…OK…?"

He leaned forward. The room seemed darker. The candles flickered.

"He understood the words."

"What do you mean?"

"If you saw the letters aphe, pitosh, heffe, and hogge, you would know it meant dog, right? If you were a mage and that was a spell, you would be concentrating on making the noises for aphe, pitosh, heffe, hogge. This man knew it said dog. No one, mage, non-mage, or anyone really, knows what words those letters make up. So that means that the words that make up spells are written in some language and the words have meaning."

"Did you ask him what the spell said?"

"Yeah. I wrote it down. It fucked me up for the rest of the night, and then, the next day, when I saw what I saw, at the ceremony, I was really thrown for a loop."

"Well, what did it say?"

"'Hear me now, one time (or it might have been one finger), shock that there, fuck him up'."

Eric blinked. "Seriously? That was the translation of the spell?"

"That's what he said."

"Ok, you are right, that is weird." Eric thought for a second. "So you've agreed to help us. And you can probably *say* the words in the spell. Don't take this the wrong way, but are you powerful enough to *cast* the spell?"

"Probably not."

They all stared at him. This was not going well.

"Look, I learned the spells that I was powerful enough to cast. I didn't pass the ceremonies. So unless, for some reason, the university deliberately keeps us from spells that we are powerful enough to cast, if I haven't heard about the spell, I very probably can't cast it…"

Eric stared at the table, despondent.

"…unless you have some object which concentrates the power from the environment."

There was silence for a moment. "What kind of object?"

"I've heard that some people who have not learnt how to harness magic can still cast spells. They use objects which harvest the power and store it, allowing them to release it at a later time."

"…like gloves?"

354

"Well, usually they are amulets, but yes, I guess you could embed the stone in anything."

"I think I might have some."

"Some amulets?"

"Wait here."

Eric rushed back to the room and returned with the satchel, emptying it on the table.

The mage's eyes went wide. He wasn't looking at the gauntlets, or the flasks of lantern oil. He was staring at the black-gray dusty stone that Eric had dug out of the pit in the ogres' tunnels. The mage looked up at each of them in disgust.

"You brought this here? You are - you really have no idea what this is?"

"...it's a stone?"

"It's a no-magic stone. That's what we call it. The professors call it something else, but that was the word we used for it. A null magic stone." Again, Oram looked from blank face to blank face. "You don't know what that is?" They wordlessly shook their heads.

"It stops magic from working. It is super rare, because the university, and all other universities, hunt these down and destroy them. There is a huge black market for them among the more senior mages, because, what would protect them from their peers and rivals? These. Look, with this you have a small chance of sneaking into the library, but you're going to get lost getting there. The first year of school is spent learning the paths between the towers, and even a lot of second years get lost when they leave the more well-trodden routes. You don't have any other magical treasures lying around, do you?"

Eric was about to guffaw and say "of course not!" when he paused. "Actually, maybe you should see something." He left again and came back shortly afterwards with the book that he'd found in the saddlebags when he had first arrived on this world. "The words move," he said unnecessarily.

The mage may have been upset at the null magic stone, but with the book, he was a little less impressed. "It's a book, usually used as a diary. It's enchanted, so the words move to disguise what is written inside - a combination of enchanted ink and a magical book. There is a password that you say to unlock it. That would make the words visible until you say the locking word. I don't know if they're attuned to the voice as well, that was the advanced version of the magic."

"Can we pick the lock or get around the magic somehow?"

"I don't know. We could try and guess the password?"

"Or maybe use the null magic stone?"

Oram shook his head. "The stone might wipe the book of all its contents. The magic protecting the book's contents sort of becomes

356

the content itself, it gets mixed up with it. So, removing the protection effectively removes what's written inside. I think."

"Like a hard drive?"

Oram looked blankly at him.

"So, using the null magic stone would be more of a last resort?" Eric asked.

"Yeah."

"Could I come? Seeing the library at Havelin will be a dream come true," Anton interrupted.

"Anton, this might be a case of the core mission taking priority over what we might like to happen. Is it possible for all three of us to go?" He turned to the mage. "Would it be best if you went alone? Sounds like you are a necessary element, but is it better to have one go, two, or all three?"

"Hoi! What about me?"

"How many of the mages are women?"

"Very, very few." Imogen pursed her lips and sat back in her chair before continuing. "Hmmm… As long as I am sent through to your world with you, I guess I can forgo the dangerous mission into the mages' library to steal a spell… Just make sure you get back with it. And with Eric, of course."

Eric smiled at her; pretty sure she was joking. Was she joking?

"So, what does the spell look like anyway? What are we stealing?"

"Well, you see, all a spell is, is a recipe, much like those for a cake or a loaf of bread. You have to say particular words, make particular pauses between the words, and make certain gestures and the right amount of power. And boom, spell cast. Small spells - few words, few pauses, few gestures. Large spells... well..."

"Got it, but what will it look like?"

Oram paused, looking at them in turn. "I'm not supposed to share this information with anyone who is not a student or graduate of the school. Upon pain of death if I graduated and on pain of... well, pain for any undergraduates."

They looked at each other.

Oram shrugged. "Well, I guess I'll figure it out later. OK. The library is actually small compared with some of the collections of books I have seen in small towns, such as Sweem or Gerton." He made a face.

Anton looked affronted and was going to say something when Eric placed his hand on his arm, with a half shake of his head. Oram continued, unperturbed.

"But the books we do have go into the theoretical discussions of certain minutiae of the cutting edge of magic theory - what is a spell? What is magic? That sort of thing. Most of our learning happens in classrooms with tutors though. In the advanced classes, it might be in the labs or on the higher towers. And spell books are books that each mage writes in himself in language that he understands, using terminology that he understands. His own shorthand for the recipe if you like. So, a Wilese would need to note the exact way that the sounds of the letters differ from what he is used to forming with his mouth. So that he doesn't mispronounce the words and miscast the spell. Whereas someone like me might focus on how many heartbeats to wait between the first phrase and the later ones so that the rhythm works. So, when you ask 'what does the spell look like', there isn't a master list of all the spells. If you know something that none of the other mages know, you will only give a short hand note of how to cast it using what you usually do."

"Hang on, does that mean that the library won't have the spell?"

There was an uncomfortable silence.

"To tell the truth I don't actually know. That's the sort of thing that they tell you after you graduate."

"For all you know, there is a master book of spells," Anton said.

A flash of anger registered across Oram's face. He was about to retort but visibly reconsidered.

"I guess you're right. All I know is that I don't know a spell that would send people between worlds. I have been in the library, and I haven't seen any reference to anything like it."

They sat in silence for a second before Eric summarized the situation. "We could get you into the library, we could read all the books, but we don't know for sure that we would find the spell. And I imagine it's dangerous to sneak into the university library."

"Without the null stone it would be suicide. With it, you have a slim chance of getting in but a very low chance of getting out. With me, we might survive."

"But there's no point if that's not where the spell is."

"True. But…"

"But?"

"But I might be able to contact my friend. The one who I saw the mote go up his nose."

"Would he help us?"

"No - he doesn't know you at all. But he knows me, and he might tell me where I could find it. Maybe. And hopefully without telling anyone."

"But you just told us that he is an official mage now – committed and loyal. One of them. What makes you think that he will forget all that and put his vows on the line?"

Oram's look was intense and between gritted teeth, he said "He owes me."

Eric wanted ask him why but judging by Oram's facial expression, he thought it best to leave that line of questioning. "OK. It just seems a very thin thread to place ourselves at such risk. Surely, better to meet your friend out of school? Get a word to see him here in a pub?"

"Who would we trust to get a message to him?"

"Surely there is a message service? Couriers and such?"

"That might just work."

Chapter 20

They arranged for a messenger to contact Oram's friend and, despite Eric wanting to be there, Oram was adamant that he could have no distractions (and no witnesses, Eric thought). So they had to rely on the post-game report after the meeting.

When they came to the inn at the agreed upon time, Oram was sitting down to an impressive serving of roast chicken and roasted vegetables. Most of the vegetables Eric recognized, but there were a few alien shapes and colors that didn't quite match his memory of roasts back home or in this world. The three of them sat at the table, looking expectantly at Oram.

"What? Have I got something in my teeth?" joked Oram. Imogen gestured to the innkeeper and, with remarkable brevity, communicated that they wanted what Oram was having. "Kidding, kidding," he continued. "It went well. I was starting to think that they had not even missed me. What's one less student mage in a school of them, right? But no - they had missed me. Not enough to scour the lands, or to share my description with the guards, but I am listed on the official rolls as absent." He paused to slice the leg of the bird from the rest of the body and negotiate it into his mouth. "I didn't have to remind my friend that he owed me. And what I was asking wasn't apparently enough to threaten his vows of loyalty. There is a second library with a lot more books, including some standardized spell books."

"Standardized?"

"Well, you know how I said that each spell book was really the mage's recipe with shorthand and notes on how to pronounce and gesture and pause? The master spell books use a standard notation for each of those."

"And you know the standard notation?"

"Well, no, but I'm hoping if they are comprehensive spell books, they will have one or two of the spells that I do know, and therefore, I'll be able to figure out the standard notation."

Eric looked at him doubtfully.

"We don't have much of an option. But if the spell is not well known or a personal discovery of whoever cast it, we will be out of luck."

"Tell me more about this other library. Is it better defended than the one that you do know about? Did you find out where it is?" With every discovery, their chances seemed to drop further and further.

"He told me where it was. I didn't ask too many questions in order to avoid raising his suspicions."

"What did you tell him? How did you explain your absence?"

"I told him that I got cold feet at the last minute and had been weighing up my options ever since. I made him think that I might take the loyalty pledge with the next intake. He was very friendly after that. I'm hoping that the wards and guards at the library can be defeated using your null magic stone."

"Why don't we do it during the day?"

"The most important reason is because we don't know who will be using the library. If anyone notices us, they may ask questions."

"Fine, ok, and what about clothing?"

"I take it that you do not have mage's robes?"

"No. Do you have another robe?"

Oram allowed that he actually had a clean robe that maybe Eric could borrow.

"OK, we have robes, you know where the library is, we don't know if the spell is there, we don't know the defenses of the library, and we only have second-hand knowledge of how to get there. If one of my staff back home came to me with a 'plan' like this, I would tell them to go back to the drawing board. But we're betting our return to Earth on it?"

"What's the alternative?"

That question haunted Eric's nights for the next two days. Right up until the night they picked as the one to act.

They donned the robes, Eric storing the null magic stone in a coin purse. He was tempted to take some coins for whatever the local equivalent of bail was, or maybe for bribes. After a second of consideration though, he decided that the potential detriment of noise was more than the possible benefit, so left his money in the saddlebags. With a deep breath, he followed Oram out into the night.

The sewer had been ruled out. The laundry avenue had been rejected. Dressed as they were, Oram had seemed surprised that they would entertain any other method of entry than the front door. And so they walked straight in through the gate that Anton had not been able to go through.

"Evening, Harold," said Oram with a nod as they passed.

"Evening, sir," came the response.

And then came the tracing of the way to the library. They mounted one of the towers quite early on, walking up the internal spiral staircase for quite a while, stopping a couple of times to catch their breath on the way. At one of the stops, Eric frowned and turned to Oram.

"I meant to ask, why don't mages wear armor? Does the metal get in the way of the spells?"

Hands on his knees, Oram continued breathing heavily for a few seconds before answering. "No, it's not that at all. It's just basic fitness. I'm not fit because I'm concentrating on... more cerebral activities. No time for exercise. And so, the last thing I want is additional weight. Armor is heavy. Or trousers which would need a belt to hold them up. Belts aren't good on... people my size. They cut into my belly. Robes are far more comfortable."

Eric nodded in understanding. Then they continued up the tower, eventually leaving through a door in the wall onto a slightly swaying rope and wooden plank bridge. The walkways above the university crisscrossed between the towers. The view of the network they formed was impressive. Some of the other students and staff were visible, some walking alone and some in pairs, making their way from one tower to another. Eric and Oram paused for Oram to confirm their location. While he was waiting, Eric pointed to a pair of mages, one in red robes and the other in blue.

"What do the blue robes mean? Do they learn a particular type of magic?"

Oram looked over, slightly annoyed. "No, it just means they like blue."

Now it was Eric's turn to frown. "And what about the one in red? It doesn't mean that they are graduates or anything?"

Oram was apparently exasperated with him. "No, the robes just mean you're a mage. Either student or staff. Maybe a graduate student, maybe not. Sometimes a student will only have one color of robes. That's usually to make sure they get the right ones back from the laundry. But, Eric, I need to concentrate on this to make sure we end up in the right building. I don't want us to end up lost or worse, walking into some guardhouse that I don't know about. We are in a bit of a dangerous spot here, OK?"

Eric held his hands up in surrender. "OK, sorry!"

Oram turned to his notes, holding them to catch the light that was coming from the windows in the tower behind them. He nodded and led them further into the university. Far above, the red moon looked down at them.

"If I'm following my notes correctly, then we are almost there. Along this walkway, left, and then into the tower."

"OK, I'm ready." Eric could have kicked himself. Ready? Of course he was ready.

They headed along the walkway. At the end of it, a door beckoned. It swung easily open, revealing a landing with one door facing them and a staircase heading down, following the curve of the wall. The door that faced them opened, revealing a well-lit room before a mage headed out, briefly wishing them a good evening, before heading down the staircase.

Eric and Oram turned and shared a look. Were they going to be that lucky? Oram opened the door, and they went inside. Torches and lanterns spotted around the walls illuminated the interior of the library. The shelves were interrupted by narrow slits, exposing them to the outside world. Eric paused, wondering how they protected the books from wind and rain. If it snowed, would enough snow build up inside to do damage to the books? Oram nudged him. "There it is," he said, gesturing to the other side of the room. Against the far wall, in a vacant spot, unblemished by windows, lanterns, or torches, supported on a plinth of white stone, stood an ornate and solid-looking book. It must have been the size of a laptop, but a lot thicker, the edges of the pages gleaming with gold. The cover was evidently leather, which was on top of some hard substance, maybe wood, with ornate metal decorations at the corners. Even if Oram hadn't been staring at it like a junkie at a needle or a yuppie at a leveraged buyout, Eric knew this must be the spell book. The spell book with the only way back home.

He moved over to stand beside the book, his back to the featureless wall, so he could watch the door through which they had just entered on the other side of the room. Oram gingerly flicked through the pages of the book. His look had such an intensity, such... lust, that Eric was a little surprised. Oram reopened the book at the beginning, the cross-hatching of the letters by now very familiar to Eric, even if the meanings continued to elude him. Evidently, Oram had found the contents and ran his finger down the pages, his lips moving slightly as he read to himself, his eyes widening occasionally as he noted the name of one or other of the spells there. Eventually, he reached a spell he thought was the one, and he turned to Eric with a grin.

"Evan's Hole Through the Fabric!" he said breathlessly, his eyes reflecting the torchlight manically.

No sooner were the words out of his mouth when the door to the room opened, and Eric saw another mage come in.

"Good evening! I thought I would be the only one here. Don't mind me," the newcomer said as he closed the door behind him.

Oram leaned close to Eric and hissed through his teeth. "Rip out the page. I'll take care of him."

The book was still open at the contents pages. Eric was about to tell Oram that he didn't know what page it was on, but the mage had already turned to deal with the newcomer. What to do? What to do? Eric jogged from one foot to another as snippets of plans flitted across his mind. He should help Oram subdue the newcomer. He could take the whole book. They should flee and come back. He heard a scuffle and a thump. He decided they couldn't leave empty-handed, so grabbed the whole book and made for the door. He had only just registered the fact that the book was a lot heavier than its apparent size when he was brought up short by an almighty tug and the jangle of a chain, and found himself unceremoniously dumped on the ground, the book lost from his grasp. He looked back and saw that the whole book was chained to the podium it sat on. Although, now it dangled on the end of its chain, mocking him.

Oram called over to him. "We should go."

"But I don't have the spell," Eric called back from his position on the floor.

Oram flashed anger. "I told you the name of the spell, couldn't you find–"

The door opened again. A head poked in, and Eric saw eyes widening. Then the head disappeared.

Oram was all action. "Let's go!"

"But the spell!"

Oram was already at the door. "If we don't go now, we will get stuck here. Forever."

Eric scrambled to his feet, holding his robes up so that he could move his legs without them getting tangled up, and sprinted after Oram. He was lucky that they went back the way they had come, so even though he couldn't immediately see Oram when he left the room, he soon caught up with him as they ran down the walkways,

370

the swaying making their progress a crazy series of lurching lunges, holding the handrails.

Eric almost overtook Oram, the adrenaline coursing through his veins giving him an extra boost. He looked over his shoulder periodically, convinced that he would feel someone's hand on his shoulder at any stage. They paused at every door, listening to check if anyone was on the other side, or, as Eric began to suspect, for Oram to catch his breath. Eric very quickly lost his bearings and experienced a blur of walkways, towers, steps, and vaulted cellars. Eventually, they popped out into the courtyard that faced the back of the gatehouse they'd arrived at an hour or so before.

"And now?" he whispered in Oram's ear.

Oram straightened, took a deep breath, smoothing out his robes before stepping forward. Without looking at Eric, he said. "We walk out the front door."

Eric started after him, forgetting momentarily that they were feigning nonchalance and so was bent into a crouch for the first few steps. He then matched Oram's swagger and calm demeanor. The guard didn't even look up.

The coolness lasted until they were down the lanes and around the first corner, out of view of the gatehouse.

"Fuccccccck!" Oram sunk to his heels with his back to the wall, holding his head in his hands. "Fuck!"

Eric placed his back to the wall and sunk down with him. He knew the adrenaline coursing through him would start to make him shake and tremor, but he knew they still needed to be on their guard. What a mess.

"Why didn't you get the page? We only needed that one page! Of all the fucking useless - do you know what you've done? Do you?" He turned to face Eric. "I can't go back now. They saw me. The guy who came into the library? He saw me, and he recognized me. He was one of my old classmates. There is zero chance that this is not reported, and zero chance that they won't be able to find me. I. Am. Fucked."

Eric stood up, ignoring the slight shaking in his legs. "C'mon, let's go. We've got to get back to the inn, we have an escape to plan, and we have to get off the streets."

Oram buried his head in his hands.

Eric put some steel in his voice. "Oram!" Oram looked up. "Come on." He slowly got to his feet, and Eric led him back to the inn, looking over his shoulder periodically.

Imogen saw them first. "My lord," she said, "how did it go?" Her smile faltered as she looked from face to face.

"Imogen, how long would it take to get three more horses and pack all our belongings?"

Her eyes widened as she realized what he was saying. "We could pack now, and at first light, I can secure us the horses."

"Good, that would be perfect, thanks. Might pay to get some food from the innkeeper as well. Unless - will the market be open at first light?"

"The farmers might be arriving, but they won't be set up just yet."

"OK, anything you can get that's horse portable would be handy."

"Why aren't we leaving now?"

"One horse, four people. So, unless we steal three horses, or maybe only steal an extra one and we go two to a horse, we will be too easy to run down." Eric paused for a second, lost in thought. "Actually, we might be ok." He turned to Oram. "Do you own any more clothes? Not mage's robes but normal clothes?"

Imogen got it immediately. "Worst case he might squeeze into one of your jackets and maybe a pair of trousers."

Oram looked over. "All my clothes are mage's robes; I am a mage."

"Got it. Imogen, are any of your tailor folk open this late?"

She was already moving for the door, pausing with it open, and looking expectantly back at Oram.

"Anton, would you and Oram mind going with Imogen? She's going to try and get you both some clothes that might fit."

Oram frowned. "I don't want new clothes; we have to get away from here as soon as we can. Tonight!"

Eric nodded. "We have one horse. How far will a mage in robes, plus three others, get on one horse? If we leave now, we might make ten miles by dawn and twenty-five miles by noon. There are two roads leaving the island. If the school sends a mage on horseback in each direction, they will have ridden us down before nightfall, and that's assuming we leave now and go through the night. It will be obvious who they are looking for because you will have your mage robes on. And Anton's librarian's robes might be confused for mage's robes. So, any farmers along the way will point us out. But four messengers, galloping down the road, who look like messengers and are dressed as messengers, will not be pointed out to anyone. You don't have any normal clothes though, and you won't fit any of mine or, I believe, any of Imogen's. So, one, clothes, two, horses, three, food. Any questions?"

"What are we doing about the spell?"

"If we get away, we will try to use the null magic stone to disable the protection on the book."

"But I already told you that is very dangerous - we might wipe all the words within the book, even if we are successful."

Eric smiled sadly. "We're out of options, I'm afraid."

Oram looked annoyed. "I don't even know how to ride a horse!" he said petulantly.

Eric smiled wryly as Oram headed toward the door. "And yet, you might not be the worst rider here."

###

If it had been Eric, he would have sent bloodhounds to track them immediately, before their scent was lost. He would have had the innkeepers interrogated, the known criminals pulled in for questioning, and the gatehouses locked down. He didn't know what spells were available for this sort of thing, but he had played enough computer games with missions where you had to follow the wafting trail of someone who had walked past, hours before. It made a great visual effect, but whether there were actual spells that did the same here was still a mystery. He kicked himself again for not being able to read. Maybe he would be able to find the reading version of his ear worm. Being able to cast magic sounded like a good ability to have, and if he had a source of power in the gauntlets, along with protection from the null magic rock, he might not be that disadvantaged from not having gone to mage school. In fact, if he had one of those eye worms, and he did enrol in the university, surely he would advance more quickly? Having the instant ability to know the alphabet and the pronunciation of the words would surely save him a year or two of school?

If they got out of town alive and stayed alive for long enough, maybe he would try and find an eye worm. The escape plans could not be improved on immediately. With Imogen equipping the team, there was nothing to do between now and morning except sleep. If he could. He laughed. He'd adventured with those who were supposed to be the best of the best and ended up escaping from the pit of the ogres, making a pretty good result from a dire situation. And that was with a Knight, a Mage, a Healer, and whatever Jhara was. And here he was orchestrating an escape from a mage university city with a maid, a boy who could read, and a student mage. He had once again put his head in the jaws of the lion with only a very brief hesitation. Was he getting better at this world?

Imogen and the others came back a few hours later with good news. She'd managed to barter for some travelers' clothes. The transformation of Anton's and Oram's looks was quite amazing. Oram was still a little overweight, but where the mages' robes had been a little effeminate, the leather trousers, shirt with vest, and jacket made him look every part the mercenary, messenger, or traveler. If anyone asked whether they'd seen a mage, they would definitely say no. With Anton, there was less of a change - his slight frame was a little more obvious, if anything.

They retired to their respective rooms. Oram took the couch in Eric's room. Since that was the only extra bed-type surface, it made the most sense. After washing his face and stripping down to his underclothes, Eric bade Oram good night and tried to sleep. Various scenarios flicked through his mind. Being hunted certainly made him paranoid and every creak of timber, scurry of vermin, or rustling in the rushes made him think of guards encircling the inn.

He was almost relieved when Oram whispered in the night. "Eric, are you awake?"

"I am." he answered.

"I can't sleep," came the reply. "I am not used to this… excitement. It's ok for you lot, you go from one adventure to another, but this is all new to me."

Eric smiled. If only he knew. "What do you want to do since you can't sleep?"

"Well, we will be on the run from dawn and might not be able to have a good look at your book. Do you think I could have a look at it now? While we are not bouncing around on the back of a horse?"

Eric cringed at the memories of being on horseback. "Yes, that might be a good idea. If you light the candle, I'll get it out of my saddlebags."

Oram grabbed the candle and unlocked the door to the hallway, returning when he had relit the candle using the lantern outside. By the time he got back, Eric had managed to get the book out, blindly feeling in the saddlebags. He blinked in the new light as Oram relocked the door and came closer. He laid the book out on the bed.

"Tell me again about the locking."

"A mage can lock the book with a word or phrase, or maybe even by just using his voice. We don't know what words might unlock it or which language the password might be in."

Eric pursed his lips. "So, it might be 'open up' or 'open sesame'?"

He paused, hoping that he'd guessed the words, but nothing had changed. "How will we know if we guess the words?"

Oram looked surprised. "It will be very unlikely to guess the phrase. There are hundreds of languages and thousands, tens of thousands, of words. Whoever this book belonged to could have used any one of them. What is sess-ah-mee?"

"It's a seed. On bread."

"Why would you–"

"A long story from my world. Never mind. What language is the book written in?"

"The one we're speaking."

"Ok, so the passcode might be words in this language then?"

"I guess so."

"So what are the words people say when they first wake up?"

"What was I drinking last night? I promise never to drink again! Uh, who's that?"

Eric smiled, continuing the jape. "Who's that? Ow, my head. Where am I?"

There was a click.

Chapter 21

Eric looked at the mage who looked back at Eric. Neither of them breathed. Eric looked down at the book. The mage opened it. The letters that before had been a moving mass of weird lettering, now had coalesced into the same cross-hatching that Eric had never been able to read. But they were not moving. They were still. Eric couldn't bear not knowing for sure. "Did it work?"

The mage frowned as he looked from Eric back to the book. He just nodded. "As long as you don't accidentally say the locking phrase, it will remain open. I guess you could always say the unlocking phrase again and that would open it, but... anyway."

"So can you flick through and see if any of the pages seem to be the spell?"

The mage blinked in surprise. "Yes, of course! Of course!" Excitedly, he turned page after page, pausing occasionally. "Spell... not it. Another spell... not it."

Eric watched him, feeling more and more anxious. If it was a diary, then maybe the spell would be closer to the end. But there was no guarantee that the mage who had sent him to this world had only just learned of the spell. It could have been sitting in his diary for years as he hunted around for ways of tapping into enough magical power to be able to cast it. So each page flicked, representing a new chance for the spell to appear but also representing one more page that definitely did not have the spell. Nerve wracking!

Oram looked up at Eric. "It looks like this is the diary of a mage who left the school before his loyalty ceremony. It only shows the spells that he learned subsequent to leaving the school - I can't find any of the spells which might overlap with the ones I know. But there are a few here that look more powerful. Maybe too powerful. One attracts clouds and forms a storm. Handy if you want rain for farmers and their fields, I guess. But this one here seems to be the one you want. 'The Gate Between Worlds', it says. It drains a huge amount of energy to cast, and apparently, you can reduce the cost by bringing back the same amount of mass as you are sending."

"Will the gauntlets provide enough power? I don't know if the original mage will be sleeping in my bed, so there might not be mass coming back the other way."

There was a pause as Oram looked skyward, his lips moving as he performed his calculations. "If I'm reading this right, I should be fine with the gauntlets."

"So you can you cast it?"

"The diary entry just before it refers to a bunch of research he had done. There's a little diagram here, look."

The sketch was of a very thinly drawn hexagon, a slightly larger circle at each of the points, the circles not uniformly the same size. There was also something that Eric originally thought was dust or some random smudges on the page but they could also have been interpreted as moons around each of the different sized circles. It was a trivial exercise to pick out where he was currently, the pair of moons being disproportionately large compared with the planet. The next one around the hexagon might have been Earth, with the moon about a quarter of the size of the planet. The next one around was surrounded by many dots, and Eric wasn't sure whether the smudge was a result of the writing process or represented some sort of phenomena around the planet. The other three were a little larger than the one Eric thought was Earth but had more surrounding moons.

"Which one is yours?"

"We're here," Eric responded, pointing to the point on the hexagon. "This is where we need to go."

The mage nodded and read something in the diary. Curiously, he then started to make gestures, looking at his hands as he did so. There seemed to be some sort of pattern required with the first two fingers on his right hand, the thumb either sticking up or folded down. Eric guessed that the diary explained some way of indicating which direction or which planet to target with the created gate.

He smiled at Oram. "It's obviously very important that you send us to the right place. I know you'll do right by us, but the objective is to go back to Earth, not to boldly explore new planets."

The mage seemed to be in two minds - to take offense or to accept the note. Eventually, he nodded. "I understand, Eric. I'll do my best."

"That's all anyone can ask for, Oram," Eric said, putting his hand on the mage's shoulder. "Now, does finding the spell make a difference to the plan? Is there anything to be gained from fleeing now? Waiting 'til the morning? Should we cast the spell from here? In this room? What do you think?"

The mage rubbed his chin. "We can't cast the spell from here. We just don't know what kind of wards the school has on powerful magic. Maybe it would work, but it would be terrible if there was something hindering the processing of the power. It could spoil the casting. Also if someone was casting something more powerful at the same time, something might affect our spell. No, we still need to get away."

"How far, do you think?"

"Well, the biggest spell I have seen cast took about five minutes. We would not want to be too close to the school. If they can see us and detect the casting of the spell, then they might spoil it somehow. So I guess if we're out of sight, we should be ok."

"So the plan doesn't change then. Up at dawn, buy new horses and food, head out the gate as messengers. And when we're out of sight of Havelin, then we'll pull off the road and cast the spell. Does it say how much power it will need? We have those gauntlets with their stones, but I don't know how much they will provide."

"It is a powerful spell, Eric. But those gauntlets are also powerful. And there are four of them."

Eric frowned. "You won't have to wear them to get access to their power, will you? Because unless you put two on your feet, you'll only be able to wear two at a time."

The mage laughed at the thought of wearing them on his feet. "No, I won't have to wear them. If I wanted it to unleash the magical fire, I would, of course. But no, as long as I can tap into the stone, then that will be sufficient."

Eric smiled. "I only wish I could see you cast more spells. The way you balance the power, the words, and the gestures looks intriguing."

The mage almost wriggled in pleasure. "Yes, my years at the school will serve me well. This is the most powerful spell I will have cast. But I am very skilled. I came second in my class on certain spell casting exercises."

"And you are sure that you can cast it?"

"I have no doubts, Eric. No doubts at all."

"OK, this is good, this is great." Eric was beside himself with excitement. After the rollercoaster of emotions with the failed heist in the city, this was good news indeed!

"So what now? Is there anything else you need for the spell?"

"Nothing, though it would help if I had some time to go over the spell when we are out... where we would be casting it. Just to make myself more familiar with it, you understand."

"Of course. Well, if there's nothing else to be done, I guess we can try and go to sleep. The sun will be up altogether too soon. And we have to have our wits about us for the spell. I'm... going to sleep with the book, I hope you understand. This is my way back home, and I can't risk a thief in the night or anything else which might get in the way of that."

"I understand, but will you let me familiarize myself with the spell before I have to cast it?"

"Of course! I just want to keep it with me tonight, in case there's a fire or - I just want to keep my hands on it. I can taste home, Oram. I'm close!"

The mage smiled back and blew out the candle. They returned to their beds, Eric wasn't sure how much sleep he would actually be able to get, he was so amped. Home! His own apartment, with a comfortable bed and Dolby 7.1. He couldn't count how many days he'd been away, assuming, of course, that time moved at the same pace. If it did, his absence would be close to three months. So… no job when he got back because he would have been counted as a no call, no show. No way they would have held his job for him. Or give it back. He should be able to find another similar job pretty easily. There were always vacancies in his field, especially with his experience. Yay, more putting himself between the ungrateful and the uncaring. For not a lot of money. Maybe he could switch to head office, or go to school to study something else. Something involving lots of books. He was really sick of not being able to read here.

And his apartment! His rent was an automatic payment between bank accounts. There was enough for a couple of payments, so they wouldn't have thrown him out or turfed his stuff, but they wouldn't be too far from doing that. He could imagine there were a few letters sitting in his mailbox with Final Demand and Warning Immediate Action Required written on the outside in big red letters. Shit! There goes his credit! Maybe if he rang the bank first thing, then he could sell his stereo and work out a payment plan. It might take a while but surely he'd be able to get back to zero. It was terrible that after all this time in the other world, he hadn't been earning anything and yet, back on Earth, he had been spending even without being there. Rent, utilities, phone, and internet were all racking up expenses. Oh! The image of the sacks of coins and gems sprang to mind. Of course, if he could take those back, then he would be sweet! He might even have enough left over for a car! Or to do some travel!

He woke with a start from a dream where he'd traveled to Niagara Falls, but he had to escape from a horde of faceless people who were chasing him along suspended walkways that crisscrossed the river from the Canadian to the American side and back again. He had gotten lost in the labyrinth of passages, and after opening a door in a tower, had ended up in a customs hall with the border patrol guard demanding to know where he had gotten the gems that were in his pocket.

It was still before dawn, but the shutters failed to hide the pale blue predawn light that filtered through the cracks. The mage was still asleep, but Eric was keen to get going. He nudged him gently with his foot, and whispered, "It's time." Then he washed his face in the bowl on the bench by the window. The water was cold, making him grimace as he dunked his face. Soon, it would be hot showers and soap. He got dressed and packed the rest of his stuff away, happy to see that the mage was doing the same, dressing in his new ensemble.

There came a soft tap on the door. Eric unlocked it and stuck his head out to see who it was. Imogen and Anton stood at the ready, each in their travel attire. "Good morning! We know what we're doing? Good. Imogen, market place, horses, and food. Anton, saddlebags and horse. Oram, breakfast and book." Eric wasn't sure what he was going to do, but the team went about their respective duties, leaving him to follow the mage down to the dining room and breakfast.

The common area in the inn wasn't empty; other travelers were also preparing for a full day on the road. The Innkeeper's wife was doing the rounds, serving various tables with small cakes that looked like the ones that Eric had last seen at the White Swan Inn, back when he had first arrived in this world. He and the mage took one of the vacant tables that was tucked in the corner of the room. There was still a lantern hanging from a hook in the middle of the room for light. When the innkeeper's wife came around, Eric was delighted to learn that the cakes she was offering were indeed the same ones, and enjoyed every bite of the three he was given. They had their backs to the wall and were in a good position to see the door. Eric wasn't sure how much advantage that would be should someone dangerous come through as this was the only way in or out. At least, they wouldn't be taken unaware. Anton was the first to return, nodding as he came in, and accepting a plate of the cakes with a smile and a word of thanks to the goodwife. He sat at another empty table that was adjacent to Eric's and Oram's so that he too could keep an eye on the door. There was no sign of panic or any other indication that the guests or staff knew anything about a ruckus at the university. Eric was hopeful that remained the case.

He'd given back his plate and was working with his tongue on a crumb that had become lodged in his teeth while the others finished their breakfast. Meanwhile, he also inspected the other travelers carefully. There were some merchants in the far corner. They would either already have their wagons loaded or they would be heading to the marketplace to buy what they needed for their next stop. The early bird gets the worm.

The other group of three were evidently messengers. Even this early in the morning, they were sharing ribald jokes as they waited for their horses to be readied. When they left, Eric heard their horses' hooves on the cobbled street outside as they passed the frosted window pane. Not long after that, Imogen came back, carrying a pair of satchels slung one over each shoulder. She nodded and turned to leave straight away. The goodwife said something to her, but she shook her head and went out the main door. Eric, Anton, and the mage got to their feet and followed. Eric paused before he left to ask for some breakfast cakes for Imogen. The goodwife smiled and passed them over to Eric, keeping the plate. He was tempted to scoff them himself but, instead, hurried after the others. By the time he got there, he could see that Imogen and Anton were already on their horses' backs, and the mage was negotiating his mount with less aplomb. He handed Imogen the cakes and licked his fingers clean, before helping the mage up. Oram and the horse eyed each other warily.

"Slow but sure, right? We are but humble messengers. Lead the way, Imogen."

They clip-clopped at a walk through the city streets. Eric was alert to anything that had the potential to be an ambush. He was the last of the troop, keeping an eye on where Imogen was going, how the mage was riding, as well as trying to constantly check over his shoulder. He felt calmer as they approached the gatehouse.

Short of a cross-country chase on horseback, this was the last chance for an ambush. Eric had been tense all night and all morning, expecting the local equivalent of a SWAT team to come bursting through his bedroom door while he was sleeping, or through the front door of the inn while he was having breakfast, or to be intercepted just outside the inn, before they could get on their horses, or on the streets of the city before the gatehouse. The fact that none of these scenarios actually happened didn't help in relaxing him - even worse, it heightened the anxiety of anticipating that the next few minutes would be their last chance to grab him, therefore making the danger seem more probable.

A wagon coming the other way from some farm, laden with sacks of flour, grain, and vegetables was halted at the gatehouse. The guards were chewing the fat with the farmer. Eric concentrated on keeping his balance on the horse, keeping his hands steady on the reins, and willing both the guards and the farmer to ignore them. Or if not that, at least for their gaze to glance off them when they were passing and return to whatever they were doing. Indeed, the farmer and guards looked up at their passing, nodded, and waved. And then they were through.

Eric let out a breath he hadn't realized he was holding, feeling some of the stress leave his shoulders. Ahead of them, the long line of the road stretched through the slight haze that surrounded the city and the vacant lands. Somewhere out there they would find a bend in the road. Then they would pull off the road, out of sight of the city, and they would cast the spell. And return home.

Imogen kicked her mount into a trot, and the other horses followed in turn. Eric's horse snorted and gently eased into the new gait, Eric concentrating on staying upright. A sudden thought sprang into his head - this had been the only time he had properly ridden the horse.

They made good time along the road, the dawn quite spectacular to their right, the snow on the mountain range far away in the distance, changing color from dark to light gray, then to white.

Shadows were racing across the plain as the sun peeked over the top of the range. There was a smattering of clouds on the opposite horizon. What could end up being Eric's last day in this world looked to be a beautiful one. There was a crispness to the air, a sign that Autumn was here. Eric was surprised to feel comfortable on the back of the horse. He had not had any pleasant riding experiences so this was a novelty. In fact, with the weather, the release of the stress of worrying about the long arm of the law, and the ease of the ride, he was really starting to enjoy himself. So when a bend came up in the road, swinging their route around a sinkhole in the otherwise barren lands, and Imogen reined her steed in, he was a little disappointed. He pulled up alongside her.

"What do you think, my lord?"

He looked back the way they had come. The city was barely discernible, the distance and the haze around it doing a good job of disguising how far away it was. He nodded. Imogen led the way off the road toward a copse of trees, a good mile away across the rocky land. They dismounted, the mage theatrically groaning as he slid, rather than climbed out of, the saddle. Eric took the book out of the saddlebags and put it into the satchel. He moved the null magic stone from the satchel to the saddlebags. Best for that to be as far away from the spell as possible. In case it disrupted the casting. He also took the sack of coins that was slightly fuller. There were plenty in the other one for Anton to get back to Gerton. There was probably enough for him to pay someone to carry him the whole way back! He also took the bag of dull stones. He suspected these might be gems even though they weren't the flashy shiny jewels he was used to seeing in advertisements or pictures of jewelry. They could just be lumps of the local version of plastic, who knew? Maybe one of the jewelers on Rodeo Drive would be able to tell him. Anton took the reins of the horses and led them into the wood, tying them to one or other of the branches of the trees.

Eric handed the mage the book and the gauntlets with a smile. "Game time!"

The mage returned his smile. "I don't know what that means, but if it means that it's time to cast the spell, then I think I'm ready. Let me reread it and get the gestures perfected. Then I'll call you over, and we'll begin."

"Perfect!" Eric headed over to where Anton and Imogen were speaking. He figured he might be interrupting something, so paused out of earshot. They hugged but stopped when they noticed him standing awkwardly.

"My lord, is it time?"

"Yes, I think we need to talk about what will happen after we go through. Anton, the horse's saddlebags have a bag of coin for you to get back to Gerton. Take good care of the horse. She seems like a good sort."

"There's a bunch of money in there. Give the mage the null magic stone, he'll get good use out of it I'm sure. Just in case the university mages come after him." He stood awkwardly, unsure what else to say. "Thanks for your service, it's been a pleasure traveling with you."

Anton smiled. "It's been an honor, my lord. I'll take good care of the horse. If I may be so bold, may I name her?"

Eric grinned. "Of course! Something complimentary I hope!"

Anton grinned back. "I'll think of something suitable."

The mage called out. "It's time!"

Eric held out his hand. Anton looked at it blankly. "In my world we shake hands when we greet people, when we make a deal, or when we want to thank them." Anton mirrored him, and they shook hands. Eric looked over to Imogen. "Ready?"

Imogen smoothed her clothes and nodded.

They walked back to where the mage stood. When they arrived, Eric got the sack of coins out of the satchel. He handed it to Imogen whose eyes widened when she felt the weight. "We're not going far, but just in case anything happens to me, this should be enough to get yourself setup on Earth." She smiled and turned toward the mage.

"Where do you want us to stand?"

"I'll cast it here, and the gate should appear there. You should have about a minute to get through. It's as simple as stepping over a line, so you should be fine. A couple of minutes to cast it, simple."

"Thanks for this, Oram. I've left you the null magic stone in the saddlebags. After we're through, you can hopefully get away from the university mages."

"Many thanks Eric, most kind."

And then it was time to go.

Chapter 22

The words made no sense. They were exclaimed before Eric even registered they'd begun and were lost in the still air almost immediately. The clouds on the far horizon started to inch closer, and the faintest of breezes picked up. At the copse, the horses' heads twitched as if they smelled something in the air. There was a pause, and then a cough.

"Sorry, I'll try that again."

Eric turned and saw the mage bent over, looking at the gauntlets, arranged very carefully in front of him. He stood up, taking deep breaths, shaking his hands, and rounding his shoulders like a boxer readying himself for a fight. "OK, let's go!"

The words were no more memorable for the repeating, in one ear and out the other. Now the breeze was freshening further, whipping the stray hair from Imogen's braid across her face. The mage was making a pattern of motions, one after another. First, a grasping motion into the air, followed by an earnest imploring motion toward the gauntlets, almost like he expected to be able to raise them off the ground, using the force of his mind alone. The stones in the gauntlets were glowing. This made Eric less worried than the false start had.

But the dull white glow from the gauntlet stones was outshone by the gathering white light that appeared. It was shaped like branches of a tree, joining the trunk, or two grandiose family trees culminating in the mage's left and right hands, the more distant ancestors merely gray-blue tendrils, but the strands turning a brighter white by the time they reached the bottom. The light flickered like a fractious fluorescent light bulb in a 7-11 at midnight.

Eric's eyes were on stalks. This was the real shit. This wasn't just a "zap-the-baddie" spell, this was world-changing stuff, and he was in a front-row seat for it. He made eye contact with Anton and Imogen. They too were watching with awe as the wind speed picked up another notch. In the distance, the three new horses had had enough and stormed off, eyes wide and manes flowing. Eric's horse somehow managed to look even more bored.

Hearing what the mage was saying was impossible, but Eric followed the gestures as he traced the outline of a vague igloo shape on the ground in front of them. The white lightning that terminated in his arms traced the equivalent of the ice bricks, crackling as they touched each other. The gauntlets were now glowing as brightly as the rest of the light near the mage's hands. There were thick white bolts of light, feeding them to the rest of the lightning that was being employed by the mage. It appeared to be working!

Through the igloo, Eric could see the ground, grass, dirt, and the odd stone here and there. The light flickered and intensified, making it hard to discern original colors, everything being washed out and vaguely strobey. The mage was now making different gestures, and possibly chanting different words. Eric recognized some of the gestures as the same ones he had seen Oram practicing when he had first unlocked the book. He hoped and prayed those were right. He was worried that there were four other planets in the mix, so the last thing he wanted was to send Imogen to one of those when he'd been promising her the relatively progressive society of modern Earth.

He needn't have worried. With a blink of the eye some of the tendrils of the magic igloo blurred and refocused with a view into his room. He had never been so glad to see the poster of a hairband on his wall and the still-blinking lights of his stereo system. At least the power bill was still being paid. Or maybe they just hadn't switched it off after making their last demands! But it was definitely home. The light flickering in this world was shining on his room's wall, casting blue-white beams across the interior of his room. As more and more of it came into view, he got a little embarrassed by the mess. The igloo now was almost half made up of a growing gap, leading to his room.

He looked over to the mage who had stopped gesturing and was now holding two thick ropes of white light. These seemed to originate equally from the sky and the ground, or more likely, from the gauntlets. The connection to the igloo made him look like he was stuck in a spider's web. A shiny white pulsating crackling electric spider's web. The mage caught his eye and nodded, before breaking into a mile wide grin. Eric guessed that this was as close to heaven as the mage would be able to get.

Eric in turn caught Imogen's eye and nodded; it was time to go. She carried the sack of coins toward the igloo, shielding her eyes from the glare and carefully stepping over the threshold. As she did so, the weirdest thing happened. One second she was fully dressed and carrying a sack of cash. The next, she had stepped over the lowest tendril into his room and was standing naked, her hand still clenched in a fist but holding no sack of coins. Her clothes and the bag of coins were in a pile, sticking out from under the igloo. It looked like the gate could handle flesh only.

Eric walked over to the entrance, more flummoxed from the magical disrobing than any sort of prurient interest. It was time to go, to return to his world of early openings and late closing, of head office ineptitude and cronyism, of young staff, making snide remarks, and customers... oh, the customers! Or staying here, where everything and everyone wanted to kill him.

He stood for a second, a mere second, with one foot raised ready to step over the barrier, not really thinking or weighing up the equation of whether to stay or go. It was more a procession of images flitting across his mind, more concepts than anything else. And then a noise from behind distracted him. He turned and saw the mage being turned inside out, reduced to dust that instead of being whipped away by the buffeting winds, was channeled into the strands of power which made up the gate. He realized in an instant that even with the gauntlets, the spell was too powerful for the mage, and that, as predicted, it had consumed its caster. He turned back to the portal, not sure if it was to leap through before it closed or just to make sure Imogen had gotten through all right, just in time to see the sand corrupt the strands of the gate, the light faltering until it got extinguished, the image of his room disappearing. The last thing he saw was Imogen's surprised face as she turned to check if he was behind her.

Eric's ears rang in the silence that followed. He looked around in a daze.

Where the gate had been were only Imogen's clothes, the large bag of coins, a money purse, and her small dagger in its sheath: no burnt grass, no other debris. It was as if the gate had never existed.

400

Behind him, the clothes of the mage smoldered, and a limb or some body part or another protruded from them. Eric didn't look too closely. His horse watched passively from a little distance. There was no sign of the other horses. Anton was watching Eric and took a few steps toward him, hesitant.

Eric blinked. Everything had happened so fast. He didn't know what to think, how to feel. He was stuck here, but he didn't feel bad about that. In fact, it made him feel good. But the mage was very, very deceased.

Oram was gone. He'd gone out on a limb for them, and he was gone. Joining the stableboy, Giran, and the others on the train who hadn't made it to Havelin. Eric waited for the wave of grief to hit him, for the uncontrollable sobbing to start, but it didn't. He wondered if he'd been exposed to too much death and was starting to adjust to this world. He didn't know if that was a good thing or not. He pinched the bridge of his nose, his sadness turning to anger. Imogen may have made it to Earth, but she was alone.

"Fuuuuck!" Eric placed his head in his hands.

"What is it, my lord?"

"Even if the language we're speaking is English, ok, she will not be totally fucked, but she doesn't know anything that she will be expected to know. And it's not. None of these languages are English. So, she will be in a world where she doesn't speak any of the languages, she won't know about cars, or the police, or any other of the one hundred and one dangers in the universe that is America, and there is zero chance she doesn't get raped, or murdered, or locked-up, or committed to some mental institution."

Anton blinked at the almost manic procession of words. "But she wanted to go, my lord."

"I was only ok with that because I could help her. I could help her speak English. I could tell her about the dangerous stuff. Who not to talk to, how to talk to the police…"

"It was her choice, my lord. She knew it would be dangerous. She knew there would be a lot to learn. She was ok with that."

"How do you know?"

"We talked. When you weren't around. We would talk. She wanted to go to your land because she knew nobody would try to woo her if she was not interested. She wouldn't be sold for political gain. She told me it was scary and dangerous, but she was still doing it because she could be herself. She wouldn't have to put up with harassment, abuse, or the feeling that she couldn't be true to herself. She could have a fulfilling career."

"Why did she think these things?"

"Because of you, my lord"

"But I hardly talked to her at all about Earth, about America. How did she get the idea that she would be able to do all these things?"

"By the way you treated her, my lord. It's like she told the Queen. She told me that you treated her like a valued advisor. Like a human with something to offer, with a set of skills to be treasured. Not as someone who's only good for your own gratification. And you never tried to use your position and take advantage of her."

Eric was silent for a while, thinking and weighing up what he had been told.

The corpse of the mage still smoked and sizzled. The gauntlets were withered husks of burnt leather, the stones missing entirely. His horse still looked bored, and now that he thought about it, the book was still there, looking a bit worse for wear, pages folded back, but by and large intact. He walked over and picked it up, smoothing out the pages and closing it to let its weight press the creases out of the folded pages. Anton came over and gently took the book from Eric's hands. "I'll take this, my lord. Let me put it in your saddlebags." Eric suspected that Anton probably thought Eric was going to try and cast the spell himself to reopen the gate. No chance of that happening! But it was only now that he realized he didn't want to go back to Earth. The only time he felt happy there was when he was stoned. This world was dangerous, and he certainly didn't really fit, but at least what he did had an impact. And to a lesser degree, he was a somebody. Even if that might change when he ran out of money. But it was interesting, it excited him. He could always try and introduce some of what he knew back on Earth to the locals. Not fast-food culture, but maybe those adventurers had a space available for someone with innovative ideas. And he might be able to remember enough details about how things worked back on Earth to make things here. A steam train maybe? Telephone? Gunpowder? Electricity? Even if he couldn't read, he could still share the ideas that Earth had shown him.

A fleeting glimmer of memory flashed across his mind. It was of computer games where you took over the world using a combination of military might and diplomacy. Of royal intrigue, subterfuge and alliances, grand schemes, and even grander empires swallowing kingdoms across continents. Eric didn't know much, but he knew in reality there was a certain person who would excel with those ambitions. A person who everyone liked. Someone who could get friends to do their bidding, who knew the right people, and who had connections. And as someone who had been in a leadership position, Eric knew that wasn't him. So while he didn't have a cause to call his own, he had… a bit of money. A horse that seemed a little too smart. One follower, unless Anton decided he wanted to head back to Gerton, of course. He would have to check with him. He knew some people who may or may not be his friends. At least, they were acquaintances. And they were people of substance, right? People who would have their own faces in a video game, not just the generic silhouette. The Queen. Jhara. The leader of the Guardsmen, Vollo. The Ogre King.

Anton came back, leading the horse. He looked a little puzzled. "Are you alright, my lord?"

Eric realized he had a silly grin on his face. "I'm fine, Anton, thanks for asking. I must admit I'm at a bit of a loss on what to do next. I was so fixated on getting a gate back to my world that I didn't think beyond that."

Anton rubbed his chin. "Well, my lord, with the book we could find another mage to try and cast it, maybe a more powerful one this time?"

Eric shook his head. "Ah, you see, I have decided that I will stay in this world. I want to find a way to check in on Imogen to make sure that she's all right, but after that, I'm not sure what I will do. What do you want to do now? Do you want to head back to your library in Gerton? Or will you try and do research in the libraries of Havelin?"

Anton looked pained. "I really should head back to Gerton, my lord…"

Eric didn't know if Anton really wanted to go back. "Anton, when the Queen gave you leave to go to this country in order to go to Havelin with me, I gave it some thought. The agreement you have with the librarian's guild, surely that was only applicable while you were in that country?"

Anton considered this. "The guild only operates in Ordost, that is true, my lord."

"And if you are outside of the country, you are free to follow your own path rather than be tied to previously made agreements? Especially with someone who would lend you out so cheaply and callously? Because that guild does not operate here, correct? So if you weren't bound by those agreements, what would you want to do? Would you become a mage? Would you travel from city to city, reading the books that caught your interest? Or would you want to open your own library? Find a town or a city where knowledge is valued, but one that doesn't have a library, and start from scratch?"

Anton blinked. "My lord is very generous to make my path his. I will have to give that some thought. In the meantime, what are we going to do with…" He waved his hand to encompass the mage's body.

"I don't know what they do with their dead bodies. Was he from here? Do they bury their dead? Or burn them on a pyre?"

"From what I know of the Messalin, I believe they return the body to the earth to nourish it with their remains."

"Then let's bury the body and try to round up those other horses." Eric bent to collect Imogen's clothes, her dagger, and the bag of gold. He took these over to the horse, stowing them in the saddlebags. He returned to the corpse and dug a shallow grave in the loose dirt with his hands. It was hard going, even when Anton returned with the horses and helped him.

They stood awkwardly beside the heaped dirt before Eric came up with some words. "Oram didn't know us but helped us with a very dangerous task that ultimately claimed his life. He knew the risks, and the generosity of his heart will be missed. We return his body to the world and hope that his soul makes the journey to whatever paradise he believed in. We will remember him and his sacrifice."

They walked in silence back to the horses. As they climbed onto them, Eric turned to Anton. "Are there any other libraries you want to check out, Anton? Preferably ones unattached to a school of magic."

Anton smiled. "There is one, many leagues to the north, my lord. Famed across the lands for the knowledge within. It's across the mountains and over the sea, but they say that if a book exists anywhere, a copy of it will be found there."

Eric nodded. "Then that is where we will head. And I will try and learn how to read the language in the book. Do you think that you could teach me?"

"I can try, my lord."

"That's all anyone can ask!"

To be continued with *The Reluctant Knight*.

A Plea

Thank you for reading *The Illiterate Prince*, I hope you enjoyed it! If so, I'd be thrilled if you left a review or star rating on Amazon and/or Goodreads.

I also run a mailing list with new releases and special offers, you can sign up for it on my website: cglambert.com.

For further reading check out the *Uncle Reggie Stories*. All available on Amazon ebook, paperback and Kindle Unlimited.

ABOUT THE AUTHOR

C.G. Lambert was born the second of seven children and raised in South Auckland, New Zealand. His pre-writing career consisted of applying for whatever job sounded interesting, leading to time as an International Banker, a Music Manager, Web Developer and Analytics Manager. He loves travel (you can read about it at etrip.tips), holds dual citizenship (NZ/UK), a Bachelor of Arts and an MBA. He currently resides in the UNESCO City of Literature, Edinburgh with his long term partner.

Acknowledgments

I'm very grateful for the team of people who helped get this book into your hands.

Thanks to my Beta reading team (Adriane Campbell, Rebecca Scharpf, Andrea Shacklee, Todd Gault, Lauryn Lambert and Angela Pearse) for their insights and guidance.

Thanks to Caitlin Jenner for her equestrian expertise.

A big shout out to Amir Nebic for his cover art.

Thanks to my editor Katerina Hristova for the challenges and corrections – much appreciated!

As always, big thanks to Ange.

Lastly, thank you to you, the reader.

The Kids Who Lived In A Hole

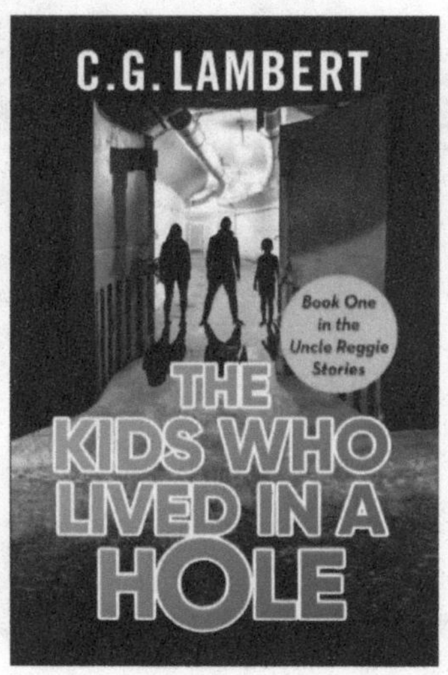

They can only escape by hiding … underground.

Fifteen-year-old Marcus Rutherford and his younger sister Zoe arrive at their Uncle Reggie's estate in idyllic Sussex. Free from having to look after his sister, Marcus explores the huge estate to learn more about his uncle's mysterious money-making schemes.

One night, the countryside erupts in violence, propelling Marcus and Zoe into a great adventure. Going into hiding, in an underground bunker – with only a strange bandaged actress for company – wasn't part of their summer holiday plan.

Will they ever make it out of the bunker? And will they ever see Uncle Reggie again?

The Man In The Hotel Ceiling

His hotel hides a secret.

When Mike, a British forensics expert, stays in an Auckland hotel apartment he inadvertently gets involved in a murder. Entrusted with a data source that proves Russian involvement, Mike hotfoots it back to London to deliver it safely into the right hands.

Avoiding poisoning by a Russian seductress and detecting mobsters disguised as scientists are the least of Mike's worries. Unwilling to let go of the case, he falls even deeper down the rabbit hole, risking his life to track down the Handler in a race against time.

Who is the Handler, how is he connected with the man in the hotel ceiling, and what does he want with Uncle Reggie?

The Girl From Wonderland

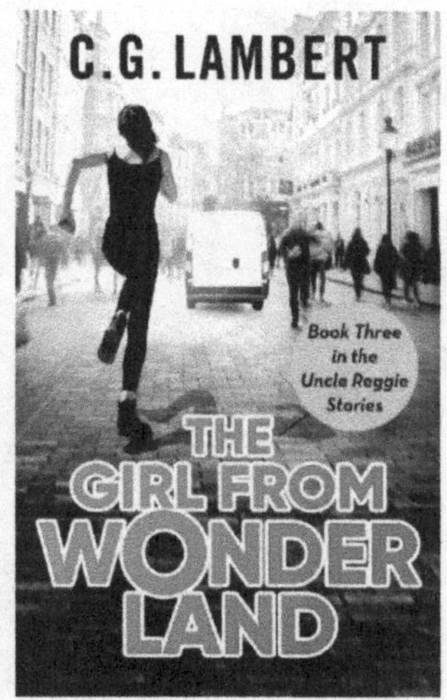

Code is her weapon, in a race against time...

England welcomes a new summer, three years after an uprising. Expert coder Alice Woodstock returns from Australia, looking for work. A chance encounter with Detective Boris McDonald leads to an all-night coding session and a headlong race across London to stop a terrorist attack.

The fallout from her efforts brings her to the attention of the Home Office who are closing in on the shadowy figure behind the historic uprising - The Handler. Alice is recruited to corner him, before realising she may be in more danger than she thought.

The Girl From Wonderland is the thrilling conclusion to the Uncle Reggie action adventure series.

9 781914 531309